CEO'S MARRIAGE MIRACLE

SOPHIE PEMBROKE

BRING ME A MAVERICK FOR CHRISTMAS!

BRENDA HARLEN

MILLS & BOON

First Published in Great Britain 2018
by Mills & Boon, an imprint of HarperCollinsPublishers,
1 London Bridge Street, London, SE1 9GF

CEO's Marriage Miracle © 2018 Harlequin Books S.A.
Bring Me a Maverick for Christmas! © 2018 Harlequin Books S.A.

Special thanks and acknowledgement are given to Sophie Pembroke for her contribution to *The Cattaneos' Christmas Miracles* series and to Brenda Harlen for her contribution to the *Montana Mavericks: The Lonelyhearts Ranch* continuity.

ISBN: 978-0-263-26548-4

1218

MIX
Paper from responsible sources
FSC™ C007454

This book is produced from independently certified FSC™
paper to ensure responsible forest management.

For more information visit: www.harpercollins.co.uk/green

Printed and bound in Spain
by CPI, Barcelona

Sophie Pembroke has been dreaming, reading and writing romance ever since she read her first Mills & Boon as part of her English Literature degree at Lancaster University, so getting to write romantic fiction for a living really is a dream come true! Born in Abu Dhabi, Sophie grew up in Wales and now lives in a little Hertfordshire market town with her scientist husband, her incredibly imaginative eight-year-old daughter and her adventurous, adorable two-year-old son. In Sophie's world, happy *is* for ever after, everything stops for tea, and there's always time for one more page…

Brenda Harlen is a former attorney who once had the privilege of appearing before the Supreme Court of Canada. The practice of law taught her a lot about the world and reinforced her determination to become a writer—because in fiction, she could promise a happy ending! Now she is an award-winning, RITA® Award–nominated national bestselling author of more than thirty titles for Mills & Boon. You can keep up-to-date with Brenda on Facebook and Twitter or through her website, brendaharlen.com.

Also by Sophie Pembroke

Island Fling to Forever
Road Trip with the Best Man
Slow Dance with the Best Man
Proposal for the Wedding Planner

Also by Brenda Harlen

Six Weeks to Catch a Cowboy
Her Seven-Day Fiancé
The Sheriff's Nine-Month Surprise
The Last Single Garrett
Baby Talk & Wedding Bells
Building the Perfect Daddy
Two Doctors & a Baby
The Bachelor Takes a Bride
A Forever Kind of Family
The Maverick's Midnight Proposal

Discover more at millsandboon.co.uk

CEO'S MARRIAGE MIRACLE

SOPHIE PEMBROKE

This book is dedicated to Auntie Barbara Roberts,
for always being my biggest fan.

CHAPTER ONE

MARIA CATTANEO—NO, she reminded herself, she was going by Rossi again now, even if it wouldn't officially be her name until after the divorce—gripped her son's tiny hand a little tighter as she stared up at the luxury chalet before her. How could something so familiar feel so strange at the same time? She'd spent Christmases and ski trips at the Cattaneo chalet in Mont Coeur for years—long before she and Sebastian had married—and on the outside, at least, the chalet had hardly changed a bit in all that time.

The same wooden veranda surrounded the oversized but traditional-style chalet, with festive greenery and berries wrapped around its beams in celebration of the season. A large green-and-red wreath hung on the front door. Inside, Maria could see lights twinkling through the windows, and knew that an absurdly huge Christmas tree would be decked out in red and gold, somewhere out of her line of sight.

Everything was the same. Everything, except her.

'Mamma?' At her side, Frankie looked up, his little face almost hidden by the hood of his snowsuit. It was freezing out, and darkness was falling; she needed to get him inside.

Which meant knocking on the door.

'Are you ready, *piccolo*?' Maria asked, forcing a smile. If Frankie sensed her unease and discomfort, he would only become distressed himself. And that wasn't going to make this enforced homecoming any easier on either of them.

'To see Papà?' Frankie nodded, his expression strangely set and serious for a two-year-old.

I'm glad one of us is ready, Maria thought, as she swept him up in her arms and climbed the steps. Then, with a deep breath, she knocked on the chalet door.

Maybe her sister-in-law Noemi would answer. Or even the mysterious new brother her husband and sister-in-law appeared to have acquired since Maria had left. Basically, anyone would be better than—

Sebastian.

The door swung open to reveal the familiar, muscular frame of her husband, and for a moment Maria was certain that nothing at all had changed. That she'd never left, that she was still in love with him, that they were happy…

She snapped out of it. *She* hadn't been happy. That was why she'd left.

Happiness was hundreds of kilometres away, back at the small cottage on the edge of her parents' estate, where she and Frankie had been living for the last year. It wasn't here, in the Swiss Alps, at the Cattaneos' luxury chalet. And it certainly wasn't with Sebastian, whatever her younger self might have hoped and dreamed.

He couldn't give her what she needed. If she'd thought for a moment that he could, there was no way Maria would have left at all. But the Sebastian she'd walked away from hadn't been capable of the love she needed. She had to keep that thought at the front of her mind this whole visit, otherwise there was just no way she would make it through with her heart intact.

When Sebastian had called and asked her to come for Christmas, with Frankie, her first instinct had been to refuse. Every other visit Sebastian had spent with his son, she'd managed to avoid, sending Frankie with his grandmother, or with Seb arranging to collect him from her parents' house when Maria was out. There'd only been two or three visits in the whole year, so it hadn't been hard to arrange.

But as difficult as it might be to go back, Maria also knew it was the right thing. Her son needed his father in his life. And Sebastian had been through so much lately… a Christmas visit from Frankie was the least she could do.

And then there had been that cryptic voicemail from Noemi on her phone when she'd landed, saying she hoped that Maria would be there tonight as she had something to discuss with the whole family.

As if Maria still counted as family. Even now.

Sebastian took a small step forward, and the light from the veranda illuminated his face. Maria held back a gasp, but only just. It had been twelve short months since she'd seen her husband, but from the weariness in his deep green eyes, and the lines forming between his brows, it could have been a decade or more. Sebastian had never really been the carefree, light-hearted sort—not like his sister Noemi—but Maria had never seen him looking quite so beaten down by the world before.

Was this because of her? She bit her lip as she waited for him to say something, but for a long moment he seemed content to just stare at her, and at Frankie, drinking them in. And she couldn't help but do the same, looking up into his once beloved face. His dark brown hair was cropped close to his head, shorter than she remembered it ever being before, and somehow it made him look even taller—although at six foot one he had always been almost a foot taller than her. She'd liked that, she remembered despite herself. Had liked resting her head against his chest and feeling his heart beat against her cheek. As if they had been connected in a way much deeper than the wedding vows their families had arranged for them to take.

This man had been such a huge part of her life for as long as she could remember. They'd grown up together, in all the ways that mattered. How could she have imagined she could cut him out completely, however far she ran?

'You came,' Sebastian said, at last, his deep voice reverberating through her body. Maria bit back a curse. She'd forgotten too how much just being near him, just hearing him speak, could affect her.

This was why she should have stayed away. But she had been unable to because…

'You asked me to.'

He gave her a small, uneven smile. 'That was by no means a guarantee that you would.'

Another sign of how little he'd really known her, Maria thought. If he'd understood how much she'd loved him once, he'd have known she could never have turned down that request. Not when he'd sounded so desperate.

Please, Maria. I need you and little Francesco here for Christmas. Everything is different now. Please come.

So, of course, she had. And at the back of her mind she had to admit that partly it was to see if 'different' meant what she'd always hoped it would. That their marriage could be what she'd once dreamed it would be.

Also because she still felt guilty—for leaving in the first place, and for not coming back sooner, when Noemi had first called with the terrible news.

'I almost came before,' Maria said, 'when I heard about your parents.' Salvo and Nicole Cattaneo had been second parents to her, too, and when she'd heard of their deaths in a helicopter accident in New York, Maria had thought she'd never stop crying. But, just like when she'd left Sebastian, she'd eventually straightened her spine and started over. The world didn't stop for grief, however much she might wish it would.

It couldn't have stopped for Sebastian either, she realised. He'd have been left dealing with not only the emotional fallout from his parents' deaths but also the practical side. Keeping the business—the world-famous Cattaneo Jewels—running like he always had would probably have proved a happy distraction from his grief, knowing Sebastian the way she did. But the news that he had a secret brother he'd never known about—one who, according to Noemi, had been left a controlling share in the family business—that couldn't have been easy for Sebastian to swallow.

She'd known how much he must be suffering, and her heart had ached for him. But still she hadn't been able to make herself return to Mont Coeur until Sebastian himself had called and asked.

After all, it was the first real sign she'd had that he'd even registered that she'd left him, that she hadn't just gone away for an extended holiday.

'Why didn't you come? For the funerals, at least?' Sebastian asked. There was no accusation in his voice, no implication that she should have been there, as his wife. Just normal curiosity.

She supposed she had to give him points for that.

'I wasn't sure it was my place. Any more.'

I wasn't sure you'd even notice if I was there.

'Maria.' Sebastian's eyes turned darker, even more serious, in the snow-lit gleam of the winter's early evening. 'There is always a home for you here. For you and for Frankie. Whatever happens. That much I can promise you.'

It's not enough. It had never been enough.

But if he hadn't understood that when she left, he wasn't going to suddenly get it now. Especially when he had so much other stuff going on in his life. So she said simply, 'Thank you.'

Sebastian turned his gaze to Frankie, whose eyes widened under the scrutiny. As Seb reached out to take him from her, Maria's hands tightened instinctively, even though her arms were aching from holding him for so long.

Frankie turned to hide his face against her shoulder with a tiny squeak of a whimper. She supposed she couldn't blame him. He'd only just turned one the last time they'd been here at Mont Coeur. His visits with his *papà* had been in Milan, close to the main offices of Cattaneo Jewels, or the villa the Cattaneos owned near her parents' estate. For all that the place and its people stirred up constant memories for Maria, for Frankie this must all seem so new and strange—and a little scary.

Seb's hand flinched away, the pain clear in his eyes.

'It's been a long day. We're both a little tired,' Maria said, trying to ease it for him, as she always had.

Seb's sad smile told her he appreciated the lie. They both knew that Frankie's real reluctance had far more to do with hardly having seen his father in a year, and then mostly on a computer screen, if Seb had managed to video chat when his son was still awake.

Maria forced the guilt to the back of her mind. It wasn't her fault that Sebastian had never lived up to his promise as a father—or as a husband. Just like she refused to feel guilty about leaving and seeking her own happiness.

How could she have possibly stayed, when staying had meant accepting that the love of her life could never truly love her back?

Knowing that Sebastian had only married her because his father had told him to was one thing. Hearing him throw it in her face that awful night before she'd left was another.

'Come on, Maria. You knew what you were signing up for when you agreed to our fathers' plans. You married me to save your family business, just like I married you to get the merger between our companies. And now you're complaining that I'm spending too much time working at that same business?'

Except she hadn't, of course. Yes, she might never have gone along with her father's insistence on the merger if the family hadn't been in such dire straits. But she'd had other plans, other ways to save it—if only they'd let her.

Instead, she'd left her business degree, come home, and married Sebastian to give her family a physical stake in the newly merged business, taking the name Cattaneo as the name Rossi had disappeared from the company letterhead.

It hadn't been how she'd wanted to do it. But she never would have done it if she hadn't already been in love with Sebastian Cattaneo—and if she hadn't believed that one day he might come to love her back.

Accepting that the love she had given him so freely and fully would never have been more than a convenience for him…that had been by far the bitterest pill to swallow. But swallow it she had—even if it had taken several years and a child to do so. She couldn't go backwards now, not when she'd worked so hard to move on.

'I'm sorry. I shouldn't be keeping either of you on the doorstep in this cold.' Sebastian stepped back, ingrained politeness obviously kicking in. He opened the door wider until the light from inside the chalet flooded out to encompass them all. 'Come in, both of you. Everyone's waiting to see you. And…welcome home.'

Maria's chest tightened just a little more as she stepped over the threshold. Mont Coeur could never be home again, even if she wished it could be otherwise.

As soon as Christmas was over, she and Frankie would be on their own again. Sebastian could keep the company—she had something far more important. Their son. And together she and Frankie would concentrate on building their own lives, far away from the Cattaneos and Mont Coeur.

And that was the best thing for all of them.

However much it hurt.

* * *

She'd cut her hair.

Seb was sure there were other changes in his wife—
and heaven knew he could see the incredible difference in
his son, from the one-year-old baby he'd been when Maria
had left to the two-year-old toddler in Maria's arms now.

But the only one he could focus on right now was the
fact that she'd cut her hair.

Those long, long ribbons of jet-black waves that had
hung almost to her waist were gone. Now her hair sat neatly
on her shoulders, curled under at the ends. Still thick and
glossy and vibrant as always, just…shorter.

And he was staring. He had to be, because Maria was
starting to actually look concerned about him, which she
hadn't been at any other point in the last year, not even
when his parents had died and he'd acquired a new sibling out of nowhere and lost control of the business and—

Hell, now he was rambling. In his mind. Which he supposed was slightly better than doing it out loud.

What had happened to the calm, collected businessman
he'd been a year ago? Oh, yes, his entire life had unravelled, that was what.

And it had all started the day he'd come home to find
Maria packing sleepsuits and her favourite pyjamas into
the suitcases he'd bought for their honeymoon years earlier.

'Sebastian?' Maria placed Frankie on his feet on the
floor as Seb shut the door behind them. Across the large,
open living space of the chalet stood his sister and surprise
brother, along with their new partners. More new people
in his life to replace all those he'd lost.

But he wasn't ready to share Maria and Frankie with
them just yet.

Maria began stripping off Frankie's bulky snowsuit.
But her questioning eyes stayed on Seb, and he felt the
weight in them.

'You cut your hair,' he said, with an apologetic half-smile. 'It suits you.'

'My life now suits me,' she said simply. The life in which she avoided him at all costs, managing to be elsewhere even when he arrived to collect Frankie from her parents' house. That life.

He was so glad it suited *one* of them, at least.

Then, as Frankie—free from his confining winter wear at last—wriggled free of his mother's grasp and took a couple of steps forward to investigate the antique nativity crib scene set up on a console table, Maria straightened and looked him in the eye.

'I want to be clear about one thing,' she said. 'Before we join the others or unpack or settle in or anything.'

Sebastian ignored the growing feeling of dread in his stomach as she spoke. 'Go on.'

'This is a visit. Nothing more. Once Christmas is over, Frankie and I will be heading home again, back to my parents' estate.' The emphasis she'd placed on *home* cut deep. This had been one of her homes once.

He had been her home.

'We're not staying, Sebastian,' she went on. 'I want that understood from the start.'

Seb forced a smile. 'Of course.' Maria's expression relaxed, and he knew he should leave it there, that to push it further would only ruin the fragile peace they seemed to have achieved.

But he couldn't help himself. He always had to try a little harder, a little longer. That was who he was. Who his father had raised him to be.

Oh, Papà, I wish you were here now to tell me what to do.

'But if you change your mind,' Seb said, ignoring the look on Maria's face, 'I wasn't just being polite when I said you always have a home here.'

'Seb...' Maria groaned.

'I know Noemi would love to have you around more. She misses you.' They'd always been close, his sister and his wife. He'd taken it as a sign that Maria was a rightful part of his family, as much as any of them.

But now Maria had gone and they had *Leo* in her place, which, as much as he'd reached a sort of truce with his unexpected brother, wasn't at all the same thing.

And apparently he'd said something wrong again, as Maria had frozen and was staring pointedly at where Frankie was about to denude the stable of sheep.

'I miss Noemi, too,' she said stiffly. 'We should go and say hello.'

Then, without looking back, she crossed the room with swift steps and removed Frankie from the antique ornaments, and carried him over to where their family was waiting instead.

At least she missed one of them, Seb supposed. It was too much to hope that she might have missed him, too, when she'd made it so clear she didn't. If she had, she'd have wanted to see him on one of his few visits. The same way he'd spent them hoping to get just a glimpse of her.

Noemi rushed forward to greet them, a huge smile on her lips, and embraced Maria immediately. Sebastian trailed behind, watching as his wife greeted his sister with considerably more enthusiasm than she had greeted him.

Then Noemi knelt down in front of Frankie. As he moved to their side, Seb could see that his son's eyes were wide as he glanced around the large room and all of the people that he didn't know. Including his own father, it seemed.

'Hey, Frankie,' Noemi said, trying to gain his attention. When he looked at her, she said, 'Can I have a hug?'

Frankie glanced up at Maria, apparently for permission.

'It's okay,' Maria said.

That was all it took for Frankie to release his mother's hand and let Noemi draw his little body to her. 'I'm so happy you're here. I've missed you tons.'

Seb's heart felt heavy in his chest. Maybe Frankie didn't truly remember his aunt Noemi either, but he'd still allowed her to hug him.

He'd been almost *afraid* of *him*. How could he have let that happen? He'd hoped his visits and video calls would have kept his memory fresh in Frankie's little mind, but apparently they hadn't been enough.

And Seb knew that those few stolen days hadn't been anywhere near enough for him. He'd missed so much already. How could he let Maria go again, knowing how much more he would miss? Just like his own parents had missed Leo's childhood when they'd sent him away for adoption.

Frankie pulled back and returned to his mother's side, and Noemi stood again, turning her attention back to Maria.

Unable to watch any longer, Seb moved away to join Leo and the others. Hopefully Noemi would get to the point of whatever it was she'd called them all there to talk about soon, and then he could pour himself a large drink and feel depressed about his life choices again. That was always a good time.

'Noemi,' Sebastian said, 'why did you call us all here? We weren't supposed to meet for another week. Is it the attorney? Does he have news for us?'

Noemi shook her head. 'This isn't about the will.'

'Then what is it about?' Sebastian's gaze moved to the man who had his arm around his sister, and then back to Noemi. 'You know I don't like guessing games.'

A sharp elbow in his ribs told him that Maria had come to stand beside him. Oh, good. She'd retained one wifely habit at least.

'Maybe we shouldn't be here,' Leo said, presumably meaning him and Anissa.

'Of course you should,' Noemi said. 'You are my brother as much as Sebastian is. Our separation as kids was a horrible mistake, but I hope that in the future there will be no distance. Because I'm going to need all of you.'

Oh, God. What now? How much more disaster could this family take?

But then Noemi smiled. 'It's nothing bad. I promise. I... I'm pregnant. You're going to be uncles.' And then glancing at the women, she added, 'And aunts.'

For a moment there was silence as everyone took in the news.

His little sister. A mother.

'And we're having twins,' Noemi added. As if one baby wasn't enough of a shock.

But she was still his sister. Stepping forward, Seb stared her in the eye and tried to think what their father would have said. Salvo Cattaneo had always known what to say.

'Are you happy?' Because, in the end, that was what mattered, wasn't it?

Noemi smiled at him. 'I've never been happier.'

He studied her face for a moment to make sure she was telling him the truth. And then he put his hands on her shoulders, like he remembered their father doing. 'Then I am happy for you, too. Congratulations.'

He pulled her into his arms and gave her a tight hug—something he wasn't sure he'd done since they'd learned of their parents' deaths. His relationship with Noemi hadn't always been without tension or frustration but he *did* love her, even if he didn't always understand her, or what she wanted from him.

When Sebastian released her and backed away, Leo stepped up to her, and Seb watched to see how the new brother would deal with the news. 'You do know that I have no idea about children or how to be a cool uncle, right?'

She smiled and nodded. 'I think you'll figure it out. In fact, I'll insist.'

She reached out and hugged him, too, which seemed to take Leo by surprise.

When they pulled apart, Noemi moved to Max's side. She placed her hand in his, lacing her fingers with his. 'Do you want to tell the rest?'

'You're doing fine,' Max replied, sounding laid-back about the whole twin situation. Really, at this point, what more news could there be?

'First, I should probably introduce Max by his proper name,' Noemi said. Sebastian frowned. 'I'd like you to meet Crown Prince Maximilian Steiner-Wolf. He is the heir to the throne of the European principality of Ostania.'

A prince? His baby sister was pregnant by a *prince*? Seb knew he'd been distracted lately, but how had he missed this much?

Noemi drew in a deep breath and then slowly expelled it. 'And he has asked me to marry him.'

Well, that was something, otherwise Max and he would have had to have words.

Then Maria said, 'You'll be a princess,' and the reality of the situation set in fully. His wife always saw to the heart of a matter first.

'Wow,' Anissa said in awe, which pretty much covered Seb's thoughts on the subject.

'Yes, she will.' Max spoke up. 'She will be the most beautiful and compassionate princess. And I couldn't be luckier. I promise you that I will do my best to make her happy.'

Sebastian looked between Noemi and Max. 'So you're moving to Ostania?' He wasn't sure how he felt about her being so far away. On the one hand, maybe they'd argue less. On the other, without Maria, and with his parents gone, and no commitment from Leo to hang around past Christmas, Seb would be on his own. Completely alone, for the first time ever.

His head spun at the thought.

'I'm afraid that my duties are increasing and after Christmas I will need to spend the bulk of my time in Ostania,' Max explained. 'I'm sorry to take your sister away from you all, but you will always be welcome at our home.'

'Don't you mean your palace?' Maria asked.

Max nodded. 'Yes. And it has a lot of guest rooms.'

'Guest rooms that I expect all of you to use regularly,' Noemi said firmly. 'Wait until you see this place. It's beautiful. And they have great skiing. But I wanted you all to know that we will be here for Christmas. It'll be a family Christmas just like Mamma and Papà would have wanted.'

With all them together—including Maria and Frankie. Even if it might be the last time it ever happened.

No. He wouldn't let that happen. He couldn't.

He had to fix things. And without his *papà* there to guide him, he was going to have to figure it out on his own.

'Now you all know everything, we can concentrate on celebrating,' Noemi said, clapping her hands together. 'Max, I haven't even properly introduced you to Sebastian's wife. This is Maria.'

'Mrs Cattaneo,' Max said, with princely suaveness as he took her hand.

'Not Cattaneo,' Maria said, too fast. 'I'm going by Rossi again now.' Wait. She'd given up his name now, too? They weren't divorced; legally she was still a Cattaneo. But the fact that she'd chosen her maiden name over his stung. Even worse was the way she'd said it so matter-of-factly, as if it were obvious.

Sebastian shot her a look. 'Did we get divorced without me noticing?'

He saw Maria's temper flare in her eyes. Good. He shouldn't be the only one angry here. 'Given everything else that happened in our marriage without you noticing, it wouldn't surprise me,' she said caustically.

'And now it *definitely* feels like a proper family Christmas.' Noemi rolled her eyes. 'Come on, Maria. Let's go show Frankie the master suite. I've had them set up the second bedroom there for the two of you.'

The second bedroom? Something primal rose up in Sebastian's chest at the idea. Maria was *his* wife, and he wanted her back where she belonged, in his bed. In his arms.

Was that so much to ask?

His objections must have shown on his face because Noemi arched her perfect eyebrows at him in amusement.

'What?' Noemi asked her brother. 'You didn't really think she was going to just move back into your room, did you?'

Yes, of course he had, when he'd let himself think about it all. Which hadn't been often. He hadn't truly believed Maria would come home until he'd opened the door to find her standing there with Frankie.

But he'd hoped. And when he'd hoped, this hadn't at all been the homecoming he'd imagined.

'Frankie can stay here with me,' he said softly. Another wish he'd had dashed this evening—a joyous reunion with his son.

He hadn't thought it possible to miss such a little human as much as he had. But now it seemed that Frankie barely even knew who he was.

'Frankie wants to see his room,' Noemi said, sweeping aside his suggestion. 'Don't you, Frankie? Come on. You come with Auntie Noemi and Uncle Max and leave Papà to sulk here alone.' She put one arm around Maria's waist, guiding Frankie forward with her other hand until he stumbled. Maria swooped down to pick up the little boy, laughing and kissing him as she did so.

None of them looked back at Sebastian.

And then they were gone, his whole family disappearing through the door in a whirl of excitement and leaving him behind.

Leaving him alone.

Again.

CHAPTER TWO

MARIA KNEW SEBASTIAN probably better than anyone in the world, even—or perhaps especially—his sister. And she was almost certain that slipping back neatly into his life, into his bed, was *exactly* what Sebastian had expected. That she'd give up her little rebellion now she'd remembered what she'd walked away from. Or that she'd have forgotten the arguments, and the loneliness, that had made her leave in the first place.

Well. The bedroom situation was only the first of many disappointments he was likely to experience during her visit, then.

'Are you okay?' Noemi whispered in her ear, quietly enough that Frankie—who was playing a peek-a-boo game with his new uncle Max—wouldn't hear.

Maria nodded, not trusting herself to tell the lie aloud.

Of course she wasn't okay. She'd never be okay as long as she was here.

How could everything have changed so much? A new brother in Leo—and soon a sister-in-law, too, given how he was looking at Anissa—Noemi becoming a princess and mother to twins… And yet in some ways nothing had changed at all.

Not when it came to Seb, or their marriage, anyway.

Noemi sighed. 'My brother is such an idiot.'

Maria didn't argue with that.

The main staircase in the chalet wound up to the second floor, all warmth and wood and local charm. 'Chalet' was a ridiculous word for the Cattaneos' home in the Alps, in Maria's opinion. A chalet sounded like a small cosy wooden cabin or a rustic lodge you stopped in just long enough to grab a hot chocolate before heading home to a *real* house.

The Cattaneos' chalet was neither small, cosy nor rustic. It was huge, spanning four floors with sprawling bedrooms with balconies, large, welcoming living spaces, a well-appointed kitchen and huge dining room for entertaining. Not to mention the heated indoor Olympic-sized swimming pool in the outbuilding.

Maria's parents had always been wealthy enough—their own business portfolio had seen to that—but next to the Cattaneos they were paupers. And when their own business had gone through a difficult time—to the point of possible bankruptcy—well, it was no wonder her father had been so keen to marry his only daughter off to the Cattaneos' only son and heir, in a merger that could not only save them but strengthen *both* their companies.

In her father's mind, Maria had been nothing more than a means to an end, she realised now. While she'd been away, studying business, discovering a flair and aptitude for it that had surprised even her, he'd been making other plans for her future. His only child, his heiress—but only if there was a business left to inherit.

Except, while she was still an only child, Sebastian was anything but. Even if she discounted Noemi—who not only had no interest in the family business, according to Sebastian, but was now apparently running off to be a princess in Ostania, wherever that was—there was Leo to take into account, too.

It had taken a lot of questions to get the full story of Leo's existence from Noemi. Maria's father had returned from Salvo's and Nicole's funerals with news of a rumour—another Cattaneo child—and had demanded that Maria stop sulking and call her husband to find out the truth of it. She hadn't, of course. She'd called Noemi instead.

It seemed that Salvo and Nicole had conceived a son together, out of wedlock, when they had been only teenagers. Their families had been scandalised and, never imagining that the couple would actually stay together, had demanded that the baby be given up for adoption.

But once they had been free of their parents' oppression, married to each other and still madly in love, Salvo and Nicole had searched for their lost son. Even after they'd had Sebastian and Noemi, for more than thirty years they'd searched. And finally they'd found him—only for them to be killed in a helicopter crash on their way to see him.

It was tragic. Heartbreaking, even.

But the only thing Maria's father had taken away from the story was that there was another Cattaneo heir now. One who, if reports were correct, had been left a controlling share in the hugely successful jewellery business.

'Maybe you were right to leave him after all,' Maria's father had said, when he'd heard the story just a few weeks ago. 'The divorce settlement should be good, and you're still young enough to marry again. We'll choose better next time.'

Maria hadn't spoken to him since.

'Here we are!' Noemi's bright and cheerful tone caught Maria by surprise, and she almost slipped on the final step leading up to the top floor.

Sebastian's floor. The one they had shared ever since their marriage. Salvo and Nicole had taken one of the smaller suites on a lower floor, smiling knowingly as they'd declared that Seb and Maria might 'need the extra room' up there sooner or later. Preferably sooner.

This particular reason probably wasn't what they'd had in mind.

She bit her lip. How could she move back in here, even

into a separate bed, and pretend that things were different? That she didn't still love her husband—and he wasn't still so indifferent to her?

But Frankie was excited to see his room and, one small hand in his aunt Noemi's, he'd barrelled on through to find out where he would be sleeping, Uncle Max chuckling as he followed behind.

Imagining their future probably—his and Noemi's. Noemi's baby bump was still relatively small, but it was there—as obvious as her excitement at starting a family with the man she loved.

And she did love Max, Maria could tell. And he loved Noemi—that was clear in every look, every smile he gave her. They would live happily ever after, just like Maria had once imagined she and Sebastian would.

How foolish she had been. Foolish, young and naive.

She knew better now, at least.

Sucking in a deep breath, Maria trailed after the others through the large open living space to the second bedroom—pointedly ignoring the archway that led to the main bedroom and the king-sized bed she remembered so well. The one where Frankie had actually been conceived, now she thought about it…

Except she wasn't—thinking about it, that was. That way madness lay.

'Well, what do you think, Frankie?' Maria asked, forcing a smile for the sake of her son. 'Will the chalet be a fun place to spend Christmas?'

Frankie, already bouncing on one of the twin beds, nodded excitedly. 'And with Papà and Auntie Noemi and Uncle Max?'

'Of course!' Maria took his hands in hers to try to calm the bouncing. 'And with Uncle Leo and Aunt Anissa, I suppose, too?'

Noemi nodded. 'We hope so, anyway. It was Mamma

and Papà's last wish—to have all their children around the table for Christmas.' Her permanent smile turned a little sad. 'I just wish they were here to see it.'

Max wrapped an arm around her shoulders, holding her close against his side, and despite her best efforts Maria felt a pang of jealousy run through her. When had Sebastian ever instinctively comforted her like that?

Never. Because that would involve understanding what she was feeling. And Seb had never drawn his attention away from the family business long enough to even *try* to do that.

She looked away, but apparently not fast enough. Noemi, obviously having caught her expression, stepped out of the circle of Max's arms, looking concerned.

Max looked between them. 'Frankie, how about you and I go downstairs and explore the kitchen? I think I saw some delicious-looking Christmas cookies in there earlier.'

Frankie's eyes widened at the mention of sugary treats.

'If that's okay with your *mamma*,' Max added, too late for her to possibly say no.

Maria felt a tightening around her heart, and it had nothing to do with Frankie eating too much sugar before bedtime. It had been just the two of them for so long now that the idea of being separated—even just by a few floors—felt strange.

'We're all family here,' Noemi murmured, taking Maria's hand and squeezing it. Her sister-in-law always had been too good at reading her. 'And Max needs the practice anyway.'

Maria gave a stiff nod, placed a kiss on Frankie's cheek, and watched as Max swept the toddler up into his arms, already talking about chocolate chips and candies baked into cookies.

'He'll be fine.' Noemi squeezed her hand one more time before dropping it.

Maria sighed. 'I know.'

'The more important question is, will you?' Noemi asked.

Sinking down onto the bed, Maria covered her face with her hands. Would she? Would she be okay, spending Christmas with the husband—and family—she'd left behind?

'I have no idea,' she admitted.

Alone.

Seb watched Maria and Frankie walk away, and felt the terrible word echoing around his mind. Through his heart.

Frankie hadn't even known him when he'd answered the door, had shied away from him when he'd tried to hold him. He'd wanted to video call more often, but it was always so hard to find a time during his son's waking hours. Maria didn't even bother answering if Frankie was already asleep, usually sending a text later to explain.

But, looking at his son now, Seb wondered how he could ever have imagined that ten minutes of video once every week or so could *ever* be enough. The baby he'd held in his arms last Christmas had gone for ever. When Maria had left, Frankie had only just begun to crawl—now he seemed to run everywhere on sturdy legs that were nothing like the podgy, squidgy baby ones he remembered. Even in the four months since he'd last visited, Frankie had grown so much. His eyes were the same bright hazel as in the photo on his desk, but they no longer gazed trustingly up at him. Instead, they were puzzled, even wary.

As if he didn't know Sebastian, his own *papà*, at all.

Seb clutched at the back of the nearest chair to steady himself. How had this happened? How could he have missed so much? And how could he ever get that time back?

You can't.

The voice in his head sounded like Maria's, like the day she'd left.

'You can't understand,' she'd said that day. 'You're not capable of it. I see that now.'

Capable of what? he'd wanted to ask. But she had already gone, leaving him behind to deal with the business, and his family, and everything else that fell on his shoulders.

But none of it, he realised suddenly, mattered as much as the year he had lost. A whole year of his son's life that he could *never* get back. Never experience as a father should.

That realisation hurt a thousand times more than learning that he had an older brother, that his parents had lied to him his whole life by never telling him about it. Hurt a million times more than learning that they'd left Leo the controlling share of the company that should have been his.

Hurt almost as much as hearing Noemi sobbing as she'd told him their parents were dead.

His parents were gone, soon Noemi would be disappearing with Max to wherever on earth his tiny country was, Maria would take Frankie away again, and all Seb would be left with was Leo—the brother he'd only discovered existed a month or so ago. And even he would probably head back to New York, and take the company Seb had given up his whole life for with him.

How had his life unravelled so completely in so little time?

Seb could feel it, spiralling out of his control, spinning his mind in tight circles until his head ached from trying to understand it all. His heart was too heavy in his chest, beating a sluggish, determined rhythm, reminding him that he, at least, still lived—even if his parents didn't. That he still had a job to do, even if the one he'd expected had been taken away. That he still wanted, and felt, even loved—even if his wife had left him and his son didn't recognise him.

God, Frankie. *Maria.*

He needed air. Cold, shocking, numbing air.

Good job he was in Mont Coeur.

Letting go of his support sofa, Seb staggered to the door and flung it open, gulping in the icy breeze as it hit his face. Then he stepped through onto the veranda, and stared out at the darkening mountains.

There was a whole world out there. So why did it feel like his had disappeared for good?

'Sebastian?' Leo's voice came from behind him as he joined him on the veranda. 'Are you okay? You look… Is it Noemi's news?'

Seb barked a laugh. Noemi, his baby sister, a princess. A pregnant princess, at that.

At least one of them had gone after the life they'd wanted and had found it.

No, two of them. Leo seemed almost offensively happy with his new girlfriend, Anissa. They'd shared secret smiles and small touches and whispered jokes since they'd arrived, too, just like Noemi and Max. So clearly a pair, a couple—in a way he and Maria never had been. No doubt Max and his sister would be settling into what had once been *his* master suite in the chalet with babies and joy, taking over his home as easily as Leo had taken over his business.

'Okay, look, why don't we sit for a moment?' Leo's voice, calm and soothing, made Seb feel instantly guilty for his thoughts. As much as Seb resented being pushed out of the family business, even he had to admit it wasn't Leo's fault. He couldn't blame his brother for the circumstances of his birth, the lies their parents had told, or even the will they had left behind them.

Much as he might wish he could.

Seb was a logical, rational man. He had to be, to be a success in his business. His father had instilled in him from birth the weight of expectation, the obligations Seb had to his family. And Seb had given everything he could to live up to them. He'd worked hard, done everything that had been asked of him.

And still it hadn't been enough.

Not for his father, not for Maria, not for anybody.

He wasn't enough.

Leo's arm over his shoulder was a heavy weight leading him to the wooden bench on the veranda and pressing him down onto it.

Maybe if he'd had a big brother all along, rather than discovering him at the age of thirty-two, things would have been different. But he hadn't.

'Do you ever feel like your whole life is unravelling in front of you, and you can't move fast enough to piece it back together?' His voice didn't even sound like his, Seb realised. Too low, too raw. Too desperate.

But Leo just laughed, a darkly amused sound Seb hadn't heard from him before.

'What do you think?' Leo asked. 'I spent my whole life thinking that no one wanted me, that my own parents had thrown me away, only to discover one day that they'd been searching for me almost my whole life. And then, when I was ready to meet them, they died before I got the chance.'

'And you got stuck with me and Noemi instead.' Yeah, that must have been a pretty big let-down.

'Actually, I kind of think of the two of you as an unexpected bonus. A silver lining maybe,' Leo said, and Seb looked up, surprised.

'What do you mean?'

'Well, I thought I'd lost any chance of ever having a family. Then I came here and met you two, and then Anissa... and now there's Max and Maria and Frankie, plus Noemi's babies. Suddenly I have more family than I know what to do with.'

'Maria and Frankie aren't staying.' Seb's mood dropped again at the reminder.

'Ah.'

'Yeah.'

Leo stretched his legs out in front of him, leaning back against the bench. Almost unconsciously, Sebastian followed suit. Leo's legs were longer than his, he realised, even though they were more or less the same height. Yeah, being the little brother really was going to take some getting used to.

'Do you remember what you told me when I called you from New York?' Leo asked, after a long moment of silence.

Seb tipped his head back and tried to remember. It had only been a handful of weeks ago now, but somehow it felt longer. Like his whole world had shifted again since then, with everyone coming home to Mont Coeur.

Leo had been in New York with Anissa, wooing her, or whatever it was that smooth, American-raised secret older brothers did. But he'd screwed it up—Seb had to admit that slight sign of fallibility had made it easier to warm to Leo—and Anissa had run when Leo had asked her to stay with him.

'I told you to wait,' he said finally.

'You said that if I loved her, I had to give her space and respect her decision,' Leo corrected. 'That I had to let love decide what happened next. And that I should let Anissa come back to me—if she wanted to.'

'And she did, of course.' And now they were blissfully happy. Good for them.

'So did Maria,' Leo pointed out. 'I mean, she's here for Christmas, isn't she?'

'Only because I called and asked her to come.' Okay, begged. It wasn't a moment his pride felt particularly good about. 'And like I said, she's not staying.'

He'd given her space. He'd respected her choices. And it hadn't made one bit of difference.

Leo sighed, and Seb couldn't help but feel he wasn't getting whatever point his older brother was trying to make.

'What I'm saying is…you gave me some good advice, and I'm glad I followed it. But I can't help but think you've been following your own advice a little too long.'

'Too long?' Seb frowned.

'Maria's been gone for, what? A year?' Leo asked.

'About that.' Sebastian couldn't bring himself to admit that he knew it was, in fact, twelve months and fifteen days.

'Well, waiting on love is all very well and good. But maybe sometimes love needs a bit of a push. A bit of effort.'

Love. He loved Maria—of course he did. She'd always been a part of his life, part of the family, and he loved her as much as he loved Noemi or his parents. But theirs had never been a romance as such.

Maybe that was what had been missing. Something to think about at least.

Leo cleared his throat, obviously a little uncomfortable about the very personal turn the conversation had taken. They didn't really know each other well enough to be baring their souls, Sebastian thought. He'd been astonished when Leo had called him from New York to ask what he should do about Anissa—until he'd realised that his brother simply didn't *have* anyone else to talk to about such things.

And neither, it seemed, did he. Noemi would be firmly on Maria's side, as always. His parents were gone, and his other friends, business acquaintances…he'd never even told them Maria had left in the first place. He'd had to keep up the facade of the perfect businessman and family man after all, even if everything about his life, family and business was crumbling around him. If anyone had asked, he'd just told them Maria and Frankie were visiting her parents for a few weeks. Making sure Frankie's grandparents didn't miss out on watching him grow up.

The way his own *papà* had.

'Actually, I didn't track you down out here to talk about your love life,' Leo said.

'I appreciate you not adding the word "dismal" in there,' Seb joked, making Leo smile. 'So, what did you want to talk to me about?' Whatever it was had to be better than the unending panic and echoing sorrow about the state of his family.

Leo took a long breath. Then he said, 'The business.'

CHAPTER THREE

WITH A SIGH, Noemi settled onto the bed beside her, and Maria smiled gratefully as her sister-in-law wrapped an elegant arm around her shoulder.

'So, are we finally going to talk about why you left?' Noemi asked. 'I mean, apart from the fact that my brother is an idiot.'

Maria felt a stab of guilt. It wasn't just Sebastian she'd left behind when she'd run—it had been her best friend, her whole family. She'd always felt closer to the Cattaneos than her own parents, and not having any siblings of her own, Noemi and Sebastian had filled that gap.

Yet every time Noemi had tried to talk to her about Sebastian over the last year, Maria had changed the subject. She just hadn't been ready to admit how stupid she'd been over the whole thing.

Who expected a marriage of convenience to blossom into true love, outside the movies and romance novels, anyway?

'Why do you think I left?' Maria stalled, knowing it was cowardly even as she did it.

'Why do *I* think you left? Or why does *Sebastian* think you left?' Noemi always had been too perceptive for her own good.

'Both, I guess.' Maria couldn't deny a certain curiosity as to Sebastian's reaction to her departure. And heaven knew he'd never talk to *her* about it.

When he'd found her packing, the day after that awful

argument, he'd asked her to stay. And when she'd refused, told him he'd never understand, he'd stood aside and watched her go. But she knew he'd been thinking she'd come back soon enough and he just had to wait her out.

Well, he'd been wrong, hadn't he? And then he'd been too proud to ask her to come back. Until now.

Noemi tilted her head to the side as she studied her, then nodded, as if satisfied by what she saw. Maria didn't dare ask exactly what that was.

'I think he thought that you were feeling neglected,' Noemi said. 'I mean, the moment you came back from your honeymoon he threw himself into the expansion, folding your family's business into Cattaneo Jewels. Even I noticed that he was working all hours—more than he had before, ever—and that didn't change when you had Frankie.'

'No. It didn't.' The memory of those lonely days was too close to the surface for her not to feel it all over again. The aching loneliness that came from being with a baby, all day long, with no support. Seb had suggested they hire a nanny, of course, so she'd have some help—it wasn't as though they couldn't afford it. But since Seb had stopped involving her in any of his business dealings or conversations the minute she'd fallen pregnant—claiming he didn't want her suffering any stress at all—she hadn't seen the point. She loved looking after Frankie, even when it was hard and lonely.

Next, he'd suggested baby groups, which she'd tried but had never really felt she'd fitted in with. Besides, all the other mums and babies in the world had been unable to give her what she'd really wanted. Needed, even.

Sebastian's support.

Sebastian's *love*.

Unfortunately, it seemed that Sebastian was incapable of giving her that.

At least until then he'd made her feel part of his family. They'd sat up talking for hours, about the business, of course, but about so many other things, too. The world around them, places they'd like to travel to, things they'd like to do.

She'd imagined them doing them all together once they were married. But for Sebastian it seemed they were only daydreams.

'As for me…' Noemi trailed off, watching Maria with a sad look on her face. 'I didn't think you wanted to go at all.'

Far, far too perceptive.

'I didn't,' Maria admitted with a sigh. 'But at the same time… I knew I had to, and I'm glad now that I did. It was the right decision for me, and for Frankie.'

'You definitely seem more…certain, if that makes sense,' Noemi said. 'Like you know what you want your life to be now.'

'Maybe I do.' It was just a shame she couldn't see any way to make sure she got it. But even if a happy-ever-after with Sebastian was off the table, that didn't mean she couldn't have a full and happy life *without* him. 'I've been learning a lot about myself since I've been away. I mean, Seb and I got married when I was so young… I'd never really been alone before. And this time I was alone with Frankie, taking care of him every day, learning what he needed—and what I needed. It's definitely been…educational.'

And hard and lonely and difficult—but also fulfilling, rewarding and so full of love that some days Maria just cried because of how *lucky* she was, instead of for everything she'd lost.

But she didn't tell Noemi that part.

'Maybe that's what seems so different about you,' Noemi said reflectively. 'You seem *grown up*. Not that you weren't before, of course, but it's different now. Like you're the adult in the room. The mother, I suppose.'

'Not the only one for long,' Maria said, with a soft smile.

'Did I tell you how incredibly happy I am for you? And for Max, of course.'

Noemi's face lit up at the mention of her fiancé and their babies. 'You did. But I'm always happy to hear it again!'

Impulsively, Maria threw her arms around her sister-in-law's shoulders and held her tight. 'I'm *so* happy for you. You give me hope.'

'Hope?' Noemi asked, frowning as she pulled away. 'What do you mean?'

'Well, if everything can work out so perfectly for you, maybe I can still find that sort of happiness one day.'

'Just not with Sebastian?' Noemi said sadly. 'Maria… I know he's a pig-headed idiot a lot of the time, but Sebastian… He means well, I think. And this last year, without you…he's just been so *sad*. And annoying and irritable, of course, but mostly sad.'

Maria looked down at her hands. Annoyed or angry, she'd expected. She hadn't expected sad. In fact, she'd imagined he'd have been frustrated for a few days and crash around the place in a black mood, then he'd get distracted by some work crisis or another and forget he'd ever had a wife or child until it was all over.

That was what he'd done when she'd been there, after all.

'Yeah, well. I was sad when I was with him, but he didn't notice that. He didn't notice anything, really. It was as if… the moment we were married I became invisible to him. Another item ticked off his "must do before thirty" list, or something. Even Frankie… I know he loves him, but sometimes I think he sees him more as an heir than a son.'

She knew why, of course, as well as Noemi did. That was how Salvo had always treated Seb—the same way Maria's father had always treated her, as an asset, to marry off as he saw best, to further his own business endeav-

ours. That was one of the things they'd had in common as
teenagers—the knowledge that their function was more
important than who they were as a person.

The only difference was that Seb's parents had adored
and loved him—even as they'd pushed him to greater
heights and bigger achievements. For Maria's father, marrying Seb was the best she could ever hope for—her entire
self-worth wrapped up in someone else's abilities.

'Maria…you know what it was like for Seb growing up.
Our parents were wonderful, loving people—especially to
me. But for Seb…our father was different with him. Seb
was in training from the moment he could see over the
counter in Cattaneo Jewels HQ. He had so much to learn,
you see, and it was so important to Papà that Seb know
everything he needed to take over the business one day—'

'And then they left the controlling share to the son they'd
not seen since the day he was born,' Maria finished, surprised at the anger she felt on Seb's behalf.

It seemed however hard she tried to leave her marriage
behind, the emotions it brought up in her still remained.

Noemi pulled a face. 'Yeah, that's all…messy. But I'm
hoping we can find a way to work it all out. I mean, we're a
family, right?' The look she gave Maria made it very clear
that she was including her sister-in-law in that statement.

A messed-up, separated, bizarre family with history
and baggage. But a family.

'Yes, we are,' Maria agreed with a sigh. The Cattaneos
had been her family long before she'd married Seb. They'd
given her a place that had felt like home when her own
had felt cold and empty, when her parents had gone away
on trips without her, or been too busy with the business
to pay her any attention. Despite Salvo's focus on training
Seb, he'd always made sure they'd had time as a family,

too. It was just a shame that seemed to be the one thing he *hadn't* taught his son.

Salvo and Nicole might be gone, but their children remained—and from the look in Noemi's eye, Maria knew her friend wouldn't let them all drift apart without their parents there. And because of Frankie, Maria would always be tied to them, whatever happened between her and her husband.

Noemi beamed, her radiant glow almost too bright to look at. 'I'm sorry. I just want everyone I love to be as happy as I am.'

'Trust me, I want that, too,' Maria replied. 'But right now I'd settle for just getting through this Christmas without having my heart broken.' Again.

Taking her arm, Noemi pulled Maria up from the bed. 'Come on. We're going to go downstairs and find your gorgeous little boy, pour you a glass of wine, and just enjoy all being together for Christmas. Okay?'

'Okay.' Resigned to making the most of her visit, Maria smiled and followed her sister-in-law back down the stairs.

And really, when Noemi put it like that, Christmas at the chalet sounded pretty good. She could enjoy this Christmas. Frankie could get to know his *papà* again, and maybe they could find middle ground between the past year and the one before it. One that gave them all what they needed to feel content at least, if not the incandescent happiness Noemi had found.

Maria could get back to the new life she'd forged for herself, and even if it never felt totally complete without Seb, perhaps he could still be enough a part of their lives to satisfy him and give Frankie the father he deserved.

It wouldn't be everything. But maybe it would be enough.

It would have to be.

* * *

Seb felt an icy chill that had nothing to do with the Mont Coeur snow sneak up his spine at his brother's words. 'The business?' he echoed.

This was it. This was when Leo told him that he wanted more than just a controlling share of Cattaneo Jewels—this was where his big brother took it over completely. Pushed him out and made the company his own.

And then what would he have left?

It made sense, in a way. Leo was the hotshot business-man—and he'd made it by himself. All his successes, wealth, everything were down to Leo. He hadn't had Salvo Cattaneo guiding his every move, telling him when he was about to screw up and helping him fix it. Leo hadn't had anyone. Not their parents, not his useless-sounding adoptive family. All he'd been able to rely on—and put his success down to—was his own hard work and natural talent.

Sebastian, on the other hand… His father had spent years drilling him in exactly what was expected from the heir to the family business, and Seb had worked like hell to prove himself. But it hadn't been enough, had it? Salvo had still left the controlling share of the business to Leo, not Seb.

No wonder Leo wanted to shake things up. He'd have his own ways of doing things, new ideas and exciting pos-sibilities.

And, sure, Seb had kept things afloat in the meantime, kept the profits ticking over nicely, thank you. But he had just been building on what was already there, not creating anything new. Even Noemi, as the face of Cattaneo Jewels, had had more influence on the shape of the company, from the outside, anyway. She'd been pushing for more, too, and as much as Seb had known she was capable of it, he'd been holding back on letting her in.

This was his responsibility, Salvo had always told him.

It was up to Seb to make the company a success, to look after his sister and his mother if anything happened to him.

How badly must he have failed for things to have come to this?

But then Leo spoke again, and Seb's understanding of the world shifted once more.

'I want to sign my shares in the family business over to you.'

Seb turned to stare at his brother in astonishment. 'You're walking away? After everything, you're turning your back on your family?'

How? Leo had admitted he'd spent his whole life without a family. How could he walk away just when he'd found them? Just when Sebastian had thought they might be finding some common ground...

But Leo was smiling. Indulgently, even.

Wait. What was he missing?

Apart from the opportunity to get back what he'd always wanted—control of Cattaneo Jewels. How was it possible that he'd missed the implications of that, even for a moment? He'd been too concerned with the idea of losing his brother when he'd only just found him.

Huh. *That* was a surprise.

'I'm not walking away from our family, Seb,' Leo said. 'I'm just putting the responsibility for the business back where it belongs.'

'With...me?'

Leo nodded. 'You're the one who has worked so hard to build the business up, to keep it flourishing even when you were grieving for our parents. You're the one who deserves it.'

'But our parents... This was their dying wish.' And as much as Seb wanted to reach out and grab what Leo was offering, now he knew it didn't mean his brother leaving, and as great as it would be to take back control of his life in some small way, he knew he couldn't deny his parents' desires like that.

'I don't think it was,' Leo said, shaking his head. He sat forward, angling his body towards Seb as he spoke, and for a moment Seb could imagine that they were young boys together, plotting an adventure behind their parents' backs.

'It was in the will,' Seb said stubbornly.

'A will that was written years ago,' Leo pointed out. 'Before they ever knew if they would find me. I've been thinking about this a lot—hell, I've been thinking about a lot of things lately.'

'Ever since you met Anissa,' Seb guessed.

Leo laughed. 'Yeah, perhaps. Anyway, the point is, that will…it was a way to bring our family together if our parents weren't there to do it themselves. And it's done that, right? We're all here, at Mont Coeur, in time for Christmas.'

'I…guess so.'

'So it's done its job. I don't need those shares to remind me I'm your brother, or that Noemi is my sister. And I hope I don't need them to earn my place in this family.'

'Of course not!' However badly he might have reacted to the discovery of a secret brother, now that Leo was there, Seb would fight anyone who said he wasn't a Cattaneo or didn't belong with them.

Leo grinned. 'Then why keep them? I've got my own businesses to run and, to be honest, you know more about the jewellery industry than I ever will. Or even want to. Jewellery isn't my thing.'

'That's true.' Seb could feel his spirits rising for the first time since he'd seen Maria standing on the doorstep and Frankie hiding his face against her coat.

'I'll speak to the lawyer tomorrow.' Getting to his feet, Leo clapped a hand on Sebastian's shoulder. 'Make it all legal as soon as the terms of the will allow me to.'

'Thanks.' Seb stared up at Leo, hoping his brother could see the sincerity in his eyes in the fading light. 'I mean it, Leo. Thank you.'

'You're welcome.' Leo started to move away towards the door of the chalet but then stopped and looked back. 'And you know, Seb, I may not have been your big brother for the last thirty-odd years. But if you need one, I'll take up the job any time you ask.'

He turned and walked away into the chalet before Seb had to come up with a response to that. Which was probably for the best, as he definitely didn't have one.

He hadn't known what to expect, meeting Leo. All he'd been told to start with was that he had a brother he'd never known existed. Then the particulars had trickled in—hotshot, self-made New York businessman. It wasn't until he'd met Leo that he'd understood some of the other aspects of his life without his family. And not until his parents' will had been read that he'd understood what Leo had meant to them.

When his parents had died, Seb had felt like he'd lost everything. After Maria leaving, and then later with the will…everything had seemed so changed and beyond his control.

But maybe he needed to start focusing on what he had left. Counting his blessings, so to speak. A sister, who was truly blissfully happy for the first time in who knew how long, and a new brother-in-law and twin nieces or nephews to go with it. A big brother, who knew when to talk and when to walk away, who wanted to be part of the family even though he had no ties to them. A business that he could take to new heights, he knew, now he had the chance.

A son he adored with every inch of his being, even if he didn't always show it. And a chance to build the father-son relationship he'd always wanted. One that kept the best aspects of Salvo's parenting but without all the pressure, perhaps.

And Maria. The only woman he'd ever imagined marrying, spending his life with. And still the most beautiful woman he'd ever seen.

Theirs may not have been a love story—no romantic nights out, falling in love—but it was *their* story, and Seb wasn't ready for it to end. Maria was his wife, and he didn't want that to change.

So maybe he didn't have her, not any more. But he *did* have a second chance to win her back. If he could figure out how.

As Sebastian opened the front door to the chalet and stood, watching his blessings as they gathered around the huge Christmas tree, he knew he couldn't squander that chance.

Maybe his marriage had been one of convenience to start with, but did that mean he couldn't make it something more? Add a little romance, find out what Maria needed from him to be happy? If he could give it, he would, to keep one small aspect of his life in order. To stop one thing spiralling beyond his control.

But most of all to give him his son back.

Maria lifted Frankie to touch one of his parents' favourite tree ornaments, his little face lit up with a joy that was reflected in Maria's smile, and Seb felt his heart contract.

Maria seemed so much more confident, and even more content than she had before she'd left. He knew that proving to her—and maybe even to himself—that they could find that same happiness together wouldn't be easy.

But he had to try.

It was what his parents would have wanted. It was what *he* wanted, if he was honest with himself. Leo was right. He'd spent too long waiting for Maria to realise that she wanted to come home. It was time to show her why she should. To prove to her that they could be happy again.

They'd been happy once, right? He smiled as he thought about their honeymoon. There had been romance *then*, at least, after their vows had been made—romantic walks on the beach, candlelit dinners and conversation, and long, lazy lovemaking at night.

That was what they needed again. What he needed to find here at Mont Coeur to remind her how they could be. Okay, maybe the beach was out—but snowy walks at Christmas in the Alps? What could be more romantic?

He could do it, he was sure. He just had to convince Maria to let him try.

'What are you doing, lurking in doorways?' Noemi asked, as she came up behind him. 'Shouldn't you be in there with your wife and son?'

Sebastian favoured her with a smile, realising that Noemi was someone else he needed to make more of an effort with. She'd be leaving with Max soon, after all. If he wanted to repair their sibling relationship, it had to be now—and when better than Christmas, anyway?

But first Maria and Frankie.

'I'm going to win her back, Noemi,' he murmured, excitement jangling through his veins at the idea. 'We're going to be happy again.'

Noemi beamed, and placed a kiss against his cheek. 'Well, it's about time,' she whispered in his ear.

CHAPTER FOUR

IT WAS SO comfortable in many ways, being back in the chalet where she'd spent so many happy times before, that it came as a surprise over and over every time something jarred with her memories of the place. A reminder that she was a guest here only, or of all the things that had changed since she'd left a year ago.

They'd all enjoyed drinks and a sort of help-yourself supper, before settling down in the main living space of the chalet together. Leo and Anissa had headed back to their own chalet—apparently Leo didn't feel completely at home with them just yet, Maria thought—but Max and Noemi had joined Seb, Frankie and her for the evening. Noemi had put some soft festive music on and kept the conversation light and inconsequential.

Maria was grateful for her friend's hostess skills. She couldn't imagine how awkward the evening would have been alone with Sebastian. It was difficult enough to relax as it was.

Maria looked up at the ornaments on the tree and remembered hanging them with Nicole in years gone by, a pang of sorrow pricking her heart again as she gazed around the room and saw the empty spaces where Seb's parents would have been.

Nicole, she thought, would have been fussing around over everyone, keeping glasses topped up and the mood merry. Salvo would have been settled in his usual chair—the one that sat empty even now—by the window, watching the snow fall and enjoying the chatter of his family around him.

And, oh, they'd both have been *so happy* at Noemi's news. Not so much the princess part particularly, or the moving away to another country. But the babies and the glow of joy that had followed her around since she and Max had figured out their future together would have thrilled them. Noemi was happy, so they would have been happy.

She had no idea what they'd have made of her and Seb now. Or even what they had thought about her leaving. She suspected Seb had told them to leave her alone, probably expecting all the time that she'd change her mind and come back if they didn't nag her.

Maria remembered the day she and Seb had told his parents that they were expecting Frankie. While Maria's own father had merely nodded and said, 'Good job,' and her mother had set about organising christening dates and invitation lists to show the baby off as soon as he arrived, Nicole and Salvo had each hugged her tightly and whispered loving congratulations in her ear.

She knew that giving them an heir to Cattaneo Jewels—along with the merger with her father's business—was the reason she'd been married off to Sebastian in the first place. But the Cattaneos had never made her feel that way, even when her own family had. They'd been genuinely happy to have her as part of the family, and delighted at the news that that family would be expanding.

She'd been *wanted* here, in a way she'd never really felt wanted back home on her parents' estate. Maybe that was the real reason why she'd agreed to the marriage in the first place.

No, she couldn't lie to herself about that. It hadn't been about business or family for her.

She'd fought against it to start with. When her parents had called her home from university, sat her down and told her she wouldn't be going back, she'd thought they were joking. When they'd explained the financial predicament the business was in, she'd thought she could fix it. She, with half a business degree, had wanted to try. To help her father turn things around.

But he hadn't wanted her to.

Instead, he'd arranged a merger with his old friend Salvo Cattaneo. One that would leave him better off and able to retire. But her father couldn't let go of Rossi Gems quite that easily—he'd wanted a physical stake in the new company.

Her.

Her marriage to Seb would give him prestige, give her and her children the company name, and leave them all wealthy and happy—at least, that had been the plan.

But even her father hadn't been able to *make* Maria marry a man she didn't want to, not in this day and age. And so she'd argued, she'd cried, she'd bargained…and in the end she'd given in. Not because it was what her parents had wanted, or because it had made good business sense, but because of the small voice at the back of her mind that had told her that this was her chance. Her shot at happiness.

Maria had agreed to marry Seb because she was already in love with him—had been for years, long before she'd left for university. Ever since an icy night another Christmas, long ago, at the Cattaneo villa near her parents' estate, when he'd made her feel like the most important girl in the world.

She'd hoped—naively, it seemed—that maybe one day he could come to feel the same way about her.

But if the other Cattaneos had welcomed her as family, she'd known deep down she'd only ever really been a convenience to Sebastian. He'd told her as much that last, awful week before she'd left. He'd needed a wife to appear the respectable businessman he was so desperate to be, and he'd wanted an heir to keep the family name alive. It hadn't been the money or the business for Seb either, she was sure. Marrying her had made his father proud—and that was always what Seb had cared about most.

But now…now Salvo wasn't there to judge Sebastian's successes or failures any more. Would that change things?

Maria couldn't help but smile at the glimmer of hope that it just might. That without his father's overbearing presence Seb might finally realise that some things mattered more than the family business.

'He's almost asleep.' Seb's deep, soft voice startled her out of her reverie, and she made a small, surprised noise. Seb chuckled. How long had it been since she'd heard that sound? 'And so are you, by the sound of it.'

'I'm awake,' Maria disagreed. 'Just thinking. But you're right about Frankie.'

The two-year-old was sprawled across her lap, his eyes starting to flutter closed. As Maria watched, his eyelids would start to fall, then he'd jerk himself awake, as if unwilling to miss a moment of what was going on around him.

'He seems…happier to be here now,' Seb said tentatively.

'Max gave him ice cream and cookies,' Maria replied. 'A sure way to any boy's heart.'

Seb's answering smile didn't reach his eyes. 'When Frankie first arrived, I was a bit worried he'd forgotten all about us.'

Maria winced. She was the one who'd kept Frankie away and, however good her reasons, she couldn't avoid feeling some guilt about that. Especially when she thought about Salvo and Nicole, and how they'd missed out on watching Frankie grow the last months of their lives. Photos and video calls weren't the same.

And now it was too late.

'It's been a long year for all of us,' she said. 'And a very long day for this little boy.'

Hoisting Frankie back into a seated position, she cuddled him around his middle. Then, leaning in, she whispered against the soft hair behind his ear. 'Time for bed, *piccolo*.'

Frankie groaned his disagreement but he didn't argue very hard, which Maria knew meant he was exhausted. Shifting him in her arms, she prepared to carry him up the stairs to their room—only for Sebastian to stand first and reach down to take him.

'Can I?' he asked, and the need in his voice made Maria's heart hurt.

She could give him this much at least. 'Papà's going to carry you up to bed, Frankie. Okay?'

'Mmm…' Frankie said sleepily. 'You come, too?'

'Of course,' she promised.

They said quick goodnights to Noemi and Max, who were also heading to their rooms—although from the way they touched each other, hand on hand or elbow, Maria suspected sleep wasn't the first thing on the agenda for them—and made their way to the stairs.

She was so preoccupied with getting Frankie settled that it didn't occur to Maria until they reached the suite that once Frankie was asleep, the moment she'd been dreading would have finally arrived.

She'd be alone with her husband for the first time in a year. And she had no idea what to say to him.

Sebastian held Frankie tight against his chest as they climbed the stairs, loving every moment of having his son in his arms. The way his small body moved in and out with every breath. The softness of his hair against Seb's cheek. The tiny hand gripping his jumper. The long lashes covering hazel eyes, sooty against his skin. Seb drank in every second of the experience until it was a wrench to place him down on the small twin bed in the suite's second bedroom.

Frankie was almost asleep now, barely able to keep his eyes open. Maria undressed him, murmuring reassurance to him the whole time, then changed him into his pyjamas with a quiet efficiency Seb couldn't help but admire. She'd always been a fantastic mother, but the closeness between her and their son appeared to have only grown while they'd been away.

He just wished he'd been there to see it.

'Could you find his fox, please?' Maria asked, motioning towards the half-unpacked suitcase on the other bed. Maria's bed, he supposed, disliking the thought even as it passed through his head.

She should be with him. Not even because he wanted her physically—although of course he did, he always had—but just because he wanted to hold her in his arms while he slept, in case he woke in the night and thought her return was nothing but a dream, and needed the reassurance that she was really here, at last.

He just wanted to hold on to her. Was that so bad?

'Seb?' Maria was staring at him. Why was she staring at him? And looking meaningfully at the suitcase…?

Oh! The fox!

With a burst of speed Seb crossed the room and started rooting through the bag for Frankie's toy fox. He'd had the stuffed animal since his birth, a gift from his grandparents, Seb's parents, and Seb was touched to discover he still slept with it, even after so long away.

His *mamma* would have liked that, Seb knew. She'd spent hours searching the toy stores for exactly the right animal for her first grandson to love.

'A first toy is important, Sebastian,' she'd told him when he'd complained. 'A first friend, a first love, a companion in this strange new world he's been thrust into. Your son has to have the right one.'

'You make it sound like a marriage, Mamma,' Seb had joked, but she'd only smiled knowingly at him.

Since she'd always known a hundred times more about the world that he ever would, he hadn't commented on it.

He missed that. Missed her. Missed being able to ask her what it was he didn't understand yet.

He held the fox against his cheek for a moment before handing it to Maria, but if she noticed, she didn't say anything.

Seb watched as Maria tucked the blanket around Frankie, even as his little hands grabbed the fox and held it under his chin, its fluffy tail brushing his cheek. For a moment he looked just like the baby Seb remembered. Like no time had passed at all.

He pressed a kiss to his son's forehead and whispered, 'Sweet dreams, *piccolo*,' just like he had every night before he'd gone to bed when Frankie had lived with him.

Then he stepped back and saw Maria's wary face, her shorter hair, her harder eyes, and knew that everything *had* changed.

And it was his job to change things back again.

Romance. That was his way in, he was almost sure. Maria had felt neglected before she'd left—had thrown it in his face when they'd argued the night before she'd packed her bags and walked out.

'You don't even see me!' she'd yelled. 'Sometimes I'm not sure you'd even notice if I left.'

But he'd noticed. Boy, how he'd noticed.

Seb may not have his mother there to set him right, but he knew exactly what she'd have said. *Take care of your wife, Sebastian. Look after your family.*

And so that was what he was going to do. Starting with talking to Maria. Listening to Maria. Letting her know how much he wanted her there, and how far he was willing to go to keep her with him.

Whatever it took.

'How about a drink by the fire?' he suggested, softly, so as not to disturb Frankie. Maria looked up at him in surprise. 'I think we've got a lot to talk about. Don't you?'

She should have thought about this more—about what she'd say once she was alone with Sebastian again. And she had, to a point. She'd been imagining this conversation for a year—ever since she'd left.

But she realised now, too late, that in her head the conversation was always Seb talking, and her unable to get a word in edgeways as he listed her faults and derided her for breaking her marriage vows. Told her what a terrible wife and mother she was. How disappointed in her he was. How he'd married her for only one reason, and she hadn't lived up to her side of the bargain.

Just like her father had done when she'd arrived home with Frankie.

She hadn't ever imagined they'd be sitting together on the squashy, cosy sofa in their old suite, drinking good red wine in front of the fire, waiting for each other to start.

Maria had never been much good at silence. She was always going to crack first.

'Look, I know we have a lot to talk about. And that you must have questions. And… I don't blame you for being angry with me—'

'I never said I was angry with you,' Seb said, so calmly she couldn't help but believe him.

'You're…not?' she asked, just to check.

'I was,' Seb admitted. 'When you first left…just ask Noemi. I was like a bear with a sore head for months.'

'She might have mentioned that.' Only with slightly less polite words when it came down to it.

'But looking at you now…' Seb shook his head, a slight

smile on his lips. 'I may not have liked it, but I can see why you had to go.'

Maria blinked at him. Did he really know? Did he, at last, understand why she'd been unable to stay, been unable to see him smile at her while looking through her every day? Did he realise how much it had hurt to be so close to him and yet feel so much difference between them?

No. Apparently not.

'I mean, you seem so much more content now. Like you've found yourself, I guess,' Seb went on, oblivious to how her heart was cracking. 'I get that I didn't give you the attention you needed, that I worked too much, that you were alone with Frankie a lot of the time.'

'That was part of it,' Maria said cautiously. But Seb didn't hear her caution, it seemed. The same way he hadn't heard her words the night before she'd left.

This isn't enough for me, Seb. And I realise now you can't give me what I need. You're not capable of it.

Not capable of love. Or not capable of loving *her*. Either way, it added up to the same thing, really.

'The thing is, I realised something today,' Seb went on. 'I don't want to be an absentee father or even a detached husband. I don't want to spend my life without you or without Frankie.' He took a deep breath, and Maria couldn't help but admire the way his broad chest moved, how handsome his profile was in the firelight.

Oh, God, was there really *no* hope for her?

'I want us to use this time, while we're all here together over Christmas, to find a better way forward,' Seb said. 'One that gives you what you need but doesn't cut me out of your lives so completely. A way for us to work together, to make our marriage what we always promised it would be. A partnership.'

Maria met his gaze, and saw the sincerity there. He wanted this for real—wanted *her*, even.

Just not the way she'd always dreamed of.

He wanted his family back together—and wasn't that only natural after losing his parents, and all the other changes he'd been through recently? She was familiar, easy. And, yes, of course he loved Frankie.

But none of that was the same as loving her.

'What do you say?' Seb shifted closer on the sofa, angling his body into her. They were so close she could smell the familiar scent of his skin, could reach out and touch his hair—kiss him, even. And it would be so, so easy to fall back into those old patterns. To let him hold her and to feel safe in his arms. To remember how they used to move together, and how incredible it had felt.

To let herself love him with her whole heart again, only to have it break even harder this time when he still couldn't love her the way she needed.

Pulling back, Maria shook her head. 'Seb, I'm not here to stay. You know that. Frankie and I... We only came for Christmas.'

'I know, I know.' Seb flashed her a devastating smile. 'But can you blame me for wanting more?'

'No, but... I have a life somewhere else now. And so does Frankie.'

Admittedly, her life mostly revolved around Frankie, and her part-time business degree. Thankfully her mother, while endlessly disappointed in her, didn't take out that disappointment on Frankie, who spent many happy days with his grandmother while his mother studied. If nothing else good had come out of this year, that at least was more than she'd truly hoped for when she'd left. And even if her relationship with her father was ruined for good after the last few months, in some ways that was a relief, too. She didn't have to try to be the Maria he wanted any more either. She could just be herself.

'Is there...? Have you met someone else?' What was it

she heard in Seb's voice as he asked that? It sounded like…
like fear, perhaps. But why on earth would Seb be afraid
of that? Unless it was his ongoing terror of not appearing
to have the perfect life.

The thing Maria had never been able to understand was
that Seb was gorgeous, rich, funny when he wanted to be,
and generally a good guy. He could have had women lining up down the street for him, especially since she'd left.

But Noemi had said he'd stayed completely alone. The
only reason Maria could think of for that was that the business and his reputation were still more important to him
than his own happiness—never mind hers or anyone else's.

That was what had convinced her, finally, that she'd
made the right decision in leaving.

But she'd never been able to take that next step herself.

'No,' she said, looking down at her hands as she shook her
head slightly. 'I mean, a couple of times people tried to set
me up on blind dates and stuff, but no. There's no one else.'

'Good. That's…that means there's still hope.'

'Hope?' Maria looked up into his eyes and saw something else there now. The same sort of determination she
was more used to seeing when he was undertaking a difficult new business deal. Or once, just after they'd married, when he'd set about finding out everything she liked
and loved between the sheets.

A determined Seb could accomplish great things. Her
body remembered. Vividly.

'Hope that I can fix this. If you'll let me try.'

God, she'd never been able to resist him when he looked
like that. Not when he focused all his attention on her so
completely, determined to do whatever it took to please her.

If only he'd looked like that more often, she'd probably
never have left.

'Okay,' she said, the word coming out raspy. She took a
sip of wine to soothe her throat and her nerves. It was only

until Christmas. On Boxing Day she and Frankie would leave, unless something fundamental shifted in her relationship with Seb. She could give him until Christmas, couldn't she? Call it his Christmas present. 'We can try.'

CHAPTER FIVE

SEBASTIAN WAS UP early the next morning—not for work reasons for once but because he was eager to start a new, even more important project.

Project Win Back Wife and Child.

Maybe it needed a better name than that, he mused as he stepped into the shower, hoping the warm water would wake him up a bit. He hadn't slept as well as he normally did. For some reason, after a year of getting used to not having Maria in his bed beside him, last night had thrown him straight back to those first, lonely days after she'd left. Rather than sprawling across the bed as he'd taken to doing over the last twelve months to make it feel less empty, he'd spent the night hours reaching for someone who hadn't been there, and waking himself up when he'd realised he'd been alone.

Clearly, he needed this project more than ever.

Maybe Project Family was the name he was looking for. He had a feeling that Noemi would approve.

He hoped so, anyway, because he was going to need her help to pull it off.

By the time Seb was showered and dressed, there was still no sign of the door to Maria and Frankie's room opening. He loitered outside for a few moments, listening, but all was quiet.

Deciding to let them sleep in, Seb headed downstairs to find his sister.

Noemi was, as he'd expected, brewing coffee in the

kitchen—decaf, in her case, it seemed, but fortunately she had some full-strength stuff on the go, too.

'Can I steal a cup of that?' he asked, settling himself on one of the counter stools to watch her work. Now he knew about her pregnancy, it was impossible to miss the slight curve of her usually slender body, or the way her clothes skimmed over it. Not to mention the glow of happiness that surrounded her.

'I was making it for Max.' She scowled at him, rather ruining the pregnancy goddess image.

'Please? I assure you, my need is greater. I need energy for my plans today.' He was wheedling, he knew, but Noemi was a soft touch sometimes, so if it worked it was worth it.

'Plans?' She poured a cup of the coffee and pushed it towards him, one eyebrow elegantly arched. 'Are these Maria plans?'

Seb nodded, taking a sip of the steaming hot drink. 'That's the idea.'

Noemi leaned forward against the counter between them, her elbows on the wooden surface. 'Then how can I help?'

Seb grinned. 'I was hoping you would ask that.'

'Because you have no idea how to win a woman over?' Noemi asked.

'Hey! She married me in the first place, didn't she?' Seb pointed out.

Noemi rolled her eyes. 'That was a business deal. No one ever denied that you were good at those.'

Well, it was the closest thing to a compliment that he was likely to get from his sister these days, so Seb decided to take it.

'It wasn't just business,' he argued, almost for the sake of it. Everyone knew that if it hadn't been for Maria's father's business troubles, she never would have married him. And he'd probably never have got around to getting married at all, too busy with the company. But business wasn't all there had ever been between them—especially after the vows had been made and he'd discovered how much he adored making love to his wife… But that wasn't the point. 'We were friends. Partners, even. And we're parents. That doesn't count for nothing, you know.'

'Hey, I'm all for you two crazy kids working things out between you,' Noemi said, lifting her coffee cup in a mock toast. 'I just think you need to figure out exactly why she left, and how you can stop screwing up so badly.'

'I'm way ahead of you.' Seb tried not to sound too smug. 'And I've always known why she left—she told me as much when we argued the night before.'

'And you listened?' Noemi asked, sounding amazed.

Seb ignored her. 'She felt ignored. Neglected. She said I didn't see her.'

'Right,' Noemi said slowly, as if there needed to be more.

'So I'm going to prove to her that I *do* see her. That if she comes home I won't ignore her. That there can be romance and that stuff in our marriage, even if it's not *why* we married.'

'"Romance and that stuff",' Noemi echoed, faintly. 'Right.'

'See! It's all going to be great.' Seb felt a lot better about his plan, having talked it through. All he needed to do was show Maria how much he wanted her there. Which was easy, because it was the truth.

'So what do you need me to do?' Noemi asked, sounding far too sceptical about the whole thing for Seb's liking. Still, he'd show her. He just needed the time to do it—and he only had until Christmas. Which meant pulling out the romance big guns from the off.

'Could you and Max watch Frankie for me today? As

much as I want to spend time with the little guy, I figure that romancing Maria comes first.' After all, if that part of the plan worked, then Frankie would be around for him to spend time with every day. If it didn't…

Well. He just wasn't going to think about that.

'Will you do it?'

'Of course,' Noemi said automatically. 'But what are you and Maria going to be doing?'

Seb grinned broadly. 'We're going on a date.'

'I'm so sorry—we slept in!' Maria bustled into the kitchen, Frankie holding her hand, to find Sebastian and Noemi sipping coffee together at the counter. 'I guess we must have been more tired than I thought after travelling yesterday.' At least, Maria assumed that was why Frankie—who was always an early-morning kid—had slept in way past his normal wake-up time. Travelling and a late night, plus lots of new people, had had him zonked out for twelve straight hours.

She, on the other hand, had spent most of the night listening to Frankie breathing and thinking about her husband in the next room, and what she'd agreed to. She'd finally passed out around three in the morning, and had apparently made up for the lack of rest by oversleeping until closer to lunch than breakfast.

Frankie, dressed in his warmest clothes, bounced on his toes beside her, still excited by being at the chalet. He'd woken up perfectly rested and had bounded onto her bed to wake her up, too, keen to start his day in the snow.

'Don't worry! You haven't missed anything yet,' Noemi said, beaming.

'In fact, we were just discussing plans for the day,' Seb added. Maria couldn't help but notice that Sebastian, at least, looked relaxed, happy and as gorgeous as ever. While she felt like a nervous wreck. How was that fair?

At least she'd have Frankie as a buffer between them today. Seb couldn't possibly want to continue last night's conversation with their son around. So all she needed to do was keep things friendly and polite—and not let him get under her skin again like last night.

Easy. Right?

But then Noemi crouched down in front of Frankie, a mischievous grin on her face. 'How would you like to spend the day with Aunt Noemi and Uncle Max, munchkin?'

Maria's gaze flew to Sebastian's face, but he was smiling serenely. This was *his* plan, then. He wanted to get her alone.

Damn him.

'Noemi, you really don't have to—'

'I'd love to!' Noemi broke in. 'And so would Max. Or he will when I tell him. I mean, it's great practice for us both.'

'Right. I know. It's just… I'm not sure that Frankie is—' Maria started again, trying to find a good enough excuse that wouldn't offend Noemi, but this time Frankie interrupted her.

'We have ice cream?' he asked, in his sweet, high voice.

Subzero temperatures and her son wanted ice cream. Naturally.

'Of course we'll have ice cream!' Noemi said gleefully. She took his hand and led him away. 'But probably not for breakfast. How about we have some pastries first, then we can go and find Uncle Max and decide what else we want to do today.'

'Okay.' Frankie sounded cheerful enough, but Maria was pretty sure he hadn't heard past 'pastries'. He loved pastries almost as much as ice cream, and at two years old he didn't have much of a handle on time just yet.

But he was happy. So she had no reason to stop him spending time with Noemi and Max. And no excuse not to spend time with Sebastian, except for the fact that she was scared of losing all the ground she'd made while she'd been away. She could feel her resistance ebbing away.

'So…lunch?' Seb asked, and Maria couldn't seem to stop herself nodding.

Ninety minutes later—after giving Noemi and Max comprehensive toddler care instructions, and explaining in great detail to Frankie the behaviour she expected from him, while knowing that despite his nodding and innocent wide eyes he wasn't going to remember any of it, then changing into something smart enough for going out and being seen around Mont Coeur with Sebastian but warm enough that she wouldn't freeze the moment she stepped outside the chalet—Seb and Maria went for lunch.

'Honestly, I'd be fine with just a burger or something,' Maria protested, as he led her towards the fanciest restaurant in Mont Coeur.

Seb gave her an amused look, as if he could tell just by looking at her that she was trying to find ways to keep this lunch short and, well, just short, really. He probably could, too. He'd always been good at reading her. On the surface, anyway. Just not when it came to the things that really mattered.

'Do you realise,' Seb said, holding open the glass door to the restaurant for her, 'this is our first ever proper date?'

'This is a date now?' Maria's eyes widened. Yeah, she really should have found a way to go snowman building with Frankie and Max.

'You, me, the best and most romantic restaurant in town… Yes, Maria, this is a date.' Seb rolled his eyes, as if waiting for her to catch up with the agenda for the day. Which she was suddenly rather afraid she had.

Seb was planning on wooing her. Romancing her. Except she knew for a fact that her husband had no experience or idea of what that should entail.

She'd known Seb since they had both been in nappies, their fathers long-time friends, neighbours and business acquaintances, with Rossi Gems providing many of the precious stones used in the Cattaneo Jewels designs. The families had grown closer as the kids had grown up together, and Maria had watched Seb change from a serious, wide-eyed boy to a gawky teenager, until he'd suddenly come into his height and build around the age of seventeen.

She'd been fifteen at the time, and definitely hadn't missed the changes in him.

When he'd left for university he'd been handsome, confident and ready to take on the business world. But he'd always been far too caught up in making his father proud to waste time on girls. Oh, she was sure he'd dated a little—and she was certain he must have had *some* experience before their wedding night, or it couldn't have been as fantastic as it had been. But women hadn't mattered to him, not the way the business did, and they'd been married less than a year after he'd finished his MBA, so it wasn't like he'd had a lot of time to play around. Besides, the idea of him taking time out from his studies to plan a dream date was sort of ridiculous.

Although a romantic restaurant was a pretty good start, she supposed. Clichéd and obvious, but at least not awful. It could have been a lot worse.

'Right.' Well, at least she knew what she was up against. Seb on a charm offensive could be quite something to watch, but she was prepared now. She could hold her own.

She frowned. Sure, she'd buy Seb not dating around much before they'd married. But… 'Wait. We *must* have gone on a date before. We've been married for years, for heaven's sake.'

'Name one,' Seb challenged.

And, of course, she couldn't. Because romance wasn't what their marriage had been about. They'd gone out, of course, but for business dinners or corporate trips or what have you. Never just to spend time in the pleasure of each other's company.

Fortunately, Maria was saved from answering by the arrival of the maître d', looking horrified that he'd missed their arrival by all of thirty seconds. He led them straight to their table, gushing over having Mr Cattaneo gracing his restaurant—and on a weekday, too!

Seb mostly ignored him, taking the offered menu and sitting down to study it as the maître d' pulled Maria's chair out for her. Copying Seb, she reached for her own menu as Seb ordered a carafe of white wine to start.

'So?' Seb peered at her over the top of his menu. 'Thought of one yet? A date, I mean.'

'What about the night we went to the theatre to see that play you were so keen on?' Maria asked. 'Doesn't that count?' Admittedly, Seb had only seen the first half because an emergency call from the office in the interval had meant he'd spent the rest of the evening on the phone in the theatre foyer, but still…

Seb put down his menu. 'I think we need to re-evaluate your criteria for a date,' he said. 'I take full responsibility—I clearly haven't been keeping up my end of the husband bargain when it comes to taking you out.'

'So, what constitutes a date by your definition?' Maria asked. Maybe there was wriggle room with one of the corporate trips…

'You and me alone—no family or business acquaintances along. Somewhere romantic, and only focused on each other.'

Huh. Well, they definitely hadn't done that—at least not since their honeymoon. And she had to admit that it didn't sound so bad. Especially if, for the first time she could remember, Seb kept his word and left work at the office. To be fair to him, he hadn't mentioned the business once since they'd left the chalet. Even now, he was smiling pleasantly at the wine waiter and tasting the white wine he'd brought them. When he nodded, the waiter poured them each a full glass.

'In that case, I agree—this might actually be our first real date since our honeymoon.' And they hadn't had any before because they hadn't needed to. The engagement had been arranged by their fathers. They'd known each other since they were children. Why would they have needed to date?

Although… Maria's mind drifted back to when she'd been fifteen, and the memory of a frosty night on a frozen lake, and Seb's hand in hers. Maybe that was the closest they'd got, and she knew for a fact that Seb wouldn't count it. He hadn't thought of her that way, even then.

But maybe now he could.

Maria lifted her glass to Seb, and he followed suit, clinking it gently against hers.

'To romance,' he said, and smiled the smile that had always made her heart flutter most.

'To romance,' she echoed.

Oh, yeah. She was in for it now.

The restaurant was everything Noemi had promised it would be when he'd asked for recommendations. The food was exquisite, the staff attentive but unobtrusive, and the atmosphere wonderfully romantic—especially with the still falling snow outside those huge glass windows.

The perfect place for his first date with his wife.

Seb watched her across the table as she delicately finished her chocolate mousse. He still wasn't used to all the changes in her.

Her hair, chopped back from halfway down her back

to just above her shoulders, looked strangely more grown up somehow, although still as dark and glossy as ever. Her bright blue eyes sparkled as they always had, but there was something wary in them, as if she was holding back. She'd lost a little weight, he thought. It made her more delicate almost, except that there was nothing fragile about the woman sitting across from him.

Her dark red knitted dress clung to her slender curves, reminding him of everything he knew lay underneath it, and he ached to learn her anew that way.

She was stronger now, he was sure. He felt it somewhere inside.

It only made him want her more.

They'd talked all through lunch—mostly about Frankie and his funny toddler ways, or about their families. He'd told her a little about Leo and their growing relationship as brothers—although not about the offer of his shares, not yet. Maria, in turn, had given him a dry account of how her parents had responded to her showing up on their doorstep with Frankie in tow.

Seb knew his in-laws. He didn't need the details to imagine the scenes.

'What about you?' he asked, as Maria put down her cutlery. 'You've told me about everyone else. But what have *you* been up to over the last twelve months?'

She looked surprised that he'd asked. Had he really been that inattentive before she'd left? Probably. He had just been so used to Maria always being there, being part of his life, he'd taken her for granted. Had skimped on the romance and attention she'd deserved.

He wouldn't make that mistake again, if she gave him the chance.

'Mostly looking after Frankie,' Maria said. 'Placating my father, that sort of thing.'

Seb waited. That couldn't be all of it. He *knew* Maria.

'And… I've been taking a course. A business course.'

'Really?' Now, that *was* interesting. 'Why?'

He knew the question was a mistake the moment he asked it—the scowl on Maria's face only confirmed it for him.

'Because I should be happy to be a wife and a mother, right? Just stay home and look pretty, rather than getting my hands dirty in business?' she snapped.

'No!' Seb's eyes widened, and he put up his hands in a mock surrender. 'That's not… I only meant that you were always such a natural at business. You understood everything I ever spoke to you about, and you gave great advice. I just wondered why you felt you needed to study it again after, well…' After she'd given it up to marry him, at her father's request. *Tactful, Seb.*

But Maria's expression softened a tiny bit anyway. 'I'm sorry. I should know better. I just… I've been spending a lot of time with my father lately.'

'Ah.' Maria's father had never wanted her involved in the family business. As far as he was concerned, her only job had been to marry well enough to bring in a *man* to deal with it—as shown by his actions when he'd run his own company into the ground, then married Maria off to fix it.

Seb knew his father would have undertaken the merger without the marriage, to help his friend. But old man Rossi had just had to have a physical marker, keeping his hand in the business, and Salvo had been happy to see his son settled so easily.

Sebastian had never had much respect for his father-in-law.

'Yeah. He didn't like me taking the course much.' She looked up and met his gaze, and Seb listened carefully, knowing whatever she had to say next mattered. A lot. 'But

I wanted to finish what I started, all those years ago. I'm a grown woman now. I make my own choices.'

'I never thought you weren't,' Seb said carefully. 'And I would never want to make choices for you.'

He'd just really like it if she made the ones he wanted her to make. Did that make him as bad as her father? He wasn't really sure any more.

'Good. I just wondered because…' She trailed off, leaving Seb to imagine what she might have been about to say.

Except he needed to know. He needed to know everything he'd done wrong so he could fix them. Otherwise in a matter of days she'd be walking away from him again—for good this time.

'Because?' he prompted.

'Back before we were married—and even after for a while, I suppose—you used to talk to me about the business. Ask my advice, let me help you work out the best way forward for Cattaneo Jewels. And I liked that. It was something we had in common, to connect us. My father, he never wanted me anywhere near the business end of things, but you did. You made me feel like you valued my opinions.'

'I did,' Seb said, quickly. 'Very much. You always knew the right questions to ask to help me work through things. You helped me get to the heart of whatever the problem was so I could figure out what really mattered.' His dad had been giving him more and more control and responsibility, he remembered, setting him up to take things over when he was ready to retire. Having Maria to talk things through with had made that less scary.

Had made him feel less alone.

'Then why did you stop?' Maria asked. 'The minute I got pregnant with Frankie, it was as if that was my only responsibility, the only thing I was good for any more. Giving you an heir.'

Seb's eyes widened. 'That wasn't… No, absolutely not. That wasn't what I was thinking at all.' What the hell *had* he been thinking? Everything had been so confused and frantic since then it was hard to remember. But he knew he had to.

'Then explain it to me.' Maria sat back in her seat and waited.

'I'll… I'll try.' Seb saw a waiter hovering, waiting to see if they wanted more drinks or whatever. 'Just…let me get the bill. I want to have this conversation properly, not here.'

He handed his card over to the loitering waiter, tipping generously as he paid, his mind still on the past—and its power over the present. So much of their history was tangled up in their fathers' actions. Could they unwind all of that to find a new path, a new future together?

This conversation could make or break his marriage, he was almost certain. He *had* to get it right.

Besides which, he wasn't ready for this date to be over yet. For the first time ever, he and Maria were being totally honest with each other. He didn't want to call a close to that—not before he had a chance to tackle the issues that really mattered between them.

Then he looked out of the window and saw the perfect way to keep their bubble of privacy and truthfulness.

Smiling, he replaced his card in his wallet and put it back in his jacket pocket.

'Come on,' he said, reaching for Maria's hand. 'I've got an idea.'

CHAPTER SIX

ONLY SEBASTIAN WOULD think that a romantic sleigh ride was the perfect place for the most important conversation she'd ever had in her marriage. Possibly in her life. He really was going all out with the romance thing, given his total lack of prior experience.

Although, she had to admit, it did at least give them privacy.

Up ahead, the two bright white horses clip-clopped through the streets of Mont Coeur, out towards the snowy fields and hills beyond, tugging their festive green sleigh behind them. Their driver wore thick earmuffs and had barely even grunted a welcome as Sebastian had helped her on board, so Maria was fairly sure he wasn't eavesdropping on their marital woes.

Still, they kept the conversation light to start with, each pointing out sights and sounds around them.

'Look! Ice skaters.' Seb pointed towards a frozen lake just beyond the village. 'Do you remember that night we crept out to go ice-skating on the lake at your parents' house?'

'Of course.' Maria smiled, a little wistfully. How could she forget the night she'd fallen in love with her husband? Even if she'd never told him.

Seb's smile was more rueful. 'I probably should have been locked up for taking you out there. It was stupidly dangerous, and you were only, what, thirteen?'

'Fifteen,' Maria corrected him. 'And I wanted to go.'

'That's why I took you,' Seb said, with a grin.

Maria looked away, settling back against the padded seat, the memory flooding back. It had been the Christmas holidays, the year before Seb had left for university. The year she'd looked at him and seen a man almost—and a gorgeous one at that. Seb and Noemi had been visiting for a weekend while their parents were away. Maria had been begging her parents all day to let them skate on the frozen lake on the estate, but they'd refused to budge. Too dangerous. Too risky.

But that was what Maria had wanted. A little risk, a little danger. Anything to make her feel less trapped in her parents' house.

That night, after everyone had gone to bed, Seb had knocked on her door, a pair of ice skates dangling from his fingers.

She'd never felt more alive than she had that night, skating in the darkness with Sebastian Cattaneo. And she'd known then she'd never love anyone else either.

But she couldn't think about that now. Not when there was so much still unsettled between them.

Dragging her attention back to the present, she made herself feel the sleigh beneath her, the icy air against her skin. She wasn't fifteen any more. She had to remember that.

'I've never been on one of these before,' she admitted, watching as the snow-capped trees flew past alongside them. 'Frankie would love it. Or be terrified. No real way of telling with toddlers.'

'We'll bring him into town to see the horses, then,' Seb said. 'See how he reacts.'

We. Together. As a family. She knew that was what Seb was getting at, what he was striving for. But she needed her answers first.

Shifting in her seat, she angled her body towards him,

her gloved hands resting on her lap. He looked so gorgeous in the bright, reflected light of the sun on the snow, his close-cropped dark hair showing off his strong jaw and handsome features. His green eyes looked thoughtful, as he stared out over the view of the Alps. Was he thinking about his answer? Or a work problem?

Probably the latter, since it was Seb.

'So. Have you thought of a reason yet?' she asked, not hiding the slight edge in her voice as she almost echoed his question from lunch. This was important to her. If they really wanted to repair their relationship—even if only so they could parent Frankie more amicably long distance—then she needed to understand what had changed for him. Why he'd started cutting her out just when she'd hoped they'd be growing closer.

'It's not so much thinking of a reason.' Seb gave her a small, apologetic smile. 'It's remembering exactly what I was thinking and feeling. I tend to act more on instinct and logic with these things, rather than thinking them through sometimes.'

She knew that. She knew him. Which meant she also knew that if he could avoid thinking about emotions and such completely and swap them for spreadsheets and profit-and-loss statements instead, he would.

But she wasn't going to let him get away with that today.

'I think… You remember how ill you were at the start of your pregnancy?' he asked.

Urgh. As if she could forget. She'd thrown up for twelve weeks straight, every day at eleven and four like clockwork. And in between she'd nursed a bottle of chilled water and a packet of plain crackers. It was *not* a time she remembered with fondness, even if it had been worth it to have Frankie.

'Of course I remember.'

'I'd never… I'd never seen you like that before. You'd never had more than a head cold the whole time I'd known you. Even when the rest of us came down with chicken-pox that year when I was about ten, you stayed immune.'

'I'd already had it as a toddler,' Maria recalled. 'So I was free to just laugh at your and Noemi's spots.'

'Yeah, well. Seeing you like that—sick and weak and emotional—it was kind of scary, I guess. I hated that it was my fault you felt that way, and hated even more that there was nothing I could do to make you feel better.'

Maria looked at him curiously. 'It was just pregnancy sickness, Seb. Millions of women go through it every day—many of them a lot worse than I did.'

'I know. But none of those other millions of women were my wife.'

She couldn't help herself. She reached over and took his gloved hand in hers, holding it on her lap. 'So that's why you stopped involving me in the business? Because I was getting sick?'

'Partly,' Seb said, and sighed. 'I suppose I felt like I had to make it up to you. I mean, of course I wasn't going to bother you with work stuff when you were feeling so lousy. But afterwards... I just wanted you to enjoy the pregnancy and then having Frankie. I didn't want to bother you with the business or my worries.'

'But you're my husband, Seb. Your worries should have been our worries.' That was what he'd never understood. She wanted a partnership. He wanted a wife and heir to trot out at business social events. 'And it's not like becoming a mother rotted my brain. I was still the same person I'd always been—I still cared about the business, too.'

'I know that *now*,' Seb replied. 'But back then...it felt like Frankie was your whole world, and my job was just to make sure that you and he were safe and secure and wanted for nothing—like my *papà* had always done for my mother.'

I wanted my husband, Maria thought. *I wanted your*

love. But she didn't say it. However cosy this romantic sleigh ride might be, she wasn't ready to admit that yet. That she wanted them to be a team, a partnership—sure, that was what they'd promised each other, privately, when they'd agreed to their fathers' plans for their marriage.

They'd never promised love, not really.

Yes, there were those pesky wedding vows—to love, honour and cherish. But that was just something they'd had to say. Besides, there were many kinds of love. And she'd never doubted that Seb loved her as an old treasured family friend. One with whom he shared a fantastic sexual chemistry, but that was just sex. She'd had his affection, his friendship, his passion, and even his son.

She'd always known it hadn't gone any deeper. He hadn't loved her with his whole heart, in that aching, all-consuming way she'd loved him.

If he had, he could never have let her leave at all.

'I just wanted what we always promised each other,' she said instead. 'I wanted us to be a team. I wanted to feel part of it all.'

All those lonely days with Frankie and then nothing to talk about when Seb came home at night except how long the baby had napped, or how much milk he'd taken. Nothing in her life beyond nappies and sleepsuits.

She'd loved her baby, loved being a mother. But she'd longed for something more, too.

'I didn't realise.' Seb shook his head a little sadly. 'I thought... I thought you wanted the sort of marriage my parents had—your parents, too, I suppose.'

Maria laughed, a little bitterly, thinking of her parents' silent, grudging marriage. 'Trust me. That was the last thing I wanted.'

Seb squeezed Maria's hand tightly through two pairs of gloves. 'I'm sorry.' He'd been an idiot as usual. Maria hadn't just felt neglected; she'd felt sidelined. Like her opinion hadn't mattered.

He'd known well enough from his earliest days in the business, trying to earn his right to be there beyond just being the son and heir, how painful that could be. Every time he'd heard someone whisper behind his back that he wouldn't have a job if he wasn't Salvo's son, or caught a comment about nepotism, he'd doubted himself over again. He'd earned the right to be there in the end, but it had taken time.

Something he didn't have with Maria.

Okay. So he couldn't fix the past. But he could try to change the future. And if all she wanted was for them to be a partnership again, he could give her that.

'I wish I'd known how you felt,' he said. 'But now that I do…we can fix this, right? If you want more of a say in the business, that's easy. I'd love to have your help and advice again.'

She'd never believe him if he told her how much he'd missed that. Even when she'd still been there, when Frankie had been a baby. Of course, she'd been busy looking after him and, quite rightly, Frankie had been her number one concern. But he'd also missed the days when they'd used to talk. About the business, yes, but about other things, too. The future. Their hopes and dreams.

He remembered his parents doing that. While Salvo had been very much the businessman, and Nicole had been content merely to *wear* the jewellery he'd sold, rather than be involved in the company, that hadn't been the case at home at all. There they had been a partnership in the truest sense of the word. They had each had their own responsibilities, but they had always worked towards a common goal—keeping their family happy, healthy and together.

He'd lost sight of that goal with Maria, he realised suddenly. She was right. Somewhere along the way they'd stopped being a team. And he wanted more than anything to get that feeling back again.

'That would be good,' Maria said, and Seb would have celebrated—except for the cautious tone in her voice that gave him pause.

'But?'

Maria sighed, turning away to look out at the snow. For a long moment all Seb could hear was the soft fall of horse hooves on newly fallen snow and the crack in the air that told him more snow would be falling soon.

And his own internal monologue, of course, coming up with increasingly awful things that Maria might say next.

But this marriage isn't enough for me.

But you're not good enough for me.

But I want to be free to find someone who can give me what I need.

But Frankie needs a better father than you.

Finally, she looked at him again and spoke over his own dark thoughts. 'But the business has always been the easy part for you.'

Seb scoffed. 'Tell that to my shareholders.'

'You know what I mean.' She pulled her hand away from his. 'Work was always what you ran to when things were difficult. Remember how many hours you put in when I was pregnant?'

'Yeah, but that was because we were in the middle of launching the new range and starting on the expansion—'

'And what does it tell you that you can remember exactly what was happening at the office at that time, but it took you twenty minutes to remember how you were feeling, or what was going on in our marriage back then?'

Seb felt heat rushing to his face, despite the chilly air. Of course he could. He could remember every milestone on his journey through the family business—from the first day that his father had taken him to the office and told him that one day he'd be in charge, through his first internship, learning the ropes, right up to the day his father had signed over a portion of the company into Seb's name and told him he was responsible now.

Cattaneo Jewels had been a part of his life since he hadn't been much older than Frankie was now. He'd grown up knowing that the company was more than his destiny or even his birthright—it was his responsibility. His burden and his joy.

If he screwed up, it wasn't just him who lost money. It was his investors, his shareholders, his board. His staff whose jobs would be on the line. His suppliers who could go out of business. His clients who would be let down.

His father, who would be disappointed in him.

Even now Salvo was gone, Seb knew that his dad's disappointment could transcend the grave. If Seb ran Cattaneo Jewels into the ground, Salvo might actually rise up to berate him for it.

But how could he explain all that to Maria?

'I guess… I know what I'm doing with the business—at least I should do by now. And it's easy to measure success or failure. It's all there in the quarterly reports. But with relationships…it's harder somehow.'

'You need a quarterly report on our marriage? Our family?' Maria arched her dark eyebrows over her sparkling blue eyes.

'Honestly? It would probably help.' Seb sighed, slumping down a little on the bench seat of the sleigh. He hadn't just lost sight of his family goal. He'd never even set it to begin with. 'Nobody ever taught me this stuff, Maria. I was just expected to *know* how to be a husband, a father. And I… I don't.'

The admission hurt. His whole life he'd tried to be ahead of the game, to make his father proud by never messing up, by pretending he already knew everything Salvo was trying to teach him. By studying harder than everyone else, striving for the right experience, the right opportunities. Knowing the answer to every question before it was even asked.

But now…if the only way to win Maria back was by admitting he was clueless?

Then he'd do it. He'd tell her exactly how little he knew—and how much he wanted to learn.

He'd tell her everything.

Did he think she'd been taken aside as a teenager and given special wife lessons? Instruction in being a great mother, beyond the basic antenatal classes? Hints and tips on how to cuddle a toddler, or how to buck up a husband who'd had a bad day at work, or how to chase away the constant fear that something would happen to one of them?

'Nobody does, Seb,' she said, softly. 'Nobody is born knowing how to…connect to other people. It's something we all have to learn.'

'*You* know.'

Did she? She'd always assumed that what she knew about loving families came mostly from hanging out with the Cattaneos practically since birth. Her father certainly hadn't given her many clues, and her mother…her mother was the perfect, doting wife, who believed whatever her husband said was law.

Come to think of it, her mother might actually be just as disappointed in Maria as her father was after the collapse of her marriage, only she was too polite to make a scene about it. Marguerite Rossi *never* made a scene about anything. Not even pulling her daughter out of university and marrying her off to avoid bankruptcy. Even then all she'd done was pat Maria's hand and say, 'Your father knows best, dear.'

And anyway, if Maria *did* know how to be a great wife

and mother, why would she be in this position? Estranged from the man she loved because he could never love her back?

'I'm not sure that I do,' she murmured.

Seb's arm was around her shoulders in less than a heartbeat. 'Maria, I've seen you with Frankie—before, and now. Trust me, you're a wonderful mother.'

'Even though I took him away from his father?' And there it was. The guilt that had eaten away at her every single day of the last year.

Did she even *deserve* Seb's love now? Maria was well aware that leaving him, and taking Frankie, might have ruined any chance of him loving her, ever.

He still wanted her back; she knew that. But how much of that was pride, or comfort and ease, and how much actual affection?

Seb looked away, out over the serene mountains. 'I... I understand, I think, why you went. More than I did, anyway. And, no, I don't like it. But maybe understanding is a good place to start.'

'Maybe it is.' Maybe this was what had been missing before.

Maybe they just needed to understand each other better. And hope that once they understood, they still liked, or even loved, each other.

It was possible.

'But I need you to know…you're not the only one who's changed this last year,' Seb said.

Maria looked at him in surprise, before realising that *of course* he would have changed. He might seem exactly the same as he'd always been on the outside, but his whole life had been turned upside down over the last twelve months.

'I know.'

Seb shook his head. 'I don't think you do. I don't think

I realised how much I'd changed until last night, when I saw you and Frankie again.'

She'd never heard him talk like this before—open and emotional and honest to a fault. That in itself was evidence he wasn't the man she'd left. But she needed more. 'Tell me?'

Seb sighed, taking a moment to find the words. Maria waited.

'When Frankie turned away from me last night... I can't explain the loss I felt. The guilt and the pain. It was like a stab to the heart. I realised in an instant how much I'd missed, not even just this last year but before that, when I'd come home from the office after he was asleep and leave before he was awake. I've missed so much, Maria, and I know I can never get it back.'

Blinking away unexpected tears, Maria placed her hand over his again, holding on tight. But she didn't interrupt. She needed to hear all of this.

'And it got me thinking about my parents, and Leo. How much they missed—his whole life, really. But not through any choice of their own, or Leo's. They'd have been together if they could. And I just couldn't bear the thought that I could blink and Frankie would be all grown up, too, and I'd have missed it all. Not when there's still something I can do about it.'

He turned to her, staring down into her eyes, and she could feel the truth and the hurt behind his words.

'Losing my parents, finding Leo... It turned my world upside down—even more than you leaving with Frankie. I couldn't be the same person any more after that, Maria. I'm a different man from the one you married. But I hope I can be one you like and respect more. One who can give you the partnership—the marriage—you need.'

Seb's arm was still around her shoulders, warm and solid and reassuring. And it would be, oh, so easy to just sink into his embrace. To accept his promises of change and fall back into her old life again. But for all they'd talked more in the last few hours than they had in the eighteen months or more before she'd left, Maria couldn't help but acknowledge how much more ground they had to cover.

She turned away.

The horses trotted on, heading back from the silent hills into Mont Coeur, and Maria knew that they weren't going to fix things with just one date. Maybe Seb had changed enough to be a better father. She certainly hoped so.

But the question still remained: could they *really* fix their marriage?

'Maria?' Seb whispered her name like snowflakes on the breeze, soft and fragile, as if he didn't want her to blow away. 'I want to get this right. I want to get back to where we used to be.'

His words were colder than the ice wind. Because wasn't that just the problem? The point at which he'd been happiest—when they were married, had Frankie, were living together, and he could have his work and his easy family life—was when she'd felt most lost and alone. When she'd felt unloved and unlovable, and he hadn't even noticed. Even if he *had* changed, would that feeling ever go away without his love?

Did she really want to go back to that? Never.

'I don't want to go backwards,' she said, her voice sharp. 'If I give you another chance—*if*, Seb—then I want it to be because we're moving forward to something new.'

A new family dynamic maybe. Because as much as she needed to protect her heart, she needed to protect Frankie, too. To give him the family—and maybe now the father—that he needed. She couldn't put her own feelings above her son's happiness. She just couldn't.

'And are you? Giving me another chance?' Seb was so close now that if the sleigh jolted even slightly she'd be in his arms, kissing him. She could feel the warmth of his breath against her cheek, could see the hope in those green eyes she knew so well.

She pulled back. 'I don't know yet. Let me sleep on it?'

Disappointment flared in Seb's eyes, but he covered it quickly. He wasn't used to not getting what he wanted, Maria thought before she realised that was wrong. He just wasn't used to things not going to plan, to not getting what he *worked* for.

But she wasn't a business deal, and their family wasn't a merger he could manage through contracts and a good business plan.

Unless…unless that was the only way to get Seb to understand what she needed from him—what *Frankie* needed from him—while still protecting her heart.

He'd said he wanted them to be a family again. And maybe, just maybe, she could live without his love as long as she knew she had his respect, his partnership, and that he valued their family above his work.

It wasn't the dream, but it was close. And in twelve months away—not to mention all the years before that— she'd never met a man who made her heart beat like Sebastian Cattaneo did.

She owed it to Frankie to try to save their marriage, if it could be saved. She owed him a chance to be with his father.

And if it didn't work, at least she could walk away guilt-free, knowing she'd given it everything she could. Knowing that Frankie would be happier with two parents who loved him but not each other, because *she* would be happier, too. And Seb would have the chance to find someone he *could* love.

She'd know, at least. As much as it might hurt. She'd know that seeking her own future was the right path—the one thing in the last year she'd never quite been certain of.

'You have an alarming look on your face,' Seb observed,

from the other side of the sleigh. 'Like you're plotting my downfall.'

'Shh,' Maria said. 'I'm thinking.'

And, besides, he was only partly right. Yes, she was plotting.

But she was plotting *survival*, not downfall. And if she could figure out a way to get this right, they could *both* get what they needed.

Or close, anyway. And sometimes good enough could be enough, right?

CHAPTER SEVEN

'Okay, I've slept on it.'

Seb blinked blurry eyes in the half-light of early morning. If it even was morning. It felt like the middle of the night.

'What time is it?' he asked, pushing himself up onto one elbow.

It must have been his imagination—or maybe he was still dreaming—but he could have sworn that Maria actually stared at his bare chest for a moment, when the sheets fell down. But seconds later she was focused on his face again, her arms folded across her pyjama top, a determined look on her face.

He knew that look. It was the one she'd worn when she'd left him.

He hated that look.

'It's morning,' Maria said, unconvincingly.

Seb glanced at his phone on the bedside table. Five thirty-five. 'Barely.'

'Frankie will be up in less than an hour, and I wanted to talk to you first.'

Seb smiled at the mention of his son. They'd returned from their sleigh ride the afternoon before to find Frankie bouncing with excitement and desperate to tell them all about the fun he'd had with Aunt Noemi and Uncle Max. Max had looked exhausted and Noemi a little triumphant, but the important thing was the babysitting had been a success—even if the date hadn't given him *quite* the victory he'd been looking for.

Frankie had fallen asleep at the dinner table, and Maria had never returned from putting him to bed. Alone, as she'd insisted.

Seb had hoped that meant she was 'sleeping on it'—her decision about their future, that was.

And it seemed he'd been right.

Shuffling up to lean against the headboard, he patted the bed. 'Sit down, at least, if we're going to talk. You're making my neck ache looking up at you.'

Maria looked conflicted, but eventually perched on the end of his bed. It wasn't *quite* how he wanted her there, but if it meant they were making progress towards her staying, he'd take it.

'So. You've slept on it. And?' Seb tried to sound relaxed about the whole thing, when in reality his heart was thumping against his ribs. This could be it. His whole future, in one conversation.

'You said yesterday that you were more comfortable with the requirements of business than the business of being a family, yes?' Maria's crisp delivery made him wonder if she'd been rehearsing these lines all night. Probably, knowing Maria. They may have had very different upbringings in lots of ways, but one thing they had in common was that both sets of parents had instilled in them a chronic fear of messing up.

He hadn't thought about that when she'd left. How hard it must have been for her to go back to her parents and admit that she couldn't make the marriage work. Whether it was fair or not, the Rossis would have seen that as a failure.

How unhappy must she have truly been to choose that over a life with him?

Maria was still staring at him. He quickly ran her last

statement through his mind again. 'Yes. I guess so. Sorry, I'm still half-asleep here.'

She bit her lip, and suddenly Seb lost all attention again, unable to focus on anything except her luscious mouth and how much he wanted to kiss it.

Until Maria said, 'In which case, I think we should make a business plan for our marriage,' and he came jolting back to the here and now.

'What?' Surely he hadn't heard that right.

'A business plan. For our marriage.' She said it more slowly this time, as if that would make it a more sensible suggestion.

'Like…with profit-and-loss statements? Or expected sales and markets?' He spent his working days—which was basically all of them—staring at those. Now he had to spend his family time doing it as well?

'With objectives and goals for the marriage. And commitments,' Maria added.

'I thought we made those when we took our wedding vows,' Seb pointed out. He refrained from mentioning the part where she'd run away and broken them, which he figured was pretty good of him under the circumstances.

They'd already *made* a deal. Their whole marriage was a business arrangement. So why did they need a new one?

'Well, clearly just *promising* to love, honour and cherish wasn't enough,' Maria snapped. 'So this time how about we do it your way?'

'My way? This is your idea—how is it *my* way?'

Except…hadn't he realised just yesterday that he hadn't chased his family goal the way his parents had? That he needed to focus on what mattered by keeping it front and centre, like he would any work goal?

'Because you're the one who—' She broke off and took a deep breath, and Seb was almost certain she was counting to ten under her breath. Yeah, that wasn't a great sign.

'Look, Seb, I'm trying to find a way to make this work. It would help if you just went along with me, rather than arguing.'

'It would help if I had coffee,' Seb muttered, scrubbing a hand over his head. He had to try. If nothing else, between now and Christmas Day he had to try literally *anything* that might help him save his marriage.

Even this. 'Okay. I'm listening. I'm open to ideas. Tell me how this would work.'

It had seemed so obvious when she'd come up with the idea. Seb knew business, so she'd turn their relationship into something he understood. And by setting the parameters herself, it gave her control over things, the better to protect her heart this time. It was perfect.

That was the problem with middle-of-the-night epiphanies—they always seemed like a good idea at the time.

But then you had to explain them to your half-asleep estranged husband at stupid o'clock in the morning, and the whole thing fell apart.

No. This was a good idea. More to the point, it was her *only* idea. If she wanted to either turn this marriage into something she could live with or be able to leave again knowing she'd given it her best, they had to follow the plan.

Once she'd explained it in terms that Seb was capable of understanding before coffee.

She contemplated actually going and fetching him coffee before she continued, but it had taken her half the night to get up the confidence to do this in the first place. She couldn't stop now.

He'd just have to struggle through un-caffeinated.

'When our fathers insisted we get married, what was their reasoning?' she said, hoping to get his mind on the same track hers was. Maybe everything only seemed obvious to her because she'd already been living with the basics since she'd first had the idea the previous afternoon. She had to take Seb through the same thought process she'd followed.

'It was…well, I guess it was a business deal.' He sounded slightly embarrassed about it, which was sweet. But it was the truth, and she'd never been under any illusions otherwise. How could she have been?

Her father had been very clear about his hopes for her future, ever since she'd become a teenager. She'd just never taken it seriously until it was too late.

When, at fourteen, she'd brought a boy home from school—not even a boyfriend, just a boy who had been a friend—he'd almost hit the roof. Her mother had calmed him down, though, and then, the next day, she'd been summoned to her father's study.

'You need to understand that you are not free to make any sort of…alliances, specifically of a romantic nature,' he'd said. 'We need more from you than just some boy you pick up from school.'

Slowly, it had dawned on her that, as a daughter, she was useless to him—or to his business. Except in one way. The right marriage. That was all her father was interested in for her—marrying her off to the highest bidder.

She'd railed against it, of course, had wanted to rebel, even—ineffectual as it might have been. Until the day her father had shown up at her university to take her away and dash all her dreams.

Except then he'd told her he needed her to marry Sebastian Cattaneo and, suddenly, against the odds, she'd started to hope again.

Now here she was, all these years later, still clinging to that hope.

Maria swallowed the memories, and tried to get her mind back on track. Their marriage, the business deal.

'Your father's business was failing, but he didn't just

want a buyout from Cattaneo Jewels. He wanted a merger,' Seb went on.

'A very physical one, since it involved me putting on a wedding dress.'

'I suppose.' Seb sounded doubtful, but that was *exactly* what they'd agreed to. Two families, and two businesses, brought together into one.

'And I got to thinking last night…maybe the mistake was trying to make this marriage something it isn't.' Or, in her case, letting herself hope it could be something more, then feeling heartbroken when it hadn't happened.

She'd known ever since her father had taken her away from the degree course she'd adored that love was off the table for her. She shouldn't have allowed herself to think otherwise, even for a moment.

Which wasn't to say Seb hadn't made mistakes, too. Ones she hoped her plan would help him rectify.

'Maria, I didn't just marry you because it was good business. You know that, right?' Seb asked, and Maria nodded her head.

'Of course I do. You married me because your father told you to.' Blunt but honest, that was the only way they were going to get through this. Get it all out in the open.

Except for the part about her falling stupidly in love with him, of course. What good would telling him *that* do? Besides, she couldn't bear to see the pity in his eyes when he realised the truth.

'That's not—' Seb cut himself off, rubbing at his eyes. She wished he'd pull the sheet up—his naked torso was simply too distracting for a conversation of this magnitude. Unfortunately, the chalet's state-of-the-art heating system meant that while she was uncomfortably hot in her thick sweater, he was likely to remain half-naked for a while.

Which was a bad thing, she reminded her treacherous body. A *bad* thing.

'We were a team, Maria. We *were*. I married you because I respect you, and more than that, I *like* you. And I don't like many people.' He looked at her balefully, and Maria felt a little of that guilt dripping back in. 'It may not have been a conventional romance, or falling head over heels in love or any of that. But our marriage wasn't nothing either.'

'I never said it was.' Sighing, Maria shifted to sit a little more fully on the bed, holding a hand out to him. He took it after a moment, and her shoulder muscles relaxed just a bit. 'Seb, if this marriage meant nothing to me, I wouldn't be trying so hard to save it.' Yes, she'd walked out. But she'd come back when he'd asked. That had to count for something.

'Okay, then.' Seb squeezed her hand then let it go. 'So, what do we do?'

'Like I said, we need a plan. Like you would for any business partnership you were entering into.' She sucked in a breath, then tried to get back on script. She'd spent half the night rehearsing it, after all. It would be a shame not to use it. 'I think part of the problem was that we went into the marriage—and parenthood, come to that—with different expectations. And we never talked about them, never discussed what we both wanted out of it.'

'And now we should?'

'And now we should.' Seb still didn't look entirely convinced. 'Think about it, Seb. What could it hurt? The worst that happens is that we realise that what we each want is incompatible, and that it can't work out between us.'

'So you walk away again and take Frankie with you?' Seb said.

'So we sit down and figure out a way forward that keeps us *both* in Frankie's life,' Maria corrected him. 'I don't want to take your son away from you, Seb. He needs you, and he deserves you in his life. But you have to make space for him, too. It can't just be video calls at eleven o'clock at night, you know. That's not fatherhood.'

He had the decency to look shamefaced at that. 'I know, I know. So I guess that's one point for our hypothetical agreement, then?'

Maria nodded. 'Only there's nothing hypothetical about this. We're going to write it all down, sign and agree it, then live by it.'

'In that case, I'm definitely going to need coffee,' Seb groaned.

But he wasn't saying no. That was definitely progress. Maria grinned. Maybe they could make time for caffeine. It might help.

'Then let's get some coffee. And my laptop.'

'I want Frankie to know me.' Seb met Maria's gaze over their coffee mugs and the kitchen counter, as her fingers hovered over the keyboard of her laptop. 'That's my number one, nonnegotiable point. I want him to be as happy and comfortable spending time with me as he is with you.'

Maria glanced across at the baby monitor between them on the counter before answering. Frankie was still asleep—mostly because it was still insanely early—and Seb couldn't help but feel that was for the best. With any luck, his parents would have ironed out all the wrinkles in his future and he'd have his family back by the time he woke up.

If Maria agreed to what he needed. And if she didn't ask for anything too unreasonable in return.

Now he had coffee, Seb had to admit this whole idea wasn't as stupid as he'd first thought. A marriage—any marriage, not just a convenient business one like theirs—*was* basically a merger, in lots of ways. And Maria was right. He knew how to handle those.

He could do this. He was almost certain.

He definitely had to give it his best shot.

'Seb… I can't give you that.' Maria sounded apologetic, which wasn't going to stop him arguing the point. But she put a hand up to stop him before he could even start. 'No, let me explain. I'm not saying I'll keep Frankie away from you or anything like that. I'm saying that your relationship with your son is down to *you*. And him, of course, but you're the adult here, so mostly you.'

Seb stared down at his coffee. She had a point. Even before she'd flown back to Italy to her parents' estate, he hadn't exactly put the time in with Frankie. He'd been more concerned with building up a successful business for his son to inherit one day than with spending time with him.

Somehow, there had to be time for both. He might have to give up sleep, but it had to be possible. What was the point otherwise? It might have taken him a while—and some huge life changes—to realise how important all those individual moments with his son were, but now that he had he wasn't going to carry on making the same mistakes.

He'd already lost enough of Frankie's childhood. And he couldn't let Frankie grow up not knowing his father, like Leo had.

'Okay. I take your point—I need to make the time for Frankie. But it would be a lot easier to do that if we were living in the same house. I want to be able to come home from work at the end of the day and hang out with him.' And, yeah, okay, so then maybe he'd put in another couple of hours in the home office after Frankie was asleep—because it wasn't as if he could just give up all his responsibilities overnight. But he could rebalance them—if Maria worked with him on that.

She gave a slow nod, but somehow it didn't feel like an agreement. 'I think that's going to depend on the rest of this document, don't you?' she said. 'I mean, if we can find a compromise that makes us both happy…'

'You'll stay,' he finished for her. But there was no nod this time. Seb gripped the handle of his mug a little tighter.

'Maria, that's why I'm doing this. Why I'm sitting here at godforsaken o'clock in the morning writing a *business proposal* for my life. What's the point of it if you don't stay at the end?'

'I'm not saying I won't!' Maria protested, although he could hear the reluctance in her voice. That was *exactly* what she meant. 'I'm just saying that there's a lot more we need to agree on first.'

Seb shook his head, anger rising up in him as the caffeine settled into his bloodstream. 'No. Frankie is what matters most—I thought we could at least both agree on that.'

'Of course we do!'

'Then I need a promise from you, before we go any further,' Seb said, his voice harsh, even to his own ears. 'If I agree to whatever plan you come up with here—'

'*We* come up with,' Maria corrected him, as if she honestly believed he wasn't just following her lead. That he wouldn't say yes to *anything* if it kept her and Frankie there with him.

'Fine, that *we* come up with. If I agree to it, if I keep to it between now and Christmas, you have to stay. You have to give us a real chance to make our marriage work again.'

Maria's eyes were huge. 'You mean, if you really make time for our family, for Frankie, and everything else... I move back here?'

'If I don't mess things up over the next two weeks between now and Christmas. Yes.' Was he being unreasonable? Seb wasn't sure. But Maria had been right about one thing—he knew business. And the most important thing in business was being able to negotiate hard.

'I'm not—'

'I need an answer, Maria, otherwise there's no point going any further with this.' Ruthless, that was the key.

There was no room for weakness in business. Or marriage, it seemed.

He could see the conflicting arguments playing out in her head, showing on her face as clearly as if she'd said them out loud. He waited, ignoring the gnawing feeling of wrongness about treating his wife this way that ate away at his stomach.

She'd wanted their marriage to be all business. He was only giving her what she'd asked for.

'Fine,' she snapped eventually. 'But you have to meet every condition we set. Every rule we make. If you mess up… I don't believe in third chances, Sebastian.'

'Right.' Seb gave a sharp nod. 'In that case, let's get down to specifics. I'm guessing you have a list? Things you need from me?'

'Actually…yes,' Maria admitted.

'Good. Because I've got some of my own to add, too.' Or he would have, by the time it was his turn to dictate terms. He just had to think of them first. After all, she'd had a twelve-hour head start on this one. 'Let's get started.'

This would be easy. Just like setting quarterly goals at work. He never missed those. He wouldn't miss these.

How could he, when the stakes were so much higher?

'Okay, then,' Maria said. 'Point One A…'

Seb reached for the coffee pot. He had a feeling this could take a while.

CHAPTER EIGHT

'WAIT—YOU PUT together a business plan for your *marriage*?' Noemi stared at her incredulously as they stood together on the chalet's sprawling wooden porch. Maria hoped that she could blame the icy air for the way her cheeks turned pink. It hadn't sounded nearly so crazy until Noemi had said it *that* way.

'Seb's a businessman,' she explained to her sister-in-law. 'I figured I needed to talk to him in terms he understood—and, well, this is what I came up with.'

And it had worked, hadn't it? It might have taken them most of the morning, but they had an actual plan, with commitments and objectives, all typed up, printed in triplicate, and signed by both of them. They'd each kept a copy, and the third had been stored away in the chalet's fireproof safe, hidden behind the fake bookcase in the snug.

'If we're doing this, we're doing this properly,' Seb had said as he'd locked it away.

Maria was just grateful that Frankie had decided to sleep in again. Apparently the cold, crisp air was tiring him out. Well, that and his aunts and uncles—who had taken over entertaining him while she and Seb had finished their negotiations.

Noemi surveyed her over the mug of peppermint tea in her hands. 'I guess that makes some sort of twisted sense. If you're you and Seb.'

'What exactly does that mean?' Maria asked, even though she had a suspicion she already knew.

Noemi shrugged. 'Just that… I don't know. It's not like your marriage was a conventional one from the start, was it?'

'We were a means to an end. A merger marriage to save my father's pride and money.' Her tone was a little too bitter for Maria to pretend it didn't still sting, but then, Noemi knew that anyway. She knew *her*.

'But you were friends first for a really long time,' Noemi reminded her. 'I mean, I know I was younger, but you and Seb always seemed so close, and I was always trailing around behind you both. Honestly, I can't remember a time you didn't feel like part of our family already.'

Tears pricked at Maria's eyes. The Cattaneos *had* been family. All of them, not just Seb. Returning to her parents' estate should have felt like going home. But it hadn't, not at all. 'Apart from the time I walked out and left you all, you mean?'

'No.' Noemi shook her head emphatically, her gorgeous hair swaying in the breeze. 'You were still family. You'll always be family, I hope you know that. Whatever happens with you and Seb, you'll always be my sister.'

Maria groped for Noemi's hand, squeezing it tight. 'Thank you.'

Noemi squeezed back, then let her go, smiling a little too brightly. 'So. What does my miserable brother have to do to keep up his end of the deal?'

Putting her mug of coffee—her sixth cup of the day, she suspected, but to be honest, she'd stopped counting at this point—down on the rail that ran around the porch, Maria ticked off the basic terms of their agreement on her fingers.

'The main thing is that he has to show me that his family is more important than his business.' Noemi raised her eyebrows at that, but Maria carried on anyway. 'He needs to include me in his life—personal and work—so that we feel like a true partnership again. He needs to spend time with Frankie—playing, reading him stories, putting him to bed, that sort of thing. He needs to learn Frankie's routine and work with it. He needs to parent according to our agreed methods, and not undermine all the work I've been doing with Frankie over the last year. He needs to talk to me before making any big decisions about his time—like lengthy business trips overseas, that sort of thing. And he needs to come up with a plan for an actual family holiday next year—no laptops, no mobile phones, just the three of us together.'

It sounded like quite a lot, put like that, Maria supposed, but really, weren't these things that any good father and husband should be doing *anyway*?

Noemi gave a low whistle. 'They are some lofty goals, my friend. I hope he can live up to them.'

'So do I,' Maria said, and realised that she meant it. Even if it meant she spent the rest of her life with a husband who would never love her the way she loved him, if she could have all that—if *Frankie* could have all that—she'd be content. She hoped.

'And it explains the current ski lesson.' Noemi tilted her head out towards the snowy ground in front of the chalet, where Sebastian was currently explaining to a snowsuited Frankie all about the mechanics and physics of skiing.

Maria was pretty sure Frankie wasn't getting much of it, but he seemed happy enough to be out in the snow with his father, all the same. That was something.

'I have to say, though,' Noemi went on, drawing her attention back, 'nothing about this plan of yours exactly screams "romance".'

'Why would it?' Maria asked. 'Like I said, we're a business partnership. Covering that up with roses and love songs doesn't change that.' And it only gave her false hope. She needed to be totally clear about what this was. A merger of their two families, and businesses, to support and nurture their child, who would grow up to inherit a share in them. Not a love story—a business contract.

It was the only way she could protect her heart if she decided to stay.

'Hmm.' Noemi didn't look convinced. 'Okay, so I've heard your demands for Seb. What did he ask of you?'

Maria resisted the urge to wince. She'd been hoping her sister-in-law wouldn't ask her that. 'Oh, you know. Regular debrief meetings over dinner without Frankie.'

'You mean date nights,' Noemi translated, sounding delighted. Maria ignored her. As long as she said they were meetings, they were meetings. Even if Seb had suggested they go back to the restaurant where they'd had lunch yesterday for the first one. But at night this time, so they could dress up and maybe go dancing afterwards.

Still, a meeting. Not a date. They'd had one of those now. How many more did they need?

She went back to her list.

'That he and Frankie get to have a boys' day every so often, just the two of them.'

'Aw, that's sweet.' It was, Maria had to agree. It was also slightly unnerving. It had been just her and Frankie for so long. The idea of letting his father take him off to do who knew what felt alien and strange.

'And that the three of us come to Ostania to visit you and Max, the moment those babies are born.'

Noemi pressed a hand to her bump, her eyes huge in her beautiful face. 'He said that? He wrote that into your contract?'

'He did.' Maria smiled. She knew that Noemi and Sebastian's relationship had been strained recently, maybe since before she'd left, but certainly since their parents' deaths and the will reading that had put Leo in charge of the business. If her return could go any small way to helping mend the rift between the siblings, it only made it more worthwhile.

'Then I can't wait for that.' Noemi beamed back at her, all sunlight on the snow and pure, unadulterated happiness.

Maria tried to ignore the envy bubbling in the pit of her stomach, and turned her attention back to Frankie and Seb, just in time to see Leo and Anissa walking up the path. As she watched, Leo bent over, scooped up a handful of snow, packed it between his hands, then lobbed it at the back of Seb's head.

Maria bit her lip as she waited to see how her husband would react. He'd never had a brother before—neither of them had—and he'd never responded well to teasing, or anything that made him look a fool. Even as a child he'd hated it—although when they'd been younger he'd sometimes played the clown to make her laugh, if it was just the two of them. But never in front of anyone else, and never since he'd taken on the business mantle of being Salvo's successor.

And for Leo to do it in front of Frankie...

But suddenly a deep, warm laugh rang over the snow, echoing back from the hills, and she saw Seb kneeling in the snow, making snowballs for Frankie to lob back at 'Uncle Leo'.

'Wow,' Noemi said. 'I didn't expect that.'

'Neither did I,' Maria said, faintly, watching as Anissa came and joined Seb and Frankie's side, all three of them teaming up to pelt Leo with snow. 'Not ever.'

Maybe Seb was right. Maybe he really had been changed by the recent turmoil in his life.

Seb hoisted Frankie up onto his shoulders to give him the height advantage, and gamely took more snowballs to the chest from Leo as Anissa supplied Frankie with his own ammunition. They all laughed and shouted and joked, and even from a distance Maria could see the joy on her son's face.

This was what she'd wanted for him. This was why she'd come back.

For family. Because however helpful and polite her mother might have been since she'd moved home, it couldn't make up for her father's cold glares and mumbled complaints. And she knew from her own childhood that their house could never provide the loving family relationship she wanted for Frankie.

She'd do her best alone, of course, and that could be enough. But why should he have to settle for just her when he could have all this?

As Seb turned and grinned at her, his cheeks pink and his eyes bright, for the first time Maria believed that maybe this could really work.

Because the Seb she'd left would never have had a snowball fight with a two-year-old. Would never have let himself appear so relaxed and uncaring about his reputation.

The Seb she'd left would have been stuck in his office and never even made it outside in the first place.

'Maybe he really has changed,' she murmured, the thought settled in her mind at last.

'Maybe he has,' Noemi agreed, sounding every bit as astonished as Maria felt. 'Who knew? Christmas miracles really do happen.' -

The minute the first snowball hit him, Seb had his usual, instinctive response to anything unexpected or unwelcome—to turn and yell first, then give whoever had attacked him the trademark Sebastian glare until he or she went away. Then Frankie had giggled, and he'd realised that his usual instincts were what had got him into this mess in the first place.

Seb turned and saw his new brother and his girlfriend waiting for his reaction. It also didn't escape his notice that Leo had another snowball packed down in his hand, ready to attack.

This was war, then.

'Throw one back, Papà! Throw another snowball!' Frankie cried, and Seb laughed—sudden and true and deep. Pure instinct and happiness.

When had he last laughed like that? Had he ever?

He couldn't remember. Which probably said more than it didn't.

So Seb bent down and made snowballs for his son to throw at his uncle, and wondered how it had taken him thirty-two years to find this kind of contentment.

Wondered how he could keep it now that he had.

The afternoon fell into a flurry of snow attacks and laughter, Anissa abandoning Leo to assist Seb and Frankie in their fight. Seb hoisted his son onto his shoulders, barely even feeling the snowballs Leo tossed at him—obviously, Uncle Leo would never throw them at Frankie, but Seb was perfectly fair game.

Somewhere in between flying snowballs Seb turned towards the chalet and saw Maria and Noemi watching them, both smiling. And then all he saw was Maria's eyes, and the hope that flared in them.

He was doing something right. But he knew, in a sudden blinding flash like sunlight on ice, it wasn't going to be enough.

He could meet every target in her business plan, achieve every goal she set him. But it still wouldn't be enough.

Because he didn't *want* a business partnership. He wanted a marriage, a family. A connection.

And even he knew that took more than a signed contract.

But how did he convince Maria of that?

* * *

Two hours later, the sun was starting to slip below the mountains, and they had all taken refuge back in the chalet to warm up. Leo slapped Seb on the back as he ran a towel over his soaking wet hair.

'No hard feelings, brother?' Leo asked, and Seb was sure he could hear just a hint of anxiety in his question.

He flashed Leo a reassuring smile. 'I was just wondering if this is what it would have been like to grow up with you.'

Leo grinned back. 'Oh, I expect it would have been much worse.'

'I think it's so lovely you're both reliving the childhood you missed out on,' Noemi said drily. 'Because two more children is absolutely what we need around here.'

'I'd have thought it was good practice for you,' Seb joked, and she rolled her eyes.

'Do you want to get a drink? We could go into town, check out that new bar that opened,' Leo suggested, and for moment something inside Seb longed to say yes. To hang out with his new brother and build on this tentative relationship they'd been building.

But there was another relationship he had to tend to first.

'Another night?' he suggested. 'I want to help Maria get Frankie to bed. Poor little guy was exhausted.' Frankie might not have learned a whole lot about skiing that afternoon, but he'd certainly had a lot of fun.

And maybe he'd learned something about family, too. Maybe they both had.

'Another night,' Leo confirmed, patting him on the shoulder again as he headed across the room towards Anissa.

Slinging the damp towel over his shoulder, Sebastian headed up the stairs to the master suite to find his wife and child.

He heard them before he saw them—the squealing and splashing leading him straight to the large bathroom attached to the master suite. Leaning against the doorpost, he watched as Maria paraded a series of ducks along the edge of the oversized bathtub. Frankie waited until they were all lined up just right, then swept an arm across to knock them all into the water, giggling manically as he did so.

'He still likes his bath, then,' he observed. That was something he remembered from when Frankie had been a baby—how he'd loved to splash about in the water when it came to bath time. Not that he'd often been there to see it, but some nights, if he'd got home early, he'd caught the end of it.

He'd loved those nights. Why hadn't he tried harder to make sure there were more of them?

Sometimes it felt like the man who had lost Maria, who had lived through that awful last argument and watched her walk away, was a totally different person. With a year's distance, he couldn't understand why he hadn't seen the same things then that he knew in his heart now. How much Maria mattered to him. How every moment with Frankie was precious.

How his marriage was something to be grateful for every day.

Maria started slightly at the sound of his voice, but turned to look at him with an easy enough smile. 'He *definitely* still loves his bath. Almost as much as it seems he likes snowball fights.'

Seb couldn't help but grin as he thought about the afternoon they'd spent together. 'He did seem to enjoy it, didn't he?'

'We have snowball fight again, Papà?' Frankie asked, looking up from his ducks.

'Maybe tomorrow, *piccolo*,' Seb replied. 'For now, I think it must be nearly your bedtime.'

'Would you like Papà to read you your bedtime story?' Maria asked. Frankie nodded enthusiastically, and Seb thought his heart might burst at the sight.

This. This was what mattered. This was *all* that mattered.

And he'd do whatever the contract with Maria said if it made sure he kept it for ever.

For ever would give him time to convince her that this wasn't just business between them. It was family.

CHAPTER NINE

'I THINK HE'S ASLEEP,' Seb whispered, as he padded through the doorway from the room she and Frankie shared, leaving the door a little open. 'His eyes were closing all through that last story.'

'How many did you read him?' Maria asked.

'Um, four? Maybe five?' Seb shrugged. 'He just kept handing me books, so I just kept reading them.'

Maria rolled her eyes—mostly to stop herself smiling besottedly at the husband she'd designated as nothing more than a business partner. 'He's normally only allowed two.' But Frankie loved his stories, so would keep going as long as someone would read them to him.

Seb shrugged again, sinking onto the sofa beside him. 'Well, I've missed out on a lot of bedtime stories. I figure I have ground to make up.'

And how was she supposed to argue with that?

'I made some hot chocolate for us,' she said instead, motioning to the mugs on the coffee table in front of the roaring fire. 'Figured you might still need warming up a bit after your snowy adventures earlier.'

'I love hot chocolate,' Seb said, reaching for his mug. 'Oh, and you even added marshmallows!'

'Of course. I didn't forget everything while I was away, you know.' She hadn't forgotten anything. But he didn't need to know that.

The smile Seb gave her was just a little bit sad. It made Maria wonder if they'd ever manage a conversation that didn't somehow come back to how she'd left him. If they'd ever move forward beyond that fact.

Maybe eventually. If she stayed long enough this time. And if Seb kept up the way he'd been that afternoon, she might have to.

He certainly seemed to be going all out so far to meet every expectation and objective she'd set him. If she'd realised sooner that this was the way to get cooperation from her husband she'd have tried it years ago.

But if he kept going on the way he had today, Maria would have to uphold her end of the bargain, too. She'd have to recommit to their business partnership marriage and stay, something that somehow both terrified and excited her.

They hadn't set time limits on what would happen after Christmas. If he met his objectives until Christmas, she'd stay and give their marriage a second chance. It didn't mean she couldn't leave again if he reverted back to the old Seb.

If she could pluck up the courage and steel her heart to leave him twice, that was. Something Maria wasn't at all sure about.

She remembered the winter she'd come home from college at twenty to visit the Cattaneos—just five months before she'd left university for good. She'd had two full years since she'd left home of trying to forget about Seb, and the way he made her feel. To forget his smile, or his hand in hers as they'd skated on the ice. To forget the way he'd look at her across the dinner table when her father said something awful, just to let her know he was on her side. To forget how hard her fifteen-year-old self had fallen for him.

He'd been away studying in London, and between that and starting work at his father's company, it had been easy to avoid him, especially with her own studies and friends to keep her occupied. To be honest, it had grown almost embarrassing to be mooning after him. Even if no one ever said anything, Maria had never been able to shake the feeling that they all *knew*, and were laughing at her behind her back. What was cute at fifteen or sixteen was frankly humiliating at nineteen or twenty.

It had been easier to stay out of his way, entertain herself flirting with other boys, work hard for a degree she cared deeply about, and build her own life. By the end of her first year at university she'd almost convinced herself that what she'd thought she'd felt for Seb had only been a childhood crush.

Then she'd seen Sebastian again for the first time in two years.

He'd been standing in the snow with his father, waiting for her, the winter sun glinting off his short dark hair. And he'd smiled, and she'd fallen all over again, harder than ever.

She'd broken away from Seb once before, only to fall deeper in love when she'd come back. And now she was afraid history might be about to repeat itself—but she had no idea how to stop it.

Maybe it was already too late.

'So, how did I do with our contract today?' Seb asked, breaking through her memories. 'Am I keeping up my end of the bargain?'

'I think we could definitely say that.' Maria reached for her own hot chocolate, thinking how happy, how *young* Sebastian had looked, playing in the snow with Frankie and Leo. She hadn't seen that Sebastian in a long time. Hadn't realised how much she'd missed him until today.

'In that case…since things are going so well to plan, perhaps we could talk about something?' Seb kept his eyes on the marshmallows bobbing in his hot chocolate as he asked, which made her a little nervous.

Maria frowned. 'Of course. But what, exactly?'

'How do you…?' Seb took a breath and started again, meeting her gaze this time as he spoke. There was a cautious reserve in his eyes. 'If you stay, if I meet all your conditions and you and Frankie stay with me…how do you see that going?'

As if they hadn't already spent the whole morning hammering this out.

'How do you mean? We've talked about this already—you will make time for family as well as business. You'll involve me in your decisions. Do I need to get the contract back out for you to read it again?'

'No, that's not…that's not what I mean.' Seb looked awkwardly around him, as if wishing he'd never started the conversation.

But he had, and now Maria really had to know what he was trying to get at. 'Is this about Frankie?'

Shaking his head, Seb put down his mug and reached for her, taking her hands in his. 'No. It's about us.'

As much as part of him wished he'd never started this conversation, Seb knew it was one they needed to have. He'd known it when they'd been hammering out the terms of their contract over coffee that morning, and he'd known it for certain when he'd seen Maria smiling at him through the snow. He just hadn't been ready to address it until now—alone, in the evening shadows, with a fire and a hot chocolate.

Although a little brandy in the hot chocolate would probably help.

If Maria stayed, he wanted more than a business partner. He wanted his *wife* back. And everything that went with that.

'What I need to know is…what sort of relationship do you see us having in the future, if you come home?' He watched Maria's eyes widen as she realised what he was asking.

'You mean…will our relationship be purely business, or will we resume, um, our physical, well…?' She trailed off, and Seb held back a laugh at the sight of his wife trying to make their sex life part of a business contract.

Then he realised how bad that sounded, and frowned. *That* wasn't what he wanted at all. He didn't want any relationship between them to be an obligation, something agreed on paper that Maria felt she *had* to do.

If he ever had Maria in his bed again, it would only be because she wanted to be there. Because she craved that physical connection between them as much as he did.

And they had connected. *Really* connected.

He may not have had any serious relationships in his life before he'd married Maria, but that didn't mean he was inexperienced. He knew how sex could be with women he was attracted to, liked, and whose company he enjoyed.

None of them had ever come close to sex with Maria.

It wasn't just her beauty, her gorgeous curves, or even the friendship they'd built over the years. There was something more there between them, something he'd never been able to pin down to a single word or phrase.

But it had been real. And it had taken his breath away, from the first time he'd touched her, and every single time since.

He didn't want that perfect memory ruined by trying to make it part of their contract.

'Maybe it's a bad idea to talk about this,' he said abruptly, dropping her hands. Yes, he wanted to know her intentions, but somehow the whole conversation had got twisted around, without ever going anywhere. Maybe he just had to wait until it happened naturally—or didn't happen.

It was just a shame he was so bad with uncertainty.

'No,' Maria said, biting down on her bottom lip. 'You're

right. Our physical relationship is an important aspect of our partnership. We *should* discuss it. I mean, we haven't even spoken about whether we'd like Frankie to have a brother or sister one day.'

Another baby. One he could get things right for, from the start. A companion for Frankie, like Noemi had been for him, like Leo could have been, perhaps would be now. Maria had never had a sibling, and he knew she'd been lonely—when she hadn't been with the Cattaneos, anyway. Of course she'd be thinking about this.

And he'd just been thinking about sex. God, no wonder she thought he needed a business plan to just be able to act like a normal human being.

His shock must have shown on his face, because Maria instantly started backtracking. 'But you probably meant something else. Like…if this is a business relationship, are we free to see other people? Recreationally, so to speak.'

See other people? That was basically the *opposite* of what he'd been thinking about.

Did *she* want to see other men? She said she hadn't dated while they'd been apart…but she wouldn't, not with things unsettled between them. He knew Maria.

If she wanted to start a relationship with someone new, she'd make sure she tied up all the loose ends with him first, so she could move on free and clear.

Was that what she wanted? Either to be free of him for ever, or to have an arrangement that gave her enough freedom to seek her own happiness?

Anger and fear and confusion all warred inside him for prominence—until he took a moment to really look at Maria before he responded.

She didn't look like a woman asking for freedom, or looking forward to being able to go out and find a new love. She looked…resigned? As if she thought this was what *he* wanted?

How often had he reacted to Maria without looking before? How much had he missed seeing?

Not this time.

'Maria.' The word came out low, and surely she must hear his desire in it? Well, he'd tell her, just in case. They'd spent too long missing each other's meanings, it seemed. 'Maria, the only woman I ever want to be with is you.'

The surprise on her face was almost comic. But he also saw doubt creeping in behind it. He couldn't have that.

'Believe me, I have no interest in other women, no desire for *anyone* except for my wife. Except for you.' He reached out to tuck a strand of her dark hair behind one ear, cupping her cheek as he did so. 'You have to know you are—and have always been—the most beautiful woman in the world to me.'

'You've never…you never told me that.' Maria stumbled over the words. 'Before.'

Because he was an idiot. Clearly.

'I should have.' He should have told her every day, and would from now on, if it meant she'd stay. 'Because it's true. You're so beautiful you take my breath away. You always have.'

Her cheeks flushed with colour, only making her more beautiful to him.

'So, if I stay…you want us to…'

'I want us to have a marriage, as well as a partnership,' Seb finished for her. 'I want us to have it all.'

Maria could feel the hope rising within her—that same optimism she'd felt after their wedding day. With each day of their honeymoon it had grown that little bit more. The two glorious weeks they'd spent together out in the Seychelles, making the most of just being the two of them, for the first time ever. No family interfering or expecting things from them. No meetings, no calls, no emails. Just them.

It had been one of the happiest times of her life, Maria realised. Learning Sebastian anew as her husband, rather than just a friend of the family. Talking about anything and everything, for hours, just because they could. Spending whole days lazing about on the beach, or splashing through the water, asking questions and listening to the answers.

And at night...that had been a whole different world to explore. It had been the one aspect of their marriage Maria had been most nervous about. After all, she knew that their families and business interests aligned, and had spent enough time with Sebastian growing up to know that they could get along well together, even if they hadn't seen much of each other over the last few years. But beyond a few simple, often observed kisses, they'd never had a chance to test the more *physical* aspects of their compatibility.

But she needn't have worried. From the moment they'd been alone, the first time Seb's lips had met hers, she'd known there were absolutely no concerns at all on that score.

She bit her lip just remembering how he'd made her body feel—like singing and sinking all at once, pleasure taking over in a way she'd never experienced before.

Or since, in fact.

Oh, sure, they'd had sex since they'd returned from honeymoon, but it had always come in second place since then. Seb would be too busy at work, coming to bed hours after she did, or distracted and checking his emails if he was there. They'd managed to conceive Frankie, at least, but ever since the honeymoon was over, Maria had completely understood why people used that saying.

The minute their plane had landed, Seb had been checking his work emails on his phone. And in some ways it felt like he'd barely looked up and seen her again since.

But he was seeing her now. Here, in front of the fire in

the suite they'd shared, their son asleep in the next room, he couldn't take his eyes off her.

He'd said he thought she was the most beautiful woman in the world, and somehow, finally, she believed it. And heaven knew she'd never seen a more gorgeous man than Sebastian Cattaneo. However hard she'd looked.

But it was too soon. So he'd managed one afternoon playing in the snow with Frankie. That wasn't enough for her to give in, to let herself get her hopes up about for ever. That way, she knew from bitter experience, led only to disappointment and heartbreak.

More than once before she'd thought it would be different. After their honeymoon, then when she'd got pregnant with Frankie and Seb had been so attentive she'd thought she'd scream if it wasn't so adorable. Even when Frankie had been born, and Seb had actually managed to make it to the hospital from the boardroom in time to be there and hold her hand—just.

But every time she'd thought she'd won his attention—and maybe even found the path to his love—he'd get distracted again, running off to deal with some sort of work crisis, or to discuss future plans for the business with his father. Anything except stay with her and enjoy their family.

It could still be the same this time. She couldn't lose sight of that. She needed to protect her heart—and her future.

If she stayed, it would be on her own terms, and without any false expectations. She could mandate that Seb spend time with her and Frankie, she could insist on partnership terms, but she couldn't make Seb fall in love with her.

Which meant she needed other things to make her happy. She had Frankie, of course, and Seb's family, she supposed. The only other thing she craved was a meaningful career. And Seb could give her that, too, if he wanted.

If she asked.

She'd never told him what she needed before, had expected him to know instinctively. And she knew now that didn't work with Seb. If she wanted something, she needed to tell him.

She had to ask.

Pulling back, Maria ignored Seb's disappointed expression and reached for her cooling hot chocolate. 'I hope we can find our way back there in time, too,' she said honestly.

Well, mostly honestly. In truth, she'd let him take her right there on the sofa if she thought it wouldn't end up with her heart getting broken in the morning.

'In time,' Seb repeated, and she supposed she had to give him a few points for not asking how much time.

He knew what he had to do to make her stay. And if he kept doing it…well, Maria suspected it wouldn't be very much time at all before she was also back in his arms and in his bed. She was only human, after all.

And in the meantime…

'I actually wanted to talk to you about something, too. Something more work related.'

Seb arched a sardonic eyebrow. 'I thought the aim of our contract was to get me focusing *less* on work, not more.'

'It is,' Maria agreed. 'But it's also about building our partnership. Finding ways to include each other in our everyday lives.'

'And my everyday life *is* the business,' Seb surmised. 'Fair enough. Ask away.'

Maria sucked in a breath, hoping the air particles included the courage she needed to make her request.

'Do you think…when I've finished my course, do you think there might be a place for me at Cattaneo Jewels?'

Both eyebrows flew up this time. 'You want a *job*?'

'Is that so unbelievable?' Maria snapped, all lust faded

now with just four words from him. 'Or I am just so un-employable?'

He waved her argument away with a flap of his hand. 'The company would be lucky to have you. I was just… surprised. You were always trying to persuade me to spend *less* time at work.'

'Well, maybe if you have help I'll achieve that aim,' she hit back, trying to ignore the warm feeling that had returned when he'd said 'lucky to have you'.

'That's true.' He gave her a half-smile. 'And it would give us something else in common. Something else to draw us together.'

'Exactly.' She beamed back, glad he'd got it.

As a colleague, she'd be more of an equal than ever. *That* was what she wanted most.

Seb sat back, draping an arm across the back of the sofa. 'Well, Cattaneo Jewels is a family business. And you're family. Of course there's a job for you if you want it. And I wasn't kidding—we'd be lucky to have you.'

'Don't you need to ask Leo first?' Maria asked. 'I mean, I know your parents' will left the majority stake to him…' A sensitive subject, she was sure. But Seb seemed relaxed enough for her to broach it now.

To her surprise, his half-smile broadened to a full-on grin. 'Actually, that might be changing. He spoke to me the other day about signing over his shares to me. Giving me control of the company again.'

Maria's eyes widened. 'That's…great.' It was. In lots of ways. It just also meant that Seb had no get-out—no one to share the burden if his family needed him more than the business did.

Seb seemed to guess her concern. Resting a hand against her thigh, he leaned close, gazing directly into her eyes as if to convince her of his honesty. 'I won't let it change anything, Maria. I swear to you. Never mind signed agreements and contracts—*this* is my promise. *Nothing* comes before our family. Not any more. Okay?'

'Okay,' Maria whispered.

And, God help her, she believed him.

CHAPTER TEN

SEBASTIAN GLARED DOWN at the paperwork in front of him. He'd hoped that printing it out would make it easier to digest than staring at it on the screen, but if anything, the last agreement Salvo had worked on in his lifetime was even more complex and concerning in hard copy.

He sighed, returned to the first page and started reading over again.

A soft knock at the door disturbed him after only a few moments, and he looked up as he called, 'Come in.' He knew he should be annoyed at being interrupted, but to be honest, the distraction was welcome. Even more so when Maria's beautiful face appeared around the door.

'Hey.' With a soft smile, she slid into the chair on the opposite side of the desk and peered across at his papers. 'What're you working on?'

'Papà's last deal,' Seb said with a groan. Then he realised. The only time Maria had come to his office at the chalet in the last week had been to fetch him when they had plans to go out. Had he forgotten some plan or another? And if so, what? He checked his watch quickly. 'Sorry, were we supposed to be doing something with Frankie? I've been lost in these documents for days, it feels like. But I'll stop now and we can—'

'Seb, it's okay.' Maria's smile was almost a grin now. 'Much as I appreciate your efforts to drop everything and spend time with your family, Frankie has been whisked off to the local toy store by his all-too-indulgent aunts and uncles. Apparently it's time for him to choose his Christmas presents.'

'And you didn't want to go?' Seb asked, surprised.

'I was told—quite firmly—by your sister that I wasn't invited.'

Seb bit back a smirk. 'So he's getting spoiled rotten while you're not there to stop them.'

'Basically.'

'Lucky Frankie.' Seb leaned back in his chair, surveying her across the desk. 'So, what are you up to?'

'Absolutely nothing.' Maria made it sound like the worst fate in the world. Whereas, to Sebastian, it sounded much more like an opportunity.

'Then you've got time to do something with me,' he said gleefully.

Maria rolled her eyes and, before he could suggest something romantic and maybe even a little bit seductive, she reached across the desk and picked up the stack of papers he'd been trying to make sense of. Her eyebrows rose steadily as she flicked through it, then started at the beginning again, just as he had.

Okay, so it wasn't romantic, but Seb couldn't help but wonder what Maria would make of the contract. So he waited.

After another minute or two she put the papers back down on the desk. 'I have trouble believing your father wrote that contract.'

'He didn't,' Seb confirmed. 'It was the other side. What gave it away?'

'It's convoluted, confusing and unclear in areas that are likely going to blow up on you later on.'

Exactly what Seb had been worried about. 'Want to help me figure out how to fix it?'

Maria beamed. 'Absolutely.'

An hour later, any doubts Seb might have had about Maria working for Cattaneo Jewels were definitely long gone. As they worked their way line by line through the deal Salvo had struck, Maria was right there with him—and often a step or two ahead—as they identified ambiguities, potential problems and possible attempts to slip something past them. Occupied with another big project at the time, Seb hadn't been in on the negotiations for the deal—the takeover of a smaller jewellery firm in Switzerland—so trying to second-guess exactly what his father had been aiming for, or had agreed, was tricky. Luckily, Salvo's assistant had taken good notes.

Finally, they reached the end of the document—now covered in scrawled notes and questions in both their handwriting—and Seb sat back, rolling his shoulders to try to release the tension that had settled there.

'You okay?' Maria asked, watching him.

'Yeah. Just glad I had you here to help me with this,' he admitted, 'otherwise it was going to take all night.'

Maria frowned, and pulled out her phone. 'It practically *is* night. Noemi and Max should be back with Frankie by now...' She swiped across the screen of her phone, and her face cleared as she scanned it. 'Except they've gone for ice creams, apparently. Noemi says they'll be back in an hour, and that Frankie has asked them to give him his bath and story tonight.'

'Really?' Seb couldn't help but smile at that. He loved how close Frankie had grown to *all* his family. 'In that case, I guess we've got a little more time to kill.'

'More work?' Maria asked, stretching out her arms in front of her, her fingers interlaced. She must ache as much as he did, but there was no hint of it in her voice.

But Seb was done with work for the day. It was time for some fun. 'I've got a much better idea.'

Darkness was already falling as Seb led Maria out of the chalet, a mysterious bag slung over his shoulder.

'Are you seriously not going to tell me where we're going?' she asked, picking her way through the snow behind him.

'It's a surprise.' Seb glanced back over his shoulder and flashed her a grin. 'I'm being romantic.'

'That's half the problem,' Maria muttered under her breath, as she followed him.

Distracted, work-focused Seb she was used to. This new version, who showered her with attention, never missed a date and read Frankie his bedtime story every night, was a complete mystery. Working with him on that contract, though…that was new, yes, but the discussion and collaboration was familiar from the first days of their marriage, when Seb had still found time to talk to her about what was going on at the office.

It had been nice to feel useful to the family business again that way. The idea of spending more time doing just that—of it being her actual job—made her glow a little inside. If things carried on going this well, Frankie could have two parents who loved and made time for him, she could have a career she enjoyed and that fulfilled her, and she could even have a partnership with a husband who respected her, and who she respected in return.

Not a bad life, by anyone's standards.

But will it be enough?

Maria shook the thought away as she realised that Seb wasn't leading them towards the town of Mont Coeur. Instead, they'd swerved off the main road and were tramping through a field towards…

'We're going ice-skating?' she asked, her voice high with excitement as she spotted the frozen lake before them.

When had she last been out on the ice? She tried to remember as Seb pulled two pairs of skates from his bag and presented one to her with a flourish. She must have skated since that night with Seb fifteen years ago, surely? But if she had, she couldn't remember it.

Whenever she thought of ice-skating, she thought of him, and remembered that night.

'Think you remember how?' Seb asked, as he laced up his own skates, perching on a low fence to do so. 'Or have you secretly been keeping up your training when I wasn't looking?'

Maria shook her head. 'No training.' There was no rink near her parents' estate, and the lake froze only rarely—plus, without Seb to sneak out with her, what was the point? The only place she'd have ever skated would be Mont Coeur, and the Cattaneos tended more towards skiing than skating, so she had, too.

'Me neither.' Seb held out a hand to pull her up from the fence, so they could totter towards the ice together. 'But if we hold hands, I'm sure we'll be fine.'

Hold my hand. I'll keep you safe.

As his fingers wrapped around hers, she could almost hear seventeen-year-old Seb saying the words, as he had that night.

Just like then, she clung on tight as they took their first steps onto the ice. But this time she wasn't holding on for fear of the ice breaking—this lake was so shallow it froze hard all winter—or of her parents catching them. This time she just didn't ever want to let go.

'Ready?' Seb asked. Maria nodded.

And then…oh, then they were flying. The cold night air stung her cheeks as they spun around in wide circles on the ice, whipping past the snow-covered trees and the silent mountains beyond. For the first time in so long, Maria felt *free*. Leaving Seb hadn't brought her that freedom she'd sought so desperately, but *he* had, just for this one night.

As she gripped Seb's hand, it was as if the whole world fell away, until all that mattered was them and this perfect moment.

Just as it had the night she'd fallen in love with him, all those years before.

Maria let out a whoop of joy as Seb spun her, and his echoing laugh filled the whole sky.

Eventually, out of breath and still laughing, they fell down onto the snow beside the lake, hands still clutched together.

'Feel better for that?' Seb asked, and Maria nodded, unable to find the words. 'Good.' Releasing her fingers, he wrapped his arms around her, pulling her up between his legs so she could rest her back against his chest. 'Me, too. Much better than contracts.'

Maria laughed. 'I never thought I'd hear you say that.'

'I should have. Spending time with you…that's always been better than any business deal or meeting could be.'

Something tightened in her chest at his words. 'I'm happy to hear that.' Did he really mean it? Because if he did…it wasn't a declaration of love, of course. But for Seb, it was pretty close.

'Can I ask you something?' Seb said, after a moment.

Maria turned her face so her cheek lay against his chest, and listened to his heartbeat. 'Of course.'

'Why did you marry me?'

It was the perfect night. Him, his wife, the moonlight and the ice. He could feel Maria's warmth pressed against him until it drowned out the chill of the snow beneath them as she relaxed in his arms.

Everything was just as it should be. Until he ruined it, like always.

'Why did you marry me?'

Maria jerked away, sitting up and turning to face him. 'What do you mean? You know why.'

Oh, well. In for a penny and all that.

Seb shook his head. 'No. I know why your father ordered you to marry me. What I don't know is why on earth you said yes.'

She could have had any man in the world. She was beautiful, intelligent, and so far out of his league that Seb hadn't believed his father the first time he'd told him the engagement had been arranged.

He'd always wondered what her father had done to force her into it—especially after she'd left him. But he'd never had the courage to ask.

Until now.

Maria stared straight into his eyes for a long moment, and Seb held her gaze. He could wait her out.

They'd laid so much about their relationship bare already, but how could they keep moving forward without unpeeling this last, vital layer?

Finally, Maria broke away, her gaze skittering off towards the mountains, and whatever lay beyond them.

'My father... I was away at university. You knew that, right?' Her voice was soft, tentative, and she paused for Seb to nod an acknowledgement before she continued. 'I was studying for a business degree, of course, and I had almost finished my second year when, one day, he showed up on the campus with no warning. I thought he must have a meeting locally or something. Thought it was nice of him to surprise me like that.

'He took me out for lunch at the fanciest restaurant in town, just like he always would. You know my father—he likes things because they're expensive, not because they're good. But then, as I was sitting there eating my overpriced starter, drinking one-hundred-euros-a-bottle wine, he said, "The company's going under. We either have to declare bankruptcy or you need to marry Sebastian Cattaneo."'

Instinctively, Seb reached out to hold her close again, silently cursing Antonio Rossi as he did so. He'd always

known the old man was a bastard, but he'd at least hoped
he loved his daughter.

Apparently not so much.

Maria nestled back into his arms like she belonged
there, and Seb allowed himself a moment of satisfaction
before she continued her story.

'I argued that there had to be another way. I wanted to
look at the books, talk to the investors, figure out a way
to save the company using everything I'd learned about
business. But he wouldn't even let me try.'

'You never told me,' Seb whispered, hating that she'd
been so desperate not to marry him, and forced into it anyway. 'When I proposed…you smiled. You said it was what
you wanted.'

'And you gave me an out.' Maria looked up at him, her eyes
wide and serious. 'You told me that if I didn't want to marry
you, I just had to say the word and you'd find another way.'

'But you didn't,' Seb replied. 'You said yes. Why?'

Maria sighed, and looked away. 'Because…because
it was the best solution. If my father wasn't going to let
me be of any use to his company, better we merge with
yours and I have a chance to make a difference there instead. Marrying you…it meant I escaped that mausoleum
my parents called home. Meant I could stay a part of the
Cattaneo family for ever, instead of just on visits in the
holidays. And you and I…we were friends, always. I figured there were a lot of things worse than marrying you.'

Hardly a ringing endorsement, Seb noted. But all those
things she'd wanted from the marriage, he could still give
her. His parents were gone, but the Cattaneos were still
very much a family. And they'd already proved they were
a great business team that afternoon. As for friends… He
hoped they could be much more than that. But if friends
was all he got, he'd take it.

A horrible thought occurred to him. One he'd had before, but had never realised the depth of before.

'I can't imagine how bad life with me must have been, then, to send you back to your parents.' The words came out choked, and Maria turned to kneel up in front of him, her cold palm pressed against his cheek. He gazed down into her dark blue eyes, shaded in the night, and realised a truth that had eluded him for far too long. Or perhaps he'd just never thought to look for it.

This woman is everything.

He had to make her happy. Had to give her the life she deserved. Had to be the *husband* she deserved, and the father that Frankie did, too.

Somehow. He'd figure it out.

Because nothing else mattered.

'It's getting better,' Maria whispered.

Then she kissed him, soft and sweet and perfect.

And suddenly Sebastian Cattaneo had hope again.

'Papà!' Frankie came flying into Sebastian's office a few days later, waving a sheet of shiny paper in his hand. His eyes were bright with excitement, and he bounced on his toes even when he came to a stop. 'Look, Papà!'

Noemi followed close behind, smiling indulgently and giving Seb the distinct impression that whatever happened next was going to be his sister's fault. Like so many other things in their childhood, actually. And this week.

Unbidden, Seb's mind flashed back to ice-skating with Maria, and the feel of her lips against his again after so long. They'd been giggling as they'd raced back to the chalet, hand in hand, ice skates clanking in the bag on his shoulder. He'd hoped—oh, how he'd hoped—that they'd have a chance to follow up their new-found closeness when they got home. Noemi and Max would have finished reading Frankie stories by then, and he should be fast asleep.

Except when they'd arrived, they'd found every light in the chalet blazing and Frankie jumping around the Christmas tree on a sugar high of excitement, amplified by an afternoon at the toy store.

Maria had dropped his hand before they were even through the door. And since then there hadn't been a moment when he'd felt the same closeness, or the same sense of possibility.

He had to find a way to get back there. And soon— because Christmas was nearly upon them.

They'd all managed nearly a week of harmony at the Mont Coeur chalet now, and things were starting to feel more relaxed, more natural, at least. He and Maria were both still keeping up their respective sides of the bargain, and Frankie was luxuriating in all the attention from his parents. Leo and Anissa had stopped in to see them almost every day, and there had been plenty of family dinners and conversations—enough to make Seb feel that just maybe they could be a real family, even after everything.

It probably didn't hurt that the Christmas spirit had infused the place so completely that even Seb was dreaming of cinnamon and pine needles.

Well, actually, that wasn't true. He was dreaming about Maria, and that kiss. Every single night, as she slept in the next room with Frankie. Without him.

But he was feeling festive, which was a whole lot more than he'd managed this time last year. And so was everyone else, it seemed. The Mont Coeur chalet was a haven of good cheer and amicability for the first time in what felt like an age.

And Frankie had come to find him, of his own accord, because he wanted to see him. What more could he ask for?

Mindful of his agreement with Maria, Seb shut his laptop, hoping that the emails he'd only just started to deal with could wait a little longer, and gave Frankie his full attention.

'What have you got there?' he asked, lifting the little boy up into his lap.

Frankie shoved the shiny paper towards Seb's nose, and Noemi snorted with laughter as he tried to prise it from his son's tiny fist.

The paper was red, gold and green—and glittery. Clearly no expense had been spared in the preparation of this flyer.

'Santa's coming!' Frankie cried, even as Seb read the words confirming that the man in red was indeed visiting Mont Coeur on the day before Christmas Eve—two days' time. Perfect.

'Will you take me to meet *Babbo Natale*, Papà?' Frankie asked sweetly, using the Italian name for Santa, and Seb couldn't help but smile at the excitement in his eyes.

'Of course I will.'

Frankie bounced himself right off Seb's lap in the resulting joy and celebration, after giving his *papà* as giant a hug as little two-year-old arms could manage. Then he bounded back towards the door to hug Noemi, and promptly crashed into his mother coming the other way.

'Mamma! Papà's going to take me to see Santa!'

Maria raised her eyebrows as she looked across the chalet's office at Seb. He waved the garish flyer in explanation. 'He wants to go.'

'Of course he does.' Maria's mouth twitched in what Seb suspected was an effort to keep from grinning. 'Are you hoping you've been a good enough boy to ask for a treat this Christmas, too?'

Heat filled his body just at the flirtatious tone of her voice. God, he was so far gone with wanting her, it was insane. He didn't remember feeling like this ever before—except maybe on their wedding day, waiting to be alone with her, waiting for their life together to start.

'Do you think I stand a chance?' he asked baldly.

For the first time since their kiss, Maria didn't pull back at the suggestion. 'Do you know, I think you just might.'

Seb's heart soared. Finally, finally, it felt like he was getting somewhere.

At this point in a business negotiation he'd know exactly what to do next—push the advantage. But could he risk it with Maria? She *had* said theirs was a business partnership...

And she was already halfway out of the door with Frankie, Noemi following behind. If he wanted to act, it had to be now.

He stood up behind his desk. 'In that case, I think you owe me another date.'

Maria paused in the doorway and raised her eyebrows at him. 'I *owe* you?'

Noemi was shaking her head at him. He ignored her.

'That was part of our deal, yes? Regular catch-up meetings in romantic settings.' He was still kind of amazed he'd got that one past her. She'd been so determined to keep everything businesslike, and he, well...hadn't been.

'I suppose I did agree to that.'

'Then tonight?' he pressed.

Maria shook her head. 'Noemi and Leo both have plans tonight, so no willing babysitter.'

Seb glanced over at his sister to check the truth of this statement.

'Sorry,' Noemi said unapologetically.

'Then we'll have the house to ourselves,' Seb said, glancing down to see Frankie still bouncing beside Maria. 'Well, us and Frankie. We'll have date night at home.'

'I...' Maria's mouth was open, but no more words were coming out.

'Dinner at eight,' Seb said. 'I'm cooking.'

That was how you won a negotiation.

CHAPTER ELEVEN

MARIA SMOOTHED DOWN the soft jersey dress she'd chosen for the evening, and hoped against hope that Frankie wouldn't choose tonight to wake up with a bad dream, or wanting another cup of milk, or whatever. She'd finally settled him down—after three books about *Babbo Natale* and his reindeer, helpfully supplied by his aunt Noemi—while Seb was bashing about in the kitchen downstairs, and then realised that if this really was a date night, she should probably change out of the jeans and jumper she'd been wearing all day.

She hadn't exactly packed for parties or fancy nights out, but she had included a forest-green jersey dress, with a twist at the waist that made her slender curvy shape into a true hourglass, and a cowl neckline that dipped low enough to show off her best lingerie.

That she was only wearing because it went with the dress. Not because she expected Seb to be stripping it from her later.

Probably.

Oh, who was she kidding? That was *exactly* what she was expecting.

Since their trip to the lake, Maria had been feeling the tension between them more than ever. Every smile Seb gave her, every look…she could feel the heat in it. Could remember the sensation of his lips under hers as she'd kissed him, his breath against her skin as she'd pulled away. The amazed look in his eyes. The way his hand at her waist had made her tremble…

And, of course, it had gone nowhere, because that was the reality of life with a toddler. But this time Frankie was asleep, the rest of the house was empty, and anything could happen. And maybe it just might.

In fact, making love with Seb tonight would be the perfect end to a pretty perfect week. Yes, Seb had still worked most days—he wouldn't be the driven and conscientious man she'd married if he hadn't—but he'd called on her to talk things through once or twice, and he'd always turned the laptop off in time for a family dinner. And he'd been surprisingly patient with Frankie's many, many interruptions during his office hours. Plus he'd actually taken whole afternoons off some days to play with Frankie in the snow, attempt more ski lessons, or just show him around Mont Coeur. They'd even managed to take him on a sleigh ride— although Frankie still wasn't sure about the huge horses that pulled the sleigh. Apparently he'd prefer reindeer, like Santa had.

In short, Seb had given her a picture-perfect view of what life could be like with him, if he stuck to their agreement.

Now it was her turn to keep to the contract.

A romantic date night. And maybe more… A shiver ran through Maria's body just at the thought.

With one last check on the sleeping Frankie, Maria headed down the stairs to the large, state-of-the-art kitchen. There was a formal dining room for special occasions— where Maria fully expected that they'd be eating Christmas dinner in just a few days—but tonight she found that Seb had laid the small table in the breakfast nook, with a delicate display of seasonal greenery in the middle, and a couple of low candles giving it a romantic air.

'I thought this was more…intimate than the dining

room.' Seb handed her a glass of white wine, and bent to kiss her cheek. 'You look beautiful, by the way.'

That was another thing. Seb had made a point of telling her how beautiful she was at least once a day for the last week. As if he was making up for all the years when he'd barely seemed to see her at all.

It was almost enough to make her believe that this time it really could all be different.

'Is Frankie asleep?' Seb asked, returning to the stove to stir whatever was in the pot that smelled so delicious.

Maria nodded. 'I think your ski lesson this afternoon wore him out. That and all the Santa excitement, courtesy of Noemi.'

Seb flashed her a smile. 'He did seem pretty excited about the idea of meeting *Babbo Natale*.'

'So did you,' Maria replied. She settled herself on a stool at the kitchen counter to watch him cook. 'This is the first year he's really understood about the concept of Santa—or even Christmas, really. So it's all new and exciting for him.'

'I can't tell you how glad I am that I get to share that with him,' Seb said.

Maria shifted uncomfortably on her stool, very aware that *she* was the reason that Seb had missed Frankie's second Christmas. They'd have to ensure that his third was a great one to make up for it.

'What are we eating?' she asked, eager to change the subject. Seb hadn't cooked for her very often—by the time he'd got home in the evenings it had usually been too late to start and, besides, Maria liked to cook. But she also knew that Nicole Cattaneo wouldn't let any child of hers out into the world without being able to cook some Italian classics.

Or knowing how to serve a perfect antipasti plate. Maria picked at the platter of cured meats, olives, roasted vegetables and cheeses, and felt her stomach rumble in anticipation. If nothing else about tonight went to plan, at least the food should be good.

'That pasta and sausage dish of Mamma's that you always loved,' Seb replied, stirring the sauce. 'Want to taste? Check it's as good as you remember?'

She nodded eagerly, and he lifted his spoon from the pan with a small sampling of sauce on the end, and held it over the counter for her to try. Maria blew to cool it, then let the delicious, spicy sauce luxuriate on her taste buds as her eyes fluttered closed.

'Okay?' Seb asked, a hint of nervousness in his voice.

'Perfect.' Maria opened her eyes to find him watching her intently. And, before she could even guess what he was about to do, Seb dropped his spoon to the counter and leaned across it, his tall frame allowing him to reach her easily.

Then he kissed her, and Maria forgot all about the taste of the pasta sauce, and let herself fall into the taste of him instead.

Oh, God, he'd forgotten how good this felt, even in the few days since he'd last kissed her. It was as if his mind couldn't believe the memory was as sensational as it truly was.

Seb cursed the counter between them, blocking his ability to sweep Maria into his arms and hold her close. But then, as they broke the kiss, coming apart just enough to breathe and stare at each other, Seb decided it might be for the best.

He'd wanted to romance her tonight. To show her how ready he was to be the kind of husband she needed—in every way. To focus on her completely.

If he took her to bed before they even got to dinner, he would kind of be missing the point.

So he pulled back, smiling at the sight of her flushed

skin, bright eyes, and her chest heaving with too-fast breaths under that gorgeously slinky dress. He was just about to think of something wonderfully suave and seductive to say when the pasta boiled over behind him.

'Hold that thought,' he said, and turned to deal with the culinary crisis.

Ten minutes later, dinner was served.

'Is it like you remember?' he asked, as Maria tucked in. He was pretty sure he'd recalled his mother's recipe correctly, but not having her there to ask had brought him down for a few minutes, the way it always did when he remembered that they were gone.

But his parents would approve of his attempts to win Maria back, he was sure. Well, his father would be worrying about him neglecting the business, but Mamma would understand, and she'd talk his *papà* round. She always did.

'It's perfect,' Maria replied, smiling. 'Just as I remember. Your mother always made this for me the first night of my visits. Do you remember?'

'I do. In fact, I took it as evidence that you were always her secret favourite, long before you actually married into the family.'

Maria laughed. 'I think she just liked cooking for an appreciate audience. You and Noemi were too used to her incredible meals. My mother liked us to pretend we could exist on air and water alone. I used to long to escape her steamed chicken and salads and come to your place for proper food.'

'I knew there had to be something that kept you hanging around us,' Seb replied. 'I was just hoping it had a little bit more to do with my charm and good looks.'

'Oh, there was definitely that appeal, too,' Maria said, with another flirtatious smile. 'But mostly…mostly I just liked the way your family felt like, well, a *real* family.

Mine was always more like three people stuck together because they had nowhere else to go.'

Seb remembered how she'd spoken about escaping her parents' home by marrying him. Which led to the memory of the first Christmas they were married, and how they'd spent it in the chilly atmosphere of the Rossi mansion. He knew exactly what she meant. There was a reason they'd agreed to always spend Christmas with Sebastian's family after that.

'Do they mind you being here for Christmas with Frankie this year?' he asked, aware that it was rather late to be asking that question. If they did, it wouldn't have stopped him asking her to come to Mont Coeur anyway. But Maria had been living with them for a full year...

'I didn't tell them,' Maria admitted, topping up her wine glass.

Seb blinked. 'You don't think they might notice you're gone? I mean, Frankie kind of fills a place with sound. If nothing else, they might remark on the sudden quiet.'

'They're away visiting with friends for the holidays. Besides, I wasn't *exactly* staying with them,' Maria said. 'I mean, the idea was to find somewhere Frankie and I could be happier. And that place was never going to be with my parents.'

That stung a little, but Seb acknowledged the truth of it. Though he felt slightly reassured that even being married to him was, in fact, better than staying with her parents. 'So where have you been living?'

'Do you remember the little cottage on the edge of their estate? Down by the lake?'

'The one we ice-skated on? Of course. I remember escaping to that cottage the first Christmas Eve we were married, and spending the evening together away from them. It was...very cosy.' It had been tiny, even by normal house standards, and Maria was used to mansions and luxury chalets. Beyond its size, the only thing Seb could really remember about it was how he'd made love to Maria in front of the fire…

'I love it there,' Maria said, breaking into his memories. 'And Frankie does, too. He spent time with my parents—well, mostly my mother—but I think we both liked having somewhere that was just ours to go home to.'

'You liked it being just the two of you?' Seb asked, his heart sinking a little. That was something he definitely couldn't give her.

'It made Frankie and me closer than we might have been otherwise,' Maria said. 'But in lots of ways it didn't feel all that much different from living with you.' She gave him a tiny apologetic smile as she spoke, but it did nothing to ease the guilt and pain eating him up inside.

Seb laid his fork on his almost empty bowl, his appetite gone. 'And now? Have you felt that this week?' *It's getting better*, she'd told him. He had to hope that was enough.

Because if she said yes, it was game over, nowhere else to go. He'd done his best—within realistic boundaries. He couldn't give up his business completely. That would never work long term. But he'd thrown himself into finding a balance that kept everyone happy.

Had it been enough?

Maria placed her fork down, too, pushing her bowl away and meeting his gaze as the candles guttered and flickered, down to the end of their wicks. 'This week…this week has felt like something completely new between us. Something I like very much.'

'I'm glad.' Relief flooded through him at her words. 'And I feel the same. In fact, I'm hoping it might continue for a very long time.'

'I hope so, too.' Maria held his gaze so long that Seb could feel heat rising in him just from the way she looked at him. Like she was seeing him anew. Like she wanted what she saw.

In which case…

'How do you feel about taking dessert upstairs?' he suggested, the final part of his plan for the evening falling nicely into place.

'To the living room?' Maria asked.

Seb shook his head. 'I was thinking the hot tub.'

The hot tub wasn't exactly the ideal place to eat tiramisu, but Maria was past caring. This wasn't about pudding anyway. This was about them.

Being husband and wife again.

While Seb transferred their dessert into something easier to eat from than the large dish he'd bought it in, Maria slipped into the bedroom she shared with Frankie and tried to dig out her swimming costume quietly. She really, *really* didn't want to wake her little boy up right now. She wanted to get changed quickly and get back out there to her husband.

Unless she didn't bother with the swimming costume part. If Seb showed up to find her naked in the hot tub, he'd definitely know he'd been good enough to make the nice list, right? No need to check it twice or anything.

After a week and a half of both of them trying to live up to the other's expectations, Maria was more than ready to say enough and just jump back into bed with her husband. Or hot tub. Wherever, to be honest. She just wanted her marriage back—new and improved, but still *her* marriage. The one she'd thought she could never have again.

With her husband. The one she loved.

That thought stopped her cold, and she held her swimming costume to her chest as she realised. She'd got so carried away with how well things were going, she hadn't even noticed that the word 'love' still wasn't on Sebastian's lips. He'd embraced the whole business partnership marriage idea—even if he had his own ideas about how much romance that might entail—and he'd been living up to the goals and objectives she'd set for him, just like he would at work.

What if she was just another job? What if he just wanted to tick 'Win back wife' off his goals-for-the-year list?

What if that was still all she was to him—another acquisition? One he had fun with, slept with, even talked and worked with—but still just another part of the Cattaneo treasury, at the end of the day.

She bit her lip, and scrunched the costume up in her hands. Did it really matter, anyway? If he never said *I love you*—if he never even felt it. As long as he kept behaving the way she wanted him to—with respect and affection for her and their family—wasn't that enough?

She could live with that. Especially if it meant she got to have sex with the most gorgeous man she'd ever met in a hot tub tonight.

Before she could change her mind, she changed quickly out of her dress and into her swimming costume, wrapping her dressing gown around her for added warmth. The chalet itself might have superb central heating, but the hot tub…the hot tub was out on the balcony. In the snow.

At least the water would be warm. And maybe the chill in the air would help her cool her overheated mind. And libido, come to that.

She stepped out of the room to find Seb already out on the balcony, two pots of tiramisu balanced on the edge of the hot tub as he finished running the water. She frowned. She knew from past experience that the tub took at least a couple of hours to fill and heat properly. Which meant he had to have been planning this from the start.

Sneaky.

But to be honest, she couldn't really blame him. If he

was feeling half as frustrated by their lack of a physical relationship as she was, she was kind of surprised he hadn't just pulled her into the bathtub because it was quicker.

And it meant he was thinking ahead *about them*. The same as with dinner—digging out her favourite recipe, her favourite wine, buying the food and making it... He was making an effort. A real, sustained effort.

And wasn't that exactly what she'd asked for, really?

Didn't he deserve the same in return?

Ducking back into the shadows, Maria watched Seb for a moment as he fiddled with the tub, until she was certain he hadn't spotted she was there. Then she shimmied out of her costume under her robe, left it hanging off the back of the sofa and strode out onto the balcony to meet her husband.

Seb turned and smiled as she closed the door behind her. 'Ready?' he asked.

'Definitely,' Maria said.

Then she dropped the robe and watched Seb's eyes widen.

The look on his face had made the risk of hypothermia totally worth it, Maria decided later. As she stretched out under the luxury sheets on Sebastian's bed, watching his chest rise and fall as he slept beside her, she knew without a doubt she had made the right decision. Maybe he never would love her the way she loved him, but the new man she'd come home to had made up for not saying the words with the quality of his actions. Respect and adoration could be every bit as wonderful as that fabled true love nonsense, she'd decided.

Especially when he could make her body sing the way he had tonight. Every inch of her still tingled with the memory. She'd half thought, over the last year, that she must have imagined how phenomenal they were, moving together in sync, their bodies as one. But if anything, it had been even better than she remembered from their honeymoon.

A perfect moment.

It might be her very own Christmas miracle. Her husband really saw her at last—and she truly believed that they could be happy together, as a family.

Maria was still smiling as she fell asleep.

But when she woke up alone, a handful of hours later, it was a very different story.

CHAPTER TWELVE

SEB HAD HAD plans for this morning. Important plans that involved waking up before his son and persuading his wife to relive their hot tub activities from the night before. Just in case he'd only dreamed how amazing it had been. He hadn't, he knew. No dream he'd ever experienced had been *that* vivid or *that* incredible.

From the moment she'd dropped that silky dressing gown, and he'd seen her perfect body again, skin glowing with the moonlight reflecting off the snow, he'd known that his Christmas was complete. Taking her into the water with him, holding her in his arms again, moving with her as they'd found their pleasure together… It had been the confirmation he'd needed that everything they'd been working towards had been possible.

She was his wife again. She trusted him with her body again, and her happiness. She would stay now; he knew it. Not because of the amazing sex but because of what it had meant for her to stand there naked on the balcony before him.

Trust. Partnership. That was what they'd wanted, and that was what they'd found again.

Maybe that partnership contract idea hadn't been so stupid after all. And he'd been looking forward to thanking Maria for coming up with it—in a rather intimate, physical way—that morning.

But instead he found himself on a private helicopter,

speeding towards Geneva to deal with a last-minute crisis with the Swiss merger.

The Italian arm of the business never had this sort of problem the day before Christmas Eve, he thought mulishly.

He hadn't wanted to go. But he simply hadn't had any other choice.

When his phone had buzzed just before five a.m. that morning, his first instinct had been to ignore it. Maria, deeply asleep beside him, hadn't seemed to be bothered by it. And when he'd planned to wake up before Frankie did, he hadn't meant quite *that* early.

But then it had buzzed again, and Maria had shifted in her sleep, giving a small moan, and he'd known he had to answer it before it woke her.

Of course, then he'd seen the screen, and the panicked text messages from his deputy, on duty in Geneva, and he'd known that this wasn't going to be anything approaching a good day.

The contract he and Maria had spent hours picking apart, the one she'd helped him make sense of—the last deal his father had ever worked on—was about to implode. And he was the only person who could stop it. So, gathering up all the notes he and Maria had made, he'd kissed her sleeping forehead, and left.

The worst part—after leaving Maria—had been having to ride in a damn helicopter.

He'd taken this trip half a dozen times before, and travelled by helicopter transfer to the Mont Coeur chalet more times than he cared to remember. But that had been before his parents had died in a helicopter crash.

He hadn't had too much time to think about it, to start with. At first, he'd just been concentrating on not waking Maria as he'd dressed, then on making sure he had all the relevant documents with him to try to salvage an almost impossible situation. This deal was only the first in a series that was supposed to secure the future of the company beyond the Italian borders. If it went south, his shares might not even be worth the paperwork it would take to sign them over.

His father had wanted a big gesture, something to show that his work was done, and Seb was ready to take over the company fully. And he'd found it—a huge expansion into new territories. He'd been so sure it was all tied up, every t crossed and every i dotted. And Seb had known that even if his father hadn't lived to see it, Salvo Cattaneo's legacy would live on through the company, getting bigger and brighter every year.

Until this morning, and a last-minute contract issue that could blow the whole thing. Worst of all, it was one that Maria had pointed out to him when they'd worked on the contract—one that he'd assured her would be fine.

It wasn't anywhere close to fine, as it turned out.

He'd screwed up again. He'd put his father's last-ever deal at risk. The whole *company* at risk. His father's legacy hung on him getting this right.

And he could never let his father down.

So here he was, sitting aboard a precarious flying machine with whirring blades that made him see his parents' terrified faces every time they rotated, preparing to fix it. Perfect way to spend the day before Christmas Eve, really.

Closing his eyes, Seb focused on Maria's face in his mind. The gleam in her eyes as she'd dropped that robe and stepped into the hot tub, stark naked. The way she'd insisted on eating tiramisu—also naked—before she'd even let him kiss her. The way she'd melted in his arms when they'd finally, finally touched...

The helicopter banked sharply to the right, and Seb clung to the base of his seat with white knuckles, his heart racing with fear.

All he had to do was get through this helicopter ride, the meeting from hell, and then one more trip back home to Mont Coeur. Then he was taking Christmas Eve off, come hell or high water. He'd fix the contract, pick up a bottle of champagne on his way back to the helipad, and then he'd go home to Maria and Frankie and enjoy Christmas, in a way he'd never hoped to again.

He just had to make it through this. Then everything would be wonderful again.

How could it not be, now he had Maria back home where she belonged?

'What do you mean, he left?' Noemi's beautiful brows crumpled up in a confused frown. 'It's the day before Christmas Eve. We all had plans. With Frankie. And You Know Who.' She mouthed 'Santa' in a deliberate manner in case Maria hadn't picked up on the inference.

She had. And even if she hadn't, how could she have forgotten the promised Santa trip, with Frankie reminding her every moment since he'd woken up?

Although Seb seemed to have managed it. Probably because he hadn't been there when Maria and Frankie had woken up.

Wordlessly, Maria handed Noemi the note Seb had left stuck to the bedside table for her to find that morning. Noemi scanned the sticky note, her eyes widening. Then she went back to the beginning and read it out loud.

'*"Had to fly to Geneva—work stuff. Hope to be back for dinner. S. x."* Well, that's…succinct.'

'Exactly.' So much for all those promises to involve her in his world—the business as well as the personal. Apparently it all fell by the wayside the moment some more interesting 'work stuff' appeared.

All of it, including their son.

Frankie sat on the stairs in the hallway, holding his toy

fox close to his chest and looking more forlorn than Maria thought she'd ever seen a toddler look. He'd been so excited about today—about seeing Santa, of course, but Maria knew the real appeal had been taking his *papà* to see Santa.

And stupid Papà was in stupid Geneva.

'He said he flew…' Noemi's face was strangely pale, and it took Maria a moment or two to connect the dots and figure out why.

'He'll have taken a helicopter,' she said faintly. Of course he would have. It was the obvious and fastest mode of transport from Mont Coeur to Geneva, and one he'd taken numerous times before when he'd been setting up the Swiss office.

But that had been before. Before Salvo and Nicole had died flying in one in New York, where they were supposed to be meeting Leo. Maria's heart pounded against her ribs at the thought of Seb so desperate to get back to work that he'd willingly climb into one again and fly away from them all the day before Christmas Eve. *How could he?*

'Have you called him?' Noemi asked. Maria could tell what her friend was really asking. *Do you think he's okay?*

'Not yet.' How could she? He'd made his choices very clear once again. Work before family, business before his wife. Just like always.

The worst part was that she'd honestly believed he'd changed. She'd thought that he'd finally seen the value of their marriage, the importance of their son. She'd thought they had a future.

Apparently Seb had simply wanted to get her into bed again, and now that mission was accomplished and he felt secure that she'd be moving home, he could get back to what he *actually* cared about most in the world. Work.

Well, at least she knew the truth now rather than later. If this had happened after their agreed trial period, once she'd already moved back in with him, had told Frankie they were staying with Papà for good…that would have been much worse. Small mercies and silver linings, she supposed. Her heart might be breaking again, but at least it was something that she found out now—before she got Frankie's hopes up. Or hers.

Seb might never have learned that lesson about counting chickens before they were hatched, but that was working to her advantage right now. And he never had been a patient man. She shouldn't really be surprised.

Unbidden, memories of their last fight, the night before she'd left, just over a year before, came back to haunt her…

'Where were you?' she'd yelled, the moment he'd breezed through the door. 'You promised you'd be here.'

'I got caught up at work.'

Seb had looked surprised she'd even noticed.

'There was a problem with one of the new campaigns, took for ever to straighten out. Does it matter?'

'Yes, it matters!'

How could she ever make him understand? she'd thought. 'You haven't even seen your son in three days. That *matters*, Seb.'

'Look, work's been crazy. Trust me, I'd rather have been here. I'm exhausted. I'll make it up to Frankie at the weekend,' he'd promised.

And she had even believed that he'd meant it.

Except he'd promised the same thing every weekend for a month.

And then she'd known. It would never happen.

She'd shaken her head. 'I don't believe you.'

With a groan, Seb had dropped his briefcase to the floor. 'Come on, Maria. You knew what you were signing up for. You married me to save your family business—just like I married you to get the merger between our companies. And now you're complaining that I'm spending too much time working at that same business?'

She'd stumbled back a few steps. She'd dared to hope that their marriage was something more, and in just a few words he'd proved that it was even less than she'd thought.

She was nothing to him.

And he was everything to her.

'You don't even *see* me!' she'd yelled. 'Sometimes I'm not sure you'd even notice if I left.'

'You're making this into something this isn't, Maria…'

But she hadn't been. For the first time she'd seen their marriage clearly.

Suddenly calm, she had forced herself to stand up straight, to look him in the eye and accept the truth.

'This isn't enough for me, Seb. And I realise now that you can't give me what I need. You're not capable of it.'

She'd known it then. And now it was happening all over again.

Time to face the truth.

'I need to pack,' Maria said, and Frankie suddenly looked up at her, his eyes wide. Maria tried to look calm and happy for his sake—she could never tell how much he understood in his little two-year-old mind. Some days the very concept of time and place seemed beyond him. Others…he seemed to understand the world around them better than she did.

'You're leaving?' Noemi asked, and Maria gave a helpless shrug.

'How can I stay?' She'd asked for what she needed to be happy. A family. A commitment from him to be a real part of that family.

And he'd flown off to Geneva instead of taking Frankie to meet Santa.

That was her answer, right there.

And she'd set *terms*, damn it. They had a *contract*. How could she hold her head up high again if she let him break it now? He'd know that he could break it again and again in the future with no repercussions.

That was no way to do business. And she was a business-woman now.

'I want to see Santa,' Frankie said suddenly, standing up on the bottom step. 'I want to see Santa *now*.'

Maria was about to give her usual lecture about asking politely, even though she didn't really have the energy, but Noemi got there first.

'Of course we'll go and see Santa, my cherub!' She wrapped her arms around Frankie's thin shoulders and held him and his fox close. 'We'll go and see him together right now. Frankie and Mamma and Aunt Noemi.'

'No!' Frankie wriggled free. 'I want to go with Papà!'

Maria sighed. Of course he did. That was what he'd been promised. And while he might forget how to brush his teeth or to say 'please' and 'thank you', Frankie never forgot a promise. Something Seb would know if he'd been paying proper attention.

'Papà's not here, *piccolo*,' she said, as gently as she could.

Not gently enough, apparently.

Frankie flew into a frenzy of sobbing, throwing himself face down on the stairs and burying his face in his hands. 'I want Papà! Papà!' he cried, and Maria's heart broke a little bit more.

Noemi looked at her with panic in her eyes. 'What shall I do? How do we fix it?'

Because she didn't know that only Sebastian could do that—and he didn't seem to want to.

'We can't,' Maria said. 'All we can do is ride it out.'

Noemi winced as Frankie gave a particularly ear-splitting wail. 'How? With earplugs?'

Maria shook her head. 'You go and get Max, and buy more ice cream. I'll deal with this. Then when he's calmer he can have ice cream with you two while I pack. It'll be a nice last memory before we leave.'

Noemi looked like she wanted to argue, but Maria kept her expression set and, after a second or two, Noemi nodded and headed towards the kitchen.

And Maria sank down onto the stairs, drew her son into her arms and pretended she wasn't crying as she whispered reassurances in his ear.

It was dark by the time the helicopter blades whirred to a stop on the Mont Coeur helipad. With a weary sigh, Seb gathered his belongings, thanked the pilot and headed back to the chalet in search of a stiff drink—and his wife.

He smiled to himself at the realisation. However awful today had been—and it had been pretty bloody terrible—he was still excited to go home and talk to Maria about it. She'd understand about how terrified he'd been of the helicopter ride. And she'd sympathise with the ridiculous contract screw-up that had dragged him out there to re-negotiate at the eleventh hour with their new partners, just to ensure the family business didn't lose millions further down the line—even if she did tell him that she'd told him so.

She'd understand. She'd pour him a drink, listen, then kiss all his cares away.

This was why he needed his wife back.

A year ago, he'd never imagined they could get back here. A year ago, he had still been replaying that last argument over and over in his head, trying to make sense of it.

He'd been so exhausted at the time he hadn't even been sure he remembered it right. It had just made no sense. Yes, he'd been late home and, yes, it hadn't been the first time. But he'd never understood what had made that time different.

He'd apologised, as always. And when she'd thrown it back at him, he'd reminded her of the truth.

This was why she'd married him. For his company.

For him to work hard, to build a new family business for them—and for Frankie. He was working *for* his son.

Just like his *papà* had worked for him and Noemi. If he could do half the job his *papà* had, Frankie would be okay.

It was just that being even half the man Salvo Cattaneo had been, living up to that impossible ideal, took time and energy—and it didn't leave a lot left over.

That was something Maria *hadn't* understood.

But now, finally, they seemed to be understanding each other at last. Now he was on the way to being the husband she needed.

When he finally reached the chalet, most of the windows were already dark. He checked his watch—it was later than he'd thought. God, this day had gone on for ever.

Then he frowned. The one light that still shone out into the night came from a room on the second floor, to the right...yes. It was his office window. Why was that room lit?

Letting himself in, he headed straight up to investigate. He had a bottle of whisky in the drawer there anyway—a result of reading too many bad detective novels as a child, Maria had always said—and there was no point turning on all the other lights in the large chalet just for a drink. He could de-stress just as well in his office, then head to bed and see if Maria was feeling amenable to being woken up.

Then he opened his office door and found his wife sitting in his chair, drinking his whisky, her feet resting on the desk beside a familiar green, red and glittery flyer.

Santa. Frankie. That was today.

Seb stalled in the doorway, leaning heavily against the frame. *Oh, God.* 'Maria, I—'

'I don't care,' she snapped. She swung her legs down from the desk and pushed herself to a standing position, resting her hands on either side of that flyer as she leaned forward. 'You promised to take your son to see Santa.

And obviously that means very little to you, but it meant everything to him. He wouldn't go without you, you realise? So he's just been miserable here all day, despite all the ice cream Noemi and Max have fed him. And then he cried himself to sleep when you still weren't back from your oh-so-important business trip.'

'It *was* important.' Seb sighed, running a hand over his hair as he tried to find a way to salvage this. He'd spent all day negotiating with idiots, and now he had to come home and do the same thing with his wife.

This was not how he'd imagined this evening going.

God, it was happening all over again. Just like last time, he was exhausted and strung out and nothing made any *sense*.

'*Frankie* is important, too.' Maria stared at him, as if she were waiting for a magical response that would make all things better. But he didn't have one.

Finally, she shook her head and straightened up. 'Look, I'm already packed. We couldn't get a flight out today or we'd be gone already, but we're booked on one at lunchtime tomorrow.'

Wait. What?

'You're leaving? You can't! You…you said you'd stay for Christmas.'

'And you said you'd put your family first for once over the holidays. You said you'd prove that if I stayed, things would be different.'

'And they *have* been different!' She'd admitted that herself last night. She couldn't take that back now, could she?

'Right up until the point where you got me into bed, yes.' Maria's expression turned hard. 'Was that what it was all about, in the end? You just wanted to prove you could have me again, and once you'd achieved that you didn't need to try any more?'

'No!' How could she think that? Well, apart from the

bit where he'd slept with her then run out on her and his obligations the next morning.

How could he have been so stupid?

'It was the contract, Maria. Remember the clause you found—'

'Look, it doesn't matter now.' Maria cut him off, and sighed. 'We tried, Seb. We really did. But I'm never going to be happy being left behind while you chase after the adrenaline high of doing business. And neither is Frankie. I thought…'

'What? What did you think?' Because suddenly Seb had the sinking suspicion that he'd been misunderstanding her from the first. That all this talk of partnerships and contracts had been hiding something else. And if he didn't know what that was, how could he fix it?

'You can't give me what I need. You're not capable of it.'

He'd given her everything. Why wasn't it enough?

What wasn't she asking for?

'I thought it could be enough. If you could live by my rules, follow the plan…if we could make all that work, I thought a business partnership marriage would be enough.' Maria looked up and met his gaze, her eyes so open and honest that he knew that, finally, they were getting to the real reason she'd left him. Yes, he'd been a lousy husband and a workaholic, and he'd forgotten important things like anniversaries and birthdays and Santa. But she'd known that and had married him anyway. She'd known that and had come back anyway, ready to give him a second chance.

So why was this time different?

'But I know now I was wrong. Yes, you messed up today. But that's not why I'm leaving.' Maria took a deep breath. 'I'm leaving because even if you met every objective I set, it still wouldn't be enough.'

There was something more, he was sure.

'Enough for what?' he asked, his voice soft. He had to *listen*. He had to *understand*.

'Enough to make up for the fact that you were never going to love me the way I'd fallen in love with you.'

CHAPTER THIRTEEN

WELL, THERE IT WAS. She'd done it now. He'd probably be grateful she was leaving. He'd wanted a business wife, one who knew the terms of the deal—entertaining clients, bringing up his heir, and basically reliving her own mother's miserable life for the next fifty years. But he'd compromised—he'd offered her a job in the company, allowed her to have a say in what *she* needed, agreed to everything she'd asked for.

And it still wasn't enough.

Because she'd never been able to bring herself to ask for what she *really* wanted—until now. Maybe she was to blame, at least a little bit, for everything that had happened between them before. She'd never been honest about what she needed.

But now she was.

She'd been furious when she'd woken alone, and had realised that Seb had skipped out on their plans and let Frankie down. But if she was honest with herself, she knew that wasn't why she was leaving.

She was leaving because, if he loved her, she wouldn't need a contract or objectives or any of the other tactics she'd used to turn him into the husband she wanted.

If he loved her, he'd have woken her up and explained, and they'd have worked it out together. She could have even gone with him and held his hand on that awful helicopter for moral support if he'd needed it. But it hadn't even occurred to him to ask.

'You…'

'Fell in love with you. Yes. Before we were even married, probably. Definitely, actually.' She may as well own her truth now it was out there. 'Seb, I've loved you since I was fifteen—since the night you sneaked me out to go ice-skating. And then I fell in love with you all over again when we got married. And since I've been back…that feeling has only grown stronger, if I'm honest.'

'Then why are you leaving? If you love me, why do you have to go?' Maria could hear the frustration and confusion in Seb's voice. Of course he didn't understand. This wasn't the deal they'd struck. And Seb only understood negotiations and deals.

They couldn't negotiate love, though.

'Because you don't love me.' It was that simple and that impossible, all at the same time.

'Of course I love you!' Seb objected.

Maria shook her head. 'Okay, I know you love me as a friend and partner. But you're not *in* love with me. You never have been.'

'I don't see what the difference is,' Seb said tiredly. 'Of course I love you, and Frankie. You're my wife. It's kind of part of the deal.' As if it were automatic, a foregone conclusion.

'That's the thing, Seb. It isn't.' Maria sighed. 'Think of it this way. When we got married, I was a business asset. And when we discovered that we actually got along and connected, well, physically, that was an added bonus, right? Then Frankie came along and you figured the job was done. You had the wife to support you and entertain clients, and you had an heir to take over the business when you were ready to retire. Right?'

Seb's uncomfortable expression told her that she'd got it *exactly* right.

'But that's not enough for me,' she said.

'I get that!' Seb exploded. 'That's why I've been jumping through hoops for the last week and a half to meet all your objectives! To give you what you want. You can have the job—hell, you can have the whole company if you want. After today, I'm not sure I'd miss it. But it's still not enough for you.'

'No,' Maria said simply. 'It isn't. Because the way I love you, Seb…it has nothing to do with business, or obligations, or expectations. It's not even about Frankie, really. It's just…all consuming. Like you're the first thing I think about in the morning and the last thing I dream about at night. Even when I was away, when I had to make a decision or wanted to try something, *you* were the person I wanted to talk to about it. But I couldn't—not because I'd left but because even before I did, you were never there to listen. You didn't see me, or hear me. But you were my whole world. And being so invisible to you, that you only saw me when you needed me…that was going to destroy me in the end, Seb. And I can't do that any more.'

Seb stepped fully into the room at last, reaching a hand out towards her, and Maria saw her chance to escape. She couldn't stay and talk about this. She just wanted to be alone.

Darting past him, she made for the door, but he wrapped an arm around her waist to stop her, holding her close—too close.

'Wait. Maria, please. Please, don't go, not like this.'

Maria wriggled to get free and he released his hold with a sigh. 'I'll email when I'm home,' she said, her words coming too fast. 'We can work out a visitation schedule for Frankie. I… I wasn't kidding about that—I want him to have you in his life. Although after today…'

'I'll make it up to him,' Seb said—automatically, it seemed. But it only made her remember all the times he'd said it before.

'You'll try,' Maria said wryly. 'You can't just buy kids off with more toys, you realise. He wanted *you* more than Santa.'

'I'll… I'll fix it, Maria, I swear.' He sounded so earnest, so desperate that Maria almost wanted to believe him. 'Look, between now and Christmas—no, now and New Year—I won't work at all. I fixed the contract thing with the Swiss team today. Everything else I can delegate! Probably. I'll sort it somehow. And it will just be you, me and Frankie for the next week, after Noemi and Max head to Ostania, and Leo and Anissa go back to New York. Just us. Our little family. Please. Just give me another chance.'

He still didn't understand, Maria realised. He never would.

It was a horrible echo of that last argument before she'd left. She'd told him he wasn't capable of giving her what she needed. Nothing had changed. And even worse, he didn't seem capable of even *understanding* what she needed. Of understanding the importance of love.

'This isn't something you can just fix, Seb. This is about who you are.' And who he was would never love her—let alone love her more than work. Living up to his father's legacy mattered too much to him.

'You're wrong. I can change. Look!' Without any more warning than that, Seb pulled his mobile phone from his pocket, strode to the window, yanked it open and tossed the device out into the snow. Then he turned to her, smiling proudly. 'See?'

Maria shook her head. 'I'm sorry, Seb. It's not enough.'

She turned, walked out of the office, and up the stairs to the room she shared with Frankie. Where, ignoring all the mostly packed cases and toys, she threw herself onto the bed and cried herself to sleep just as Frankie had done hours earlier.

It was over. For good this time.

* * *

Seb stared at the empty doorway for a long moment. And then he reached for the whisky bottle.

She loved him. Truly, deeply, properly loved him. The way his mother had loved his father. The way Leo loved Anissa and Noemi loved Max.

The way love was supposed to be.

The way he'd never imagined he'd get to experience.

He'd never told Maria, but it wasn't as if he hadn't thought about it over the years. The first time his father had raised the possibility of a union with his business buddy's daughter, he'd turned it down flat. He'd pointed out that Salvo had got to marry the love of his life. Why shouldn't he?

Except…there *was* no love of his life. No time to focus on anything but the business, being the success that Salvo expected him to be. And, honestly, most of the time the business was more fun than half the women he dated anyway.

Which had led him back to Maria, whom he'd last seen when she'd still been a teenager, two years younger than him and just an old family friend. But then she'd come home from university, twenty and poised and so, so beautiful… and he'd thought, why not? He had been twenty-two. His parents had been in love for years already by the time they'd been his age—hell, they'd even got married and had him by that point. Why wait for some mythical true love when he could marry the most beautiful woman he'd ever seen, make his father proud, save *her* father's business and inch closer to his long-term goal of taking over the company.

It had been everything he'd needed, all wrapped up in one gorgeous package. He'd have been an idiot to turn it down.

Finding out that Maria was still good company, and had seemed to be as attracted to him as he was to her…that had just cemented the fact that the marriage was a great idea. So he'd told his father yes, had bought a ring and gone through all the traditional motions.

And he'd known it wasn't love. He'd known that Maria had had her own reasons for agreeing to the marriage—reasons that had nothing to do with how she'd felt about him. So he'd never let himself think about what it *wasn't*. Love had been off the cards for him—and how could he complain when he'd had everything else he wanted?

So he hadn't thought about love. Not once.

But now it was all he could think about. A question he had to find the answer to if he was ever going to fix this.

She loved him. She'd loved him since they were teenagers. Suddenly her answers about why she'd married him, from their night at the lake, rang false—or at least incomplete.

She'd said yes because she'd hoped he'd fall in love with her. But she'd never told him—so he'd never even considered it as a possibility. Had never *let* himself consider it.

Did he love her? He'd always loved her as a partner and friend. And he'd admitted to himself this week that she mattered more than *anything* in his world. That she was *everything*.

Was that love? The way she said she loved him?

He'd never even thought about it. Even after she'd left a year ago, he'd not considered it. He'd just assumed that eventually she'd come back to him. Like he'd told Leo, sometimes when you loved someone, you had to give them space. Because *of course* he loved Maria. He'd just never stopped to think about *how* he loved her.

Because she was already his wife, so what did it matter?

Except now it mattered. It mattered a lot. To her. And so it mattered to him.

Taking a long swig from the bottle, Seb tried to imagine waking up every day without Maria there. Tried to picture coming home without the promise of her to talk to about his day. It wasn't hard to do. He'd already lived it for the last year.

Then he shifted his focus. Pictured rushing home from work early just to spend time with her and Frankie—and maybe a younger sibling or two. Thought about crossing the hall from his office to hers at work to talk through the details of some deal or another. Considered that holiday they were going to take next year, just the three of them and the sunshine.

Most of all, he imagined kissing Maria good morning *every single* morning, and goodnight *every single* night. He thought about her happy, and realised with a shocked start that it was the only thing in the world he truly, desperately wanted.

Not the deal for the Swiss office, not the accolades and success for expanding the business, not Leo's shares in Cattaneo Jewels. Not even his father's approval, if he were still here to give it. And that was the only thing he'd ever fought for before now.

Now he had a new fight.

He wanted Maria to be happy.

Just that. Just Maria, and, of course, Frankie. The two of them happy. If he had that, he didn't need anything else at all.

And that was his answer, right there.

Because he loved her. *Exactly* the way she loved him, even if it had taken him too bloody long to realise it. Even if he didn't behave like he did. Even if she didn't believe it.

He, Sebastian Cattaneo, was in love with his wife. And suddenly he understood a fundamental truth that his father had failed to teach him—probably because he'd thought it was too obvious to need to be said.

His family, and their happiness, was the greatest achievement he could ever hope to attain.

No other goal, objective or business plan could come close.

But it wasn't one he could achieve on his own. He needed help.

He needed people who had been down this hole before, and knew the way out. People who'd fallen so desperately in love and had found a way to make it work. To be happy together.

He needed his parents. But in their absence...

He reached for his phone, before realising he'd already thrown it out of the window. Never mind—the person he needed most was already in the chalet. He just hoped she didn't mind a late-night wake-up call, especially since it was all for the highest of causes.

Seb stoppered the bottle and headed for the door, certain at last of what he needed to do next.

He needed to find his sister, and then his brother. And his brother-in-law-to-be and sister-in-law-to-be, come to that.

And probably a Santa suit.

Maria woke on Christmas Eve, bleary-eyed and sore-headed, to find Frankie clambering into bed beside her. As she snuggled his little body close, she tried to find the courage and energy to face the day ahead.

They were leaving. In just a few hours she and Frankie would be on their way back to that little cottage on her parents' estate in Italy, ready to spend Christmas together, just the two of them.

And she was glad about that. Really.

Glad that she'd made a decision at least. Glad that she wasn't going to spend the rest of her life waiting for Seb to wake up and see the woman he'd married. Glad that she could look to her future and—

Oh, who was she kidding? She hated it. But that didn't change the fact that it was the right choice.

She'd asked for what she needed at last. Had opened up and given him the chance to be the husband she needed.

And he'd thrown his phone out of the window instead. As if that equalled all the 'I love you's she'd never hear from him.

'Come on, *piccolo*,' she said, nudging Frankie to sit up. 'Let's go and find your aunt Noemi for a last play before we have to go home.'

Frankie nodded sleepily—apparently he hadn't been entirely awake when he'd crawled into her bed. He snuggled some more with his fox while she got washed and dressed, then decided that Frankie could stay in his pyjamas a little while longer at least. She listened at the door to make sure that Seb wouldn't be waiting to ambush her. Then, satisfied that he was either still asleep or had already left for the office, she led Frankie out and down the main stairs of the chalet, heading for the kitchen.

Only to stop and stare as they reached the top of the flight of stairs to the ground floor.

Beside her, Frankie gasped, clasping his hands together and looking up at her with wide eyes, before turning his attention back to the scene below again.

There, beneath the giant Christmas tree with all its glistening ornaments and lights, was a pile of presents in shiny wrapping paper. And standing next to the presents was—

'Santa!' Frankie cried, looking completely overcome by the whole situation.

Maria didn't blame him. But Leo in a Santa suit wasn't what was surprising her most about the whole tableau.

That was Sebastian in an elf costume next to him, with Anissa in a matching girls' version, while Max and Noemi both wore headbands with reindeer antlers. She almost didn't want to know what Seb had held over his siblings and sister-in-law-to-be and brother-in-law-to-be to get them to take part in this. Especially since it had been gone midnight when she'd walked out on Seb, and it was barely six in the morning now.

Apparently Seb really could pull off anything he set his mind to. He'd promised to make it up to Frankie, and he was. This was basically the dream, and a lovely way to finish the trip, since they wouldn't be there for actual Christmas Day tomorrow. This was fine—if utterly bizarre.

And it didn't change her decision one bit.

'Can I, Mamma?' Frankie asked, and she nodded, watching as he skipped down the stairs towards Santa. He stopped a few steps away as he recognised Santa's chief elf, though.

'Papà?' he asked, baffled.

Seb crouched down beside him. 'That's right, Frankie. I'm so sorry I wasn't here to take you to meet Santa yesterday like I promised.'

'Santa's here now, though?' Frankie glanced between the elf that was his *papà* and the man in the big red suit with the white beard next to him.

'That's right, Frankie,' Leo said, in a suitably booming Santa voice, the beard disguising him well enough to fool a two-year-old. 'Your *papà* told me how sorry he was, and how much you wanted to meet me, so I made a special trip back to be here this morning—and made him promise to help me by being my special elf for the day. Now, how would you like a present?'

That was, of course, the magic word. As much as she'd told Seb he couldn't just bribe kids with toys, they weren't exactly likely to turn them down either.

Leo picked up the first parcel next to him, one with bright green shiny paper, and handed it to Frankie—who was almost the same size as the box. Max and Noemi both darted in to help him and Maria thought, not for the first time, how lucky their twins would be to have them as parents. Prince or not, she could tell how much Max loved Noemi, and how much effort he would put into always being there for her.

Which thought, of course, drew her back to Sebastian, who stood beside Frankie—but his eyes were on her. As soon as she looked his way, he took a step towards her, obviously wanting to continue their conversation from the previous night.

Maria shook her head, hoping he got the hint. There was nothing he could do now to change her mind anyway.

But then Santa looked up, too, a large envelope in his hand. 'Now, Frankie, it looks like this present is for your *mamma*. Would you like to give it to her?'

Frankie, engrossed in the toy train set he'd just unwrapped, shook his head. 'Papà do it.'

With a smirk that twisted his fake beard up, Leo handed the envelope to Sebastian, who smiled. So did Noemi and Max. And Anissa.

Oh, Maria didn't like how this was going one little bit.

'Why don't you take it into the other room to open it?' Noemi said, gesturing to the doorway to the snug with her antlers and giving Seb a little push in that direction, so Maria had no choice but to follow if she wanted her present.

She wasn't at all sure that she wanted her present.

But Frankie wanted her to open it. 'Go on, Mamma. I stay here with Santa.'

Okay, then. 'I'll be right back,' she promised.

Then she followed Seb into the next room, feeling suspiciously like she was heading into the lion's den.

CHAPTER FOURTEEN

Seb held the door to the snug open for Maria as she walked through it, rehearsing what he wanted to say one last time. He hadn't slept in over twenty-four hours, he was dressed as a freaking elf, but, heaven help him, he was *not* going to mess up what had to be his last-ever chance to win his wife back.

Maria turned to face him, leaning against the back of the small sofa in the snug. 'Seb, look, this was a nice gesture for Frankie. And I appreciate it. I do. But I think we said everything we needed to last night, don't you?'

'No,' Seb disagreed. 'You may have done, but I have a lot more to say. Starting with this.' He held out the envelope on which Noemi had stuck a giant bow, even as she'd nagged at him to tell her what was inside. He hadn't, and Leo—the only one who knew about the contents by necessity—had kept his secret.

He wanted Maria to know this first.

She took the envelope gingerly, staring at the garish bow. 'You know, Seb, you can't buy me with gifts either.'

'I swear to you that is not what I'm trying to do.' Although now he thought about it rationally—or as rationally as he could after so little sleep—it could definitely look that way. 'Just…open it. And then let me explain, please. Okay?'

Maria nodded and peeled off the bow. Seb held his breath as she lifted the flap and pulled out the thick, creamy paper inside. 'This is another contract?'

'Not exactly.'

Her eyes widened as she read through it. 'This is…this is a controlling share of Cattaneo Jewels. You're giving me Leo's shares?'

'Well, Leo is, as soon as he's allowed to. Once it goes through, the family business will be more yours than mine.'

'Why…why would you *do* that?' she asked, exasperation leaking out in her tone. 'Seb, I told you, you can't buy me back. That's not what I want. I just—'

'You want to be free to find someone who loves you, the way my parents loved each other, the way Leo and Noemi have found someone, right?' Maria nodded, and Seb allowed himself a small smile. 'See, I do listen sometimes.'

'I know. And I appreciate this gesture, Seb. I do. And I know I'll always be in your life because we'll always have Frankie. But I don't need this. And I don't think… I don't think it would help, working so closely with you.'

'That was sort of the idea,' Seb muttered, and Maria's gaze turned suspicious.

'Wait, you gave me this to keep me here, didn't you? To buy me off. Because you can't give me what I *really* need—you don't love me that way. But you don't want anyone else to have me either, because I'm your *wife*. Seb, this is…this is low.'

'No!' Oh, hell, this was all going wrong. Very wrong. This was what happened when he planned a grand gesture on no sleep, clearly. 'That's not what this means, okay?'

Scrubbing a hand over his head—and dislodging his elf ears—Seb sank onto the sofa, his whole body aching with exhaustion. After a moment Maria sat down next to him.

'Okay, then. Tell me what it does mean. And why you're dressed up as an elf, come to that.'

Seb huffed a laugh. 'The elf thing was more for Frankie than you, unless you have some strange tastes you never mentioned before. And because Leo wouldn't wear the Santa suit unless I dressed up, too.'

'Ha! No. Although I think Anissa was secretly impressed with Leo's costume.'

'And she looks a lot better as an elf than I do,' Seb commented. Maria didn't disagree with him, which wasn't a surprise.

'So. Explain?' Maria asked. 'Everything, preferably. Starting from when I left you last night.'

Seb sighed. How to explain it in a way that she would believe? It felt like the realisation of his love had come on so slowly, over the years, then had sped up over the last week and a half. But would she believe that? If he just said 'I love you', Maria would think they were just words to make her stay, like she had with the shares.

It wasn't enough to just say the words. But he also knew the words were what would mean the most to her.

'When you left last night,' he started slowly, thinking his way through as he spoke, 'I realised that you were right about some things, and that I'd been dead wrong about others.'

'Like?'

'You said I didn't see you.' The memory was almost as painful as the words had been, especially when he knew what he'd been missing. 'And in lots of ways you were right. When we got married, I believed our relationship was one thing—a business deal, a partnership. And I never looked beyond that. In my head, I'd assigned you to the role of "wife of heir to Cattaneo Jewels", and looked forward to the day you'd be the "wife of the CEO of Cattaneo Jewels". And it never occurred to me to rethink that, until last night.'

'I noticed,' Maria said drily.

'But that doesn't mean that was all you were to me.' Seb twisted on the sofa so he was facing her, needing her to see the sincerity on his face. 'Just because I never assigned words to it the way you did, or even gave it too much thought… Maria, you were never just a convenience to me. You were a friend, a trusted confidante and partner, the mother of my child, and the most beautiful woman I've ever seen. With all those amazing qualities…of course I fell in love with you. So in love that you became an integral part of my life, and I'd jump through any hoop, meet any target you asked me to in order to keep you there. It just never occurred to me that, when you asked for those things, what you really wanted was my love. Because that was yours all along, even if I didn't realise it until now. I love you, Maria. Not as a friend or anything except as the woman I love. My wife.'

Maria froze, trying to take in his words. First Leo's shares, now declarations of love. Seb really was pulling out all the big guns to try to make her stay.

'Is this…? I have to ask. Are you just staying this to keep me here?' she asked, hating that it was even a question. But after everything…it was.

'No! Maria, I…' Seb stopped, looked down at his hands, then started again. 'You know what you said last night? About me being your first thought and last dream? I'd like to… Can I tell you about my day yesterday?'

His day? The day where he'd sneaked off to work in the early hours and skipped out on seeing Santa with their son? And he thought that was going to *help* his cause?

'I guess so,' she said, confused.

'I woke up yesterday morning to my phone buzzing, and all I wanted to do was ignore it and curl back up with you. But it wouldn't stop and I didn't want to wake you, so I checked my messages and…the deal my dad was working on before he died—the one you helped me work through the contract for? Well, you were right. That clause I dismissed… it was about to bring down the whole deal.'

'I told you so,' Maria said absently. Salvo's last deal. His legacy. Seb's last chance to make his father proud.

Suddenly Seb rushing off to Geneva to save it made a lot more sense.

He *had* been thinking about family, just in a different sort of way. And living up to his father's expectations had always been what had mattered most to him.

'It was…it was what Dad had been working towards for years. Our biggest expansion yet. He always said that once it was sorted, he was going to hand the whole company over to me and retire.'

'Only he never got the chance,' Maria murmured.

'Exactly. And I couldn't… I just couldn't let this one go down without a fight. You know?'

Maria nodded. 'So you went to Geneva.'

'I had to take a—a helicopter.' Seb's voice almost broke on that word. 'And I couldn't stop thinking about my parents, or what had happened to them. And I was just praying I could make it through and get back home to you, because I knew everything would be okay then. I was thinking of you and of Frankie the whole way there. How much I wished I was here with you. Or that you were there with me, distracting me, holding my hand, anything. I just wanted you there. No one else. Only you.'

Maria bit her lip. 'When I realised you must have taken a helicopter… I wished I could have been with you, too. But it didn't even occur to you to ask me to go with you.'

'How could I?' Seb asked. 'I was disappearing to take care of work stuff on our Christmas holiday. I mean, I'd forgotten all about Santa, I'll admit, but even so, I knew I was cutting it close with the rules and regulations you'd set.'

'*That* was why you didn't ask me?' Not because he hadn't thought of her, or because she wasn't important to him, but because he'd thought that was what she wanted.

Because she'd set impossible rules that he couldn't help but follow.

Something, somewhere had got very messed up in their marriage.

'Yeah. Of course. Why else?' Seb looked at her, confused. 'Anyway, I *really* wished you could have come with me when I arrived in Geneva. All these idiots were up in arms about this contract, and I just knew that if you were there to talk it all through with them we'd have had it sorted in half the time. You were always so great at making these problems that looked huge more manageable, and you made far better sense of that contract than I could.'

'I… It's just about breaking things down into what really matters.' Which was basically the opposite of what she'd done when she'd arrived at Mont Coeur. She'd given Seb some convoluted and taxing targets to meet, and had never stopped to focus on what really mattered most to her—whether he loved her. 'Once you get to the heart of what both parties really want, it's easier to figure out where there's room to manoeuvre.'

'Exactly,' Seb said, his voice soft. 'Anyway, by the time I flew home again, I was frustrated, exhausted, and all I wanted was to come home to you. To tell you about my day—and how it would have been better if you had been there with me. But then I realised about the Santa thing, and I just… I knew I'd failed. I'd spent my whole life trying to make my dad proud, and my whole day trying to salvage his last deal, and in the end it was going to cost me what matters most in the world to me. You and Frankie.'

What matters most. Not his father's legacy. Not Salvo's expectations.

Her. Their family.

A small, warm thing that felt a lot like hope started to unfurl in her chest.

'So you called Leo and asked him for his shares and a

Santa suit. And he said yes.' Maria shook her head. 'Seriously, he has taken to brotherhood amazingly well.'

Seb laughed, then sobered quickly. 'Actually... Leo said something else last night, something that got me thinking.'

'Oh?'

'He said...maybe the expectations I was trying to live up to weren't mine to meet.'

Maria tilted her head as she looked at him. 'What do you think he meant by that?'

'I think... I never knew about Leo until Papà and Mamma were gone. But now that I do... I wonder if the... pressure I felt was more about Papà's guilt over losing Leo than what he expected from me.'

'Salvo couldn't live up to his own expectations as a father because Leo wasn't there for him to be a father *to*,' Maria said, thinking out loud. 'It makes a lot of sense, you know.'

Seb shrugged. 'Maybe. I don't know. I need to think about it some more. But sometimes I wonder if I was trying to be two sons rolled into one. If that was why I was never enough.'

Maria reached over to grab his arm. 'You were enough for them, Seb. Salvo and Nicole...they loved you, so much. Not as a replacement for Leo but for yourself.'

'I know.' Seb glanced away, then cleared his throat. 'But we were talking about last night.'

Maria let go. One emotional breakthrough at a time. If she stayed—*if*—there'd be time to deal with Seb's feelings about his parents later. 'You called Leo?'

'Actually, no. I couldn't call, because I'd thrown my phone out into the snow in some sort of misguided romantic gesture.'

Maria winced. 'Of course.'

'So instead I had to knock on Noemi and Max's door and get *them* to call Leo and Anissa, and by that point everyone wanted in on the *next* grand gesture and…here we are.'

'They all wanted to be part of it?' Maria asked, a little touched.

'They all want you to stay,' Seb replied. 'Not as much as I do, of course, but maybe close. Apparently I'm a lot nicer to be around when you're here. Plus they all love you, too. They're your family as much as they're mine.'

Family. Wasn't that what she'd wanted when she'd married Seb in the first place? To have a place she belonged, where she was loved? And it was definitely what she wanted for Frankie, more than anything.

And she could have it if she stayed. If she trusted that Seb was telling the truth when he said he loved her.

She knew they couldn't be happy the way they had been before, and while the last week and a half had been better, it still wasn't what she really wanted from a marriage. She didn't want to have to hold her husband accountable to quotas and objectives every day of their lives. But she didn't want him to get so consumed with work that he forgot about them again either.

Which meant they needed a new plan. A new negotiation.

Starting with what mattered most this time.

Starting with love.

'If I stay,' Maria started, and Seb felt his heart rise, light with hope. '*If.* If I stay…we need a new plan. Not a contract or objectives like before,' she added quickly.

'Good. Because… I want to be the husband you deserve, and the father Frankie needs—really I do. And I want you to tell me what you need that to be. But I'd rather it happen because we're a team, working together to get where we want to go. Not because we both have our separate objectives to meet or we're going to fail.'

He'd spent too much of his life afraid of failing already. Too much of his life not being the son his father had given away, and not being good enough to make up for that loss.

Now he wanted to focus on being happy instead. On making Maria and Frankie happy, every single day.

'A team.' Maria smiled at him. 'That's what I want, too. You and me against the world. Well, you, me and Frankie.'

'Exactly. Plus… I've been thinking about this a lot lately, especially since we found out about Leo,' Seb said. 'I think… I think the only way to fail at being a family is to stop trying. As long as we want to be together…'

'And I do.' Maria grabbed hold of his hands suddenly, and Seb was surprised to see that there were tears in her eyes. 'That was always the problem, you see. I wanted to stay so badly. But I knew that if I stayed as things were, I'd never be happy. But now…'

'Now I'll make it my life's work to keep you happy. That's my only objective,' Seb promised. 'But… I'm going to need some promises from you, too.'

'Yeah?' Maria raised her eyebrows at him. 'Objectives? Goals?'

'I like to think of them as…vows. New wedding vows for us both. What do you think?' He barely remembered what he'd promised the first time round—he'd been too busy staring at how beautiful Maria was in her bridal gown, and feeling the gazes on the back of his head of the hundreds of people their mothers had insisted on inviting.

But this time…this time he knew the vows they made would stick with him through the years. That he'd think of them every morning, and live by them every day.

Even if there was no one else there to hear them make them, and he was dressed in an elf suit rather than a tuxedo.

These were the vows that mattered.

'Vows,' Maria said, with a smile. 'I like it. So, what

were you thinking? You want to promise to love, honour and obey me?'

'Ha! No. You didn't even promise that last time.' He frowned. 'Did you?'

'Of course I didn't,' Maria said, rolling her eyes. 'But what, then?'

'How about… I promise to always keep you first in my heart, and in my mind?'

'I like that one.' Maria shifted closer, and he lifted an arm to place it around her, stroking her shoulder gently. 'And I promise to always tell you what I need, and let you find a way to meet that need. I think that sounds better than goals and targets, don't you?'

'Much,' Seb agreed. This was progress. But then his hand stilled on her shoulder. Next was the hardest one. 'And speaking of needs… Maria, I need you to promise not to run again. If things get hard, or I'm not being what you need, talk to me first. Please. I can fix anything if you stay long enough to let me. But the thought of what would have happened if you'd been able to get a flight out before I got back from Geneva…' That would have been the end of them. The end of this. Seb shuddered at the thought of it.

'I won't run.' Maria twisted and knelt up on the sofa, taking his face between her small, soft hands. When he looked into her eyes, he saw nothing but love, and marvelled again at how he'd never seen it before. 'I promise you, Seb. No, I vow. From here on, no running. We stick together and we work through things as a team.'

'That's all I need from you,' he replied.

Maria grinned. 'Then I think it's about time I got to kiss the groom.'

With that, she leaned in and brought her lips to his, soft and loving and for ever.

And at last Sebastian felt the knot around his heart

loosen, and he knew that everything would be all right from now on. Just as long as they were together.

'Wait!' Maria said suddenly, pulling away from the best kiss of Sebastian's life.

'What?' he asked, panicked. They'd come so far. What else could there possibly be to keep them apart now?

But Maria was already on her feet, crossing the room to the fake bookcase, moving it out of the way and opening the safe.

The contract. Their first misguided attempt at fixing their marriage. Of course.

Maria shut the safe again, and brought the thick signed document towards him. 'Do you want to tear it up, or shall I?'

'I've got a better idea,' Seb said, taking it from her.

With one last look at the document that had almost saved—and almost destroyed—his marriage, Seb tossed it unceremoniously onto the fire.

'Now,' he said, gathering Maria back into his arms, 'where were we?'

'Right about here,' Maria said, and kissed him.

CHAPTER FIFTEEN

IT WAS ANOTHER half an hour or so before Maria and Seb emerged from the snug. She almost dreaded to think how many presents Frankie would have opened by now, but she just couldn't bring herself to tear herself away from her husband's arms now she'd found her way back into them at last.

He loved her. Truly loved her.

Time would tell if they could find a balance with the rest of it, but she was hopeful—which was something she hadn't been in a long time before this week.

'I gave you Leo's shares not as a bribe,' he'd explained between kisses, 'but so we could have a real partnership. Working together as well as playing together. I figured that way we're always on hand to remind each other of what really matters most when we get lost in the business.'

And he was right. What she'd wanted all along had been a more equal partnership, and now she was getting one. Their lives would no longer be separate, kept apart by work commitments and a family model that didn't suit them or their family.

They'd be a real team. And together she was sure they could take on the whole world.

Outside, under the Christmas tree, Leo, Max and Frankie had set up the most complex wooden train track Maria had ever seen. It snaked all the way through the large open-plan living area, with a bridge over a coffee table, before heading back through to the hall and looping round the tree. At some point Leo had clearly excused himself to change out of the Santa suit, but Max was still wearing the antlers, much to Maria's amusement.

Frankie sat, still in his pyjamas, right in the centre of the whole mess, watching his uncles push tiny wooden trains around the track and making train noises.

It was pretty much perfect.

'Aren't you glad you stayed to see this?' Noemi handed Maria a cup of coffee as she and Anissa came closer to watch the boys playing with their toys. Seb, Maria noticed, was already adding a side track with a turntable and another bridge.

'I am, actually,' Maria admitted, unable to hide her smile.

How close had she come to missing all this? By running the first time then trying to run again yesterday? If there had been a flight out then, she might have never seen Frankie playing trains with his uncles. Might never have known that Seb loved her.

If that wasn't a good enough reason to stop running when things got hard, she didn't know what was.

Noemi arched her eyebrows. 'So? Is all well in Maria Land? Do we get our final Christmas miracle after all?'

Maria watched as Seb knelt down to help Frankie set up a small forest of tiny wooden trees off to one side of the track. One by one, they methodically laid out the models, and every time Frankie knocked one over Seb would patiently pick it up and start again.

For a moment Maria couldn't help but see one or two more little people there with Seb. A whole little family, with siblings that Frankie could rely on and call for help, the same way Sebastian had today. Her future, in one perfect image.

Noemi was right. It was a Christmas miracle.

'Do you know, I think we just might,' Maria said, her eyes still on her little family.

Noemi and Anissa both gave a small celebratory whoop and clinked their coffee mugs together, making Maria smile even wider. She looked away at last, and turned to the women who were, to all intents and purposes now, her sisters.

'Thank you, both. For everything.' She pressed kisses to first Noemi's cheeks and then Anissa's. 'I know Seb couldn't have pulled this off without the two of you, and Max and Leo. And it's meant so much to Frankie.'

'I'm glad,' said Anissa.

'But you know we didn't just do it for him, right?' added Noemi.

'I know.' Maria ducked her head, warmth coming to her cheeks.

'If there's one thing I've learned over the last six months, it's that when times get hard, you need your family behind you. Whether they're blood relatives, or the people you grew up with, or just new friends who become family before you have time to even realise it.' Noemi was smiling at Max as she said that, Maria realised. 'Family is what matters.'

'And I can't tell you how happy I am to have mine back again,' Maria admitted.

'I'm just glad you found a way to get what you need, here, with Seb,' Noemi replied.

Seb fished under the tree for one last present, and handed it to Frankie. With a little help he unwrapped it to reveal a green wooden sleigh, just like the one she and Seb had ridden on, pulled by two reindeer with impressive antlers. 'Wow!'

He added it to the tableau of trees and trains with a proud expression on his face, then launched himself into his *papà*'s lap for a cuddle.

'Yeah,' Maria said softly. 'I think everything's going to be just fine.'

* * *

Christmas Eve, Seb reflected later, had been about as picture perfect as it could be. Between his new vows with Maria that morning, the relief of burning that bloody contract, Frankie's joy at Santa and his new train set, and just spending the day together as a family…it was all Seb had ever wanted. Tomorrow would be the more formal Christmas dinner—the whole family around the dining table for the first time since their parents had died (not to mention Leo's first time at a family Christmas dinner ever). But today had been…fun. Something Seb was starting to suspect had been sorely missing from his life for too long.

After a long afternoon of playing, Maria had swept Frankie away to eat something that didn't involve sugar, and Max and Anissa had gone with her. Max was apparently planning to make some sort of traditional Ostanian cocktail that sounded perfectly lethal, and Anissa had a secret supply of ingredients for making her grandmother's Christmas Eve cookies that she planned to bake and bring out to soak up the cocktails.

Which left just Sebastian, Noemi and Leo—the three Cattaneo siblings—sitting together under the lights of the Christmas tree, a small battery-powered train chugging slowly around the track surrounding them.

'So what was in the envelope?' Noemi asked, kicking her leg lazily over the arm of her chair. That was how she'd used to sit as a teenager, Seb remembered, and for a moment it sent him back in time—until he noticed the changes, showing how time had moved on. Her pregnancy bump was really on display at this angle, and Seb couldn't help but smile at the idea of his little sister as a mother.

He hoped she was half as happy as he was as a father. Looking at her, and watching her with Max, he was certain she would be.

He just wished their parents were there to see it. Still,

he knew Nicole and Salvo would be proud of what they were all doing, and the choices they'd made—in their partners and in their futures. Even in the gift he'd given Maria that morning.

'Leo's share of the company,' Seb told his sister, and waited for the explosion.

Noemi bolted upright, at a speed that couldn't possibly be good for the babies. 'What?'

'I offered to sign my shares over to Sebastian as soon as I legally can,' Leo explained. 'I don't need them to feel a part of this family, and he knows the business better than I do.'

'That part I get. But… Seb? You gave them away— gave away the *controlling* share in our family business. To *Maria*?' Noemi's eyes were wide with amazement and… something else Seb couldn't put his finger on.

'Uh, yes. Are you…angry?' It seemed as good a guess as any. Maybe he should have talked to Noemi first. Now they were getting along again, he really didn't want to ruin it so soon.

But Noemi laughed—high and tinkling and happy— and Seb's shoulders relaxed again. 'Of course I'm not angry! I think it's wonderful. You always loved that company more than anything…and now you love Maria most. That's exactly how it should be. I'm actually proud of you, big brother.'

'Well, okay, then. I'm glad you approve.'

'That said, though…' Noemi gave him and then Leo a calculating look. Then she nodded firmly, whatever decision she was working on clearly made. 'We should sign my shares over to you and Maria, too. I mean, I'm about to become a crown princess. It's not like I need the income. And to be honest…' she smiled, as if at a private joke '…I think I'll have enough wonderful things going on in my life as it is.'

'Well, if you're sure...' Seb said.

'I am.' Noemi glanced over at Leo, who hadn't said anything. 'And, actually, now is probably the perfect time to discuss that other thing I mentioned to you, don't you think, Seb?'

Now it was Seb's turn to grin. 'Absolutely.'

Leaning forward, Noemi twisted the ring on her right hand a few times until it popped off. Then she placed it in her palm and held it out to Leo, who stared at it, confused.

'It was our mother's engagement ring,' Seb explained, rather enjoying seeing his new-found brother dumbfounded for once. 'We want you to have it. For Anissa.'

'And before you start, it's totally obvious you're going to propose to her soon,' Noemi added. 'We think you should do it with this.'

'I... Well, yes. Actually, I was planning to...but I can't,' Leo said, shaking his head. 'This was your mother's ring. She left it to you, Noemi.'

'And I'm giving it to you.' Noemi placed the ring firmly in Leo's hand, then held on to his fingers for a moment. 'Listen. We have a lifetime of memories of our mother. I don't need a ring to remind me of her. But you missed out on all that. And this ring...it can't make up for that. But it can be that reminder for you.'

'Why would I need a reminder when I have you two?' Leo joked, but Seb could see the affection in his eyes. 'Thank you. Both of you.'

'Now you just need her to say yes,' Seb said, grinning at his brother. 'If you need them, I have some ideas about proposals...'

'Given that your last idea involved me dressing up in a Santa suit at six in the morning on Christmas Eve, I think I'll handle this one myself, thanks,' Leo said, smiling back.

Noemi shrugged. 'I don't know. I think Anissa liked the Santa suit...'

* * *

'"Merry Christmas to all, and to all a good night,"' Maria read, shutting the book quietly as the story came to a close.

Frankie was already mostly asleep on the bed beside her, lulled by the rhythm and rhyme of the classic festive story.

'He's had a long day,' Seb observed from the doorway. Then he yawned.

'Not as long as you have,' Maria replied with a low chuckle. The poor man couldn't have slept in thirty-six hours or more.

Tucking the blanket securely around Frankie, Maria placed the book back on the shelf and crossed the room to be wrapped in her husband's arms.

'Tomorrow we'll give him the most perfect Christmas,' Seb whispered in her ear, and Maria huffed a soft laugh.

'He already opened all his presents today.'

'Not all of them,' Seb muttered, and Maria rolled her eyes, even though he couldn't see her do it. Clearly, one of the things their team was going to have to discuss soon was not spoiling the children. Well, child for now. But maybe soon… 'We had to save some for epiphany. It's traditional.'

'Fair enough. And good call on the train track, by the way,' she said, to stop her mind running away with the possibilities of siblings for Frankie. 'He loves it.'

'I used to have one when I was little,' Seb said. 'Papà and I would play with it for hours.'

'And now you'll play with Frankie with his.' Maria thought about all the men playing trains that afternoon. 'And probably his uncle Leo and uncle Max, too.'

'He'll have so many people to love him,' Seb whispered. 'Even if his grandparents aren't here to see it.'

Tears stung Maria's eyes as she thought about how much Seb had lost this year. How much more she'd almost taken from him.

'Hey.' Seb tucked a finger under her chin and tilted it to make her look up at him. 'Don't cry. Things might not be perfect, but I know the future is going to be wonderful. Okay?'

'How do you know that?' Maria asked, dabbing at her wet eyes.

'Because I've found my Christmas miracle,' Seb said simply. 'You came home, and that was all I ever needed.'

Maria stretched up on tiptoe to kiss him, love burning bright in her heart.

'You're all I need, too. You, Frankie and me. Together.'

'Always,' Seb promised, and kissed her again.

CHAPTER SIXTEEN

On Christmas Day, just as Salvo and Nicole Cattaneo had hoped, all three of their children sat down around the huge dining table at Mont Coeur together, with their families and loved ones, to share a festive feast.

Before they tucked in, Sebastian got to his feet, wine glass in hand, and waited for the others to fall silent.

'I just wanted to say a few words before we eat, if that's okay?' he said, acutely aware that, really, as the oldest sibling, it was Leo's place to do so. But Leo was so wrapped up in his girlfriend—no, *fiancée* as of last night, it seemed—that it fell to Seb to say what mattered most.

As the others settled in to listen, Seb searched for the right words.

'This year has been a difficult one for all of us,' he acknowledged, watching as heads nodded around the table. 'We've lost our parents—in Leo's case, before he'd even got to know them. We've faced crises of confidence, business disasters and relationship issues. And there were so many times when any one of us could have given up on our families, on love, on our own happiness and just walked away.'

Leo wrapped an arm around Anissa's shoulders at that, pulling her close against him, a sign that he'd never let her go again.

'But we didn't. We fought on for everything that matters most to us. And it paid off for all of us. We each got more than we dreamed was possible as a result, and we're all here today to share our stories, and our Christmas dinner—just as Mamma and Papà hoped we would be.'

At that, Noemi leaned her head against Max's shoulder but reached a hand out to take Leo's. The brother they'd never known they had—and Seb already couldn't imagine ever being without him again.

'So today I'd like to thank you all for being part of my family. For knowing what I needed when I didn't. For supporting me when I needed it most. And for going above and beyond the call of family to help me fix the biggest mistake I ever made in my life—letting Maria walk away from me.'

Seb looked down and met his wife's gaze and held it, silently promising once more that he'd never let that happen again. He'd made his new vows, and he would keep them. However hard that was, and whatever happened next.

He knew what mattered most now. At last.

'But most of all, I'd like to raise a toast to absent friends.' Seb glanced up at the wooden ceiling, and imagined that if he looked hard enough, he could see his parents looking down on them all together. 'Mamma, Papà, we miss you. And I wish you were here today to see how far we've all come. I think you'd be very proud.'

Around the table, everyone raised their glasses. 'To absent friends.'

Seb sat down with a thump, the emotion of the day overwhelming him.

'Nice toast,' Maria said, pressing against his side. 'Your parents *would* be so proud of you, you know.'

'I hope so.' It had been so easy to say but harder to feel the truth of.

'I know so,' Maria said.

'Oh? And how is that?'

'Because I am.' Maria leaned across and pressed a kiss

to the corner of his mouth. 'I'm so proud to call you my husband, Sebastian Cattaneo,' she whispered.

'Not half as proud as I am to have you as my wife,' he replied.

On the other side of the table, Noemi leaned forward, reaching around Leo to take Anissa's left hand and study the ring there.

'It suits you perfectly,' she said, beaming. 'Mamma would be so happy to see you and Leo engaged, you know. And Seb's right—she'd have loved to have us all here at Mont Coeur, together, for Christmas.'

'Not to mention preparing for a royal wedding next year,' Maria added, as Max placed a hand over his fiancée's baby bump, a reminder of the exciting future they had ahead of them.

Seb smiled at the thought of both his siblings happy and settled, though he just knew that they could never be as happy as he was to have Maria back in his life.

'Oh!' Maria jumped up suddenly. 'We forgot the cranberry sauce! Hang on.'

She dashed off to fetch it, and Seb watched her go. Then he spotted something hanging in the doorway between the dining hall and the kitchen.

'Dare I ask which one of you was responsible for that?' he asked, motioning to the mistletoe hanging there, waiting for unsuspecting couples to pass underneath.

Noemi shrugged her elegant shoulders. 'Well, at one point yesterday we really weren't sure if you'd need the extra help.'

'If I were you, I'd take advantage of it anyway,' Max said with a grin.

Seb considered, but only for a moment. And then he jumped up to wait for his wife under the mistletoe.

'We've got ordinary cranberry sauce or cranberry sauce with apple— Oh!' Maria gasped, as Seb caught her around the waist and kissed her thoroughly in the doorway, as Noemi whooped and even Leo gave a small cheer.

'Mamma! Papà!' Excited by all the noise, Frankie jumped down from his chair to join them. 'Frankie hug, too!' He wrapped his little arms around their legs, and Seb broke away, laughing, to embrace his son as well as his wife.

This Christmas was nothing like he'd dreamed it would be. But now it was here, he couldn't imagine it any other way.

All his Christmas wishes had come true. And Sebastian knew he'd appreciate the Christmas miracle that had brought his family together—all of them, even the brother he'd never known he had—all year long.

'Just think, next Christmas we'll have twins to add to the chaos,' Noemi joked, making everyone laugh.

But Seb just smiled, and placed a kiss on Maria's cheek as he ruffled Frankie's hair. 'Well, I for one can't wait. After all, Christmas *is* a time for family. Isn't it?'

* * * * *

BRING ME A
MAVERICK FOR
CHRISTMAS!

BRENDA HARLEN

This book is dedicated to Ryan. I know you stopped
writing letters to Santa a lot of years ago, but
as you finish up your first term at university,
I'm making three wishes for you this season:

1. that you eternally believe in the magic of Christmas;

2. that you always know how proud I am of you; and

3. that you forever remember how much I love you. XO

Chapter One

"No way in ho-ho-hell," Bailey Stockton said, his response to his brother's request firm and definitive.

"Hear me out," Dan urged.

"No," he said again. He'd been conscripted to help with far too much Christmas stuff already. Such as helping Luke decorate Sunshine Farm for the holidays and sampling a new Christmas cookie recipe that Eva was trying out (okay, that one hadn't been much of a hardship—the cookies, like everything she made, were delicious). His youngest brother, Jamie, had even asked him to babysit—yes, babysit!—so that he could take his wife into Kalispell to do some shopping for their triplets and enjoy a holiday show.

In fact, Bailey had been enlisted for so many tasks, he'd begun to suspect that his siblings had collectively made it their personal mission to revive his holiday spirit. Because he couldn't seem to make them understand that his holiday spirit was too far gone to be resurrected. They'd have better luck planning the burial and just letting him pretend the holidays didn't exist.

"But it's for Janie's scout troop," Dan implored.

Janie was Dan and Annie's daughter—the child his brother had only found out about when he returned to Rust Creek Falls not quite eighteen months earlier. Since then, his brother had been doing everything he could to make up for lost time. Which Bailey absolutely understood and respected; he just didn't want to be conscripted toward the effort.

"Then *you* do it," he said.

"I was planning to do it," Dan told him. "And I was looking forward to it, but I'm in bed now with some kind of bug."

"Is that a pet name for Annie?"

"Ha ha," his brother said, not sounding amused.

"Well, you don't sound very sick to me," Bailey noted.

"That's because you haven't heard me puking."

"And I don't mind missing out on that," he assured his brother.

"I need your help," Dan said again.

"I'm sorry you're not up to putting on the red suit, but there's got to be someone else who can do it."

"You don't think I tried to find someone else?" Dan asked. "I mean, no offense, big brother, but when I think of Christmas spirit, yours is not the first name that springs to mind."

Bailey took no offense to his brother speaking the truth. But he was curious: "Who else did you ask?"

"Luke, Jamie, Dallas Traub, Russ Campbell, Anderson Dalton, even Old Gene. No one else is available. You're my last resort, Bailey, and if you don't come through—"

"Don't worry," Annie interrupted, obviously having taken the phone from her husband. "He'll come through. Won't you, Bailey?"

He hated to let them down, but what they were asking was beyond his abilities. And way outside his comfort zone. "I wish I could, but—"

That was as far as he got in formulating a response before his sister-in-law interjected again.

"You can," she said. "You just need to stop being such a Grooge."

"A *what*?"

"A Grooge," she said again. "Since you have even less Christmas spirit than either the Grinch or Scrooge, I've decided you're a Grooge."

"Definitely not Santa Claus material," he felt compelled to point out.

"Under normal circumstances, I'd agree," Annie said. "But these aren't normal circumstances and your brother needs you to step up and help out, because that's what families do. And that's why I know you're going to do this."

Chastened by his sister-in-law's brief but pointed lecture, how could he do anything else?

But he had no intention of giving in graciously. "Bah, humbug."

"I'll take that as a yes," Annie said.

Bailey could only sigh. "What time and where?"

"I'll meet you at the Grace Traub Community Center in an hour."

* * *

And so, an hour later, Bailey found himself at the community center, in one of the small activity rooms that had been repurposed as a dressing room for the event. Annie bustled around, helping him dress.

"Is this really necessary?" he asked, as she secured the padded belly.

"Of course, it's necessary. Santa's not a lean mean rancher—he's a toy maker with a milk-and-cookies belly."

He slid his arms into the big red coat and fastened the wide belt around his expanded middle.

"Now sit so that I can put on your beard and wig and fix your face," Annie said.

He sat. Then scowled. "What do you mean—fix my face?"

"Relax and let me do my thing."

"'Do my thing' are not words that inspire me to relax," he told her.

But he clenched his jaw and didn't say anything else as she unzipped a pouch and pulled out a tube that looked suspiciously like makeup. She brushed whatever it was onto his eyebrows, then took out a pot and another brush that she used on his cheeks.

"I can't believe I let you talk me into this," he grumbled.

"I know this isn't your idea of fun, but it means a lot to Dan that you stepped up."

"I didn't step," he reminded her. "I was pushed."

Her lips curved as she recapped the pot and put it back in the bag. "Now the beard," she said, and hooked the elastic over his ears.

"No one's going to thank me for this when I screw it up," he warned her.

"You're not going to screw it up."

"Beyond *ho ho ho*, I don't have a clue what to say."

"This might be a first for you, but it's not for the kids," she told him. "And if you really get stuck, I have no doubt that your wife will be able to help you out."

Wife? "Who? What?"

"Mrs. Claus," she clarified.

"You didn't say anything about a Mrs. Claus."

And he didn't know if the revelation now made things better or worse. On the one hand, he was relieved that he wouldn't have to face a group of kids on his own. On the other, he was skeptical enough about his ability to play a jolly elf, but a jolly elf with a wife?

"I didn't think any kind of warning was necessary," Annie said now. "It was supposed to be me—I was going to be the missus to Dan's Santa, but when he got sick, well, I couldn't leave him to suffer at home alone, so I asked a friend to fill in. But you don't have to worry. Mrs. Claus will be here to hand out candy canes and keep the line moving—no romantic overtures are required."

"Thanks, I feel so much better now," he said dryly.

"Good," she said, ignoring his sarcasm. "And speaking of spouses—I should get home to my husband, who isn't feeling better but is feeling grateful."

"Do you want me to drop off this costume later?"

"No, I'll come back and get it," she said.

When she'd gone, Bailey chanced a hesitant glance in the mirror. He was afraid he'd look as stupid as he felt—like a kid playing dress-up—and was surprised to realize that he looked like Santa.

There was a brisk knock at the door. "Are you just about ready, Santa?" The scout leader poked his head in the doorway. "Wow, you look great."

"Ho ho ho," Bailey said, testing it out.

The scout leader grinned and gave him two thumbs-up. "The kids are getting restless."

"Mrs. Claus isn't here yet," he said. Although he hadn't originally known there was supposed to be a Mrs. Claus, he now felt at a loss on his own.

"Maybe she got caught up baking cookies at the North Pole," the other man joked.

Whatever she was doing, wherever she was, his missus was nowhere to be found, reminding Bailey of the foolishness of depending on a spouse—even a fictional one.

"Okay, then." He exited the makeshift dressing room and followed the scout leader backstage. Though the curtains were closed, he could hear the excited chatter of what sounded like hundreds, maybe thousands, of children. All of them there to see Santa—and getting stuck with a poor imitation instead.

He felt perspiration bead on his brow and his hands were clammy inside his white cotton gloves. The leader handed him a big sack filled with candy canes and nodded encouragingly.

It was now or never, and although Bailey would have preferred to go with the never option, he suspected his brother would never forgive him if he chickened out.

Just as he was reaching for the curtain, he heard footsteps rushing up the stage stairs behind him.

Mrs. Claus had arrived.

He didn't have time to give her much more than a cursory glance, noting the floor-length red dress with faux fur trim at the collar and cuffs, and a white apron tied around her waist. Despite the white wig and granny glasses, he could tell that she was young. Her skin was smooth and unwrinkled, her lips plump and exquisitely shaped, and her eyes were as bright and blue as the Montana sky.

"Good, I'm not late." She was breathless, obviously having run some distance, and paused now with her hand on her heart as she drew air into her lungs.

Of course, the action succeeded in drawing his attention to her chest—and the rise and fall of nicely rounded breasts.

"Are you ready to do this?" she asked.

He nodded. *Yes. Please.*

She sent him a conspiratorial wink, and suddenly he felt warm all over. Or maybe it was the bulky costume and the overhead lights that were responsible for the sudden increase in his body temperature.

Then she stepped through the break in the curtains and began to speak to the children.

"Well, we ran into a little bit of rough weather on our way from the North Pole, but we finally made it," she said.

The crowd of children cheered.

Bailey listened to her talk, enjoying the melodic tone of her voice as she set the scene for their audience. He didn't know who she was—he hadn't thought to ask his sister-in-law—but it was immediately apparent to Bailey that Annie had cast a better Mrs. Claus than her husband had a Santa.

"I know you've all been incredibly patient waiting for Santa to arrive and everyone wants to be first in line to whisper Christmas wishes in his ear, but I promise you, it doesn't matter if you're first or last or somewhere in the middle, everyone will have a turn."

They had a wide armchair set up on the stage, beside a decorated Christmas tree surrounded by a pile of fake presents. All he had to do was walk through the curtain and settle into the chair. But his feet were suddenly glued to the floor.

"While Santa finishes settling the reindeer," she said, offering another explanation for the delay of his appearance, "why don't we sing his favorite Christmas song?" She looked out at the audience. "Who knows what Santa's favorite Christmas song is?"

Through the narrow gap between the curtains, he could see hands immediately thrust into the air.

Mrs. Claus listened to several random guesses as the children called for "Jingle Bells," "Let It Snow" and "All I Want for Christmas," shaking her head after each response.

"Okay, I'm going to give you a clue," she said. Then, in a singing voice, she asked, *"Who's got a beard that's long and white?"*

The children responded as a chorus: *"Santa's got a beard that's long and white."*

It was an upbeat and catchy tune with call-and-response lyrics that made it easy for the kids who didn't know the words to sing along anyway, and Bailey found his booted foot tapping against the floor along with the music.

The young audience was completely caught up in the song, and he was reluctant to interrupt. But when Mrs. Claus asked, *"Who very soon will come our way?"* it seemed like an appropriate time to step out from behind the curtain.

"Santa very soon will..."

The response of the chorus faded away as the singers noticed that Santa was, in fact, here now. Several clapped, others pointed and many whispered excitedly to their neighbors.

"And here he is," Mrs. Claus said, then smiled warmly at him and gestured for him to take a seat.

Bailey nodded as he made his way to the chair. He was too nervous to smile back, although she probably couldn't tell if he was or wasn't smiling behind the bushy mustache that hung over his mouth anyway.

He settled into his seat as the leader announced that the young Tiger Scouts would get to visit with Santa first. There were craft tables at the far end of the room for groups waiting to be called and refreshments available.

Bailey felt his palms grow clammy again as the kids lined up, but it didn't take him long to realize that his sister-in-law had been right: the kids knew what they were doing. In fact, most of them didn't expect much from him beyond listening to their wishes and offering them a "Merry Christmas."

There were a lot of requests for specific toys and new video games. A couple of requests for puppies and kittens, building blocks and board games, hockey skates or ballerina slippers. Some of the kids asked questions, wanting to know such random facts as "who's your favorite reindeer?" or "how old is Rudolph?"

He gave vague responses, so as not to contradict anything else they might have been told by their parents, and he was careful not to make any promises, assuring each child only that he would do his best to make their wishes come true.

And if he was a little stiff and unnatural, his supposed wife was the complete opposite—warm and kind and totally believable. She did more than move the line along and hand out candy canes. She seemed to instinctively know what to say and do to put the little ones at ease.

He was about halfway through the Bear Scouts and finally starting to relax into his role when a scowling boy climbed into his lap.

Bailey, anticipating one of the usual requests, was taken aback when the boy said, "Christmas sucks."

"Yeah," Bailey agreed. "Sometimes it does."

Mrs. Claus gasped and the boy's eyes immediately filled with tears.

"You're not s'posed to agree," the child protested. "You're s'posed to tell me that it's gonna be okay."

Since Bailey didn't know what *it* was, he didn't feel he should make any such promises. But he belatedly acknowledged that he shouldn't have responded the way he did, either. Being called out by the child was only further proof that taking his brother's place as Santa had been a bad idea.

"Now, Santa," Mrs. Claus chided. "I told you not to take your grumpy mood out on the children or I'll have to put *you* on the naughty list."

This threat served to both distract and intrigue the little boy, who eyed her with rapt fascination.

"I'm sorry, Owen," she continued, speaking directly to the child now. "Santa's a little out of sorts today because I warned him that he has to cut down on the cookies if he wants to fit down the chimneys on Christmas Eve."

Then she sent Bailey a pointed look that had him

nodding in acknowledgment of her claim as he rubbed his padded belly. "I really like gingerbread," he said, in a conspiratorial whisper to the boy his "wife" had called Owen. "But I definitely don't want to end up on the naughty list."

"Can she do that?" Owen asked.

He nodded again, almost afraid to do otherwise. "So tell me, Owen, is there anything Santa can do to help make the holidays happier for you?"

"Can you make Riley not move to Bozeman?" he asked hopefully.

This time Bailey did shake his head. "I'm sorry."

The child's gaze shifted toward Mrs. Claus again. "Can *she* do it?" Because apparently the boy believed Mrs. Claus not only had authority over her husband but greater magical powers, too.

"I'm sorry," he said again.

Owen sighed. "Then maybe you could leave a PKT-79 under my tree at Christmas and I can give it to Riley, so that he'll have something to remember me by."

It wasn't the first request for a PKT-79, and though Bailey still had no idea what it was, he was touched by the child's request for the gift to give to someone else.

"I'll see what I can do," Santa told him. "Merry Christmas."

"Yeah," Owen said, his tone slightly less glum. "Merry Christmas."

Mrs. Claus held out a candy cane to the boy.

Owen paused to ask her, "You'll make sure Santa can get down my chimney, won't you?"

"You bet I will," she promised, with a wink and a smile for the boy.

Bailey paid more attention after that, to avoid another slipup. When all the children had expressed their wishes to Santa, he and his wife wished everyone a Merry Christmas and headed backstage again.

By the time he made it to the dressing room, Bailey was more than ready to shed the red coat and everything it represented, but Mrs. Claus walked into the room right behind him.

Closing the door firmly at her back, she faced him with her hands on her hips. "I don't know why anyone would ask someone with such an obviously lousy disposition to play Santa, but you have no right to ruin Christmas for the kids who actually look forward to celebrating the holiday."

Bailey already felt guilty enough for his unthinking response to Owen, but he didn't appreciate being taken to task—*again*—by a stranger, and instinctively lashed out. "A lecture from my loving wife? Now I really do feel like we're married."

"I'd pity any woman who married you," she shot back.

His ready retort stuck in his throat when she took off the granny glasses and removed the wig, causing her long blond hair to tumble over her shoulders, effecting an instant and stunning transformation.

Mrs. Claus was a definite hottie.

Too bad she was also bossy and annoying. And… vaguely familiar looking, he realized.

She twisted her arm up behind her back, trying to reach the top of the zipper, but her fingertips fell short of their target.

While she struggled, Bailey removed his own hat, wig and beard.

She brought her arm around to her front again and

tried to reach the back of the dress from over her shoulder, still without success.

He should offer to help. That would be the polite and gentlemanly thing to do. But as his sister-in-law had noted, he was a Grooge and, still stinging from Mrs. Claus's sharp rebuke, not in a very charitable or helpful mood. Instead, he unbuckled his wide belt, removed the heavy jacket and padded belly, eager to shed the external trappings of his own role.

Finally, she huffed out a breath. "You could offer to help, you know?"

"If you need help, you could ask," he countered.

"Would you *please* help me unzip my dress?" she finally said.

"Usually I buy a woman dinner before I try to get her out of her clothes." He couldn't resist teasing. "But since you asked…"

Chapter Two

She turned her back to give Bailey access to the zipper, but not before he saw her roll her eyes in response to his comment. "Do you have to work at being offensive or is it a natural talent?"

"It's a defense mechanism," he said, surprising them both with his honesty. "I screwed up in there—I know I did. I knew I would. That's why I didn't want to put on the stupid suit and pretend to be jolly."

"You ever try actually *being* jolly instead of just pretending?" she asked, as he tugged on the zipper pull.

"Yeah, but it didn't work out so well."

"I'm sorry." She pulled her arms out of the sleeves and let the bodice fall forward, then stepped out of the skirt to reveal her own clothes: a snug-fitting scoop neck sweater in Christmas red over a pair of skinny jeans tucked into knee-high boots.

A definite hottie with curves that should have warning signs.

He looked away from the danger zone, pushing the suspenders off his shoulders and stepping out of Santa's oversize pants, leaving him clad in a long-sleeve Henley and well-worn jeans. He picked up the flannel shirt he'd shed before donning the Santa coat and put it on over the Henley.

She neatly folded her dress and tucked it into a shopping bag. He watched her out of the corner of his eye, unable to shake the feeling that, though he couldn't think of her name, he was certain he knew her from somewhere.

Before he could ask her if they'd met before, there was a knock at the door.

"Come in."

They both said it at the same time, then she smiled at him, and that easy curve of her lips only increased her hotness factor.

The door opened and Annie poked her head in.

"Oh, Serena, I'm so glad to see that you made it."

"I did. Sorry I was almost late. There was some excitement at the clinic this morning."

Serena.

Clinic.

The pieces finally clicked into place and Bailey realized why the substitute Mrs. Claus looked familiar. She was Serena Langley, a vet tech at the same clinic where his sister-in-law was the receptionist.

"What kind of excitement?" Annie asked, immediately concerned.

"Alistair Warren brought in a fat stray that he found

under his porch. The cat turned out not to be fat but pregnant and gave birth to nine kittens."

"Nine?" Annie echoed.

Serena nodded. "Exam Room Three is going to be out of commission for a while, because Brooks doesn't want to disturb the new mom or her babies."

"I can't wait to see them," Annie enthused. "But right now, I want to hear about the substitute Santa's visit with the local scout troop so that I can report back to his more-sick-than-jolly brother."

Bailey turned to Serena again. Truthfully, his gaze had hardly shifted away from her since they'd entered the dressing room. He'd thought it was because he was trying to figure out where they might have crossed paths before, but even with that question now answered, he found his attention riveted on her.

He waited for Serena to say that the substitute Santa had sucked and that the event had been a disaster—although maybe not in terms quite so blunt and harsh. At the very least, he anticipated her telling his sister-in-law that Bailey had screwed up and almost made a kid cry. And he couldn't have disputed either of those points, because they were both true.

But Serena seemed content to let him respond to the inquiry, and he did so, only saying, "It was...an experience."

His sister-in-law's brows lifted. "I'm not sure how to interpret that."

Bailey looked at Mrs. Claus again.

"Everything went well," Serena assured her friend.

Annie exhaled, obviously relieved. "Of course, I knew the two of you would be able to pull it off."

"If you were so confident, you wouldn't have rushed

over here to interrogate us," he pointed out. "Although I suspect your concerns were really about Santa and not Mrs. Claus."

"Well, you were the more reluctant substitute," she told him. "Serena didn't hesitate when I asked her to fill in."

"I'm always happy to help a friend," Serena said. "But now I should be on my way."

"What's your hurry?" Annie asked.

"I'm not in a hurry," she denied. "It's just that I left early this morning and...well, you know that Marvin doesn't like it when I'm gone all day."

She seemed a little embarrassed by this admission, or so he guessed by the way her gaze dropped away.

Bailey frowned, wondering about this Marvin and the nature of his relationship with Serena. Was he her husband? Boyfriend? How did he express his disapproval of her absence? Did he give her the cold shoulder when she got home? Or did he have a hot temper?

The possibility roused his ire. Lord knew he wasn't without faults of his own and tried not to judge others by their shortcomings, but he had no tolerance for men who bullied women or children.

"You worry too much about Marvin," Annie chided.

"You know I can't stand it when he looks at me with those big sad eyes."

"I know you let him use those big sad eyes to manipulate you," Annie said. "You need to stand firm and let him know he's not the boss of you."

Bailey didn't think his sister-in-law should be so quick to disregard her friend's concerns. No one knew what went on behind closed doors of a relationship.

"Is Marvin your...husband?" Bailey asked Serena.

In response to his question, Annie snickered—inappropriately, he thought—and Serena's cheeks flushed with color as she shook her head.

"No, he's my, uh, bulldog."

"Your bulldog," he echoed.

She nodded, the color in her cheeks deepening.

Well, the *big sad eyes* comment made a lot more sense to him now. As the humor of the situation became apparent, he felt his own lips curve.

"He's a rescue," she explained. "And very...needy."

"Only because you let him be," Annie said. "Not to mention that you have a doggy door, so he can go in and out as required."

"Well, yes," Serena admitted. "But he still doesn't like to be alone for too long."

Which led Bailey to believe that there wasn't anyone else at home—husband or boyfriend—to put the dog out or deal with his neediness.

Not that it mattered, because he wasn't interested in any kind of romantic relationship with his sister-in-law's friend and colleague.

Was he?

"I hope Danny is feeling a lot better before Tuesday," Annie said as she picked up the bags containing the costumes.

The worry was evident in her friend's voice, compelling Serena to ask, "What's happening on Tuesday?"

"We're supposed to play Santa and Mrs. Claus for a visit to the elementary school."

Which gave Annie's husband only two days to recuperate from whatever had laid him up.

"I'd be happy to fill in again," Serena immediately offered.

"Oh, that would be wonderful," Annie said. "And such a weight off my shoulders to not have to worry about finding a replacement at the last minute again. Thank you both so much."

"Both?" Bailey echoed. "Wait! I never—"

But his sister-in-law didn't pause long enough to allow him to voice any protest. "In that case, I'll leave the costumes with you and just pop over to Daisy's to pick up some soup for Danny. Fingers crossed, he'll be able to keep it down."

"—agreed to anything," he continued.

Of course, Annie was already gone, leaving Serena and Bailey alone again.

She wasn't surprised when he turned toward her, a deep furrow between his brows. "I never agreed to anything," he said again.

"I know, but Annie probably couldn't imagine you'd object to doing a favor for your brother," she said reasonably.

"*Another* favor, you mean."

"Was today really so horrible?"

"That's not the point," he said. "But you're the type of person who's always the first to volunteer for any task, aren't you?"

She shrugged.

It was true that she hadn't hesitated when Annie asked her to fill in as Mrs. Claus. Although she generally preferred the company of animals to people, she was always happy to help a friend. And when she'd acceded to the request, it had never occurred to her to

ask or even wonder about the identity of the man playing Santa Claus.

But even if Annie had told her that it was Bailey
Stockton, Serena wouldn't have balked. Because how
could she know that she'd have such an unexpected vis-
ceral reaction to her friend's brother-in-law?

After all, this was hardly their first meeting. She'd
seen him at the clinic—and even once or twice around
town, at Crawford's General Store or Daisy's Donut
Shop. He was an undeniably handsome man. Of course,
as far as she could tell, all the Stocktons had been ge-
netically blessed, but there was something about Bailey that set him apart.

Maybe it was the vulnerability she'd glimpsed in his
eyes. It was the same look of a puppy who'd torn up
the newspaper and only realized after the fact that he'd
done something wrong. Not that she was really compar-
ing Bailey Stockton to a puppy, but she could tell that
Bailey had felt remorseful as soon as he'd agreed with
Owen's assessment that the holidays sucked.

Serena knew as well as anyone that Christmas wasn't
all gingerbread and jingle bells, but over the years, she'd
learned to focus on happy memories and embrace the
spirit of the season.

But now that she and Bailey were no longer surrounded by kids pumped up on sugar and excitement
about seeing Santa, now that it was just the two of them,
he didn't seem vulnerable at all. He was all man. And
every womanly part of her responded to his nearness.

When he'd unzipped her dress, he'd been doing her a
favor. There had certainly been nothing seductive about
the action. But she'd been aware of his lean hard body
behind her, and his closeness had made her heart pound

and her knees tremble. And although she was wearing a long-sleeved sweater and jeans beneath the costume, she'd felt the warmth of his breath on the nape of her neck as the zipper inched downward, and a shiver had snaked down her spine.

While she was wearing the costume, she could be Mrs. Claus and play the role she needed to play. But now that the costume had been packed away, she was just Serena Langley again—a woman who didn't know how to chat and flirt with men. In fact, she was completely awkward when it came to interacting with males of the human species, so she decided to do what she always did in uncomfortable situations: flee.

But before she could find the right words to extricate herself, Bailey spoke again.

"And what if I have plans for Tuesday afternoon?" he grumbled. "Not that Annie even considered that possibility."

"If you have plans, then I'll find somebody else to fill in," she said.

In fact, that might be preferable, because being in close proximity to Bailey was stirring feelings…desires…that she didn't want stirred. And while she liked the idea of a boyfriend who might someday turn into a husband, her track record with men was a bunch of false starts and incomplete finishes.

Well, not really a bunch. Barely even a handful. But the number wasn't as important as the fact that, at the end of the day, she was alone.

"Do you have other plans?" she asked.

"No," he reluctantly admitted. "But that's not the point."

"If you don't want to help out, say so," she told him.

"I just don't think I'm the best choice to fill the big guy's boots," he said.

"You managed okay today."

"I'm not sure Owen would agree," he remarked dryly.

"A bump in the road," she acknowledged. "But I'm confident you won't make the same mistake again."

"You're expressing a lot of faith in a guy you don't even know," he warned.

"I'm a pretty good judge of character."

Except that wasn't really true with respect to men. Canines and felines, yes. Even birds and rodents and fish. And while most people would doubt that fish had much character, she'd had a dwarf puffer for four years that had been a true diva in every sense of the word.

"But if you really don't want to do it, that's fine," she said to him now. "I'm sure I can find someone else to play Santa."

And that would probably be a better solution all around, because he was clearly a reluctant Santa and she was reluctant to spend any more time in close proximity to a male who reminded her that she was a woman without a man in her life.

Most of the time, she was perfectly happy with the status quo. But every now and again, she found herself thinking that it might be nice to share her life with someone who could contribute something other than woofs and meows to a conversation. And then she'd force herself to go out and try to meet new people. And her hopes and expectations would be dashed by reality. Again.

But Bailey surprised her by not immediately accepting this offer. "Well, I'm not sure that what I want really matters, since Annie will tell Dan that I agreed to do it and then, if I don't, I'll have to explain why and how I wriggled my way out of it."

"Are you saying that you *will* do it?" she asked, half hopeful, half wary.

"I guess I am," he agreed.

"Then I guess, unless Dan makes a miraculous recovery, I'll see you at the school on Tuesday."

"Or maybe now," Bailey said, as Serena moved toward the door. Because for reasons he couldn't begin to fathom, he was reluctant to watch her walk away. Or maybe he was just hungry.

She looked at him blankly. "Maybe now what?"

"Maybe I'll see you now—which sounded much better in my head than it did aloud," he acknowledged ruefully. "And which was supposed to be a segue into asking if you wanted to get something to eat."

"Oh." She seemed as uncertain about how to answer the question as he'd been to ask it.

"I was so nervous about the Santa gig that I didn't eat lunch before, and now I'm starving."

Serena offered him a leftover candy cane.

"I think I'm going to want something more than that," he said. "How about you? Are you hungry?"

"Not really."

Her stomach rumbled, calling her out on the fib.

His lips curved. "You want to reconsider your answer?"

"Apparently I am hungry," she acknowledged, one side of her mouth turning up in a half-smile.

"Do you want to grab a bite at the Gold Rush Diner?"

She hesitated.

"It's a simple yes or no question," he told her.

"Like…a date?" she asked cautiously.

"No." His knee-jerk response was as vehement as it was immediate.

Thankfully, Serena laughed, apparently more relieved than insulted by his hasty rejection of the idea.

"In that case, yes," she told him.

Since nothing was too far from anything else in the downtown area of Rust Creek Falls, they decided to leave their vehicles parked at the community center and walk over to the diner. Even on the short walk, the air was brisk with the promise of more snow in the forecast.

The name of the restaurant was painted on the plate-glass front window of the brick building. When Bailey opened the door for Serena, a cowbell overhead announced their arrival.

Though the diner did a steady business, the usual lunch crowd had already cleared out and he gestured for her to choose from the row of vacant booths. She slid across a red vinyl bench and he took a seat opposite her.

After a quick review of the menu, Bailey decided on the steak sub and Serena opted for a house salad.

"Your stomach was audibly rumbling," he reminded her. "I don't think it's going to be satisfied with salad."

"I'm supposed to be going to a dinner and dance at Sawmill Station tonight. The salad will tide me over until then."

"The Presents for Patriots fund-raiser," he guessed. "I've been working with Brendan Tanner on that this year."

"Dr. Smith bought a table and gave the tickets out to his staff."

"Then I'll see you there."

"Unless I decide to stay home with Marvin, Molly and Max."

"I know that Marvin's your dog," he said. "But Molly and Max?"

"Cat and bunny," she admitted.

"You have a lot of pets," he noted.

"Animals are usually better company than people."

"Present company excluded?" he suggested dryly.

Her cheeks flushed. "Maybe it would be more accurate to say that I'm better with animals than with people."

"You were great with the kids today," he assured her.

"Thanks, but kids are generally accepting and easy to please. Especially kids who are focused on something else—such as seeing Santa Claus."

"That reminds me," he said. "What do you know about this PKT-79 all the kids were asking about?"

"It's an upgrade of the 78 that came out in the spring."

"The 78 *what*?"

"An interactive pocket toy that communicates with other similar toys," she explained.

"And where would I find one?" he asked.

"You won't," she told him. "They're sold out everywhere."

"They can't be sold out everywhere," he protested, nodding his thanks to the waitress when she set his plate in front of him.

"It was a headline on my news feed last week—'Must-Have Toy of the Year Sold Out Everywhere.'"

He shook salt over his fries as he considered this setback to his plan.

"Of course, you could always ask Santa for one," she said, tongue in cheek, as she stabbed her fork into a tomato wedge.

"Do Santa's elves have a production line of PKT-79s at the North Pole?"

"They might," she allowed. "The only other option is an aftermarket retailer."

"Like eBay?" he guessed.

She nodded. "But you won't find one reasonably priced," she warned. "Supply and demand."

"I was hoping to get one for Owen," he confided. "To give him a reason to believe that Christmas doesn't suck."

"And because you feel guilty?" she guessed.

"Yeah," he admitted.

"Well, it's a really nice idea," she said. "But I promise you, he'll have a good Christmas even without a PKT-79 under his tree."

"How do you know?"

"Because I know his family, and yes, it's going to suck that his best friend is leaving town after the holidays, but he'll be okay."

"I guess I'll have to take your word for it," Bailey decided. "And since I'm apparently going to do this Santa thing again, I could use some pointers on how to interact with the kids."

"Just try to remember what it was like when you were a kid yourself," she suggested. "Remember the anticipation you felt in those days and weeks leading up to the holiday? All of it finally culminating in the thrill of Christmas morning and the discovery of what Santa left for you under the tree?"

But he didn't want to think about the anticipation leading up to Christmas. He didn't want to think about the holidays at all. Because thinking about the past inevitably brought to mind memories of his parents and all the ways that they'd made the holidays special for their family.

With seven kids to feed and clothe, Christmases were never extravagant, but there were always gifts under the tree—usually something that was needed, such as new work gloves or thermal underwear, and something that was wanted, such as a board game or favorite movie on DVD.

He was so lost in these thoughts—of what he was trying *not* to think about—that he almost forgot he wasn't alone until Serena reached across the table to touch his hand.

The contact gave him a jolt, not just because it was unexpected but because it was somehow both gentle and strong—a woman's touch. And it had been a long time since he'd been touched by a woman.

He deliberately drew his hand away to reach for his soda, sipped. "Remembering those Christmases only serves to remind me of everything I've lost," he told her. "Not that I expect someone like you to understand."

Serena sat back. "What do you mean…someone like me?"

There was a slight edge to her voice that he might have heard if he hadn't been so caught up in his own misery. But because he was and he didn't, he responded without thinking, "Someone who can't know that happiness and joy can turn to grief and despair in an instant."

She reached for her own glass, sipping her soda before she responded. "You should be careful about making assumptions about other people." Then she meticulously folded her napkin and set it beside her plate.

"Thanks for lunch, but I really do need to get home to my pets."

And then, before he could figure out what he'd said or done to put her back up, she was gone.

Chapter Three

By the time she got home, Serena had decided to skip the Presents for Patriots Dinner, Dance & Silent Auction. Though it was barely four o'clock, she'd had a full day already and had no desire to get dressed up and go out. Or it could be that she was looking for an excuse to stay home and avoid seeing Bailey Stockton again.

As she climbed the stairs to her apartment above an accountant's office, the urge to put on a pair of warm fuzzy pajamas and snuggle on the sofa with her pets was strong. And made even stronger when she opened the door and was greeted with so much affection and enthusiasm from Marvin that she couldn't imagine leaving him again.

After giving Marvin lots of ear scratches and an enthusiastic belly rub, she made her way to the bedroom— and found Molly curled up in the center of the bed. She sighed, the exasperated sound alerting the calico to her presence. The cat blinked sleepily.

Serena tried to establish boundaries for her pets—the primary one being that they weren't allowed on her bed unless and until specifically invited. Marvin mostly respected her rules; Max was usually content in his cardboard castle; but Molly roamed freely over the premises.

"Off," she said firmly, gesturing from Molly to the floor.

The calico slowly uncurled herself, yawning as she stretched out, unashamed to have been caught breaking the rules and unwilling to be hurried.

Marvin, having followed Serena into the room, finally noticed Molly on the bed and barked. Molly hissed, as if chastising him for being a tattletale. The dog plopped onto his butt beside Serena and looked up at her with adoring eyes.

"Yes, you're a good boy," she told him.

His tongue fell out of his mouth and he panted happily.

"And you—" She wagged her finger at Molly, then let her hand drop to her side, acknowledging that there was no point in reprimanding an animal who wasn't motivated to do anything but whatever she wanted. As much as the attitude frustrated Serena at times, she couldn't deny that she admired Molly's spirit.

The cat, having made her point, nimbly jumped down off the bed and sauntered toward the door. Marvin started to follow, then turned back to Serena again, obviously torn.

She chuckled softly. "You can go with Molly. I'll be out as soon as I put my jammies on."

But when she opened the closet to put her sweater in

the hamper, her gaze was snagged by the dress hanging in front of her.

The dress she'd planned to wear to the Presents for Patriots Dinner, Dance & Silent Auction tonight had been hanging in her closet for eleven months. She'd bought it on sale early in the new year—an after-holiday bargain that she'd been unable to resist—and she'd been excited for the opportunity to finally wear it. Because as much as she usually preferred the company of her animals over that of people, she also enjoyed getting dressed up every once in a while.

She lifted a hand to stroke the crushed velvet fabric. It was the color of rich red wine with a scoop neck, long sleeves and short skirt. She sighed, silently acknowledging that if she skipped the dinner and dance tonight, it might be another year—or more—before she had the opportunity to wear the dress.

Not to mention that Dr. Brooks Smith's table would already be short two people, as Annie, the clinic receptionist, was at home caring for her sick husband. Which meant that if Serena didn't show, a third meal would go to waste.

But while Annie and Dan would miss the event, Dan's brother would be there—and she wasn't sure if Bailey's attendance was a factor in favor of going or staying home.

When Bailey Stockton left Rust Creek Falls thirteen years ago, he'd thought it was forever. His life and family were gone—torn apart by *his* actions—and he hadn't imagined he would ever want to return. He'd tried to move on with his own life—first in various parts of Wyoming, then in New Mexico—certain he could find a

new path. After a few years, he'd even let himself hope
that he might make a new family.

That hadn't worked out so well. Though he'd had
the best of intentions when he'd exchanged vows with
Emily, it turned out that they were just too different—
and too stubborn to compromise—which pretty much
doomed their marriage from the start.

And then, last December, he'd heard that his brother
Luke had made his way back to Rust Creek Falls, and
he'd impulsively decided to head in the same direction.
He'd arrived in town just in time to witness their brother
Danny exchange vows with his high school sweetheart.
At the wedding, Bailey had reconnected with most of
his siblings, who had persuaded him to stay—at least
for a while.

Eleven and a half months later, Bailey was still there.
He was living in one of the cabins at Sunshine Farm now
and filling most of his waking hours with chores around
the ranch. Still, every few weeks he felt compelled to
remind himself that he was going to head out again, but
the truth was, he had nowhere else to go. And while he'd
been certain that he wouldn't ever want to return to the
family ranch that held so many memories of the parents
they'd lost and the siblings who'd scattered—he'd been
wrong about that, too.

When Bailey, Luke and Dan left town, they'd believed the property would be sold by the bank to pay off
the mortgages it secured. They'd been shocked to discover that Rob and Lauren Stockton had insurance that
satisfied the debts upon their deaths—and even more
so to discover that their maternal grandfather had kept
up with the property taxes over the years. And while
they would all have gladly given up the farm to have

their parents back, they were now determined to hold on to the land that was their legacy.

Of course, holding on to the land required a lot of work—and his brothers had started with the barn, because that was the venue where Dan and Annie had promised to love, honor and cherish one another.

The simple but heartfelt ceremony Bailey had witnessed was very different from the formal church service and elaborate ballroom reception that had marked his own wedding day, but he was confident now that his brother's marriage was destined for a happier fate.

On the day Dan and Annie exchanged their vows, though, Bailey had been much less optimistic about their prospects. Still smarting from the failure of his own union, he'd felt compelled to caution another brother when he saw the stars in Luke's eyes as he'd looked at his date.

Luke and Eva had gone their separate ways for a short while after that. Bailey didn't know if his advice had played a part in that temporary breakup, but he was glad that his brother and new sister-in-law had found their way back to one another. Luke and Eva had gotten engaged last New Year's Eve and married seven months later.

In addition to being committed to one another, they were committed to using Sunshine Farm to spread happiness to others. In fact, Eva's childhood friend Amy Wainwright had recently been reunited with her former—and future—husband, Derek Dalton, at the farm, resulting in the property gaining the nickname Lonelyhearts Ranch.

Bailey couldn't deny that a lot of people were finding love in Rust Creek Falls, including four of his six siblings. But he had no illusions about happily-ever-after for himself. He'd already been there, done that and bought the T-shirt—then lost the T-shirt in his divorce.

But he was happy to help out with Presents for Patriots. He would even acknowledge that he enjoyed working with Brendan Tanner—because the retired marine didn't try to get into his head or want to talk about his feelings, which was more than he could say about his siblings.

Bailey believed wholeheartedly in the work of Presents for Patriots. He had the greatest respect for the sacrifices made by enlisted men and women and was proud to participate in the community's efforts to let the troops know they were valued and appreciated. Maybe sending Christmas gifts was a small thing, but at least it was something, and Bailey was pleased to be part of it.

He was less convinced of the value of this dinner and dance. Sure, it was a fund-raiser for a good cause, but Bailey suspected that most of the guests would be couples, and—as the only single one of his siblings currently living in Rust Creek Falls—he was already tired of feeling like a third wheel.

Not that he wanted to change his status. No, he'd learned the hard way that he was better off on his own. No one to depend on and no one depending on him. But it was still awkward to be a single man in a social gathering that was primarily made up of couples.

He looked around the crowd gathered at Sawmill Station, hoping to see Serena in attendance. She'd said that she had a ticket for the event, but considering the abruptness with which she'd left the restaurant after lunch, he had to wonder if she'd changed her mind about coming.

Her plans shouldn't matter to him. After all, he barely

knew her. But he couldn't deny there was something about her—even when she was admonishing him for his admittedly inappropriate behavior—that appealed to him.

In fact, while she'd been scolding him, he'd had trouble understanding her words because his attention had been focused on the movements of her mouth. And he'd found himself wondering if those sweetly curved lips would stop moving if he covered them with his own— or if they'd respond with a matching passion.

Yeah, he barely knew the woman, but he knew that he wanted to kiss her—and that realization made him wary. It had been a lot of years since he'd felt such an immediate and instinctive attraction to a woman, and he would have happily lived out the rest of his days without experiencing that feeling again. Because he knew now that the euphoric feeling didn't last—and when it was gone, his heart might suffer more dings and dents.

So it was probably for the best that she'd walked out of the diner before he'd had a chance to ask her to be his date tonight. Because while he wasn't entirely comfortable being a single man surrounded by couples, at least he didn't have to worry about the stirring of unexpected desires—and the even more dangerous yearnings of his heart.

Just when he'd managed to convince himself that was true, he turned away from the bar with a drink in hand and saw her. And his foolish heart actually skipped a beat.

The silky blond hair that had spilled over her shoulders when she'd removed the Mrs. Claus wig was gathered up on top of her head now. Not in a tight knot or a formal twist, but a messy—and very sexy—arrangement of curls. Several loose strands escaped the knot to frame her face.

She was wearing a dress. The color was richer and deeper than red, and the fabric clung to her mouthwatering curves. The skirt of the dress ended just above her knees, and she wore pointy-toed high-heeled shoes on her feet.

He took a few steps toward her and noticed that there were sparkles in her hair. Crystal snowflakes, he realized, as he drew nearer. She'd made up her face, too. Not that she needed any artificial enhancement, but the long lashes that surrounded her deep blue eyes were now thicker and darker, and her temptingly curved lips were slicked with pink gloss.

"You look… Wow," he said, because he couldn't find any other words that seemed adequate.

Her cheeks flushed prettily. "Back atcha."

He knew his basic suit and bolero tie were nothing special, particularly in this crowd, but he smiled, grateful that she didn't seem to be holding a grudge. "I wasn't sure you were going to come."

"Neither was I," she admitted.

"I'm glad you did," he told her. "And I hope you brought your checkbook—there's a lot of great stuff on the auction table."

"As soon as I figure out where I'm sitting for dinner, I'll take a look," she promised.

"You can sit with me," he invited.

"I think I'm supposed to be at Dr. Smith's table."

He shook his head. "There are no assigned tables."

She looked toward the dining area, where long wooden tables were set in rows on either side of the dance floor.

The decor was festive but simple. Of course, Brendan and Bailey had left all those details in the hands of the event planners, who had adorned the tables with evergreen branches and holly berries, with tea lights in clear glass bowls at the center of each grouping of four place settings. The result was both festive and rustic, perfect for the venue and the occasion.

"I've never been here before," Serena confided. "But this place is fabulous. You and Brendan did a great job."

Bailey immediately shook his head. "This was all Caroline Ruth and her crew. The only thing me and Brendan can take credit for is putting her in charge," he said. "And picking the food."

"What will we be eating tonight?" she asked.

He plucked a menu off a nearby table and read aloud: "Country biscuits with whipped butter, mixed greens with poached pears, candied walnuts and a honey vinaigrette, grilled hand-carved flat iron steak, red-skin mashed potatoes and blackened corn, with huckleberry pie or chocolate mousse for dessert."

"And that's why I had salad for lunch," she told him.

He chuckled as he steered her toward the table where Luke and Eva were already seated, along with Brendan Tanner and his fiancée, Fiona O'Reilly, and Fiona's sister Brenna and her husband, Travis Dalton.

Conversation during dinner covered many and various topics—Presents for Patriots, of course, including the upcoming gift-wrapping at the community center—but Brendan and Fiona's recent engagement was also a subject of much interest and discussion.

"So how long have you and Serena been dating?" Brenna asked, as she dipped her spoon into her chocolate mousse.

Bailey looked up, startled by the question. "What?"

Serena paused with her wineglass halfway to her lips, obviously taken aback, as well.

"I asked how long you've been dating," Brenna repeated.

"They're not dating," Eva responded to the question first. "But they're married."

"Really?" Brenna sounded delighted and intrigued by this revelation.

"Not really," Serena said firmly.

"I don't know." Eva spoke up again, winking at Bailey and Serena to let them know she was teasing. "There were a lot of people at the community center today who believe you are."

Serena rolled her eyes. "Only because we were dressed up as Santa and Mrs. Claus."

"There's nothing wrong with a little role-playing to spice things up in the bedroom," Brenna asserted.

Serena shook her head, her cheeks redder than the dress she'd worn during their role-playing that afternoon. "I should have stayed home tonight."

"I'm just teasing you," Brenna said, immediately contrite. "Although Travis and I fell in love for real while we were only pretending to be engaged."

"I cheered for both of you on *The Great Roundup*," Serena admitted.

"Then you saw me win the grand prize," Travis chimed in.

Bailey frowned. Though reality shows weren't his thing, it would have been impossible to be in Rust Creek Falls the previous year and not follow the events that played out when two local residents were vying for the big money on the television show. "It was Brenna who won the million dollars."

"That's true," Travis confirmed, sliding an arm across his wife's shoulders and drawing her into his embrace. "But I won Brenna."

She smiled up at him. "And I won you."

"And I need some air," Bailey decided.

"Me, too," Serena said, pushing back her chair.

They exited the main reception area but didn't venture much farther than that. Leaving the building would require collecting their coats and bundling up against the frigid Montana night.

"They don't mean to be obnoxious," Bailey said when he and Serena were alone. "At least, I don't think they do."

She laughed softly. "I didn't think they were obnoxious. I thought they were adorable."

"Really?"

"Yeah. I mean, I watched *The Great Roundup*, but you never know how much of those reality shows is real, how much is staged, how much is selectively edited. It's nice to see that they truly are head over heels in love with one another."

"For now," Bailey remarked.

Serena frowned. "You don't think they'll last?"

He shrugged. "I don't think the odds are in their favor."

"Love isn't about odds," she said. "It's a leap of faith."

"A leap that frequently ends with one or both parties hitting the ground with a splat."

"Spoken like someone who has some experience with the splat," she noted.

He nodded. "Because I do."

"Of course, most people don't make it through life without a few bumps and bruises."

"Bumps and bruises usually heal pretty easily," he said.

Bailey's matter-of-fact statement told Serena that the heartbreak he'd experienced had left some pretty significant scars. She also suspected that the romance gone wrong had reopened wounds caused by the loss of his parents and the separation from his family when he was barely more than a teenager.

"Usually," she agreed.

"I'm sorry," he said, after another moment had passed.

The spontaneous and unexpected apology surprised her. "Why are you sorry?"

"Because I obviously said something that upset you at lunch today."

"I can be overly sensitive at times," she admitted.

"Does that mean I'm forgiven?" he asked hopefully.

She nodded. "You're forgiven."

"That's a relief," he told her. "We wouldn't want the kids of Rust Creek Falls Elementary School to worry about any obvious tension between Santa and Mrs. Claus."

"I'm not sure they care about Santa's marital status so long as he delivers their presents on Christmas Eve."

"Which he wouldn't be able to do if the missus got possession of the sleigh and custody of the reindeer in the divorce," Bailey pointed out.

"Then he better do everything he can to keep her happy," she suggested.

"If Santa had a secret formula for keeping a woman happy, it would top every man's Christmas list," he said.

"Ha ha."

"I'm not joking," he assured her. "But in the interests of keeping you happy, can I buy you a drink?"

"No, thanks. I had a glass of wine with dinner and that's my limit."

"One glass?"

She nodded.

"Okay, how about a dance?"

"The words sound like an invitation," she remarked. "But the tone suggests that you're hoping the offer will be declined."

"Maybe, for your sake, I'm hoping it will," he said. "Because I'm not a very good dancer."

"Then why did you ask?"

He shrugged. "Because it might seem like everyone else is paired off, but I have noticed that there are a few single guys in attendance and I know they're just waiting for me to turn my back for a second so they can move in on you."

"Should I be flattered? Or should I get out my pepper spray?"

"Maybe you should just dance with me," he suggested.

So Serena took the hand he proffered and let him lead her to the dance floor. But the minute he took her in his arms, she knew that her acquiescence had been a mistake. Being close to him, she felt those unwanted feelings stir again.

She'd had a few boyfriends in her twenty-five years, and even a couple of lovers, but she'd never really been in love. And though she didn't know much about Bailey, the intensity of the attraction she felt for him warned her that he might be the man she finally and completely fell for.

But she also knew that he didn't want to be that man, and his brief and blunt comments about his marriage gone wrong should serve as a warning to her. Which was too bad, because she really liked being in his arms. And notwithstanding his claim that he wasn't a good dancer, he moved well.

As the last notes of the song trailed away, she tipped her head back to look at him.

The heels she wore added three inches to her height, so that if he lowered his head just a little, his mouth would brush against hers.

She really wanted him to kiss her.

But they were barely more than strangers and in a very public setting. And yet, in that moment, everyone and everything else faded into the background so that there was only the two of them.

Then he did tip his head, so that his mouth hovered a fraction of an inch above hers. And she held her breath, waiting...

A guitar riff blasted through the air—an abrupt change of tempo for the couples on the dance floor—and the moment was lost.

Serena stepped back. "I—I'm going to check out the auction items."

So Bailey returned to the table without her.

"Watching you and Serena on the dance floor, I could see why Brenna thought that you guys were together," Luke commented.

"Why were you watching us instead of dancing with your wife?" Bailey asked his brother.

"Because I was working at Daisy's at 4:00 a.m.," Eva responded to the question. "And my feet are very happy to *not* be dancing right now. But he's right," she continued. "You and Serena look good together."

"Except that we're not together," he reminded his brother and sister-in-law.

They exchanged a glance.

"Denial," Eva said.

Luke nodded.

"Look, it's great that the two of you found one another and happiness together, but not everyone else in the world wants the same thing," Bailey told them.

"You mean they're not ready to admit that they want the same thing," Eva said.

Bailey just shook his head.

"A year ago, I was a skeptic, too," Luke said. "And then I met Eva."

The smile she gave her husband was filled with love and affection. And maybe it did warm Bailey's heart to see Luke and Eva so happy. And Danny and Annie. And Jamie and Fallon. And his sister Bella and Hudson. And maybe he was just the tiniest bit envious.

But only the tiniest bit—not nearly enough to be willing to risk putting his own heart on the line again.

Thankfully, he was saved from responding by the sound of—

"Is that dogs barking the tune of 'Jingle Bells'?" Eva asked.

"That's gotta be Serena's phone," Bailey noted.

Luke picked it up from the table, his brows lifting when he looked at the case. Then he turned it around so Eva and Bailey could see the image of a bulldog wearing a Santa hat.

Bailey wasn't going to judge her for loving Christmas as much as she loved her dog, especially when the call had provided a timely interruption to an increasingly awkward conversation. He took the phone from his brother and went to find Serena.

"This would send Marvin into a frenzy of joy," she told him, gesturing with the pen in her hand to a Canine Christmas basket filled with toys and treats that had been donated by Brooks Smith and his wife, Jazzy.

Bailey glanced at the bid sheet. "Looks like there's already a bidding war between Paige Traub and Lissa Christensen."

"And now me, too," she said, as she scrawled her offer on the page.

He lifted his brows at the number she'd written. "You doubled the last bid."

"It's for a good cause," she reminded him.

"So it is," he agreed.

"Is there anything here that's caught your eye?" she asked.

He knew she was referring to the auction table, but the truth was, he hadn't been able to take his eyes off *her* since she'd arrived.

"I'm still looking," he told her. But as he'd very recently reminded his brother and sister-in-law, he wasn't looking for happily-ever-after.

"There's a lot to look at," she said. "Everything from kids' toys and knitted baskets to a weekend getaway at Maverick Manor." She sighed. "Unfortunately, the bids on that are already out of my price range."

And yet she was willing to overpay for some dog toys to support a good cause and make Marvin happy.

"Is this Marvin?" he asked, holding up her phone.

She smiled. "No, it's a stock photo, but I bought the case because it looks a lot like him."

"Well, you might want to check your messages," he said. "Because you missed a call."

Serena finished writing her contact information on the bid sheet, then took her phone from him. "I can't imagine who might be calling me. Almost everyone I know is here tonight," she told him, as she unlocked the screen with her thumbprint.

He was surprised to see her expression change as she scanned the message. The light in her eyes dimmed, her lips thinned. She texted a quick response, then said, "I have to go."

"Now? Why?"

"My mom's at the Ace in the Hole."

"And?"

She just shook her head. "Long story."

"Do you want me to come with you?" he asked.

She seemed surprised that he would offer. "No," she said, but softened the rejection with a smile. "I appreciate the offer, but it's not necessary."

He took her phone from her again, then added his name and number to her list of contacts. "Just in case you change your mind."

"Thanks," she said, and even managed another smile. But he could tell that her mind was already at the bar and grill down the street—and whatever trouble he suspected was waiting for her there.

Chapter Four

Serena found a vacant spot in the crowded lot outside the Ace in the Hole and shifted into Park. She pocketed the keys as she exited her vehicle, the sick feeling in the pit of her stomach increasing with every step she took closer to the oversize ace of hearts playing card that blinked in neon red over the front door. She could hear the music from the jukebox inside as she climbed the two rough-hewn wooden steps. The price of beer was subject to regular increases, but the ancient Wurlitzer still played three songs for a quarter.

There were a few cowboys hanging around outside, cigarettes dangling from their fingers or pursed between their lips. She held her breath as she walked through their cloud of smoke and ignored the whistles and crude remarks tossed in her direction as she reached for the handle of the old screen door with its rusty hinges.

Once inside, her gaze immediately went to the bar that ran the length of one wall with stools lined up along it. Booths hugged the other walls, with additional tables and chairs crowded around the perimeter of the dance floor.

She made a cursory scan of the bodies perched on the stools at the bar. The mirrored wall behind the rows of glass bottles allowed her to see their faces. She recognized many, but none belonged to her mother.

Rosey Traven, the owner of the Ace, was pouring drinks behind the bar. Catching Serena's eye, she tipped her head toward the back. Serena forced her reluctant feet to move in that direction.

She found her mother seated across from a man that Serena didn't recognize. A friend? A date? A stranger?

Amanda Langley mostly kept to herself. For the past couple of years, she'd worked as an admin assistant at the mill, but outside of her job, she didn't have a lot of friends. And as far as Serena knew, she didn't date much, either.

She was an attractive woman, with the same blond hair and blue eyes as her daughter, but a more boyish figure and a raspy voice courtesy of a fifteen-year pack-a-day habit that she'd finally managed to kick a few years earlier.

The man seated across from her wasn't bad looking, either. He had broad shoulders, a shaven—or maybe bald—head, and a beard and moustache that were more salt than pepper.

Serena hesitated, trying to decide whether to advance or retreat, when her mother glanced up and saw her. Amanda looked surprised at first—and maybe a little guilty? Then she smiled and beckoned her daughter over.

Serena made her way through the crowd to the table. "Rena—what are you doing here?"

She bent her head to kiss her mother's cheek. "I think the more important question is what are *you* doing here?"

"I'm having dinner with…a friend."

Serena looked again at the man seated across the table. Up close, she could see that his twinkling eyes were blue and his good humor was further reflected in the easy curve of his lips. She added well-mannered to her assessment when he stood up and offered his hand. "Mark Kesler."

She took it automatically. "Serena Langley."

"It's a pleasure to finally meet you, Serena," he said. "Your mother's told me so much about you."

"That's interesting, because she's told me absolutely nothing about you."

"Serena." Her name was a sharp rebuke from her mother.

But Mark only chuckled. "It's okay, Amanda. In fact, it's nice to know that your daughter looks out for you."

"Is that what you're doing, Serena?" her mother asked.

"I can't seem to help myself," she admitted.

Because it was warm in the bar, she unwound the scarf from around her neck and unbuttoned her coat. Then she reached across the table to pick up her mother's glass and tipped it to her lips.

"If you want a drink, you can order your own soda," Amanda said dryly.

"I just wanted a sip," she said.

"And did that sip satisfy your…thirst?"

They both knew that what her mother really meant

was *curiosity*, but Serena refused to feel guilty for needing to know what was in her mother's glass. And she wasn't going to apologize, either.

"As a matter of fact, it did," she said.

Amanda picked up a fry from her plate, nibbled on it. Then she said quietly, "Mark knows I'm an alcoholic."

The man in question reached into his jacket pocket and pulled out a coin, then slid it across the table for Serena to look at.

She immediately recognized it as a sobriety coin. Her mother had recently earned one with the Roman numeral V on it, commemorating five years without a drink. The numerals inside the circle inside the triangle of this coin read XXV.

"I understand, more than most, that sobriety is a daily challenge for addicts," he told her.

"Then why would you bring her here?" she wanted to know.

"Because the Ace has the best burgers in town," Mark said.

Serena couldn't deny that, but she still worried about her mother's ability to resist the temptation that beckoned from the assortment of bottles lined up behind the bar. Gin had always been Amanda's preferred poison, but beggars weren't usually choosers, and for a lot of years, she drank anything she could get her hands on.

"But I forgot how much food they give you here," Amanda said now. "And while I managed to finish the burger, I barely touched my fries." She nudged the plate toward her daughter.

Serena shook her head, declining the silent offer. "I ate at the Presents for Patriots event."

"That's why you're all dressed up," her mother realized. "Did you go with a date?"

"No." But she thought about Bailey now—about how much she'd enjoyed chatting with him during the meal. And how much she'd savored the security of his strong arms around her on the dance floor, and the heat of his lean hard body close to hers, stirring long-dormant desires inside her.

But sitting at the same table and sharing a single dance didn't make a chance encounter a date. Maybe if he'd kissed her... And for a brief moment at the end of the song, she'd thought he might. But he didn't.

"Oh," Amanda said, obviously disappointed by her daughter's response. Then to *her* date, she said, "If Serena spent a little less time with animals and a little more with people, she might find a nice young man to settle down with."

"Maybe she doesn't want to settle down," Mark suggested.

"Thank you," Serena said, grateful for his acknowledgment of the possibility.

It wasn't the truth, of course. She *did* want to settle down—but she had no intention of settling. She wanted to fall in love with a man who loved her just as much, then get married and raise a couple of kids and grow old together.

"She wants a husband and a family," Amanda insisted, as if privy to her daughter's innermost thoughts. "But she has some trust issues that get in the way of her getting too close to anyone. Totally my fault," she acknowledged ruefully.

"Not totally," Serena said, because she couldn't deny that her childhood experiences continued to influence her expectations of adult relationships. "My father bears equal responsibility for walking out on both of us."

"And then I made things worse."

"I don't think there's anything to be gained by assigning blame," Mark protested, reaching across the table to cover Amanda's hand with his own, a tangible gesture of his support.

"Step Five—admitting the nature of our mistakes."

Mark started to say something else, but his attention was snagged by the vibration of his cell phone on the table. He glanced at the screen, then at Amanda. "I'm sorry but—"

"Go," she said. "You don't need to apologize, just go."

"Excuse me," he said to Serena, as he slid out of the booth, already connecting the call.

"Mark is an active AA sponsor," Amanda explained when the man in question had moved out of earshot.

"Is that how the two of you met?" Serena asked.

"We met at a meeting," her mother confirmed. "But he was never my sponsor."

"But he was an alcoholic," she noted.

"*Is* an alcoholic. Sober for more than twenty-five years, but still an alcoholic."

Serena nodded. Aside from her own experience with Amanda, she'd attended enough Al-Anon meetings as the daughter of an alcoholic to know that the battle against addiction was ongoing.

She also knew that her mother had worked hard to get and stay sober, and she deserved credit for that. "I'm sorry I overreacted," she said now.

"I'm sorry, too," Amanda said. "Because I know you have valid reasons to be concerned."

"Mark seems nice," she acknowledged.

"And you're worried that if I get emotionally involved and it doesn't work out, I'm going to lose myself in the bottle again?" her mother guessed.

Serena didn't—couldn't—deny it, so she remained silent.

"We both worried about the same thing," Amanda confided. "It's why we fought against our feelings for one another for so long."

"How long have you known him?" she asked curiously.

"Twelve years."

Her brows lifted. "How long have you been dating?"

"We've been spending more and more time together over the past few years, but tonight was our first official date," her mother told her.

"And your daughter crashed it."

Amanda smiled. "I'm always glad to see you."

It was a sincere statement, not a commentary on the scarcity of their visits, but she felt a twinge of guilt nevertheless. Over the past five years, her mother had made a lot of efforts and overtures that Serena had resisted—not as punishment or payback, but simply out of self-preservation.

She'd lost track of the number of times that she'd given her mother "one more chance" to be the mother that she wanted her to be, and somewhere along the line, she'd stopped believing that Amanda could ever be that person. Now, however, Serena acknowledged that she hadn't always been the daughter that her mother wanted her to be, and maybe it was time to work toward changing that.

When Mark finished his phone call and came back

to the table, Serena wished them both a good-night and headed out. She caught Rosey's eye again as she passed the bar and gave the other woman a thumbs-up. Rosey nodded and continued to pour beer.

The time displayed on the Coors Light clock on the wall assured Serena that it wasn't too late to go back to the dinner and dance—and check on her bids—but her emotions were raw and she didn't think it was wise to seek out the company of a man whose mere presence churned her up inside.

No, the smart thing to do would be to go home to the animals who would shower her with unconditional love—or, in Molly's case, tolerant affection.

So resolved, she buttoned her coat up to her throat and braced herself for the slap of cold as she walked through the door and into the night. A different group of smokers huddled outside now—willingly braving the frigid air for a hit of nicotine.

Serena kept her head down and moved briskly toward her vehicle, parked at the far edge of the lot. As she drew nearer, she saw a tall broad-shouldered figure leaning against the tailgate of the truck in the slot beside her SUV.

She thought about the guys who'd been hanging around outside when she arrived and wondered—with more than a little bit of trepidation—if one of them had decided to wait by her vehicle until she came out again.

Her heart pounded against her ribs, and she considered going back into the bar and asking Mark to escort her to her SUV. Instead, she drew in a steadying breath and slipped her hand into her pocket to retrieve her keys. She held them in her fist, so that the pointed ends protruded between her knuckles as her grandmother had taught her to do, and walked purposefully, projecting more confidence than she felt.

Though the figure was mostly in shadow, as she got closer, she sensed that there was something familiar about his shape.

"Bailey?"

He turned, and the light in the distance provided enough illumination of his profile to confirm that her guess was correct. Her heart continued to hammer against her ribs, though its frantic rhythm was no longer inspired by fear but relief—and pleasure.

"I know you didn't call, but I also know that the crowd here can get a little rowdy on weekends, and I wanted to make sure you were okay," he said, answering her unspoken question.

"I'm okay," she assured him.

"Do you want to talk?"

"No," she replied automatically, having grown accustomed to dealing with everything on her own since her grandmother had retired down to Arizona three years earlier. Then she reconsidered. "Maybe."

"We could go back inside to have a drink," he suggested.

She shook her head. "Definitely not."

His brows lifted.

"I wouldn't say no to hot cocoa at Daisy's, though."

"Hot cocoa at Daisy's it is," he agreed.

Daisy's Donut Shop was practically a landmark in Rust Creek Falls. Originally renowned for the best coffee—and the only donuts—in town, the owner had eventually responded to the demand for a wider range of food options. As a result, Daisy's menu now included a rotating selection of soups and sandwiches, but it was the mouthwatering sweets on display in the glass-fronted cases that continued to draw and tempt the most customers.

There were several people lined up at the counter ahead of them when they arrived.

"I think we came in with the last of the movie crowd," Serena noted.

Bailey had almost forgotten that movies were shown at the high school on Friday and Saturday nights—but only so long as the Wildcats didn't have the gymnasium booked for a game, in which case the bleachers would be filled with residents cheering on the local team.

"Waiting in line gives us more time to check out the desserts Eva made today," he said, gesturing to the glass-fronted cases.

Of course, it was late, and the offerings that remained were limited—but still tempting.

"Just a regular hot cocoa for me," Serena said, stepping up to the counter.

Bailey looked dubious. "Just regular hot cocoa, like you could make for yourself at home?"

She shook her head. "I've tried all kinds of hot cocoa mixes. I've even tried making it from scratch, but it's never as good as Daisy's."

"Secret recipe," the server said with a wink.

"Coffee, decaf, for me," Bailey said. "And I've got to have one of those cheesecake-stuffed snickerdoodles."

"Didn't you already have dessert at Sawmill Station?" Serena asked him. "In fact, I'm pretty sure you ate your chocolate mousse and finished your sister-in-law's huckleberry pie."

"I did," he confirmed. "But that was more than two hours ago."

She smiled as she shook her head.

"Anything else for you?" the server asked.

"No, thanks," Serena said.

"Whipped cream and chocolate drizzle on your cocoa?"

"Mmm, yes," she agreed.

When they were seated with their hot beverages—and Bailey's enormous cookie—Serena wrapped her hands around her mug and announced, "My mother's an alcoholic."

"Ahh," he said, understanding now why she'd raced away from the silent auction when she learned that her mother was at the town's notorious drinking hole. "Was she...drunk?"

Serena shook her head. "She was drinking diet cola and eating a cheeseburger."

"Strange place to go for a diet cola," he noted. "Best place in town for a burger."

Now she nodded.

"So why are you all wound up?"

She couldn't deny that she was. Not when her hands were clutching her mug like it was a buoy keeping her afloat in stormy seas—but maybe that was an apt analogy for her life at the moment.

"I can't help it," she admitted. "I get a message like that, and the memories—years and years of horrible memories—play through my head like a horror movie on fast-forward."

"Who told you that she was there?"

"Rosey made the original call. Then Shelby sent a text when I was already on my way."

"I don't think I know a Shelby," he said.

"She used to be Shelby Jenkins, but she married Dean Pritchett a few years back," she told him. "She's worked at the Ace for a long time and has good instincts about people—and knows which customers to keep an eye on."

"Gives a whole new meaning to neighborhood watch," he remarked.

"Over the years, Rosey and Shelby have had a front-row seat to some of my mother's struggles—and mine," she explained. "And five years of sobriety hasn't helped me forget more than a decade of drinking."

His brows lifted.

She sighed. "And I guess two years of weekly therapy didn't quite succeed in helping me work through my anger and frustration and fear."

"That's why you wouldn't have more than one glass of wine tonight," he guessed.

She nodded. "Some scientists believe there's a genetic component to addiction, and I don't want to take any chances. Although—" she lifted her mug "—it wouldn't be wrong to say that I'm addicted to chocolate."

Then she sipped her cocoa, ending up with a whipped cream moustache that she swiped away with a stroke of her tongue.

The gesture drew Bailey's attention to the temptation of her mouth again, and he silently chided himself for not taking advantage of the opportunity he'd had to kiss her when they were on the dance floor.

But that opportunity had passed, and he owed her the courtesy of paying attention to what she was saying without being distracted by his own fantasies.

Except that a tiny bit of whipped cream clung to the indent at the center of her top lip, and it was driving him to distraction. He finally reached across the table and brushed his thumb over her lip, wiping away the cream.

He heard her sharp intake of breath, watched her eyes widen with awareness. And maybe…arousal?

Or maybe he was projecting.

"Whipped cream," he explained.

"Oh." She reached for her napkin and wiped her mouth. "I probably should have skipped the whipped cream and chocolate sauce—they're messy."

"There's nothing wrong with messy," he told her, imagining that they could have a lot of fun getting messy together with whipped cream and chocolate sauce.

Serena blushed, making him wonder if her thoughts had gone in the same direction as his own.

There was definitely a zing in the air—a sizzle of attraction that ratcheted up the temperature about ten degrees whenever he was with her.

He'd been back in Rust Creek Falls for almost a year, and during that time, he'd crossed paths with any number of undeniably attractive women. Several had flirted with him, a few had offered more than a phone number, but he hadn't been tempted by any of them.

But after only a few hours with Serena Langley, he hadn't been able to get her out of his mind. When she'd left the Gold Rush Diner earlier that day, he'd counted the hours until the fund-raiser in anticipation of seeing her there. And when she'd excused herself from that event, he could tell she was upset about something. And because he'd worried about an attractive single woman walking into a place like the Ace alone, he'd followed her, just to make sure she was okay.

Now he was sitting across from her at Daisy's Donut Shop, watching her sip hot cocoa and trying to resist the temptation to imagine her naked. He was feeling better about life, the universe and everything than he'd felt in a very long time—maybe even since he'd left Rust Creek Falls following the deaths of his parents thirteen years earlier. Which confirmed a crucial fact: Serena Langley was a dangerous woman. And if he wasn't careful, her sparkling eyes, warm smile and open heart could pose a significant threat to the walls he'd deliberately built around his own damaged vessel.

So he would be careful, he resolved. He would take a step back—maybe several steps—to avoid the danger of another emotional splat. But those steps could wait until tomorrow, he decided, as he popped the last bite of snickerdoodle into his mouth.

Because tonight, he was really enjoying being with her.

Chapter Five

"I know, I know," Serena said, as she kicked off her shoes inside the door. "I promised I wouldn't be late, but I got caught up."

Marvin didn't move from the spot where he'd been sitting when she opened the door, his big sad eyes filled with silent reproach.

"I'm sorry," she said, crouching down to rub his ears.

He closed his eyes, savoring her touch.

Then she sighed. "Actually, that's a lie. I'm sorry you missed me, but I'm not sorry I'm late, because I had a really good time with Bailey tonight."

Marvin tilted his head.

"Am I forgiven?" she asked, continuing to scratch where he liked it best.

His licked her hand.

"Thank you," she said, and kissed the top of his head

before rising to her feet again and moving toward the bedroom to change.

On the way, she checked on Max, who was sleeping soundly in his bed. She found Molly curled up on *her* bed again, but Serena pretended she didn't see her there, because attempting to reprimand the stubborn calico only proved to both of them that the cat was the one calling the shots.

Instead, Serena hung her dress back up in the closet and finally donned the warm fuzzy pajamas that had beckoned to her hours earlier. After brushing her teeth, she wanted nothing more than to climb beneath the covers of her bed, but she felt guilty for neglecting Marvin through most of the day and night, so she returned to the living room. She played some tug-of-war with him and his favorite knotted rope, then a few minutes of fetch—he'd always been good at finding and retrieving the ball, but not so good at returning it to her.

When he finally tired of the game and crawled into her lap, she lifted her hand to his head to rub his ears, and he sighed contentedly and closed his eyes.

"I think I'm developing a serious crush," Serena confided to her pet.

He opened one eye, as if to assure her that he was listening.

She smiled as she continued to stroke his short glossy fur.

"I know it's crazy," she admitted. "I barely know the guy. And yet…there's just something about him.

"Or maybe it's just been so long since I've spent any time with a man that I'm making this into more than it is. I mean, it wasn't even a date—we just both happened to be at the same event. But it felt like a date.

And it was so nice to talk to a guy who seemed to listen to what I was saying.

"Of course, you're a good listener, too, but sometimes it's nice to talk to someone who actually talks back."

Marvin responded with a low growl.

She laughed softly. "I'm not denying that you know how to communicate," she said, attempting to placate her pet. "But we really don't share a dialogue. And, if I'm being completely honest, I like to look at him, too. Because Bailey Stockton is hot. And the way he looks at me, I feel like I'm more than a vet tech or a pet owner or 'the girl who lives upstairs,' as Mr. Harrington calls me. I feel attractive and desirable, and I haven't felt that way in a long time."

Marvin tilted his head to lick her hand.

"I know you love me," she said. "And I love you. But as sweet as your doggy kisses are, they don't compare to real kisses. At least, I don't think they do. Of course, it's been so long since I've been kissed by a man, I can't be sure."

But there had been that almost-kiss moment, during which she'd experienced so much joyful anticipation she was certain that sharing a real kiss with Bailey Stockton would make her toes curl inside her shoes.

"And even though I was gone all night, I was thinking about you," Serena told Marvin. "And hopefully my bid on the— Well, I can't tell you what it was, because if my bid was successful, it will be your Christmas present and I wouldn't want to ruin the surprise. Anyway, tomorrow I will be home all day," she promised. "Maybe I'll even make some of your favorite treats."

Marvin's head lifted at the last word, and she laughed again.

"And, because you sometimes get too many *t-r-e-a-t-s*, we'll go for a nice long walk."

He immediately dropped his head again and closed his eyes, faking sleep so he could pretend he hadn't heard her.

"People told me to get a dog, they said I'd be more active. I swear, I got the only dog on the planet that's even lazier than me," Serena lamented. "But a walk will do both of us good—and I definitely need one because I had hot cocoa with whipped cream and chocolate sauce tonight."

And her lips tingled as she recalled the sensation of Bailey's thumb brushing over her lip to wipe away a remnant of the cream.

She pushed the tempting memory aside and refocused her attention on Marvin, who continued to fake sleep.

"I know you don't love to walk in the winter," she acknowledged. "But we'll put on your new Christmas sweater to keep you nice and warm."

Of course, Marvin hated wearing sweaters or coats, but it really was too cold to take him outside without one.

"And since you're obviously too tired to keep up your end of this conversation, I guess it's bedtime," Serena said.

Bedtime was another familiar word to him, and Marvin immediately hopped down off the sofa and raced over to the doggy door. But he sat obediently on his mat until she said "okay," then pushed through the flap and went outside to do his business.

A few minutes later, he was back, and immediately went to his bed in the corner.

Serena retreated to her bedroom—where Molly was still curled up in the middle of the mattress.

"You could at least move over and give me some room," she grumbled.

Of course, the cat didn't budge. Not until Serena had fluffed up her pillows and tucked herself in under the covers.

Then Molly crawled up to snuggle against Serena's chest, and purred contentedly.

Serena would never reject the calico's affection, but she couldn't deny that she longed for a different kind of company in her bed. As she drifted off to sleep, she was thinking of Bailey's strong arms around her, his heart beating in sync with her own.

Tuesday morning, Bailey spoke to Dan's wife on the phone. Annie had assured him that her husband was feeling better, but they agreed it wasn't worth the risk of exposing the kids to any remnants of the virus that might be lingering.

He should have dreaded the fact that he had to don the Santa suit again. Instead, Bailey found himself whistling as he drove to the elementary school, where he'd made arrangements to meet Mrs. Claus in the parking lot.

They walked into the school together and were directed to the teachers' lounge to change into their costumes. He zipped up Serena's dress and tied her apron; she secured his padding and whitened his brows. It was almost like they were a real married couple, helping one another get ready for a social engagement.

Only a few days earlier, he'd been sweaty and nervous and not at all looking forward to stepping out from behind the curtain and facing the group of children waiting in the community center. Today, there was no curtain. Today, they walked through the double doors of the gymnasium, but he felt much more comfortable and relaxed with Serena beside him.

He caught Janie's eye when he entered the gym, and the way her smile widened, she'd obviously recognized Uncle Bailey as the man behind Kris Kringle's white beard. But, of course, she didn't reveal his identity to anyone.

When the principal invited him to say a few words, he took advantage of the opportunity to explain that Christmas wasn't just about what they wanted to find under their trees the morning of December 25 but also about giving, and he encouraged them to talk to their parents about supporting Presents for Patriots in any way that they could.

As the afternoon progressed, he thought everything was going well. And then one of the kids—a little girl in second grade with reindeer antlers mounted onto a headband set in her curly red hair—climbed up onto his lap.

"Ho ho ho," Bailey said. "And what would you like for Christmas?"

Unlike most of the other kids who'd made a request for the usual variety of toys and games, she looked at him with big green eyes filled with worry and sadness and said, "I want my daddy to come home."

Which, of course, wasn't a wish that even the real Santa—if he existed—could grant.

Bailey was at a complete loss because he didn't have

any idea where the child's father was or what could be preventing him from being with his family for the holiday. Maybe the little girl's parents were separated or even divorced. Maybe the father was traveling on business or serving overseas in the military. It was even possible that the child's father had passed away, ensuring that her wish was never going to come true.

He glanced, helplessly, hopelessly, at his missus.

And, once again, she came to his rescue and saved the day.

Crouching beside his chair, Serena spoke quietly to the child. "Your daddy's got an important job to do, Harley, and he can't come home until it's done. But I promise that he misses you and your mommy and your brothers as much as you miss him, and I know his wish for you would be that you have happy Christmas memories to share with him when he calls home."

The little girl nodded solemnly, eager to believe every word that Mrs. Claus said to her.

"So is there anything special you'd like to find under the tree on Christmas morning?" Santa asked her again.

This time, she responded without hesitation, confirming that although her first wish was to spend the holiday with her father, she was still a child. "A Stardust Stacie doll would be something good to tell daddy about."

"I'll see what I can do," Santa promised, even as he wondered if the doll would be more readily available than the pocket toys that Serena had told him were so popular this season.

Thankfully, Harley's request was the only snag in Santa's visit to the school. After all the children who wanted to share their wishes with Santa had done so,

Mr. and Mrs. Claus retreated to the staff lounge to change out of their costumes and assume their real identities again.

"Who was the little girl who asked about her father coming home for Christmas?" Bailey asked Serena, as he rolled up his enormous red pants.

"Harley Williams," she said. "She's the youngest of three kids. Her mom works at the library and her dad is a marine, currently stationed in Syria."

"Do you know everything about everyone in this town?" he wondered aloud.

"Hardly," she told him. "But the family also has two cats—Bert and Ernie. You'd be amazed how much you learn about people when you help take care of their pets."

"So it would seem," he agreed, stuffing the pants and jacket into the costume bag. "And it seems that I owe you thanks for bailing me out—again."

"It was my pleasure."

"Actually, it was kind of fun today," he acknowledged.

She laughed at the surprise in his voice. "Yes, it was."

He wanted to say something else, something to prolong their conversation and give him an excuse to spend a few more minutes in her company.

It was strange to think that he'd only met her four days earlier, but between the Santa gigs and the Presents for Patriots event and the hot cocoa at Daisy's, they'd spent a lot of time together over those few days. And when he hadn't been with her, he'd been thinking about her.

He suspected that Serena was equally reluctant to part company with him, because after he'd stuffed the costumes in his truck, she asked, "Do you want to go for a ride with me? I'll bring you back here after."

"After what?"

She just smiled, and the sweet curve of her lips was like the sun breaking through the clouds on a gray day.

"Are you game to come with me or not?" she challenged.

Hmm…go back to Sunshine Farm and the chores that were always waiting? Or spend another hour—and maybe more—in the company of a bright and beautiful woman?

It was a no-brainer.

Because the more time he spent with Serena, the more he wanted to be with her. There was something warm and sincere about her that appealed to him. And okay, she was gorgeous and sexy, too, and he was far more attracted to her than he was ready to acknowledge—even to himself.

His romantic history wasn't particularly extensive or successful. Prior to meeting and falling in love with Emily, he'd only dated a few women. Growing up in Rust Creek Falls, he'd spent most of his waking hours at Sunshine Farm, doing any of the endless chores that filled the hours from sunup to sundown. And when those chores were finally done, he was usually too exhausted to go out and do anything else.

The one night he'd let Luke convince him that they deserved to have some fun had ended up being the worst night of his life.

He shook off the weight of those memories and focused his attention on the present—and the woman presently waiting for a response to her question.

"Why don't I drive and bring you back to your vehicle after?" he suggested. Because yeah, he was one of those guys who liked to be in the driver's seat—both literally and figuratively.

"After what?" she teasingly echoed his question.

He shrugged.

"And that's why I'm driving," she said. "Because I know where we're going." She thumbed the button on her key fob to unlock the doors.

He went to the driver's side first. She pulled back the hand that held her keys, as if she expected him to try to take them from her, but he only opened the door for her.

"Thank you," she said, appreciative of the gesture.

"You're welcome," he said, waiting until she'd slid into the driver's seat to close the door for her.

After he was buckled in, she turned her vehicle toward the highway, heading out of town.

After only a few minutes, Bailey figured out that they were making their way toward Falls Mountain and the actual Rust Creek Falls that gave the town its name. They passed a picnic area and signs that guided visitors to a viewing area for the falls. She continued to drive farther up the mountain, finally turning off the main road to park in a small gravel lot at the base of the trail that led to Owl Rock—the lookout point named for the large white boulder that resembled the bird and protruded out over the falls, as if keeping watch over them.

During the spring and summer months, vehicles would be packed closely together and the trails would be busy with hikers and families. But it was early December and too cold for most people, aside from the most hardy outdoor enthusiasts. Apparently Serena was one of those enthusiasts.

"Nice day for a hike," he commented, as he followed her up the trail.

And it was, because although the air was frigid, the sun was shining. Also, he had a spectacular view of her shapely butt, encased in snug-fitting denim.

"I haven't been up here since I was a teenager," he told her, as they arrived at the lookout point. "In fact, I'd almost forgotten this place existed."

"It's one of my favorite places in Rust Creek Falls," she confided, sitting down on a flat outcropping of rock with her legs crossed beneath her. "My grandmother brought me here when I first came to Rust Creek Falls, and whenever I'm feeling down, I find myself drawn back. Being close to nature always lifts my spirits."

"Why did you want to come here today?" he asked her.

She was silent for a minute before responding. "Because Harley's request about her dad brought back some painful memories."

As a man who carefully guarded his own secrets, he was reluctant to pry into hers. On the other hand, she'd invited him to come here with her today, which suggested that she wanted someone to talk to.

He lowered himself onto the rock beside her, sitting close enough that their shoulders were touching. "What kind of memories?"

"When I was just about Harley's age, I went to see Santa and asked him to bring my sister home from the hospital in time for Christmas."

"I didn't know you had a sister," Bailey admitted, surprised by her revelation.

"I don't." She unfolded her legs and drew her knees

up to her chest, wrapping her arms around them. "Not anymore."

He didn't prompt her for more information. She would tell him more when she was ready.

"I was an only child for the first six years of my life," she began. "An only child who *begged* for a brother or sister. And when my parents finally told me that there was a baby in my mommy's tummy, I couldn't wait for her to be born.

"I don't know if my parents knew for sure that they were having a girl, but I always thought of her as my sister. It was probably wishful thinking on my part, because I was seven, and I thought boys were mostly gross and dumb and I really wanted a sister."

She paused for a minute, gathering her thoughts—or maybe her composure.

"Then something went wrong, and my mom had to go into the hospital early. It must have been just before Halloween, because I was sucking on a lollipop that I'd stolen out of the bucket of candy my mom had bought for trick-or-treaters when Grams came into my room and told me that she was going to be staying with us for a few days.

"Miriam was born six weeks before her due date. I remember asking my grandmother why she didn't seem happy when she told me the news. She said it was because the baby was too small and that she might not make it.

"I didn't understand what she meant. The only information that registered with me was that I finally had a sister.

"So my grandmother bluntly told me that Miriam

might die. I refused to believe it. Babies didn't die. Old people died. And I demanded to meet my sister.

"A few days later, Grams finally gave in and took me up to the hospital to see my parents and the baby. Miriam was in an incubator, though of course I didn't know what it was at the time. I only knew that she had tubes stuck in various parts of her body and she didn't look anything like a baby—at least nothing like Mr. and Mrs. Wakefield's baby, the focus of everyone's attention and well wishes at church earlier that morning.

"I think I started to cry, because my dad picked me up and tried to soothe me. And my mom got mad at Grams for bringing me to the hospital, but she argued that it was important for me to see my sister, in case anything happened.

"This made my mom cry and my dad told her to go. But I got to stay for a while, snuggling with my mom while my dad told us that everything was going to be fine, because Mimi—that's what we called her—was strong, just like me. And he promised that we'd all be celebrating Christmas together in a few weeks.

"And he was right, although it wasn't really as simple or easy as that. Mimi had to stay in the hospital until she was a lot bigger and stronger, and the doctors warned that could take several weeks or even months.

"One night, in mid-December, my dad said that he had a surprise. Instead of going to the hospital, he took me to the local mall to see Santa." Serena nudged Bailey playfully with her shoulder. "Back then, it was what you did to see the big guy, because we didn't have a community center in town or any handsome cowboys willing to put on a padded red suit."

Taking his cue from her deliberate attempt to lighten

the mood, Bailey lifted his brows. "You think I'm handsome?"

"To quote Ellie Traub, 'all those Stockton boys are handsome devils.'"

"Good to know," he said, equal parts flattered and embarrassed by the older woman's assessment. "But you were telling me about your visit to Santa."

"Right," she agreed. "My dad took me to see Santa and I thought of all the wishes I'd carefully printed on my Christmas list to decide which one I wanted most of all. That year, it was a toss-up between Mouse Trap, the board game, and a new pair of ballet slippers. But when it was finally my turn, all I could think was that I wanted my baby sister to come home from the hospital for Christmas."

"Did Santa deliver?" he asked gently.

She nodded. "Mimi came home the afternoon of December 24. It was as if we got our very own Christmas miracle. The next morning, I didn't even race downstairs to see if Santa had left any presents under the tree. Instead, I rushed across the hall to the nursery, to make sure she was still there.

"And she was. The Mouse Trap game and ballet slippers that I unwrapped later were bonuses—all I really wanted was my sister. Of course, she needed a lot of attention," Serena continued. "And I was happy to give it to her. Happy to finally have the sister I'd always wanted.

"If she cried, I wanted to be the one to pick her up. If she was hungry, I wanted to give her a bottle. Even when she was content to sit in her high chair or play swing, I was there, reading to her or singing the songs I'd learned at school. Long before she could talk, she would clap her hands and kick her feet whenever she listened to music."

She smiled at the memory. "And Christmas carols were her favorite. Maybe not that first Christmas," she acknowledged. "That year she mostly seemed fascinated by the colored lights and sparkly ornaments on the tree. But by the following year, when she was thirteen months old, she was munching on sugar cookies and tearing the bows and paper off presents. The year after that, she shook colored sugar onto the cookies before she ate them and even helped hang some sparkly ornaments on the tree."

Serena dropped her chin to her bent knees, her gaze focused on something in the distance—or maybe something in the past. "And then, just a few weeks after her third birthday, she disappeared."

Chapter Six

Disappeared?

Just when Bailey started to think he knew where the story was leading, it took a major detour. He caught the sheen of moisture in Serena's eyes, noted the tension in the arms that hugged her legs tight. He shifted on the rock so that he was sitting behind her, his legs splayed to bracket her hips, his arms wrapped around her.

"My parents had planned a special trip for all of us," she continued. "We went to Missoula to participate in the Parade of Lights and enjoy a performance of *The Nutcracker*. Of course, Mimi was too young to understand the show and she fidgeted through the whole thing, but I'd been dancing for five years by then, and I was completely entranced. Next to Mimi, that was the best Christmas present I'd ever received.

"The morning of our planned return to Rust Creek

Falls, we stopped at the Holiday Made Fair so that my parents could do some last-minute shopping. It was crowded with booths and toys and goodies and lots of people. I was under strict instructions to hold tight to Mimi's hand, and I did." She swallowed. "Until I didn't."

He hugged her a little tighter, a wordless offer of comfort and encouragement.

"She saw the doll first," Serena said, resuming her narrative. "It was a replica of the Sugar Plum Fairy and she pulled me to it. There was a whole bin of them, and Mimi tugged her hand from mine so that she could pick one up. And I picked up another one, admiring the intricate details of her costume, and I turned to show Mimi something, but she wasn't there anymore.

"It happened that fast," she said, her voice hollow. "She was right beside me…and then she was gone. My parents were, of course, frantic. We didn't celebrate the holidays—we were too busy looking for Mimi. But she'd disappeared without a trace. The police got all kinds of tips and followed countless leads, but nothing ever panned out. As days turned into weeks and weeks into months, we began to lose hope that she would ever come home again.

"I know she's out there somewhere," Serena insisted. "And I believe with my whole heart that she's alive… just lost to us.

"By the summer, my mother was self-medicating with alcohol. I didn't know what that meant, except that I heard my dad say it to my grandmother. I did know that my mom stumbled around a lot, ran her words together so that sometimes I couldn't understand what she was saying, and slept a lot. And, of course, my parents fought. All the time. Several months later, before Christmas the following year, my dad took off."

And only a few days earlier, Bailey had accused Serena of not understanding that happiness was a fickle emotion that could be snatched away without warning. No wonder she'd cautioned him about making assumptions, because she did understand. Because she'd experienced a loss as profound as his own.

"He left a note," she continued. "It wasn't like when Mimi disappeared. But the note didn't say much more than that he felt as if he'd failed his family, and every day with us—without Mimi—was a reminder of that."

"I'm so sorry, Serena." The words sounded so meaningless, even to his own ears, but they were all he had to offer.

"There wasn't anything joyful about Christmas that year, either," she said.

"I can only imagine how difficult it would be to celebrate anything after losing a child," he acknowledged.

"Mimi's disappearance was devastating for all of us," Serena agreed. "But my parents had two children—and they didn't lose both of them."

But Serena had effectively lost both of her parents after the disappearance of her sister. And Bailey suspected that she'd been deeply scarred by it.

"Of course, my mom's drinking got even worse after my dad left. And Child Protective Services got involved in the New Year after my teacher called to report that I frequently wore the same clothes to school several days in a row and sometimes didn't have any food in my lunch box.

"That's when my grandmother came to stay with us again. She tried to get my mother back on track—and

Amanda tried to stop drinking. But inevitably, after a few weeks—or sometimes not more than a few days—she'd decide that she needed 'just one drink' to take the edge off her pain and emptiness. Of course, one drink always turned into two and then three, until eventually she'd end up passed out on the sofa."

Bailey had been there—alone in that dark place where it seemed that nothing could take the edge off his aching emptiness and the only recourse was to drown his sorrows. He didn't do that anymore, but he could appreciate that it was a slippery slope and he was grateful that he'd managed to find his footing before he'd slipped too far.

"After a few such incidents, my grandmother talked her into going to rehab. She completed a thirty-day inpatient program and, when she came home, assured us that she'd turned a corner. A few days later, on what would have been her thirteenth wedding anniversary, she got drunk again."

"Significant dates and special occasions are triggers for a lot of people," he observed.

Serena nodded. "But as much as my grandmother was worried about her daughter's downward spiral, she was even more worried about me. So she packed up all my stuff and brought me to Rust Creek Falls to live with her. And she told my mother that, when she was ready to prove that her daughter was more important than the contents of a bottle, she would be welcome to stay with her, too."

"Sounds like a strong dose of tough love," Bailey remarked.

"It was tough on Grams, too. She wanted to make everything right, but she couldn't fight Amanda's addiction. So she focused her attention and efforts on me. I had sporadic contact with Amanda over the next few years," she confided. "I still feel guilty saying this out loud, but those were some of the most normal—and best—years of my childhood. Maybe it was a little strange that I lived with my grandmother rather than my mother or father, but I had no cause for complaint. I had regular meals and clean clothes, willing help with homework and even a chaperone for occasional school trips."

"I'm glad you had her," Bailey said.

"I was lucky," Serena acknowledged.

He hadn't had the same fortune when he lost his parents. In fact, Matthew and Agnes Baldwin had essentially told their three oldest grandsons to fend for themselves—and allowed their two youngest granddaughters to be adopted, forcing the split of seven children grieving the deaths of their parents.

"Does your grandmother still live in Rust Creek Falls?" he asked Serena now.

She shook her head. "A few years ago, after I'd graduated from college and she was sure my mother's life was back on track, she decided her old bones couldn't handle the cold any longer, and she moved to Arizona." She smiled a little. "It's been good for her. She's taken up golf, plays bridge and does water aerobics—and she's got a new beau."

"You can be happy for her and still miss her," Bailey assured her.

"I do miss her," she admitted. "But I've also realized that I maybe relied on her too much. I don't think the warmer climate was her only reason for leaving Rust Creek Falls. I think she wanted me to stand on my own two feet—not to see *if* I could, but to show me *that* I could. Because she always had a lot more confidence in me than I had in myself."

"I'd say her faith was well-founded."

"My grandmother's a wise woman," she acknowledged. "She's the one who taught me to focus on my happy memories of the holidays."

"That couldn't have been easy," he noted. In fact, considering how much heartache she'd endured—and so much of it focused around this time of year—he might have found the task impossible.

"It took me a while to look past all the bad stuff and remember the good stuff," she confided to him. "Although we only celebrated three Christmases together with Mimi, those were the happiest Christmases of my life. Every memory of my sister is a happy memory, and she loved everything about Christmas."

"You're an amazing woman, Serena Langley."

"I'm not sure about that," she said. "But focusing on the happy memories is the one thing—the only thing—I can do that helps me get through. And in remembering Mimi's holiday joy, I've rediscovered my own."

Her outgoing and optimistic demeanor had led him to make certain assumptions about her, but those assumptions couldn't have been more wrong. Not knowing what to say to her now, certain there were no words to express his regrets and sympathy, he merely pulled her closer.

Serena dropped her head back against his shoulder, and when her lips curved a little as she looked up at him, he knew that he was forgiven for what he'd said the other day.

And then his head tipped forward…and his lips brushed against hers.

He hadn't consciously decided to kiss her. Sure, he'd given the idea more than a passing thought. And yeah, he'd wondered if her lips would be as soft as they looked or taste as sweet as he imagined. And maybe, when they'd been dancing at the Presents for Patriots fundraiser, he'd considered breaching the scant distance that separated their mouths.

But he'd resisted the impulse, because he knew that kissing her was a bad idea for a lot of reasons. First, after the breakdown of his marriage, he was wary of any kind of romantic involvement. Second, even if he was looking to get involved, it would be a mistake to hook up with a woman who was both a colleague and friend of his sister-in-law. Third—

He abandoned his mental list in favor of focusing on the moment—and the fact that Serena was kissing him back. And her lips were as soft as they looked, and their taste was even sweeter than he'd imagined.

And he realized that sitting on Owl Rock and kissing Serena was the absolute highlight of his day. His week. His month. Possibly even his whole year.

He lifted a hand to cup the back of her head, his fingers diving through silky strands of hair, tilting her head so that he could deepen the kiss. She didn't protest when his tongue slid between her lips but met it with her own.

He wrapped his other arm around her middle and dragged her onto his lap. Her arms lifted to his shoulders. Her legs wrapped around his waist. He wanted to touch her; he wanted his hands on her bare skin. But they were outside in Montana in December, which meant there were at least a half dozen layers of clothing and outerwear between them.

After a while—two minutes? Ten? He didn't know,

he'd lost all track of time while he was kissing her—she drew her mouth away from his.

"Maybe we should...slow things down," she suggested a little breathlessly.

He took a moment to draw the sharp cold air into his own lungs. "That would probably be the smart thing to do," he agreed. "But it's not what I want to do."

"Right now, it's not what I want, either," she admitted. "But I haven't had much success with romantic relationships and I don't want to jeopardize our fledgling friendship by trying to turn it into something more."

"I suck at relationships, too," he told her. "I'm not sure I'm much better at friendships."

"You seem to be doing okay so far."

He appreciated the vote of confidence, but he remained dubious. "You think we're friends?"

"I think we could be," she said.

"Hmm," he said, considering.

"Unless you have so many friends that you don't want another one?"

He chuckled softly. "Before I came back to Rust Creek Falls last year, I'd been gone for a dozen years and lost touch with not just my family but my friends."

"It was after your parents were killed that you left town, wasn't it?"

The surprise he felt must have been reflected in his expression, because she explained, "I've worked with Annie for almost three years, and when Dan came back—just a few months before you did—it sent her whole life into a tailspin. And sometimes, if we were on break together, she'd talk to me about it."

"So how much of the story do you know?" he wondered.

"I don't know all the details—and most of those that I do know are from her perspective. Essentially that you, Luke and Dan were of legal age, and your grandparents decided that you were able to take care of yourselves so they didn't have to."

He nodded. "That about sums it up," he agreed. "What really sucks is that we all assumed that Sunshine Farm would be lost. Our parents struggled for a lot of years and without my dad around to run the ranch, we couldn't imagine making a go of it. If we'd known that the mortgage was insured, we might have stayed." Then he shook his head. "Who am I kidding? We wouldn't have stayed. We couldn't have. Not after that night."

That night was the night both of his parents had been killed by a drunk driver. And the events of that night continued to haunt him and would undoubtedly do so forever.

"Look," Serena said, holding out a hand to catch a delicate flake on her palm. "It's snowing."

"So it is," he agreed, noting the fluffy flakes falling from the sky. "It's also getting colder by the minute."

"I know. I can't feel my butt anymore."

"I could feel it for you," he suggested, in an obvious effort to lighten the mood.

"I appreciate the offer, but maybe another time," she said, as she untangled her legs and rose to her feet. "We should be heading back now, anyway."

"You're probably right," he agreed, understanding only too well that driving conditions on the mountain roads could turn hazardous quickly.

But as they turned back toward the trail, he asked, "Did Owl Rock work its magic for you today?"

She nodded. "It's always so peaceful up here. But even better today was having someone to talk to."

"Glad to be of service," he told her.

At the top of the narrow trail, Bailey insisted on taking the lead so that he could check for slippery patches on the descent. But he also took her hand, to ensure she didn't fall behind.

The weather in Montana wasn't just unpredictable, it could change fast—and had done so while they were up at Owl Rock. By the time they got back to her vehicle, she had to pull her snow brush out to clear off her windows.

"You get in," Bailey instructed. "I'll take care of this."

She didn't object to that but handed him the brush and slid in behind the wheel, turning on the engine and cranking up the heat.

A few minutes later, Bailey put the brush away and took his seat on the passenger side.

"I'm happy to drive, if you want," he told her.

Her only response was to shift into Drive and pull out of the gravel lot.

At the midway point of their return journey, Bailey said, "Since we almost go right past Wings To Go on our way back to the school, why don't we stop in there to grab some dinner?"

"I can't," Serena said regretfully. "I've got animals waiting to be fed at home."

"Do you have dinner waiting, too?"

She shook her head. "I wasn't thinking that far ahead when I left home this morning."

"Do you like wings?"

"Who doesn't?"

"Well, here's an interesting fact about Wings To Go,"

he said. "Customers can actually place an order...and then take it away from the restaurant."

"No kidding," she said, sounding bemused. "I'll bet that's what the To Go part of the name refers to."

"And with that in mind, here's plan B," he said. "After you take me back to my truck and go home to feed your animals, I'll pick up wings and bring them over to feed us. What do you think of that plan?"

"I think I like that plan," she agreed. "Especially if it includes honey-barbecue wings."

After dropping Bailey off at his truck in the elementary school parking lot, Serena hurried home. Not just because she knew Marvin, Molly and Max would be waiting for her, but because she wanted to tidy up a little before Bailey showed up. She didn't think her apartment was a mess, but earlier in the day she'd been so focused on the anticipation of seeing Bailey that she honestly couldn't remember if she'd left her lunch dishes in the sink or her pajamas on the floor in the bathroom.

As she raced around the apartment, tidying a stack of mail on the counter, wiping crumbs—and a smudge of something sticky—off the table and pushing the Swiffer around, Marvin chased after her, delighted with what he assumed was a new game.

"It's not a game, it's housework," she told him. "And I do this at least once a week."

But she didn't usually clean at such a frantic pace, and Marvin refused to believe she wasn't playing with him.

She gave him his dinner, hoping the food would take his attention away from the Swiffer. The diversion worked—for the whole two minutes that it took him to empty his bowl. But she finished putting her apartment in order—and even managed to run a brush through her hair and dab on some lip gloss before she saw Bailey's truck pull into one of the designated visitor parking spots at the back of the building.

Marvin raced toward the door a full half minute before the bell rang, having been alerted to the presence of a visitor by the sound of feet climbing the stairs. Though he could easily have gone through the doggy door to greet the newcomer, Serena had been strict in his training to ensure his safety and that of her guests. So now he waited in eager anticipation, his entire back end wagging.

"No jumping," she admonished firmly as she opened the door.

Bailey's eyes skimmed over her, a slow perusal from the top of her head to the thick wool socks on her feet. "I wasn't planning on jumping," he drawled. "But I can't deny that the idea is intriguing."

"Ha ha," she said, taking the bag from his hands so that he could remove his boots.

As he reached down to unfasten the laces, Marvin whimpered.

"You must be Marvin," Bailey said, and offered his hand for the dog to sniff.

Marvin sniffed, then licked, then shoved his snout into the visitor's palm. Bailey chuckled and scratched the dog's chin.

Serena set plates and napkins on the table. "What can I get you to drink? I've got cola, root beer, real beer, milk or water."

"Cola sounds good," he said.

"Glass or can?"

"Can works."

She retrieved two cans from the fridge and set them on the table, then glanced back at the entranceway to discover that Bailey was sitting on the tile floor with Marvin sprawled across his lap. The dog's belly was exposed and his tongue lolled out of his mouth as his new best friend gave him a vigorous belly rub.

She shook her head. "Such an attention whore."

"I am not," Bailey denied.

"I was referring to the dog."

"Oh." He gave Marvin a couple more rubs, then carefully heaved the dog off his lap and stood up. He made his way into the kitchen and washed his hands at the sink. Marvin kept pace with him, practically glued to his shin.

"I'm the one who feeds you," Serena felt compelled to remind her canine companion.

Marvin wagged his whole body, but he didn't move away from Bailey.

And when Bailey took a seat at the table, Marvin settled at his feet.

"I feel like I talked your ear off when we were up at Owl Rock today," Serena said as she used the tongs to transfer several wings from the box to her plate. "But the truth is, I don't often talk about my sister or her disappearance. In fact, I doubt if more than a handful of people in this town even know what happened before I came to live with my grandmother all those years ago."

"Your secrets are safe with me," he promised.

"I'm not worried," she said. "But I'm thinking that it's your turn to tell me your life story."

"There's not much to tell." He took the tongs she offered, then proceeded to pick out half a dozen wings. "And you already know the highlights."

"I know why you went away, but I don't know anything about where you went or what you did when you left Rust Creek Falls."

"Me, Luke and Danny headed to Wyoming together and found work on a big spread in Cheyenne. We stayed there for about six months together before we parted ways."

"Why?" she wondered aloud.

He shrugged. "Maybe because we had different goals and ambitions. Or maybe because we shared the same guilt and regrets."

She picked a piece of meat off the bone. "Where did you go after Cheyenne?"

"Jackson Hole for a while, then Newcastle and Douglas."

"So you stayed in Wyoming?"

"For a few years," he acknowledged. "Then I made my way to New Mexico."

"That was quite a move," she remarked.

He licked honey-barbecue sauce off his thumb. "There was a girl," he admitted.

"Ahh, I should have guessed."

He shook his head. "I promise you, I'm not in the habit of chasing women halfway across the country. That was the first—and absolute last—time."

"Putting aside the fact that New Mexico isn't really across the county but directly south of Wyoming, she must have been someone really special."

"Actually, she was my wife."

Chapter Seven

Wife?

Serena nearly choked on a mouthful of cola.

Bailey watched her cough and sputter, his brow furrowed with concern. "Are you okay?"

"Yeah." She coughed again. "I'm fine." She took a careful sip of her soda. "I didn't realize you'd been married."

"Only because I was young and foolish enough to believe that love conquers all."

"I'm sorry it didn't work out," she said. "But at least you were willing to take a chance on love."

"I was young and foolish," he said again.

"And now you're old and wise?" she teased.

"Older and wiser, anyway. No way am I ever going to make that mistake again."

"You don't believe in love anymore?"

"I don't know," he said. "I mean, each of my brothers

and even my sister Bella seems to have found a forever match, so maybe it's just me. Maybe I'm not capable of loving somebody that way."

"You must have loved your wife."

"I thought I did," he acknowledged. "But in the end, whatever I felt for her wasn't enough."

"It takes two people to make a relationship work," she pointed out. "Or allow it to fail."

"So it would seem," he agreed.

"Then again—" she picked up another wing "—what do I know?"

"You've never been in love?"

She shook her head. "The longest relationship I've ever had is with Molly."

His brows lifted. "Molly?"

"My cat," she reminded him.

"That's right. You've got Marvin, Molly and…"

"Max," she supplied.

"So where are Molly and Max?"

"Hiding," she admitted. "They're both leery of strangers. And—" she glanced at the bulldog under the table "—*not* attention whores."

"Why all the animals?" he wondered aloud.

She shrugged. "I've always loved animals."

"That would explain why you became a vet tech," he commented. "Not why you've turned your home into a mini animal shelter."

"And…they love me back. Unconditionally."

"That's something a lot of human beings have a problem with," he said.

"Yeah. Sometimes even the ones who are supposed to love you."

"Like your dad," he guessed. "And my grandparents."

She nodded. "All my animals want from me is a roof over their heads, food in their bowls, some interaction and playtime, and the occasional lazy Sunday morning snuggle in bed."

"They sleep with you?"

"No. They have their own beds, but sometimes, if I'm feeling lazy and slip back between the covers after feeding them their breakfast, they'll follow me into the bedroom and want to cuddle with me."

"Even the cat?"

She nodded. "Molly is a surprisingly affectionate feline at times—at least with me," she clarified. "And Max. She absolutely adores the bunny. She's less fond of strangers."

"Marvin doesn't consider me a stranger," he noted.

"Marvin is forever devoted to anyone who gives him an ear scratch or belly rub. Or *t-r-e-a-t-s*," she said, purposely spelling the word so that the dog wouldn't get excited about the possibility of getting one. "Which reminds me—I guess my bid didn't win the Canine Christmas basket at the silent auction?"

Bailey shook his head. "You were outbid by Lissa Christensen."

"That's good for Presents for Patriots, but sad for Marvin," she said.

"And then Lissa Christensen was outbid by me."

"*You* bought the basket?"

He nodded.

"Why?"

"Because I know how much you wanted it," he said.

"You bought it for me?"

"Well, for Marvin, actually."

"That was really sweet," she said, then laughed when

he winced. "How much do I owe you? I don't know how much cash I have, but I could write you a check."

"You're not writing me a check," he protested.

"Worried it might bounce?"

He shook his head. "I mean you're not paying for the basket."

"But you bought it for my dog."

"That's right," he said. "*I* bought it for you to give to him."

"Then I'll say thank you, and check Marvin's name off my shopping list."

"Yeah, I guess I should probably get started on mine," he acknowledged.

"You haven't even started your shopping yet?"

"It's only December 4," he pointed out.

"No," she denied. "It's *already* December 4."

"To-may-to, to-mah-to," he said.

"You'll be saying something different when you're fighting the frantic and desperate masses of last-minute shoppers at the mall on Christmas Eve."

"I won't wait until Christmas Eve. Probably."

She shook her head despairingly. "I'm planning to go into Kalispell to do some shopping on Saturday," she told him. "You're welcome to come with me, if you want."

"I guess it wouldn't hurt to get a head start this year."

"You'll be one of the early birds," she said dryly.

Bailey just grinned. Then he said, "Seriously though, I appreciate your offer to let me tag along."

"It's not a problem," she assured him. "But you're not allowed to complain if we're gone most of the day."

"I can't make any promises there," he said.

"Then I can't promise that you'll get a ride back home again."

* * *

When all the wing bones had been picked clean and the dishes cleared away, Bailey thanked Serena for her hospitality and made his way to the door.

He could have come up with an excuse to linger; he could have requested a cup of coffee before he hit the road or offered to take Marvin for a walk or asked her to turn on the TV to check the score of the game—because there was always a game of some sort playing—and then allowed himself to get caught up in the action on the screen for a while. But when he realized that he was searching for a reason to stay, he knew it was time to go. Because the more time he spent with Serena, the more he wanted to be with her, and that was a dangerous desire.

Besides, he was going to see her again on Saturday.

Yeah, Saturday was four days away, but maybe a little space and time was what he needed to give himself some perspective and remember that he wasn't going to get involved.

Not with Serena. Not with anyone. Not ever again.

But when she walked him to the door, he was more than a little tempted to kiss her goodbye.

But she'd asked him to slow things down. She wanted to be *friends*. He had his doubts about that possibility—mostly because he really wanted to get her naked, and in his experience, lust tended to get in the way of friendship—but he decided to try it her way for a while.

So he didn't kiss her goodbye, but the memory of the kiss they'd shared at Owl Rock teased his mind and heated his body as he climbed into his cold truck and drove away.

But before he could head back to Sunshine Farm, he had one more stop to make. He'd promised to return the costumes to Annie after the visit to the elementary school—a promise he'd nearly forgotten until he spotted the bulky bags in the back seat.

"There he is," Annie said when she responded to his knock on the door.

"Who is it?" Janie asked from somewhere inside the house.

"Uncle Grooge," her mother responded.

"Bah, humbug," Bailey said, playing along as he held out the costume bags, and heard Janie giggle.

"Hmm…" Annie took the bags and stepped away from the door so he could enter. "That doesn't sound quite as cynical as it did a few days ago. Maybe this suit has magic powers."

He ignored her comment to focus on his niece, seated at the table with her schoolbooks open in front of her. "Homework?" he guessed.

She nodded. "Science," she said, her expression and her tone reflecting displeasure. "Dad was helping me, but Mom ordered him to go rest when you showed up."

"I ordered him to rest because he's still recuperating," Annie said in a no-nonsense mom voice.

"Oh, right."

The exchange struck Bailey as a little odd, but his sister-in-law didn't pause long enough for him to ponder it.

"Considering that school let out almost five hours ago, I hope you're not just getting back from the Santa gig now," she remarked.

"Of course not. Me and Serena went for a drive afterward," he admitted. "And then we decided to get some dinner."

"Like a date?" Janie asked.

"No," he immediately replied.

"Sounds like a date to me," his niece insisted.

"What do you know about dating?" he asked her.

"Nothing," she said with a sigh. "Nothing at all."

"Homework," Annie said, in an effort to redirect her daughter's attention. Then to Bailey, "But your non-date with Serena is interesting."

"What's so interesting about it?" he challenged.

"Just that, as far as I know, you haven't dated anyone since you came back to Rust Creek Falls."

"And I'm not dating anyone now," he said firmly.

His sister-in-law sighed. "Well, thank you again for filling in for your brother today."

"How's he doing?"

"Much better. In fact, he's in the living room watching TV if you want to say hi."

So Bailey went through to the living room, where his brother was stretched out on the sofa. Shifting his gaze to the screen, he saw that, sure enough, there was a game on.

"Hey," Dan said, clicking the mute button on the remote. "How'd it go today?"

"Pretty good," Bailey allowed.

"Janie said you were a very believable Santa Claus."

"Ho ho ho," he said, affecting the persona.

Dan nodded. "Not bad for a Grooge."

Bailey just shook his head.

"Seriously though, I appreciate you filling in for me again," his brother said.

"It wasn't really that big a deal," Bailey said.

"It was to me. For too many years, when I was living on my own, I forgot what it meant to be part of a family, to know there were people I could count on to help me out."

"I'm sorry I bailed on you all those years ago."

Dan shook his head. "That's not what I'm saying."

"I'm sorry anyway."

"We all made mistakes. And it really did mean the world to me that you found your way back to Rust Creek Falls for my wedding."

"That was just unfortunate timing on my part," Bailey said, not entirely joking.

"So you've said—on more than one occasion," his brother acknowledged dryly.

"But you and Annie…you really do work," he said. "Not just as a couple but a family."

"Coming home was the best thing I ever did," Dan said. "I only wish I'd found the courage to do so a lot sooner—then maybe I wouldn't have missed the first eleven years of Janie's life."

Yeah, it sucked that his brother had lost so much time with his daughter. And though Bailey didn't doubt that they'd hit some rough spots as they got to know one another, they were growing closer every day.

If Dan held on to any resentment because his daughter also continued to be close to Hank Harlow, who'd raised her as his own for the first decade of her life—even after divorcing Annie—he was smart enough not to show it. And if Bailey could believe his brother, Dan was sincerely grateful that Hank had been there for Janie during those years that her biological father wasn't.

"I'm hoping that it won't take too much longer for you to figure out that coming home was the best thing you ever did, too," Dan said.

Bailey shrugged, deliberately noncommittal.

When he'd shown up in Rust Creek Falls the previous December, he'd had no intention of staying for any length of time. He only wanted to touch base with his siblings before he moved on again. Almost twelve months later, he was still in town, still trying to figure out a plan for his own life.

He should be on his way, but things felt…unfinished. Though he'd reconnected with all of his brothers and two of his sisters, he knew that there would be a void in all their lives until Liza was found.

Bella's husband, Hudson Jones, had willingly bankrolled the search for his wife's missing siblings. Of course, Hudson had all kinds of money to throw around and there was no doubt the multimillionaire would do anything for Bella. In fact, it was the bigshot PI he'd hired—David Bradford—who'd managed to track down their brother Luke in Cheyenne, notwithstanding the fact that a payroll glitch had caused him to be working under the name Lee Stanton at the time.

Bailey had come back to Rust Creek Falls of his own volition a few weeks after Luke. But while the PI continued to look for their youngest sister, he'd yet to make any significant progress in that search.

"Anyway," Bailey said, not wanting to dwell on past mistakes or current problems, "I'm glad you've finally kicked back at that virus or flu or whatever knocked you down."

"Not as glad as I am," Dan said. "I don't mind staying in bed all day if my beautiful wife is there with me, but fever and chills sure can put a damper on a man's enjoyment between the sheets."

Bailey held up a hand. "I really don't want to hear about your bedroom activities."

"You're just jealous that I have a love life," Dan teased.

Maybe he was envious—not so much of his brother's bedroom activities, but the obvious and deep connection he shared with both his wife and newfound daughter. Dan was part of a family again, and thriving in the roles of husband and father.

Dan and Annie had fallen in love when they were teenagers, and somehow their love had survived not only a dozen years apart but Annie's marriage to another man during that time. Bailey knew there had been issues for them to work through when Dan finally returned to Rust Creek Falls—and a lot of hurts to be forgiven—and he wondered what it would be like to share that kind of relationship with someone.

Bailey had thought he was in love with Emily and wanted to build a life with her, but it quickly became apparent that he and his wife had very different ideas for their future together. He'd taken a chance and he'd blown it. He had no desire to open up his heart and let it be kicked around again.

But even as he reminded himself of that fact, he found his thoughts drifting again, and an image of Serena formed in his mind, tugged at his heart. She was obviously a lot stronger and braver than he was. She'd suffered the loss of her sister and subsequent breakup of her family, and somehow she still managed to greet each day with a smile on her face. Not only that, but she actually looked forward to celebrating the Christmas season and sharing her joy with others—including him.

"So you didn't mind partnering with Serena Langley?" Dan asked, breaking into Bailey's thoughts.

"No, it was fine," he said cautiously.

"Just fine?"

"What do you want me to say?"

His brother shrugged. "I just wondered what's going on with the two of you."

"*You* wondered what's going on?"

"Okay, Annie was wondering," Dan admitted. "You know she and Serena are friends as well as coworkers."

"I do know," Bailey confirmed. "And if your wife wants to know what's going on, maybe she should ask her friend and coworker."

"Believe me, I wouldn't be hassling you if Annie had had any success with her inquiries."

"Maybe Serena hasn't told her anything because there's nothing to tell," Bailey suggested.

"Luke said you danced with her at the fund-raiser— and that sparks were flying."

"Maybe between him and Eva," he countered. "But it's nice to know that my brothers have nothing better to do than gossip about me."

"Since you don't tell us anything, it's the only way we can keep up with what's going on in your life."

He wanted to protest that there was nothing to share, but then he remembered the kiss. That kiss had definitely been something, and it made him want more. A lot more.

But that wasn't something he had any intention of sharing with his brother for Dan to then share with the rest of the family.

Even if it was kind of nice to be reunited with his siblings and to know that they cared.

* * *

Serena was waiting for Bailey to pick her up for their shopping trip Saturday morning when her phone rang. She intended to let the call go to voice mail, but a quick glance at the display identified the caller as Janet Carswell, causing her to snatch up the receiver.

"Hi, Grams."

"I got your Christmas card in the mail yesterday," her grandmother said. "The pretty winter scene on the front didn't make me miss the snow, but I do miss you."

"I miss you, too," Serena told her.

"How is everything in Rust Creek Falls?"

"Cold and snowy," she said.

"Nothing new?" her grandmother prompted.

"Well, I saw my mom last week."

"How is she?" Grams asked cautiously.

"Good," Serena said, and proceeded to fill her grandmother in on the conversation she'd had with her mother—and on Amanda's new boyfriend.

"I'm glad to hear that my daughter's doing well," Grams said. "But I really want to know what's been going on with my granddaughter and her new man."

"You've been talking to Melba Strickland," she guessed.

"Well, someone needs to keep me up to date with the happenings in Rust Creek Falls."

"I talk to you every week," Serena reminded her grandmother.

"But you always censor the good stuff."

She chuckled. "You only think I do. The truth is, there isn't any good stuff to censor."

"Maybe that's why I worry about you, Rena."

"You don't need to worry about me—I'm doing just fine," she assured her.

"You're alone," Grams said in a gentle tone.

"Hardly."

"Your pets don't count."

"Don't tell them that," Serena cautioned.

Grams sighed. "You've got so much love to give, but you're afraid to give it."

"I'm not afraid."

"It's understandable." Her grandmother forged ahead as if Serena hadn't spoken. "You've been hurt, and deeply, by so many people who were supposed to love you."

"You're the one who always said that whatever doesn't kill us makes us stronger."

"I was paraphrasing Nietzsche," Grams confessed.

"Still, I think there's a lot of truth in that statement."

"And I think you're one of the strongest women I know," her grandmother said. "With one of the softest hearts. But you don't let many people into your heart."

"I let plenty of people into my heart."

"You know what I mean," Grams chided. "You've hardly dated anyone since you broke up with Bobby Ray."

It was true. It was also true that she never should have let herself fall for a man who everyone knew was still carrying a torch for his high school girlfriend— notwithstanding the fact that she'd moved on and moved away and was now married to someone else.

But Serena had a habit of falling for men who were emotionally unavailable. Before Bobby Ray Ellis, she'd dated Howard Shelton, a widower with a gorgeous lab-radoodle. Before Howard, she'd gone out with Kevin

Nolan, an attorney from Kalispell who'd been so focused on his billable hours he'd rarely had any time left for her.

And since she was thinking about time, she glanced at the clock and realized she didn't have much before Bailey was due to arrive.

"I've gotta go, Grams, but I'll call you next week," she promised.

As she hung up the phone, she couldn't help but wonder if she was making the same mistake with Bailey that she'd made so many times previously.

She knew that he had an ex-wife, but she didn't know any other details about his marriage or why it had ended. Was he still in love with the woman he'd married? Was her growing infatuation with the sexy cowboy going to end with more heartache?

Possibly…and yet, she couldn't stop her heart from doing a happy little dance when she saw Bailey's truck pull up in front of her building now.

Chapter Eight

Bailey had called Serena on Friday night to confirm their plans for shopping the next day—and to offer to drive. She'd teasingly accused him of being worried that she might actually leave him at the mall, but she didn't oppose his plan. She did, however, request a slight detour when he picked her up Saturday morning.

"I have to stop at Crawford's before we head out," she told him, as she buckled her seat belt.

"You don't think that whatever you need from the general store could be picked up in Kalispell?"

"No, because what I need is a tag from the Tree of Hope."

He looked at her blankly. "The what?"

"The Tree of Hope," she said again. "It was Nina's idea," she said, referring to the woman who'd been born a Crawford but was now married to Dallas Traub, with whom she was raising his three sons and her daughter. "It started about five years ago, when families were struggling to recover from the catastrophic flooding that summer, and so many people had nothing left to put presents under a Christmas tree—if they even had a Christmas tree."

She went on to explain that gift tags marked with the age and gender of the intended recipient were hung on the branches of a decorated tree inside Crawford's General Store. Customers would choose one or more of the tags, purchase appropriate gifts and return them to the store with the tags. Then Nina—and any other volunteers that she managed to recruit—would wrap and deliver the gifts.

"Rust Creek Falls really does take care of its own," Bailey noted, pulling into a parking spot near the General Store.

"Sometimes we need a little help from our neighbors," Serena acknowledged, unbuckling her belt. "After the flood, we were fortunate that a lot of folks from Thunder Canyon came to town to help with the cleanup and rebuild."

"That's the second time you've mentioned a flood," he observed as he opened her door for her.

"I guess the news didn't make its way down to New Mexico."

"I guess not," he confirmed.

"It was five years ago, around the Fourth of July. There were torrential rains in the area, and a lot of homes were ruined by the floods. Several public buildings were destroyed, the Commercial Street Bridge was washed away, the Main Street Bridge was impassable, and Hunter McGee, the former mayor, died of a heart attack after a tree crushed the front of his car. That led to a battle between Collin Traub and Nate Crawford to fill the vacant office which, you could probably guess, Collin won, as he's still the mayor today."

"I had no idea about any of this," Bailey confessed.

"The devastation was unlike anything I've ever seen," she told him. "Afterward everyone pitched in to help with the cleanup and rebuild, but it still took months. And that," she said, passing through the door he held open for her and entering the store, "is the not-so-short story about the floods that led to the creation of the Tree of Hope."

Bailey followed Serena to the holiday display and the tree that appeared to be empty of tags. On closer inspection, he found two. "There are only a couple of tags left."

"It is only a couple of weeks until Christmas," she pointed out.

He reached for the nearest tag and removed it from the branch to read the information on the back. "Male, seventy-two-years, diabetic, shoe size ten."

"There are some older residents in town who don't have any family around to celebrate with, so Nina added them to the Tree of Hope to ensure they aren't forgotten during the holidays."

"Do you think you can help me find a gift for a seventy-two-year-old diabetic man who wears a size ten?"

"Sugar-free candy and warm slippers," she immediately suggested.

He nodded and held on to the tag.

Serena took the last one from the tree.

"What did you get?" he asked.

"Seven-year-old boy." She approached Natalie Craw-ford, who was organizing a display of building block sets nearby. "Did Nina happen to put a tag from the Tree of Hope aside for me?"

"Oh, hi, Serena," Natalie said. "And yes, she did." She finished stacking the boxes in her hand, then moved toward the cash register. Opening a drawer beneath the counter, she retrieved a tag that had been stored there for safekeeping. "Here you go."

"Thanks." Serena slid both tags into the side pocket of her handbag, then turned back to Bailey. "Now we can go."

"Are you going to tell me what that was about?" Bailey asked, when they were back in his truck and en route to Kalispell.

"You mean the tag that Natalie gave me?" Serena guessed.

He nodded.

"If there's a three-year-old girl who needs a gift, Nina will put that tag aside for me," she confided. "I know it's silly, but—"

"No," he interjected. "It's not silly at all. It's a good way to remember your sister at the holidays, at least until you find her again."

She was grateful for his understanding—and his confident assertion that she would one day be reunited with her sister. But she'd been hoping for exactly that for so long, she knew she had to accept the possibility that it might never happen. "*If* I ever do," she clarified.

"I didn't think I'd ever come back to Rust Creek Falls," he reminded her. "But here I am."

"And your family's thrilled to have you home," she said.

"I don't know about that, but it has been good to reconnect with most of my siblings. I haven't been able to spend much time with Dana, of course, because she's still living in Oregon with her adoptive family," he noted. "And we still don't know where Liza is, though Hudson's private investigator insists he's making progress."

"You don't believe him?"

He shrugged. "I think if I were a PI with a client whose pockets were as deep as Bella's husband's, I'd want to stay on his payroll, too."

"I don't think Hudson Jones is foolish enough to pay someone without results," she told him.

"You're probably right," he acknowledged. "But I know Bella would feel a lot better if she actually saw results, preferably in the form of our youngest sister."

"I'm sure you'll *all* feel better when you find Liza," she said, as he pulled into the parking lot of the shopping mall. "But right now, you need to focus on finding an empty parking spot."

"I hate Christmas shopping," Bailey announced several hours later as he followed Serena up to her apartment, his arms heavy with the weight of the bags he carried.

"What is it that you hate?" she asked, as she slid her key into the lock. "The festive decorations? The seasonal music? The shopkeepers wishing you happy holidays?"

"The crazy drivers racing for limited parking spots, the desperate shoppers pawing through boxes of toys and piles of clothes, then pressing toward the cash registers like teenage girls rushing the stage at a Justin Bieber concert."

She smiled at the image painted by his words as she carefully sidestepped an excited Marvin, who seemed determined to get tangled up in her feet.

"The key," she told him, "is not to let yourself get caught up in the chaos."

"Easy to say, not so easy to do when the chaos is all around."

"But you can't deny it was a successful day."

He unloaded his shopping bags on the floor, then dropped to his knees to give Marvin some of the attention he was begging for. "Except that apparently I now have to wrap all that stuff."

"Yes, you do," she confirmed. "But you'll see that I already have a wrapping station set up on the table, so you can get started while I heat up the sauce and put a pot of water on to boil for the pasta."

"Or I could make the spaghetti and you could do the wrapping?" he suggested as an alternative.

She shook her head. "I'll help you *after* dinner."

Marvin, even in a fog of canine euphoria induced by Bailey's belly rub, recognized that last word and immediately scrambled to his feet and raced over to his bowl.

Bailey chuckled.

"Yes, it's almost time for your dinner, too," she assured the eager bulldog. "Although I doubt you've worked up much of an appetite, hanging around inside the apartment all day."

"He could probably use some exercise," Bailey decided. "Do you want me to take him out for a walk before dinner?"

Poor Marvin didn't know whether to lie down and

feign exhaustion—his usual response to hearing the word *walk*—or remain seated by his bowl in anticipation of his *dinner*.

Serena shook her head. "If you'd really rather *w-a-l-k* the dog than wrap presents, his leash and sweater are on the hook by the door."

"Sweater?" he echoed dubiously.

"It's December, and his short hair doesn't do much to keep him warm."

Of course, Marvin hated the idea of the sweater as much as Bailey did, but with Serena's help, they managed to get it over the dog's head and his front legs through the appropriate holes.

When Serena returned to the kitchen to stir the sauce, Bailey clipped the leash onto his collar and said, "Let's go."

But Marvin did not want to go. In fact, he sat stubbornly on his butt and refused to move, even with Bailey tugging on the leash.

"I think your dog's broken," he said to Serena.

"He's not broken, he just hates the snow."

"You could have told me that when I first offered to take him out," he noted.

"I could have," she agreed, making no effort to hide her amusement. "But he really does need the exercise."

"Did you hear that, Marvin? You need the exercise."

Marvin dropped his head, as if ashamed, but his butt remained firmly planted on the floor.

So Bailey bent down and picked him up.

"Jeez, he's gotta weigh at least fifty pounds."

"Fifty-five at his last checkup," Serena told him.

"Well, at least I'll get some exercise hauling him

down the stairs." Then to Marvin, he said, "But when we hit street level, your paws are on the ground."

Whether or not Marvin understood any of that, Bailey had no idea, but for now, the dog snuggled into the crook of his arm to enjoy the ride.

Serena held up her end of the bargain.

After Bailey and Marvin returned from their walk and the humans and animals had eaten, she helped him wrap the presents he'd bought.

Their efforts were occasionally impeded by her pets. Molly's curiosity about Bailey finally proved stronger than her wariness of strangers, and she ventured out from hiding to jump from chair to chair—and occasionally even onto the table—and knock various items onto the ground. Max somehow got tangled up in a length of curling ribbon, but after Serena untangled him, he mostly stayed out of the way, content to nibble on an empty wrapping paper tube. Marvin was the worst offender. Despite his pre-dinner walk with Bailey—who assured her that yes, he did make the dog walk—he remained full of energy and determined to cause mischief.

When Bailey folded the sweater he'd chosen for Bella and positioned it in the center of the paper he'd already cut, Serena shook her head.

"What?" he asked.

"You need a box."

"Why?"

"Because clothing should always go in a box—and because boxes are easier to wrap," she explained.

"You didn't make me put the pj's I bought for the triplets in boxes."

"Because you want kids' presents to be easy to open," she explained.

"There seem to be an awful lot of rules about gift-wrapping," he noted. "Maybe you should write them down for me."

She selected an appropriate-size box from her stock, lined it with tissue, refolded the sweater—after removing the price tag—laid it inside the box, closed the lid and handed it back to him.

He wrapped the paper around the box and fastened it with a piece of tape.

Serena picked up the gift she'd finished wrapping and looked beneath it, then under the table. "Did you take that bow?"

"What bow?"

"I had a green bow that I was going to put on this one."

"You have a whole box of bows," he pointed out.

"And I picked a green one out of the box and set it on the table right here," she said, indicating the spot. Then a movement caught her eye and she sighed. "Molly."

Bailey glanced over to see the cat in the middle of the living room, batting the missing bow around the floor.

Serena stepped away from the table just as Marvin decided to race ahead of her, knocking her off balance. Bailey instinctively reached for her—his arms wrapping around her and hauling her against him.

"Sorry." Her cheeks burned with embarrassment over her clumsiness, and her breasts—crushed against his chest now—tingled with awareness and arousal.

"I'm not," he said huskily, his arms still around her.

Then he lowered his head and touched his lips to hers.

Maybe she should have resisted the seductive pressure and the intoxicating flavor of his kiss. But the moment his mouth made contact with hers, her only thoughts were:

Yes.

This.

And, *More.*

He gave her more.

Parting her lips with his tongue, he deepened the kiss. He slid his hands down her back, then beneath the hem of her sweater. She shivered as his callused palms moved over her bare skin, an instinctive reaction that caused her breasts to rub against his hard chest, sending arrows of pleasure from her peaked nipples to her core.

He nibbled playfully on her lips, teased her with strokes of his tongue that made her tremble and ache with want. Her whole body felt hot, so hot she was sure her bones would melt.

And then he abruptly tore his mouth from hers. "What the—"

She drew in a slow deep breath and willed her head to stop spinning. "What?"

He looked down at his feet, where Molly was innocently licking her paw and rubbing it over her face.

But Serena knew better. "Molly," she said reprovingly.

"I think she left her claws in my skin," Bailey said.

"She's not overly fond of strangers," she admitted. "And she is somewhat protective of me."

He reached down to rub his shin. "Well, it's going to take a bigger cat than that to scare me away," he promised.

"Maybe she did us a favor," Serena suggested.

"I'm not feeling grateful."

"But we agreed we weren't going to do this," she reminded him.

"Why was that again?"

"Because neither one of us has had much success with relationships."

"That's true," he acknowledged. "And while I know I'm not so good with the opening up and sharing my emotions part, I promise you that I can muddle through the naked physical activity part."

"You sure do know how to tempt a girl, don't you?"

"Are you saying that you're *not* tempted?"

"I'm more tempted than I should be," she confessed.

"Obviously not tempted enough or we'd be doing it instead of talking about it," he told her.

"You've still got presents to wrap," she reminded him.

"I'd rather unwrap *you*."

The words were accompanied by a heated look that made her knees weak—and her resolve even weaker. She consciously steeled both, picked up a roll of paper and pointed it at him. "Wrap."

Bailey took the paper—and the hint.

He was undeniably disappointed that she'd put on the brakes *again*, but he didn't really blame her. Although they'd spent a lot of time together over the past week, they'd really only known each other a week.

So while Serena went to retrieve the bow Molly had stolen, he tried to focus on measuring and cutting the paper—and not stare at the sexy curve of her butt.

"Tell me about your marriage," she suggested, as she affixed the bow to the wrapped gift.

"Well, that question effectively killed the mood," he noted.

"That wasn't my intention."

"Are you sure? Maybe you want to hear about all the reasons my marriage failed so that you can feel justified in pushing me away."

"I'm not pushing you away," she said. "But I'm also not in the habit of jumping into bed with a man I just met."

"I've told you more about me than a lot of other people know," he confided.

"So why won't you tell me about your marriage?"

He shrugged to indicate his surrender. "What do you want to know?"

"How long were you married?"

"Almost two years. And before you say, 'that's not very long,' believe me, it was long enough for both of us to know it wasn't working."

"I'm sorry. I didn't mean to pry. I didn't realize it was such a touchy subject."

He sighed. "It's not really. I just don't like admitting that I failed—and it was my failure. Because from the day we exchanged vows, I was waiting for everything to fall apart."

"Why were you so sure that it would?"

He shrugged. "Maybe because of what happened to my parents."

"They were killed by a drunk driver."

"Yeah," he acknowledged. "And before that, they were happy together, running the farm and raising a family. And then everything changed."

"Because of a tragic accident."

"Because of *me*," he said.

Serena frowned. "What are you talking about?"

"It was my fault they were on that particular road at that particular time on that particular night."

And he proceeded to tell her about the events of that fateful evening. How his older brother had invited him to go to an out-of-town bar. Although Bailey wasn't yet of legal drinking age, Luke assured him that he knew of a honky-tonk dive that didn't care if their customers had ID so long as they had cash to pay for their beer. Bailey was always happy to tag along with his brother, and when Danny heard they were going out, he refused to be left behind.

The bartender didn't blink when Luke ordered a pitcher of beer and three glasses, which he carried over to the table where his brothers waited. But Danny, always a rule follower, went back to the bar to get a soda.

When Bailey had emptied the pitcher into his glass, Danny suggested that they leave and asked for the keys. Bailey, who had driven, refused, unwilling to let his little brother call the shots. Besides, a trio of young women had just settled around the neighboring table and immediately began to chat up the three cowboys.

"But Danny—devoted to Annie—was even less interested in flirting than in drinking," Bailey continued his explanation. "And when me and Luke refused to heed his warnings and pleas, he went to the pay phone outside and called our parents."

Even after so many years, the memories were clear, the pain sharp. Everything had changed that night. Not just for Bailey, Luke and Danny, but their four younger siblings—and especially their parents.

"They were on their way to get you," Serena realized.

He nodded. "Because I was too stubborn, too arrogant, to let my little brother have the keys."

"And you've been carrying the guilt of that decision for more than a dozen years," she realized.

"Because it was *my* decision."

"It was your decision to hold on to the keys," she acknowledged. "And Danny's decision to call your parents. And their decision to come after you. But the only one responsible for their deaths is the drunk driver who hit them."

"So why can't I let go of the feeling that it's my fault?"

Chapter Nine

Serena understood guilt. She'd carried her fair share of it for a lot of years, and though she'd managed to let go of most of it, there were still moments that she wondered *what if*, still occasions when she felt sharp pangs of regret. So she wasn't going to tell Bailey to "let it go" and expect that he'd be able to do so. She knew it wasn't that easy, but she also knew that holding dark and negative feelings inside only strengthened their hold.

"I don't know," she said. "But I do know that talking about it can sometimes help."

"Like I said, I'm not good with the sharing feelings thing," he reminded her.

"Like anything else, it gets easier with practice," she promised.

"I don't know that that's true," he said. "But I do know that I find it easy to talk to you."

"I'm glad."

"In fact, all that stuff I just told you, about the night my parents were killed…I never told Emily," he confided.

"Why not?" she wondered aloud.

"When she asked about my family, I told her that my parents were dead and my siblings were scattered—though even I didn't know how scattered at that point. And she didn't seem interested in knowing anything more." He shrugged. "Probably because she was so close to her family, and me not having a family simplified our life. There was never any question about where we would spend the holidays—always with her family."

"How were those holidays?" Serena asked carefully.

"Fine," he said.

"Why is it, whenever someone gives that answer, it usually means not fine?"

"No, it was fine," he insisted. "I mean, I never got into the celebrations, but that was my fault. I had disconnected from my family and I didn't know how—or maybe I didn't want—to connect with hers."

"Did that become a source of friction between you?"

He shook his head. "There really wasn't friction between us. There really wasn't much of anything. In fact, I'm not even sure she noticed that I didn't connect with her family."

Now it was Serena's turn to frown. "What do you mean, she didn't notice?"

"She was the youngest of three kids and the only girl, Daddy's little princess and her mother's best friend, doted on by her brothers, close with both of their wives and a favorite aunt to the kids. She was accustomed to being the center of attention and basked in that attention.

"It all came to a head when her youngest brother's wife had their first baby. We, of course, raced over to the hospital to celebrate the big event, and Emily immediately fell in love with her new niece. I braced myself for what I knew was coming next—or what I thought was coming next."

Serena nodded, undoubtedly anticipating the same response that he had.

"She looked at her brother and sister-in-law with their newborn and said, 'That's what I want.' A baby, I guessed, having resigned myself to that eventuality, because after marriage comes kids, right? Well, not always in that order," he acknowledged, responding to his own question. "But she surprised me by shaking her head. 'Yes, I want a baby,' she told me. 'But I want more than that.'

"Of course, I'm not very good at reading between the lines, so I said, 'You mean, two kids?' 'No, I mean the whole package,' she said. 'I want a husband who looks at me the way Matt looks at Tanya. A husband who wants to have a baby with me because he knows that child will be the best of both of us and a bond that ties us together forever.'

"Or words to that effect," Bailey said. "The point was, we both knew that husband wasn't ever going to be me. And that was the end."

"Are things better now?" Serena asked.

"If you consider being divorced better," he said dryly.

"I meant, are you both satisfied with the decision to end your marriage?" she clarified.

"I assume so," he said. "I haven't seen or spoken to her since I filed the divorce papers three years ago."

"You haven't had any contact with her in three *years*?"

"I thought a clean break would be best," he confided.

"I think you need to talk to her," Serena said. "And she probably needs to talk to you."

"Why?"

"For closure."

He scowled. "What does that even mean?"

"It means understanding how and why the relationship ended, so that you can accept that it has ended and move on," she explained patiently.

"We're divorced," Bailey reminded her. "I don't think either of us is under any illusions that the relationship isn't over."

"But have you moved on?" she prompted gently.

"I'd say the fourteen hundred miles I moved proves that I have."

"Have you dated much since the divorce?"

"Not really," he admitted.

"That's a rather vague response."

"Do you want to know the specific number of dates?"

"A range would suffice," she said.

"Then I guess it would be…more than zero and less than two," he confided.

"Only one?" she asked, surprised.

"And only if we're counting this as a date."

"This is a date?"

"Well, it was prearranged, I picked you up, we shared a meal—and a kiss. Doesn't that tick all the boxes?"

"I guess it does," she said, though she still sounded dubious.

"Or we could say it's not a date."

"I don't have a problem with the label," she said. "I'm just not sure how I feel about being your rebound girl."

"It's been three years," he reminded her. "I'm not on the rebound."

"Three years of not dating suggests you might have been more heartbroken over the failure of your marriage than you wanted to admit."

"Or maybe I'd finally accepted that I was so damaged by the mistakes of my past that I had nothing left to offer a woman."

"So what's changed to make you want to start dating again now?" she wondered aloud.

"I met you."

Those three simple words melted Serena's heart.

She was still thinking about them the next day as she slid the last tray of sugar cookies into the oven. Marvin, who'd been snoring in the corner, suddenly picked his head up, his ears twitching.

"Do you hear something?" she asked him.

He responded by leaping off his bed and racing toward the door. Serena wiped her hands on a towel and followed the dog, pulling open the door before she heard a knock.

"This is a surprise," she said, when she saw Bailey standing there.

"I left a message on your voice mail and sent a couple of texts, but you didn't respond, so I thought I'd take a chance and swing by after I ran some errands," he explained.

She stepped away from the door so that he could enter. "That's strange—I didn't hear my phone ring at all." And then a thought occurred to her. "Of course, I didn't plug it in last night, so chances are, the battery's dead."

"Is it okay that I stopped by?"

"Well, Marvin's certainly happy to see you," she said, with a pointed glance at the dog who had rolled over to display his belly.

Bailey chuckled as he bent down to give her pet a one-handed belly scratch. His other hand held up a padded envelope. "When I got home last night, this was on my doorstep."

"What is it?" she asked him.

"Another Christmas present that I need to wrap—and that I'm hoping you'll deliver for me."

She took the envelope and peeked inside. "You got a PKT-79?"

"Two of them," he told her. "For Owen and his friend Riley."

"I can't believe you managed to get your hands on not just one but two of the most popular toys of the season," she said.

"I took your advice," he admitted.

"eBay?"

He nodded.

"I'm not going to ask what these cost you."

"Good, because I'm not going to tell you," he said.

"You do know this wasn't necessary, right?"

"I know," he confirmed. "But it was something I wanted to do."

"It will definitely restore Owen's faith in Santa Claus," Serena murmured.

"I hope so," Bailey said. "Because spending time

with you seems to be restoring my faith in the spirit of the season."

She smiled at that. "All the wrapping stuff is still on the table—I haven't got around to putting it away yet."

"It looks like you've been busy with other things," he said, glancing around the kitchen. Then he lifted his head and sniffed the air. "Cookies?" he asked hopefully.

She nodded. "But nothing as fancy as your sister-in-law makes."

"Cookies don't need to be fancy to taste good," he noted, as he washed his hands at the sink.

She lifted one off the cooling rack and offered it to him.

He picked up a towel to dry his hands, but instead of taking the cookie from her, he lowered his head and bit a piece off.

"Mmm," he said around a mouthful of cookie. "That is good." Then he took another bite, and another, until he was nipping at her fingers, the teasing nibbles making her blood pulse and her knees weak.

She took a step back and wiped her hands down the front of her apron, brushing the crumbs away.

He grinned, no doubt aware of the effect he had on her.

"So," he said, moving over to the table and selecting a roll of wrapping paper, "what are your plans for the rest of the afternoon?"

"The afternoon's almost over," she pointed out to him.

"Okay, what are your plans for tonight?"

The oven timer buzzed and she slid her hands into the padded mitts and retrieved the hot tray of cookies.

"After I get the kitchen cleaned up, I'm going to pop

a big bowl of popcorn and snuggle up on the sofa with Marvin, Molly and Max to watch one of my favorite holiday movies."

"I don't see Molly as a snuggler," he said. "Of course, that might be because I can still feel her claws digging into my leg."

"She really is a sweetheart, once you get to know her."

He snorted, a clear expression of disbelief.

Serena filled the sink with hot soapy water and began washing her dishes.

"You didn't mention any plans for dinner," Bailey commented as he finished taping his present.

"I figured I'd skip dinner, because I've been sampling cookies all day," she confided.

"Or I could go over to the Ace and pick up burgers."

"I really don't need a burger." But now that he'd put the idea in her head, her mouth was watering.

"But do you want one?" Bailey asked, his tone suggesting that he already knew the answer.

"Now I do," she admitted.

"Fries?"

"No," she said firmly.

He chuckled. "Okay, just a burger."

"Cheeseburger," she clarified.

"Anything else?"

She started to shake her head, then paused. "Yeah—why are you doing this?"

"Because I'm hungry?" he suggested.

"I don't just mean the food. I mean why are you here?"

He held up the package he'd finished wrapping.

"You expect me to believe that Eva didn't have wrapping paper?" she asked.

"Okay, so maybe that was just an excuse to see you."

"You shouldn't need an excuse to visit a friend," she told him.

He sighed. "You're still determined to stick me in that friend zone, aren't you?"

"I think friendship is always a good place to start."

To start what? Bailey wanted to know.

But he didn't ask the question. He had no right to demand answers from Serena about the status or direction of their relationship when he hadn't yet figured out what he wanted.

But he knew that he wanted *her*. And the more time he spent with her, the stronger the wanting grew.

A smart man would realize that the key to getting a woman out of his head—and his hormones back in check—would be to put some distance between them. A smart man would have ignored the impulse that drove him into town and then steered him toward her apartment.

Apparently he was not a smart man.

Instead, he picked up burgers—and fries for himself—from the Ace in the Hole. When he got back to Serena's apartment, Marvin went nuts all over again, as if Bailey had been gone for days rather than forty minutes.

Growing up, there had always been a dog or two at Sunshine Farm and several cats hanging around the barn, but Bailey hadn't had a pet since he'd left Rust Creek Falls thirteen years earlier. He hadn't wanted the responsibility. But he was beginning to see how much joy an animal companion could add to life—at least an animal like Marvin. He was still skeptical about Molly and undecided on Max, who mostly kept to himself.

While he was gone, Serena had cleared off the dining room table so they had somewhere to sit and eat. Then Bailey took Marvin outside while she made popcorn and set up the movie.

He hadn't asked what they would be watching— because it really didn't matter. He just wanted to hang out with her, and if that meant watching Bing Crosby and Danny Kaye sing and dance with Rosemary Clooney and Vera-Ellen, so be it.

He was admittedly surprised when, instead of the instrumental notes of a classic Irving Berlin song, the screen filled with an image of an airplane coming in for a landing against the backdrop of an orange sky.

"*Die Hard* is your favorite Christmas movie?" he asked. *"Really?"*

"It's a Christmas classic."

"I don't disagree."

"But you thought I'd want to watch *White Christmas*," she guessed.

"Maybe," he acknowledged, happy to be proven wrong.

He settled on the sofa, the bowl of popcorn in his lap. Marvin scrambled up onto the sofa beside Serena and promptly fell asleep. Max positioned himself by her feet, where he nibbled on a carrot-shaped pet chew. Molly was apparently in hiding, which didn't hurt Bailey's feelings at all and allowed him to focus on the woman seated beside him.

Because he sure as heck couldn't focus on the movie—not with Serena so close. Not when his fingers brushed against hers every time he reached into the bowl. Not when her hair tickled his chin when she tipped her head back. And definitely not when he inhaled her tantalizing scent with every breath he took.

But the woman who was the center of his attention seemed oblivious, her gaze fixed on the movie. When only a few unpopped kernels remained in the bottom of the bowl and the first staccato bursts of gunfire erupted on the screen, Molly sauntered into the living room, the tip of her tail high in the air, flicking side to side.

The cat made her way toward the sofa, then froze, her pale green eyes narrowing to slits. Apparently Bailey was in her spot, and she wasn't happy about it, as evidenced by the way she hissed at him.

"Molly!" Serena scolded.

The cat continued to stare at him, unaffected by the reprimand.

"I'm sorry," Serena apologized. "She's never…okay, not never…but she rarely does that." Her brow furrowed as she considered. "And it's only ever been when I have male company—which isn't very often," she hastened to add.

"She's protective of you," he said, echoing her earlier remark.

She glanced at the snoring lump pressed against her thigh. "Unlike Marvin, who would sell me out for a belly rub."

Bailey chuckled at that.

Serena leaned over to scoop up the cat, holding her so that she was nose to nose with the feline.

"Bailey is our friend," she said, her tone firm but gentle. "And you need to be nice to our friends. No biting, no scratching, no growling, no hissing."

The demon cat gently bumped her nose against Serena's, then rubbed her face against her cheek—and actually purred.

"I told you she can be affectionate," she said.

"Is she really being affectionate?" he wondered aloud. "Or is she just gloating?"

"What?"

"She's cuddling up to you but looking at me, as if to rub it in that she's your favorite."

Serena laughed at that. "Do you feel as if you're in competition with my cat?"

"Well, I can't help but notice that she's a lot closer to you than you've let me get."

"Molly's been with me eleven years," she reminded him. "I've known you just over a week."

"I hope you're not suggesting that it's going to take me another ten years and fifty-one weeks to get to second base."

She shook her head, but a smile tugged at her lips. "I'm suggesting that we should watch the rest of the movie."

So they did. But it seemed all too soon that the credits were rolling on the screen, and Bailey knew it was time to say good-night and head back to his cold empty cabin at Sunshine Farm. His reluctance was a little unnerving. He was accustomed to being on his own and had always been content that way. Now it seemed that he might prefer Serena's company—and possibly even that of her furry menagerie.

"Thanks for letting me hang out with you tonight," he said when she walked him to the door.

"It was fun," she agreed.

"Maybe we could do it again next weekend," he suggested. "But instead of staying in, we could go out for dinner and a movie."

"I'd like that," she said. "Although this time of year, movie nights at the high school generally feature holiday films."

"Or we could drive into Kalispell and see a new release in a real theater."

"That sounds a lot like a date," she mused.

"It does tick all the boxes," he confirmed. "What time do you finish work on Friday?"

"Four o'clock."

"I'll pick you up at six," he said, already counting the hours.

Amanda Langley was seated inside Daisy's Donut Shop when Serena arrived to meet her at noon on Friday. They'd chosen the restaurant because of its proximity to the veterinarian clinic as Serena only had an hour for lunch—and because the food was as good as the service was prompt.

"I'm glad you were available to meet me today," she said to her mom, as she slid into the seat across from her.

"I was grateful for the invitation," Amanda replied.

Serena set aside her menu. She ate at Daisy's often enough that she already knew what she wanted, and the waitress immediately appeared to take their orders.

"I wanted to apologize to you," Serena said when the server had gone.

"Apologize?" Amanda echoed, sounding surprised. "For what?"

"Interrupting your date last Saturday night."

Her mother waved a hand dismissively. "It was fine. And Mark was glad that he finally got to meet you."

"So you did tell him about me?"

"I've told him everything," Amanda assured her.

"You have?"

Her mother nodded. "I've learned that keeping things inside isn't good for me—and that I need to stop doing things that aren't good for me." Then she smiled. "Mark is very good for me."

Serena chose to ignore the obvious implication, saying only, "Well… I'm glad you have someone you can talk to."

"Do you? Have someone that you can talk to, I mean?"

"Sure," she said, because she knew it was true. It was also true that she didn't usually like to talk about the past.

And yet, for some reason, she'd had no trouble opening up to Bailey. In fact, she'd *wanted* to tell him about Mimi. But even more surprising was the realization that he was a good listener. Understanding and empathetic.

And a really great kisser.

Of course, that probably wasn't something she should be thinking about right now. Not just because she was having lunch with her mother, but because she was the one who had told him that they should slow things down. Although she was admittedly a little disappointed that he hadn't tried to kiss her goodbye when he'd left her apartment the other night.

"It's still so hard, not knowing," Amanda said.

The softly spoken remark drew Serena back to the present. She nodded, understanding that her mother was thinking about Mimi and that tragic day when she'd gone missing.

"There are so many possibilities…most of them too horrible to think about," her mother noted.

"So don't think about them," she urged.

"I try not to," Amanda admitted. "I want to believe that she was taken by somebody—a woman or even a couple—who desperately wanted a child but couldn't have one of their own. And maybe it seemed unfair, that I had two beautiful little girls—" she lifted her napkin to dab at the tears that trembled on her lashes "—so they took one home."

It was the same scenario that Serena clung to—the one that allowed her to sleep at night. It couldn't change the fact that her sister had been cruelly ripped from the arms of her loving family, but she desperately needed to believe that, wherever she was now, Mimi was loved and cared for and didn't miss her real family at all.

She reached across the table and touched her mother's hand.

"She was such a sweet child," Amanda said, turning her palm over to clasp her daughter's hand.

Serena nodded, feeling as if their joined hands were squeezing her heart.

"I should have held on to her tighter," her mother said.

"I was—" Serena swallowed. "I was holding Mimi's hand," she reminded Amanda.

Her mother's brow furrowed, as if she was struggling to remember, then she shook her head. "You were a child yourself. I never should have made you responsible for your sister."

"I thought you blamed me," she said. "I thought that's why…"

"Why I turned into an alcoholic?" Amanda guessed. She nodded again.

"I hate knowing that you could ever believe such a thing," her mother said, her eyes bright with unshed tears. "That I ever let you believe such a thing."

"I blamed myself," Serena confided.

"It wasn't your fault. Please tell me you know that none of what happened was your fault," Amanda implored.

"I do know. Now," she said. "Most of the time, anyway."

Her mother gave Serena's hand a gentle squeeze before releasing it as the waitress approached with their plates.

"You were the only light in my darkest days," Amanda said when the server had gone. "You were never responsible for any of the wrong choices I made, but you were the biggest part of the reason why I was finally able to get sober."

"I didn't do anything," she said, and she'd always felt a little bit guilty about that.

"You always were, and still are, my sweet, beautiful daughter. And I want to earn the right to be your mother again, to be worthy of your love again."

"You always were, and still are, my mother. And I have always, and still do, love you," Serena told her.

Amanda's lips started to curve, then her smile wobbled. "Dammit," she said, and lifted her napkin to dab at the tears that trembled on her lashes. "I promised myself that I wasn't going to get weepy today."

Serena's own eyes were watery as she picked up her

fork. "So tell me more about Mark," she said, suspecting they'd both appreciate a change in the topic of conversation.

"He's asked me to go with him tomorrow to cut down a Christmas tree," her mother said.

Serena sipped from her glass of water while she considered this information. For most people, it would be a traditional holiday event, but she knew that holiday events were often triggers for her mom.

"How do you feel about that?" she asked cautiously.

"Scared," Amanda admitted. "I find it's easier to get through the holidays if I pretend they don't exist."

"Not easy to do when the whole town is decked out in red and green," Serena noted.

"Well, apparently, the world does continue to turn through the whole month of December—at least for everyone else."

"You know, you can tell him no," she said. "If you're not ready."

"I've been saying no for the past three years," her mother confided. "I think it's time to say yes. I want you to know that I'm strong enough to say yes."

"Don't do this for me," Serena said. "Please."

"I'm not. I'm doing it for Mark, and for me. Okay, and maybe a little bit for you…and for Mimi."

Serena swallowed another sip of water—along with the lump in her throat. "Then you better get a huge tree and decorate it with hundreds of twinkling lights and tons of sparkly ornaments."

"We will," her mother promised.

And Serena trusted that they would.

Chapter Ten

There'd been plenty of chores around Sunshine Farm to keep Bailey's hands busy throughout the week, but the physical labor hadn't stopped him from thinking about Serena, wondering what she was doing and wishing he was with her instead of fixing fence, moving hay or cleaning tack. But he knew that she was busy, too, with her responsibilities at the vet clinic, preparations for the holidays and, of course, her animals.

By Friday, he could hardly wait for their date that night. In the afternoon, he slipped away from the ranch for a few hours to meet Brendan Tanner at the community center.

"This town is truly amazing," Brendan remarked, after they'd sorted through the gifts that had been donated for Presents for Patriots.

"You must not get out much," Bailey said dryly.

The other man chuckled. "I've been to a lot of places—bigger cities, prettier towns." He sighed wistfully. "Places with pizza delivery."

"There is something to be said for the luxury of food brought to your door," Bailey agreed.

"On the other hand, people who don't have that option are forced to go out and interact with other people," Brendan noted. "Maybe that's why there's such a strong sense of community in Rust Creek Falls."

"I don't think pizza delivery would jeopardize the town's identity."

"It's something to think about, anyway," the retired marine said.

Bailey stood back and looked at the pile of gifts. "Where did all this stuff come from?"

"Rumor has it that Arthur Swinton donates the majority of these gifts every year," Brendan remarked.

"Since when do you put any stock in gossip?" Bailey asked.

His friend shrugged. "It seems to be a favorite pastime in this town."

"Because there's not much else to do."

"Well, it's a fact that Swinton bankrolled this whole place," Brendan told him, gesturing to their surroundings. "The Grace Traub Community Center was made possible by his generous support."

"Who is this Swinton guy?"

"The former mayor of Thunder Canyon who went to prison for embezzlement several years back."

"He built this place with stolen money?"

Brendan chuckled. "No, I'm pretty sure he paid that back."

Bailey was captivated by this tidbit, but he wasn't

nearly as interested in history as he was the future. More specifically, his future plans with Serena. He surveyed all they'd accomplished. "Looks like we're done here. Is it okay if I take off?"

"Hot date tonight?" his friend teased.

"Just heading into Kalispell to grab a bite and catch a movie," he said, deliberately not answering the question.

"By yourself?"

"No," he admitted. "With…a friend."

"Serena Langley?" Brendan guessed.

"Yeah."

"I guess the rumor mill got that one right, too."

"I don't want to know," Bailey told him.

His friend chuckled again. "Well, have a good time tonight."

Bailey planned on it.

He'd made reservations at a popular steak and seafood restaurant in Kalispell and previewed the movie listings so they could discuss their options over dinner. He'd been looking forward to this date with Serena all week, and he hoped that she had been, too.

So he was understandably surprised when she opened the door in response to his knock and he saw that she was dressed in flannel pajamas with fuzzy slippers on her feet.

"I don't think the restaurant has a dress code, but considering that it's only twenty degrees outside, you might want to put on a pair of boots."

"Restaurant?" she echoed, then winced. "Oh, right. Dinner and a movie."

"You forgot our date," he realized, surprised and more than a little disappointed.

"I did. I'm sorry. It was just a really lousy day, and when I got home, all I wanted were my pj's. And ice cream," she admitted.

He looked closer, saw the puffiness lingering around her eyes. "You've been crying."

"I'm out of ice cream," she said, her eyes filling with fresh tears.

"You had lunch with your mom today," he suddenly remembered.

She nodded. "But that was fine. My mother's really doing well."

"So what happened after lunch?" he asked.

"Thelma McGee came in with Oreo," she said.

"I'm not yet seeing the connection between your tears and cookies," he confided.

She managed a smile as she shook her head. "Oreo is—*was*—Thelma's black-and-white cat."

The *was* finally clued him in to the cause of her distress. He drew her into his arms, a silent offer of comfort.

She choked on a sob. "I'm sorry."

"There's no need to apologize," he assured her.

"Believe it or not, I'm getting better at dealing with the loss of an animal," she told him. "But it's never easy. And Thelma had Oreo for seventeen years."

"That's a pretty good life span for a cat, isn't it?"

"It is," she confirmed.

But he understood that when you loved something—or someone—and your time together came to an end, it was never long enough.

"She was sitting with him in the exam room, waiting for the doctor to come in, holding Oreo close to her chest, silent tears falling. And Oreo lifted a paw to her cheek, as if to comfort her."

Listening to Serena recount the story now, even he felt as if his chest was being squeezed. He could only imagine how much more heart-wrenching it had been for her in the moment.

"I love my job," she told him.

Bailey continued to rub her back. "I know you do."

She sighed. "But sometimes...I really hate my job."

"That's understandable," he assured her.

She sniffled again. "I need a tissue."

He pulled one from the box on the sideboard, offered it to her.

"Thanks." She wiped her nose. "I can't believe I completely forgot about our plans for tonight."

"It's not too late, if you want to go put some clothes on."

"I'm sorry," she said again. "But I really don't feel up to going anywhere tonight."

"Do you feel up to company?" he asked.

"You want to stay?"

"Well, I know for a fact that you've got a decent movie collection. And popcorn."

"But no ice cream."

"Do you want me to go get you some ice cream?"

She nodded her head against his chest.

"What kind?"

"It doesn't matter, as long as it's real ice cream."

"I didn't know there was such a thing as fake ice cream," he told her.

"Low-fat ice cream, frozen yogurt, sorbet—they're all fake ice cream."

"I'll get the real stuff," he promised.

* * *

He wasn't gone long, and when he came back, he offered her a ribbon-tied paper bundle.

"I meant to pick up flowers for you earlier, but I forgot."

"At least you didn't forget our date," she said, as she unwrapped the bouquet of red carnations and white chrysanthemums with accents of red berries and seasonal greens. "And these are beautiful, thank you."

"My pleasure," he said.

"What else have you got there?" she asked, noting the two grocery bags he set on the counter.

"Ice cream."

"That's a lot of ice cream," she remarked.

"I picked up a couple frozen pizzas, too, in case you get hungry for food. That way, we won't have to go out." He opened the freezer and stowed the pizzas away, then unpacked the ice cream.

Four different flavors of ice cream: chocolate chip cookie dough, mint chocolate chip, black cherry and butterscotch ripple.

She took a couple bowls out of the cupboard, then retrieved spoons and a scoop from the utensil drawer.

"Why don't you scoop up the ice cream while I put these flowers in some water?" she suggested.

He took the scoop she handed to him. "What kind do you want?"

"How am I supposed to decide when there are so many options?"

"A scoop of each?" he suggested.

"That would probably be a little overindulgent." She found a vase under the sink, filled it with water. "Maybe a little bit of mint chocolate chip and a little chocolate chip cookie dough."

While he dished up the ice cream, she snipped the stems off the flowers, arranged them in the vase, then set the bouquet in the center of the dining room table.

He handed her a bowl of ice cream. She noted that he'd gone for the butterscotch.

"Die Hard 2?" she suggested.

"Sounds good to me."

So they sat down with their ice cream and prepared to watch Bruce Willis fight bad guys at Washington Dulles International Airport.

When the British jet crashed on the runway, Bailey caught a flickering motion in the corner of his eye and realized it was Molly's tail twitching from side to side. Apparently the cat had overcome her distrust of him, at least enough to climb up onto the table beside the sofa and lap the remnants of ice cream from his bowl.

"Is she allowed to have that?" he asked Serena.

"Do you want to take it away from her?" she countered.

"No," he admitted.

She smiled. "A little bit of ice cream isn't going to hurt her."

"But will it make her like me?"

"That remains to be seen."

"How about you?" he asked, sliding his arm across her shoulders. "Did I earn points for feeding you ice cream?"

"You did." Then she dropped her head back against his chest and turned her attention back to the movie.

Though he'd wanted to take her out on a "real date" tonight, he realized that he was more than content to be here with her now. He couldn't remember ever feeling so comfortable and relaxed with his ex-wife. Emily was a social creature who'd always wanted to be going somewhere and doing something, and Bailey had almost forgotten that it could be fun just to relax.

"I'm going to preheat the oven for pizza," he said, after the hero had ejected himself from the cockpit of a plane.

"Why does it seem like you're always feeding me?" Serena asked when Bailey had completed his task and returned to his seat beside her.

"It's just frozen pizza."

She shifted slightly to face him. "Which doesn't answer my question," she pointed out.

He shrugged. "We seem to hang out together around meal times. And you made dinner for me after our shopping trip last week," he pointed out.

"That was once."

"Are we keeping score?" he asked, sounding amused.

"No." Then she revised her response, "Maybe."

He chuckled. "If you're really concerned about balancing the scales, you could offer to cook for me again sometime."

Serena considered this idea in conjunction with other thoughts nudging at her mind—and desires humming in her veins. "How about breakfast?" she suggested impulsively.

"Breakfast?" Bailey echoed.

"You know—the meal generally served in the morning," she clarified, her deliberately casual tone a marked contrast to the frantic beating of her heart. "Maybe after you've spent the night."

Heat supplanted the humor in his gaze. "When were you thinking you might make me this breakfast?"

The kisses they'd already shared assured her that the attraction she felt was reciprocated and gave her the courage to boldly respond, "Tomorrow."

Then, because she wanted him more than she wanted to watch a movie she'd seen a dozen times before, she breached the scant distance between them and touched her mouth to his.

That first contact was all it took to have desire pour through her system like molten lava, heating every part of her. What she'd intended to be a quick and easy kiss quickly changed, their mutual desire growing stronger and more intense. When he eased her back onto the sofa, she lifted her arms to link them behind his head, drawing him down with her, welcoming the weight of his body pressing her into the cushions. Her lips parted willingly when he deepened the kiss; her tongue dipped and dallied with his.

His hands skimmed down her sides, scorching her skin even through the fabric of her pajama top. She wanted to strip away her clothes and feel his hands on her bare skin; she wanted to strip away his clothes and use her hands on his bare skin. She wanted—

Beep-beep-beep.

Bailey drew in a ragged breath and eased away from her. "I better get that pizza in the oven."

After taking a moment to catch her own breath, Serena opened her eyes and found all three animals sitting in a row, staring at her.

"You have no right to judge me," she told them, reaching for the remote to pause the movie.

"Especially you," she said, pointing the control at

Marvin. "Because you'd show your private parts to any-one for a belly rub." He pressed his wet nose to her leg, an acknowledgment more than an apology.

"And you act like you don't like him," she said to Molly. "But that didn't stop you from licking his ice cream bowl." The calico lifted her butt in the air and extended her front paws out in front of her, stretch-ing lazily.

Max looked at her, his nose twitching. She gently scratched behind his ears. "And you'll cuddle with any-one, in your own time and on your own terms."

"Were you talking to me?" Bailey asked, returning to the living room.

"No," she said.

Thankfully he didn't require more of an explanation as he settled beside her on the sofa again. And though the press of his thigh against hers was enough to jolt her pulse again, she hit the play button to resume the movie.

Twenty minutes later, they were eating pizza and the animals were cowering from the noise of the firefight playing out on the TV screen.

And then they were kissing again.

She wasn't sure how it happened, or even who made the first move this time, she only knew that she didn't want him to ever stop kissing her. Or touching her.

She drew her knees up so they bracketed his hips, then lifted her pelvis to rub it against his. She could feel his erection straining against his jeans and gloried in the friction of the denim against her flannel pajama bottoms. He groaned softly as he ground into her, giv-ing her a preview of what she wanted, what they both wanted.

She gasped with pleasure—then shock, as a wet doggy tongue swept across her cheek.

"Maybe we should move to the bedroom—and close the door," she suggested.

He stood up, as if eager to accept her invitation, and offered his hand to help her to her feet. But when she started to lead him down the hall, he paused.

"What's the matter?" she asked.

"You said you wanted to slow things down," he reminded her.

"That was last week. Ten days ago, in fact." She didn't want to slow down anymore. She wanted to move full speed ahead—with Bailey. She wanted his hands on her body. All over her body. And she wanted to explore every inch of his in return.

"I can't believe I'm saying this, but ten days isn't so long," he pointed out. "And if this happens tonight, I might worry afterward that it only happened because you were trying to balance the scales."

"If this happens tonight, it's because I want it to happen—not because you brought ice cream or pizza or even flowers," she assured him.

"You had a lousy day," he reminded her.

"I'm pretty sure getting naked with you would make me forget about the lousy day."

"I'm pretty sure getting naked with you would make me forget my name," he told her. "But it's not the answer."

But before he left, he kissed her goodbye.

It was a long, lingering kiss that assured her that he desired her as much as she desired him, despite his insistence on giving her time she no longer wanted or needed.

And when he finally drew away, she watched him go when she really wished she'd been able to convince him to stay.

Ten days before Christmas, volunteers gathered at the community center to wrap Presents for Patriots. The event was the culmination of many hours of work by many hands, and by seven o'clock, the room was bustling with activity and practically overflowing with volunteers.

For the residents of Rust Creek Falls, the annual gift-wrapping was very much a social occasion—a welcome opportunity to get together with their neighbors and catch up on what was going on. As Bailey looked around, he had to agree with Brendan's assessment: this was an amazing community.

More surprising to him was the number of people that he recognized from years ago and others whose acquaintance he'd made more recently. Mallory and Caleb Dalton were in attendance, as was Caleb's sister Paige with her husband, Sutter Traub. Will and Jordyn Clifton were working at a table alongside Will's brother Craig and his fiancée, Caroline Ruth. Claire and Levi Wyatt were at an adjacent table, Lani and Russ Campbell at another. Even the mayor and his wife had helped with the wrapping for a short while before they had to slip away to another holiday party.

At one point, Winona Cobbs popped in, and while the eccentric psychic was sipping some of the complimentary hot apple cider, she told Bailey that his life was going to change before the night was over—but only if he was willing to let it. Everyone in town knew the old woman was more than a little odd, so Bailey tried not to let her words unnerve him.

Throughout the evening, he overheard some snippets of conversation and learned that Thelma McGee had already offered to foster cats for the animal shelter. She wasn't ready to replace her beloved Oreo, but she was eager to help out.

There were also murmurs, but no confirmation, that Paige and Sutter were expecting their second child, and that Paige's sister Lani was expecting her first.

There were sighs of relief, and some chuckles, when it was revealed that the heart attack that caused Melba Strickland to rush her husband, Gene, to the hospital in Kalispell turned out to be indigestion.

Christmas music played softly in the background throughout, and there was a refreshment table that offered not only hot apple cider but coffee, tea and hot cocoa, plus an assortment of seasonal cookies and treats—all donated by the generous folks of Rust Creek Falls. There was certainly plenty going on to keep the volunteers busy, and Bailey mostly hovered in the background.

Although he'd been involved in the planning and organization of the event almost from the beginning, he still felt like an outsider in the community. Of course, that was his own fault. He'd mostly resisted getting involved because, as he'd been reminding his family for almost twelve months, he didn't intend to stay.

And yet, he'd still made no plans to go.

He restocked the tables as wrapping supplies dwindled, collected finished packages and cleared away debris, and regularly found his attention shifting to the door. He told himself that he wasn't looking for anyone in particular, but when his gaze zeroed in on Serena and his heart bumped against his ribs, he was forced to acknowledge the truth.

He'd been watching for her.

And he'd been thinking about her almost non-stop since he'd declined the invitation to her bed. All the way home, after he'd kissed her goodbye at her door last night, he'd cursed himself for being a fool. It was little consolation to his aching body to know that he'd done the right thing. And he couldn't help but wonder if she'd ever give him another chance to make a different choice.

"I didn't see your name on the volunteer list," he said, after he'd crossed the room to meet her.

"Did you look for it?" she asked, a teasing glint in her eye.

He had, because he'd wanted to see her. And now she was here, but he wasn't quite ready to put all his cards on the table. "I looked at all the names," he said.

"Then you know there were more than enough people signed up for the wrapping," she explained. "So I thought I'd come late to help with the cleaning."

"We had more than enough people sign up for that, too."

"I can see that," she acknowledged. "Are you going to send me away?"

"Of course not." Instead, he dipped his head and touched his mouth to hers. "I'm glad you're here."

The unexpected—and unexpectedly public—gesture surprised Serena. She'd wondered, after he'd left her apartment the night before, if she'd misinterpreted the situation. His kiss, in addition to making her lips tingle and spreading warmth through her veins, reassured her that she had not.

She smiled at him. "*That* made the walk over here totally worthwhile."

He drew back to look at her. "Why on earth would you walk over here in twenty-degree weather?"

"So that I could ask you for a ride home."

"I'd be happy to take you home," he assured her. "But I'm not sure how much longer I'm going to be stuck—"

"As of right now, you're unstuck," Brendan interjected, obviously having overheard at least part of their conversation. "Fiona already agreed to stick around and, no offense, but she's much prettier than you."

Bailey chuckled. "No offense taken, and Serena's much prettier than you, too, so I guess we both win."

Brendan held out his hand. "Thanks for all your help."

"It was my pleasure," Bailey said, clasping his hand and grasping his other shoulder.

Not quite a man-hug, but a gesture that spoke of the friendship and camaraderie that Serena guessed had developed between them over the past few months.

"Have you been here all day?" she asked, as she and Bailey exited the community center together.

"No, just since two," he said.

"Still, that's a lot of hours."

"Yeah, but it was a good day," he told her. "Being away from Rust Creek Falls for so long, I almost forgot what it was like to be part of such a tight-knit community."

"Did you miss it?"

"I didn't let myself," he admitted, opening the passenger door of his truck for her. "Not the town. And definitely not my family."

"Why did you finally come back?" she asked, when he was settled behind the steering wheel.

He turned the key in the ignition, then cranked the defroster to clear the windshield and warm up the truck's cab. "After my marriage fell apart, I was kind of at loose ends. I could have stayed in New Mexico, but I didn't want to, so I decided to make my way back to Wyoming, to see if I could track down Luke and Danny again.

"Of course, they were both gone by then, but the foreman at the ranch where Luke had last been working told me that he'd gone to Rusty River."

"Rusty River?" she echoed, amused by the bastardization of the town's name.

He shrugged. "Not a lot of people outside of Montana have heard of Rust Creek Falls, and the Rusty part was at least close enough that I was able to figure out where he'd gone—although I couldn't imagine why he'd want to come back to the town we'd said goodbye to forever."

"Well, whatever his reasons, I'm glad he came home," she said, as Bailey pulled into a vacant parking spot behind her building. "Because then you came home, too."

She unbuckled her belt, and he did the same, then came around to help her out of the truck.

"I didn't plan on staying—in Rust Creek Falls," he clarified, as they started up the steps to her apartment. "Even as the days turned into weeks and then months, I was sure I'd pack up and head out again."

"But you're still here," she noted.

"And right now, I don't want to be anywhere else."

She unlocked her door, then turned to face him. "Did you want to come in for hot cocoa and cookies?"

"I don't know," he said. "I seem to recall you once telling me that I needed to cut back on the Christmas cookies."

"I seem to recall that was an attempt to cover for your ill-tempered comment to a little boy."

"You don't think I need to worry about staying in shape?"

She splayed her palms on his chest. Even through his sheepskin-lined leather jacket, she could feel the hard strength of his muscles. "I don't think a couple of cookies are any cause for concern."

"What about the cocoa?"

She slid her hands over his shoulders to link them behind his head. "Maybe we should skip the cocoa," she said, and drew his mouth down to hers.

Chapter Eleven

They bypassed the kitchen and headed straight to her bedroom. On the way, Serena almost tripped over Marvin, who had eagerly raced ahead and jumped on the bed.

She sighed. "He thinks it's playtime."

"I was hoping the same thing," Bailey said. "But just between me and you."

She smiled at that, then turned to Marvin and in a firm tone said, "Off."

His excitement leaked out of him like air escaping from a punctured balloon, and he dropped his head and crawled to the edge of the mattress. He paused then, as if giving her an opportunity to rescind her banishment. Serena pointed to the door. Marvin reluctantly jumped down off the bed and retreated from the room.

"This is a new feeling for me," Bailey said.

"What's a new feeling?"

"I'm torn between the anticipation of finally getting you naked and guilt that you sent the dog away."

"If it makes you feel any better, I promise that Marvin doesn't hold a grudge. In fact, he's probably curled up on Molly's pillow already."

"So you're telling me it's okay to focus on the getting you naked part?"

"I'm suggesting we focus on getting one another naked," she said.

He smiled and pulled her into his arms. "That works for me."

Then he kissed her again. His tongue slid between her lips, to tease and tangle with hers. His hands slid under her sweater, searching for skin, and found a soft cotton T-shirt instead.

"Damn Montana winters," he grumbled, as he yanked the shirt out of her jeans and finally put his hands on *her*. His callused palms moved over her skin, stroking her body, stoking her desire.

She fumbled with the buttons of his shirt, desperate to touch him as he was touching her, and discovered that he was wearing a thermal tee beneath. "Damn Montana winters," she echoed his complaint.

He chuckled as he yanked the shirt over his head and tossed it aside. The rest of their clothes quickly followed. Then he eased her down onto the mattress, covering her naked body with his own.

Her hands slid up his arms, tracing the muscular contours. Her palms stroked the shape of his bare shoulders, so broad, so strong. Then trailed over the hard planes of his chest and his stomach. He had the body of a rancher, lean and tough, and she wanted to lick every bit of it. But for now, she reached down and wrapped her fingers around him.

He sucked in a breath.

She immediately loosened her grip. "Did I hurt you?"

"Oh, yeah," he said. "But in the very best way."

She stroked his rigid length, slowly, from base to tip, then back again, and watched as his eyes darkened and a muscle in his jaw flexed as he clenched his teeth together. She stroked him again, and he caught her wrist as his breath shuddered out between his lips.

"I can't take much more of that," he warned.

"Then take me," she suggested. "I want you inside me."

"I want to be inside you," he assured her, but he lowered his head to nibble on her earlobe, kiss her throat.

"So why aren't you there?"

"Because it's been a while for me," he admitted. "And I want to make sure that it's good for you."

"It's been a while for me, too," she told him. "And I don't want to wait another minute to have you inside me."

"In that case, give me fifty-five seconds," he suggested.

"What?"

"It's less than a minute," he pointed out, as his hands leisurely traced her curves.

He continued the exploration with his mouth, kissing her breasts, her belly. He parted the soft folds of flesh at the apex of her thighs, opening her to him. Then he lowered his head and touched the sensitive nub at her center with his tongue, a slow, deliberate lick that made everything inside her tighten in glorious anticipation.

"Bailey…you don't have to—"

"Shh," he whispered against her slick flesh. "I've only got another forty seconds."

She might have smiled at that, but his mouth was already on her again, licking and nibbling, tasting and teasing. Instead, she let her head fall back against the pillow, biting down on her bottom lip to prevent herself from crying out with shock and pleasure.

She tried to hold it together. She didn't want to come apart like this. She wanted to wait until he was inside her.

Her fingers curled, fisting the cover beneath her, and she closed her eyes and tried to count down the last thirty seconds. But the numbers blurred together in her mind, as the desires and demands of her body shoved aside everything else.

"Isn't—" her breath hitched "—your time up?"

"Not just yet," he said, and continued his intimate exploration.

She couldn't fight the onslaught of sensations any longer. The tension inside her had built to a breaking point, and she shattered into a million pieces.

When her body finally stopped shuddering with aftershocks, he sheathed himself with a condom and rose up over her, then buried himself inside her.

She gasped as he filled her. Deeply. Completely.

She braced her heels on the mattress and lifted her hips, taking him even deeper, drawing a low groan of satisfaction from his throat as her muscles clenched around him.

He began to move, slowly at first, a steady rhythm that stroked deep inside her. Then faster, harder, deeper. Her hips rose to meet him and her fingernails scraped down his back as he drove them both to the pinnacle of pleasure—and beyond.

Bailey had barely managed to catch his breath when he heard Marvin's plaintive whimper through the bedroom door.

"Does he need to go out?" he asked, mumbling the question into Serena's hair.

"He has a doggy door," she reminded him.

"So why is he whining?"

"He was probably a little confused by the noises we were making," she admitted.

"You mean the noises *you* were making," he teased.

"I'm gonna plead the Fifth on that one."

He turned his head to nibble on her ear. "You were pleading something very different twenty minutes ago."

She lifted a hand to shove at his shoulder, but she didn't put much force behind the motion. "A gentleman should never embarrass a lady."

"I'm not a gentleman, I'm a cowboy," he told her.

"Well, cowboys have a code, too," she pointed out.

"Uh-huh," he agreed. "A cowboy must never shoot first, hit a smaller man or leave a woman unsatisfied."

She choked on a laugh. "I think you made that last part up."

"But did I honor the code?"

"You know you honored the code."

"Good." He lifted his head to brush his lips over hers. "Because you totally rocked my world, too."

"Yeah?"

"Oh, yeah," he confirmed.

She smiled at that. "I'm glad I walked over to the community center tonight."

He kissed her again, softly, sweetly. "I'm glad you invited me up for cocoa and cookies."

"We never had the cocoa and cookies."

"I know." Another kiss, longer, lingering. "And I'm thinking we should not have cocoa and cookies again."

"Right now?"

"Right now," he agreed.

Bailey had known that sex with Serena would be good, and he hadn't been exaggerating when he'd told her that she'd rocked his world. Of course, she was the first woman he'd been with since he'd ended his marriage, so he suspected that the extended period of celibacy had something to do with the intensity of the experience.

Except that the second time with Serena had been even better than the first. And the third had exceeded all his expectations yet again. And even after three rounds of lovemaking, his desire for her had not abated in the least.

It was that realization that caused the first hint of panic to set in. His subconscious reference to their physical joining as *lovemaking* only exacerbated it.

He wasn't in love with Serena.

He wasn't foolish enough to go down that path again, especially not with someone he'd only known a few weeks.

Sure, she was an amazing woman. Beautiful. Smart. Sexy. Passionate. Compassionate. Resilient. Caring. He could go on and on enumerating her many wonderful qualities—qualities that proved she was too good for him.

And yet, by some stroke of luck, she'd chosen to be

with him. And he was selfish enough to take whatever she was willing to give, for as long as she was willing to give it.

He fell asleep with her head nestled against his shoulder—and woke up with what felt like a ten-pound weight on his chest.

Turned out it was a ten-pound cat.

"I thought you said the animals don't sleep in your bed," he remarked, when Serena returned to the bedroom from the adjoining en suite bath.

"They don't," she confirmed.

"Well, don't look now, but there's a cat on my chest."

"A wide-awake cat who wants her breakfast."

"She's not the only one," he said. Then he looked at Molly and, utilizing the same command that Serena had used so effectively with Marvin the night before, said, "Off."

The cat just stared at him, those pale green eyes unblinking.

He pointed to the floor and tried again. "Off."

Molly continued to stare at him.

"Your cat doesn't listen very well."

"She's a cat," Serena said, sounding amused.

"I can practically hear the thoughts going through her head." Then he changed the tone and pitch of his voice to recite those imagined thoughts. "I'll move my tail when I feel like moving my tail."

Serena laughed as she tied the belt of her robe around her waist. "I admit that I talk to my animals, but I don't pretend they talk back."

"Look at her and tell me that's not what she's thinking," he demanded.

She tilted her head to look at the cat. "That's not what she's thinking."

"Then what's she thinking?" he wanted to know.

"She's hoping that Santa will leave a little catnip in her stocking this year."

"Catnip, huh?"

Serena headed toward the door. "Come on, Molly."

And the damn cat followed her.

Shaking his head, Bailey pushed back the covers and climbed out of bed.

"Do I smell coffee?" he asked, when he joined her in the kitchen after he'd showered and dressed again in last night's clothes.

She handed him a mug filled with the hot fragrant brew. "What would you like for breakfast?"

"You don't have to cook for me," he said. "Or is this about balancing those scales you're so worried about?"

She laughed softly. "It's about the fact that I'm hungry and I thought you might be, too."

"I am," he confirmed.

"Eggs okay?"

"Eggs are always okay."

"Bacon?"

He nodded emphatically. "The only thing I like more than eggs."

They cooked breakfast together and ate breakfast together, and it was all very nice and domestic. And maybe it did make Serena wish she had someone with whom to share not just a single morning but the rest of her life. And maybe, if she let herself, she could imagine Bailey being that someone.

But she didn't let herself because she knew that one

night did not a relationship make. She was hopeful, however, that one night might lead to two, and maybe more.

She'd just gotten up from the table for a coffee refill when the landline phone rang. A glance at the display made her pause.

"Are you going to answer that?" Bailey asked when the phone rang again and she only continued to stare at it.

"I don't know who it is," she confessed, carrying the coffeepot to the table to top up his mug. "The area code is Arizona, which is where my grandmother lives, but the number isn't familiar."

So she let the machine answer. And because she had an old-fashioned answering machine hooked up to her landline, the message transmitted clearly through the speaker.

"Hi, Rena, it's Grams. I know you said you'd call next week when I talked to you last week, but, well, I'm not actually home right now." Then her voice dropped to a loud whisper. "I'm at George's place."

Bailey's brows lifted.

"We had the best time last night," Grams continued, and then she giggled. "And this morning."

Serena buried her face in her hands.

"Honestly, the therapeutic effects of orgasm cannot be overrated, and I know you're under a lot of stress, which is why you need to grab hold of that Stockton boy and—"

She leaped from her chair and snatched up the receiver, cutting off the recording.

"Grams, hi." She turned her back to Bailey, so that

he wouldn't see that her cheeks were flaming. "I, uh, just got out of the shower."

Which wasn't technically the truth, since she'd showered when she woke up, but it wasn't exactly a lie, either.

"Do you have one of those massaging shower heads?" her grandmother asked. "I'm not saying they can replace a man's touch, but desperate times and all that."

Serena groaned inwardly. "So…tell me what's going on in your life," she said, desperate to change the subject.

For the next several minutes, her grandmother proceeded to do precisely that—in great and unnecessary detail—while Serena silently prayed that the ground would open up and swallow her. But of course that didn't happen.

"Just remember your own last rule," Serena said, when Grams paused to take a breath.

"I remember all my rules," her grandmother assured her.

"But do you follow them?"

"Oh, I've gotta run," Grams said. "George is signaling that breakfast is ready."

And before Serena could reply, she'd disconnected.

"That was your grandmother, huh?" Bailey said, amusement evident in his tone.

"That was my grandmother," she confirmed.

"And 'that Stockton boy'…that would be me?"

"So much for hoping you might pretend you hadn't heard that part," she muttered.

"Sorry," he said, not sounding sorry at all. "But now I'm wondering what you told your grandmother about me."

"Nothing," she immediately and emphatically replied.

"And yet, she apparently wants you to grab hold of me and... What exactly was it she suggested you should do?"

"You're enjoying this a little too much."

"Not as much as I enjoyed last night," he assured her. "But that phone call certainly added something to the morning after."

"Can you please just forget about the phone call?"

"Okay," he agreed. "But tell me about your grandmother."

"What do you want to know?" she asked warily.

"It's obvious the two of you are close."

"I lived with her growing up," Serena reminded him.

"And has she always offered such interesting advice?"

She nodded. "Grams has often been exasperating and opinionated, but she loves wholeheartedly and unconditionally. She also had some pretty strict rules for anyone living under her roof."

"Like what?"

She ticked them off on her fingers as she recited: "Tell where I'm going and who I'm going with. Call when I get there. Be home by midnight. Never leave a drink unattended. Never drink and drive. Never share naked pictures. And never have sex without a condom."

"Those sound like some pretty smart and savvy rules," he remarked.

"Grams is a pretty smart and savvy lady."

"So is her granddaughter," he said.

"You think so?"

"Well, she gave me some pretty good advice."

"What advice was that?" she wondered aloud.

"About talking to Emily," he confided.

"You called her?"

He nodded. "I did."

"Was she surprised to hear from you?"

"Yeah, she was surprised to hear from me. And then she shared some surprising news."

"What was that?"

"She got married again. Six months ago."

"That's big news," Serena noted.

"And the even bigger news—she's pregnant."

"Wow."

He nodded again.

"How do you feel about that?" she asked him.

"It has nothing to do with me."

"Your ex-wife is expecting a baby with her new husband—you have to feel something."

"I'm happy for her," he said. "Really. And…relieved."

"Why relieved?" she asked, curious.

"Because there was part of me that wondered if I'd ruined her life."

"Because you divorced her?"

He shook his head. "Because I married her."

"You loved her," she reminded him.

"Or thought I did, anyway," he acknowledged. "But in retrospect, I think my decision to marry Emily was also an attempt—and not a very successful one—to take back control of my life."

"What do you mean?"

"The night my parents were killed…in addition to the grief and the guilt, I felt such an overwhelming sense of helplessness. They were gone, and there was absolutely nothing I could do to change what had happened, to fill the empty space in all of our lives.

"And then our grandparents told us there was no way that they could take in seven kids, so my two brothers and I were essentially on our own. We had no choice about that, but we chose to leave Rust Creek Falls and make our own lives. Yeah, it was a hollow victory, but we needed to feel like we had control over something.

"Everywhere I went after that, every job I took, every decision I made, was an effort to prove to myself that I was in charge of my own destiny. Then I met Emily, and I decided that I wanted to get married. But was I motivated by my feelings for her or a desperate desire to be part of a family again?"

He shrugged, as if he still wasn't certain of the answer to that question. "And does it really matter? Because I never managed to fit in with her family. I never got what I wanted. My fault, I know. Because I never really tried. Because it didn't take me long to realize that I didn't want to be part of *a* family again, I wanted *my* family back. And that was never going to happen."

He was silent for a minute, no doubt pondering those revelations. "But the point of all of that is that you were right," he continued. "There were too many things left unsaid, and saying them will, I think, help both of us put that chapter of our lives behind us."

"I'm glad," she said sincerely.

He finished his coffee and carried his empty plate and mug to the kitchen. Setting the dishes on the counter, he pulled his cell phone out of his pocket and sighed. "Four text messages from Luke in the past hour."

"Is something wrong?" she asked, immediately concerned.

"Nah, he's just nagging me for not being there for morning chores."

"My fault," Serena realized. "Sorry."

He smiled. "I'm not." He kissed her then, softly, sweetly. "But I do have to go."

She nodded. "I know."

"I had a really good time last night."

"Me, too."

And though he'd said he had to go, he didn't move. "I'm not sure what else to say here," he confessed.

"You don't have to say anything else," she told him.

"I want to say something else."

"What do you want to say?"

"Well, I'd like to ask if I can see you again tonight, but I don't want you to think that I'm making any assumptions...or have any expectations...that we're going to do what we did last night. Again, I mean."

She took a moment to untangle his words. "So you're saying that last night was a one-night stand?"

"No," he immediately replied. "I mean, I hope not."

"That's good," she said. "Because I hope not, too."

"So...can I see you tonight?"

"I'll be decorating my Christmas tree tonight."

"I was surprised that you didn't have one yet," he admitted.

"Me and Grams always went to get one on December 16, so I carry on that tradition," she told him.

"Where do you go?"

"Just over to the tree lot in town."

"I've got a better idea," he suggested.

"What's your better idea?" she asked warily.

"Come to Sunshine Farm with me now and we'll cut one down together and bring it back here."

"You're already late for morning chores," she reminded him.

"They'll be done before I get back."

"And you figure that your brother will be less likely to yell at you if I'm there?" she guessed.

"Do you want to hassle me or get a Christmas tree?"

She gave him a cheeky smile. "Both. But I guess I need to put some clothes on for the latter."

He gave her a playful pat on the butt. "Be quick."

Chapter Twelve

"Are you still going to pretend that there's nothing going on between you and Serena Langley?" Dan asked Bailey.

It was Monday afternoon and the brothers had all been recruited to repair a section of downed fence at Sunshine Farm. The repair hadn't taken as long as they'd anticipated, and they were back at the barn now, attempting to warm their frozen hands with hot coffee.

"Why do you think I'm pretending?" he asked, not really denying the fact so much as wanting to know what his brother knew—or thought he did.

"Because your truck was parked outside her apartment overnight," Dan noted.

"Saturday *and* Sunday," Jamie chimed in.

"Only one of the things I forgot that I hate about small towns," Bailey grumbled.

"So what's the status of the relationship?" Luke asked.

"I don't know that I'd call it a relationship," he hedged.

"You're spending your nights in her bed," Dan said again.

"Two nights." So far. "And even in a small town, I don't think that's illegal."

"In a small town, people talk," Jamie reminded him. "And Serena's not that kind of girl."

Bailey felt a twinge of uneasiness—and not his first—as he silently acknowledged the truth of his brother's claim. Of course, he hadn't thought about the potential repercussions for her reputation when he'd accepted the invitation to go up to her apartment after the Presents for Patriots event Saturday night. He hadn't thought about anything but how much he wanted to be with her.

On the other hand, it's not as if he had a reputation for bed-hopping in town. In fact, he didn't have a reputation for much of anything, except being one of *those Stockton boys* who had returned to Rust Creek Falls after so many years away. And in the twelve months that he'd been back, Serena was the first woman he'd been with. In fact, she was the first woman he'd been with since his ex-wife—not that he had any intention of admitting as much to his brothers.

"I know you probably think this is none of our business," Luke began.

"Bingo," Bailey said.

"But it is," Dan insisted. "Not just because you're our brother, but because Serena is a friend—a good friend—of Annie's."

"I'm aware of that," he assured his brothers. "I'm also aware that she's an adult capable of making her own decisions."

Dan held up his hands in a universal gesture of surrender. "I'm not suggesting otherwise."

"Then this conversation is over," Bailey said, looking at each of his brothers in turn.

They exchanged glances, shrugs.

"Just…be careful," Luke urged.

"I always am," he said.

But their words and warnings continued to niggle at the back of his mind throughout the rest of the day. And even when he met Serena after work, as they'd planned, to take a reluctant Marvin for a walk, followed by dinner together again.

So maybe it wasn't surprising that Serena sensed his preoccupation. Or maybe he didn't do a very good job hiding it, because when she took his hand to lead him into the living room after the dishes had been cleared up, he balked.

"What's wrong?" she asked.

"I'm wondering if I should go," he admitted.

"Oh." She immediately released his hand. "If that's what you want."

"It's not," he assured her.

"Then why are you wondering about it?"

"Because people are already talking about the fact that my truck was parked outside your apartment last night," he said. "And the night before."

"Really?" She seemed surprised by this revelation—then surprised him by smiling again. "Good."

"Why is that good?"

"Because I've always been a good girl, never giving anyone reason to speculate or gossip."

"Well, they're speculating now," he told her.

"Grams will be so proud."

"Please tell me you're not going to tell your grandmother."

"I won't have to. She'll most likely hear it from Melba Strickland—if she hasn't already."

He winced at the thought. "And then she'll wonder, along with everyone else, what a nice girl like Serena Langley is doing with an aimless boy like Bailey Stockton?"

She lifted her arms and linked her hands behind his neck, her fingertips playing with the hair that curled over the collar of his shirt. "I don't think you're aimless," she said. "You're just taking some time to figure things out."

"So what are you doing with me?" he asked her.

"I know what I want to do." She rose up onto her toes to whisper her idea in his ear.

"Your wish is my command," he said, and scooped her into his arms to carry her to the bedroom.

After that first night with Bailey, Serena knew that she was well on her way to falling in love with him. When he'd invited her to cut down a Christmas tree at Sunshine Farm, where he'd undoubtedly participated in the same ritual with his parents and siblings for the first twenty years of his life, she felt the first glimmer of hope that maybe he was starting to feel the same way.

But she didn't want to get too far ahead of herself, because she knew that he'd put shields up around his badly damaged heart, and that he might never let them down enough to fall in love again. In the meantime, she tried to enjoy just being with him and making new memories with him as they participated in all the usual holiday rituals.

Unfortunately, she couldn't spend every minute of every day with him, because they both had jobs and responsibilities. In fact, she was clipping the nails of a Great Dane Wednesday afternoon when a knock sounded on the door, then Bailey stepped into the exam room.

"Annie said it was okay for me to come in," he explained.

"Sure," she agreed. "Tiny is always happy to meet new people." The Great Dane's tail thumped noisily against the surface of the metal table, but otherwise, the animal didn't move as she continued to work.

Bailey made a show of looking around the room. "Where's Tiny?"

She smiled. "*This* is Tiny."

"I doubt that animal was ever tiny, even as a puppy," he remarked.

"Norma Wilson has a fondness for irony," Serena explained. "Her other dog is a Chihuahua named Monster." She clipped the last nail. "All done."

Tiny nimbly hopped down off the table. Standing, his head was level with Serena's midriff. Then he dropped to his butt on the floor, sitting patiently, expectantly.

She retrieved a treat from the pocket of her lab coat and fed it to him. "Good boy," she said, and rubbed the top of his head.

"Do I get a treat?" Bailey asked.

She offered him a doggy cookie.

He lowered his head and kissed her instead.

"That's what I wanted," he told her.

"That was nice," she agreed. "But I suspect you didn't come into town just for a kiss."

"No," he agreed. "Not that one of your kisses wouldn't make the trip worthwhile, but Luke asked me to pick up some stuff at the feed store. And since I was here, I thought I'd check in to see if you wanted to reschedule the dinner and a movie that we missed last week. How's Friday night?"

"Actually, I already have plans for Friday night," she confided.

"Oh." He frowned. "What kind of plans?"

"The Candlelight Walk."

He looked at her blankly.

"Maybe you weren't back in town yet when it happened last year," she acknowledged. "It's exactly what the name implies—residents carry lit candles in a processional down Main Street."

"Yeah, I guess I missed that," he said.

"You don't sound too sorry," she noted.

He shrugged. "You know all that Christmassy stuff isn't really my thing."

"Which is why I didn't ask you to go with me."

"But if my only options are a Candlelight Walk with you or spending Friday night alone… Well, there's no contest."

"Really? You want to go with me?"

"I really want to go with you," he said.

She was used to feeling butterflies in her tummy.

The first time she'd ever met Bailey Stockton, a brief and impromptu introduction at the clinic one day when he'd stopped by to see Annie, Serena had felt flutters in her belly. And again, a few months later, when she'd crossed paths with him at Crawford's. And of course, the day that they'd played Santa and Mrs. Claus at the community center.

They'd spent a lot of time together since then, and yet, all it took was a look, a smile or a touch to have those butterflies swooping and spinning again.

As she got ready for the Candlelight Walk, she felt as if those familiar butterflies had multiplied tenfold—and then OD'd on caffeine. Because Serena knew that showing up at tonight's event with Bailey would make a statement about their relationship that would carry as much weight as a headline in the *Gazette*.

Even as she added a spritz of her favorite perfume, she wondered if this was a bad idea. If she was making their relationship into more than it really was. When she was with him, she was usually having too much fun to worry that she might be the only one emotionally invested in the relationship. It was only when she was on her own, with the holidays looming, that the doubts and insecurities raised their ugly heads.

Because each day that passed was a day closer to December 25, and Bailey had said nothing about his plans for Christmas—or asked about hers.

Not that she had any plans. While many residents of Rust Creek Falls were busy running here or there to spend time with family or friends, Serena was accustomed to being on her own with her pets. And that was okay. It was her own tradition—a day of quiet reflection and counting her blessings.

It was another tradition to spend the day after Christmas with her mother, *if* Amanda felt up to it. But her mother was spending the holidays with Mark this year, and although they were keeping their celebrations low-key, they'd invited Serena to join them. Of course, she'd declined. Not only because she didn't want to intrude on their first Christmas together, but because she was—perhaps foolishly—optimistic that she might be celebrating her own first Christmas with Bailey.

But she had accepted an invitation to Mark's house for lunch on Sunday, just two days before Christmas, and she'd ordered a Dutch apple pie—her mother's favorite—from Daisy's as her contribution to the meal. She'd told Bailey of her plans, emphasizing the fact that she didn't celebrate Christmas Day with her mom, but he hadn't taken the hint.

Of course, he'd only reunited with his family the previous year, so it was understandable that they'd be the focus of his plans. It was also possible that he planned to invite her to celebrate with him but hadn't yet done so.

Maybe tonight, she thought—fingers crossed—as she retrieved her hat and mittens from the closet. Then she reached for her boots, and Marvin immediately went to hide.

She laughed, then winced a little as she tightened the lace of her right boot. She'd had a little mishap at the clinic the day before and twisted her ankle. Although she'd iced and wrapped the joint, it was still a little sore—but not sore enough to keep her from participating in one of her favorite holiday events.

She'd just finished buttoning her coat when Bailey knocked at the door. He kissed her lightly, then looked at the floor by her feet. "Where's Marvin?"

"Hiding," she said.

"Why?"

"Because these are my *w-a-l-k-i-n-g* boots," she explained. "And not even the promise of a belly rub would entice him out for a second *w-a-l-k* in one day."

"That dog has issues," he told her.

"And his exercise phobia is only the tip of the iceberg," she admitted, as she closed and locked the door behind her. "He's also afraid of horses, cows and pigs."

"You're kidding."

"Nope." She shook her head as she descended the stairs beside him, trying not to put her full weight on her right foot. "One day when we were out, there were a couple of young girls riding horses on a trail, and he darted between my legs and would not move."

"Then that might be another reason he's hiding," Bailey suggested, as he led her around to the front of the building.

She halted in midstep. "What's this?"

"What does it look like?"

"It looks like a horse-drawn sleigh."

"Got it in one," he told her. "More specifically, it's a two-seat Albany sleigh."

And it was gorgeous, with gleaming bronze accents and tufted velvet seats and ribbon-wrapped pine boughs adding a festive touch.

"*Where* did you get it?" she asked him now.

"I borrowed it from Dallas Traub. And Trina—" he gestured to the gorgeous horse harnessed to the sleigh "—from his stables."

"Okay," she said. "But *why* did you borrow a horse-drawn sleigh for the Candlelight *Walk*?"

"Because Annie told me that you sprained your ankle at work—which you didn't mention to me," he said pointedly.

"Because it's fine," she assured him.

He just lifted a brow.

"And it's wrapped."

"But I don't imagine it will feel very good tomorrow if you're on it all night tonight."

"Probably not," she acknowledged. "But I didn't want to miss the walk."

"And now you don't have to," he said, taking her hand to help her climb into the seat.

"This is so…thoughtful."

"And romantic?" he suggested.

"Unbelievably romantic," she assured him.

And it was.

The walk started at the high end of Main Street, where volunteers from the city council handed out lighted candles in tall glass jars. Bailey left her in the sleigh while he went to get a candle for her, then they took their position at the rear of the crowd. Of course, night fell early in December, but the flicker of so many candles created a beautiful golden glow as the processional made its way slowly toward the park, where the bonfire would be lit.

Bailey held the reins in one gloved hand and Serena's free hand with his other.

"People are going to talk," she warned.

"People are already talking," he reminded her.

"And you just added fresh fuel to the fire."

"With this?" he scoffed, lifting their joined hands. "I doubt it. But maybe—" he tipped her chin up and brushed his lips over hers "—that will do the trick."

"If the trick is making me want to skip the bonfire and take you home to have my way with you, then yes."

"Participating in tonight's festivities was *your* idea," he reminded her.

"So it was," she confirmed.

And she was glad he'd agreed to come. Not only because he'd so thoughtfully provided transportation that allowed her to rest her sore ankle, but because she always enjoyed being with him.

At the end of the route, after the bonfire had been lit, eliciting gasps and cheers from the crowd, they caught sight of his brother Jamie with Fallon and the triplets, Henry, Jared and Katie.

The kids were excited to see "ho-zees," and after checking with Serena first, Bailey offered the reins to his brother so that he and his wife could take their kids for a little ride.

While they were gone, Bailey and Serena mingled with the crowd. And it was a crowd. The O'Reillys were in attendance en masse: Paddy and Maureen, their sons, Ronan and Keegan, and their daughters, Fallon, Fiona and Brenna, along with their respective partners. There were several representatives of each of the Crawford and Traub families, and even more Daltons.

They stopped to chat for a minute with Old Gene and Melba Strickland, the latter asking about Serena's grandmother. And though Serena was tempted to point out that Melba probably talked to Janet Carswell more than her granddaughter did, she managed to bite back the cheeky retort and simply assure the older woman that Janet was doing well.

Shortly after that, Jamie and Fallon returned and they traded places again, then Bailey directed Trina to take them back to Serena's place.

"Tonight was…amazing," Serena said, after he'd carried her up the stairs to her back door.

"I'm glad you had a good time."

"I suppose you have to get the horse and sleigh back to the Triple T," she said, naming the Traub ranch where Dallas and Nina lived with their four children.

"I do," Bailey confirmed.

"Do you want to come back here after you've done that?" she asked him.

He tightened his arms around her. "What horse and sleigh?"

She laughed softly. "I'm flattered. I know you wouldn't really neglect Trina after she dutifully escorted us around town all night, but I'm flattered."

"I'll be back as soon as I can," he promised.

"I'll be here," she assured him.

He kept his promise.

And when he made love to her that night, it was beautiful and magical and Serena finally acknowledged a truth she'd been trying to deny: she was in love with Bailey Stockton.

The realization filled her heart with joy—and her belly with trepidation. Because she knew that Bailey wasn't looking for a serious relationship. He'd been honest about that from the very beginning. But she'd fallen in love with him anyway.

She'd never felt like this before, and she was torn between wanting to tell him and worrying that if she did, the confession of her feelings would act as a wedge rather than a bridge between them. So for now, she resolved to keep the words to herself.

But as their bodies merged together in the darkness of the night, she knew that the truth and depth of her feelings were evident in every touch of her lips, pass of her hands and press of her body.

* * *

"You know, the first pie I ever made for Luke was an apple," Eva said conversationally, as she boxed up the dessert Serena had ordered.

"Proving that the way to a man's heart is through his stomach?" Serena guessed.

"Well, I can't argue with the results." The other woman grinned as she fluttered the fingers of her left hand, where a glittery diamond nestled against the wedding band on the third finger.

Serena smiled back as she passed her money across the counter.

"So are you going to tell me what this pie is for?" Eva prompted. "Or are you going to make me guess?"

"I'm going to lunch at my mother's boyfriend's house." It felt strange to say those words—*mother's boyfriend*—but Amanda and Mark seemed to have clearly defined their relationship, while Serena and Bailey had not.

"I would have guessed wrong," the baker said. "Is Bailey going with you?"

Serena shook her head. "No."

"Why not?"

"Because I didn't invite him."

"Why not?" Eva asked again.

"Because I'm not even sure *I* want to go," Serena admitted. "I certainly wouldn't drag anyone else into the center of my family drama."

"Every family has drama," Eva assured her. "And nothing shines twinkling lights on it like the holidays."

"Isn't that the truth?" she agreed.

"So…what are your plans for Christmas Eve?"

"Oh, the usual," Serena said, deliberately vague.

"What's the usual?"

"Hanging out with Marvin, Molly and Max," she confided.

The other woman's eyes narrowed. "Isn't Marvin your dog?"

Serena nodded. "My dog, my cat and my bunny."

"You don't spend Christmas Eve with your mom?"

"That would be too much drama even for me."

"In that case, you should come out to Sunshine Farm," Eva said.

"Oh." Serena was taken aback by the other woman's impulsive offer—and undeniably touched by the invitation. "Thanks, but I wouldn't want to intrude on your family celebrations."

"Don't be silly," the baker chided. "Everyone will be happy to see you."

"I don't know," she hedged. "Bailey hasn't said anything to me about his plans for the holidays." He certainly hadn't given any indication that he wanted to spend them with her.

"Because he's a man. He doesn't know how to make plans any more than twenty-four hours in advance of an event."

Serena smiled, but she wasn't convinced—especially since Christmas Eve was less than twenty-four hours away.

"Say you'll come," Eva urged. "It will be a lot more fun than hanging out with Marvin, Molly and Matt."

"Max," she corrected automatically. "And our holiday snuggles are something of a tradition."

"But I bet you'd rather snuggle with Bailey," his sister-in-law teased.

Serena couldn't deny it.

And Eva, confident that she'd made another sale, said, "Dinner will be on the table at six."

Two days before Christmas, Bailey wrapped the last of his gifts—this one for Serena.

It wasn't anything fancy or expensive, just a simple eight-by-ten enlargement of a photo of the animals that he'd snapped with his cell phone one day when he was at her apartment. In the picture, Marvin was sprawled out on his belly—his back end on his pillow, his shoulders and head on the floor; Max was stretched out beside him but facing the opposite direction; and Molly was curled up with her face right beside Max's and one paw on his back. The candid shot attested to the camaraderie and affection between the animals, and he was confident Serena would love it.

He had yet to decide how and when he was going to give it to her. Because holding hands and stealing kisses in public was one thing, while sharing a major holiday took a relationship to the next level, and he wasn't sure they were ready to go there—or that they ever would be.

He always had a great time with Serena, and he thought of her often when they were apart, but that didn't mean he was ready to commit to a capital-*R* relationship. And spending Christmas together definitely implied Relationship, which was why he'd decided to fly solo over the holidays.

And why he was taken aback when Luke's wife told him what she'd done.

Chapter Thirteen

"You did what?" Bailey said, certain he must have misunderstood or misinterpreted Eva's words.

"I invited Serena to come over on Christmas Eve," she repeated.

"Why?" he demanded to know.

She frowned, obviously not having anticipated his less-than-enthusiastic response to her announcement. "Because she came in to Daisy's and when I asked about her plans for the holidays, she admitted that—aside from hanging out at home with her pets—she didn't have any."

"She loves hanging out at home with her pets," he informed his sister-in-law. "It's kind of her thing."

"And because I thought you'd want her to be here," Eva added.

"You should have asked me before you asked her," he grumbled.

Her expression shifted from bafflement to concern. "Do you not want her here?"

"I just don't want her to think an invitation to spend Christmas Eve with my family means anything more than that."

"Serena doesn't strike me as the type of woman who would assume a casual invitation from her boyfriend's sister-in-law is a green light to start planning the seating chart for your wedding," she said dryly.

"I'm not her boyfriend," he said through gritted teeth.

"So what are you?" she challenged. "Just a guy who's bouncing on her bed for as long as it suits his purposes?"

That was all he'd wanted, but to hear his brother's wife put it in such blunt terms sounded harsh. And untrue.

"Why does everyone want to put a label on our relationship?" Because as much as he hadn't wanted a relationship, he couldn't deny that he was in one.

He cared about Serena. He enjoyed being with her. And yes, he enjoyed sex with her. But even he couldn't deny that their relationship was about more than sex. He liked talking to her, he appreciated the comfortable silences they shared, he even liked hanging out with her pets. Although Marvin was undeniably his favorite, he had no issues with Max and felt reasonably confident that he'd reached a détente with Molly.

But he wasn't ready for another Relationship. Or maybe he didn't trust himself not to mess up with Serena the way he'd messed up his marriage.

"Do you want me to uninvite her?" Eva asked him now.

"Is there any possible way to do that without an incredible amount of awkwardness?" he wondered aloud.

"Probably not," she admitted. "But I'd rather have an awkward conversation with Serena today than have her feel uncomfortable or unwelcome tomorrow."

"Don't bother," he said. "It's fine."

But Serena was right. Saying "it's fine" didn't make it so, and Bailey decided to go for a drive to clear his head.

Although he had no destination in mind when he set out, he wasn't really surprised when he found his truck slowing down as he approached the cemetery.

His heart was pounding hard against his ribs and his palms were clammy as he shifted into Park and turned off the ignition. He hadn't been here since that awful day his parents were put in the ground, and he was immediately swamped by a wave of memories and emotions. He pushed open the door and stepped out into the cold.

Someone had put an evergreen wreath decorated with holly berries and pinecones on an easel in the ground beside the headstone. Bella, he guessed. It was the type of thing she would think to do. He knew that she visited the cemetery regularly, and throughout the summer tended to the flowers she planted in the spring.

He took a couple steps forward and dropped to his knees in the snow, his watery gaze unable to focus on the names and dates etched in the stone. It didn't matter—the details were forever etched in his mind. The regrets forever heavy in his heart.

"I've screwed everything up," Bailey said, somehow managing to force the words through his closed-up throat. "Starting with that night in the bar, thirteen years ago." He shook his head. "I was so careless, so thoughtless. So stupid."

That long ago night, he'd ignored Danny's urgings to leave because there were pretty girls to dance with and beer to drink. And yeah, he'd actually thought it was funny that his little brother was such an uptight mother hen.

I've already got one mother. I don't need another one, he'd chided his brother.

Danny's expression had darkened, but Luke had laughed—sharing the joke, the good times.

Then the sheriff's deputy had walked into the bar, and the laughter had stopped.

"It was my fault," Bailey confessed to his parents as he stared at the headstone. "But they don't blame me. I don't know how or why, but Bella, Jamie, Dana…even Luke and Danny…don't blame me for what happened that night. But I know the truth. It was my fault. Serena thinks I'm still punishing myself. That I won't let myself be happy because I don't believe I deserve to be happy.

"She might be right," he acknowledged. "I never told Emily about that night, because I was afraid she'd look at me differently. At least, that was the justification I gave to myself. But maybe I wasn't ready to let go of any of my guilt and grief enough to share it."

It was a possibility he hadn't considered until right now. A truth that suddenly seemed unassailable.

"But somehow, I found myself telling Serena everything. Maybe because she's had to overcome devastating losses of her own. And yet, despite that, she is one of the most optimistic people I've ever met. Determined to find happiness in every day—and adding joy to mine whenever I'm with her.

"I really wish you could have met her—and that she'd had the chance to know you. She really is amazing.

Beautiful and smart. Sexy and sweet." His smile was wry. "And undoubtedly too good for me."

Of course, there was no response to his monologue. But when Bailey finally rose to his feet again, his heart felt lighter. And for the first time in a long time, he felt hopeful about his future and willing to not just appreciate but embrace the joy that Serena brought to his life.

For a dozen years, Bailey hadn't thought he had any reason to celebrate the holidays. Last year, his first back in Rust Creek Falls after twelve away, he'd felt awkward and uncomfortable, like an imposter in his sister's home. Not that Bella had done or said anything to make him feel less than welcome. Just the opposite, in fact. She'd gone out of her way for him, even ensuring there were presents with his name on them under the tree Christmas morning.

But this year, being with his siblings again, along with their significant others and kids, he truly felt as if he was where he belonged. Even Dana had made the trip from Oregon—with the blessing of her adoptive parents—to spend the holiday with her brothers and sister.

Of course, the entire family wasn't there, but those who gathered together found pleasure in their renewed and strengthened childhood bonds and remembered those who weren't with them at Sunshine Farm. They all hoped that Liza would also be brought back into the fold someday, but for now, Bailey focused on being grateful for what he had—including the beautiful woman by his side.

"So tell me how you and Bailey met," Dana said to Serena.

"Well, I actually met him several months ago at the

vet clinic where I work with Annie," she said. "But I didn't really get to know him until Dan went down with the flu. Bailey had to fill in for him playing Santa, and I did the same for Annie as Mrs. Claus, so she could take care of her sick husband."

"I guess it's lucky for both of you that Dan got the flu," Dana remarked.

Janie, only hearing the last part of her aunt's remark as she came into the living room from the kitchen, stopped in the entrance and looked worriedly toward the sofa, where her parents were seated. "Dad's got the flu?"

"Not now," her mother hastened to assure her. "He's fully recuperated now."

Janie looked puzzled. "When was he sick?" she wondered aloud.

"When Uncle Bailey had to fill in as Santa at the community center," Annie said.

"And your school," Dan chimed in.

"Oh, right." Janie chuckled, remembering. "Your fake flu."

Bailey frowned. "Fake flu?"

"Yeah," his niece confirmed, apparently oblivious to the can of worms she was opening. "Mom and Dad thought that forcing you to play Santa would help put you in the holiday spirit."

A heavy silence followed Janie's revelation, until Fallon spoke up. "Did you hear that?" she asked, though no one had heard anything. "I think the kids are starting to wake up. Janie, can you help me with them?"

"Sure," the tween agreed, always happy to lend a hand with her toddler cousins.

"I'll help, too," the triplets' father said. "Three sets of hands are always best with three kids," Jamie explained.

Bailey waited until they'd gone before he turned to Dan. "You *faked* being sick?"

"I did have a bit of a cold," Dan said defensively.

"You told me you were throwing up," Bailey reminded him. Then he turned to his brother's wife. "And you acted so concerned—going to Daisy's to get him soup. You even had Serena fill in for you because you couldn't risk leaving your oh-so-sick husband alone." He shook his head. "And now I find out it was all just part of the act."

"Or was it a romantic setup from the beginning?" Eva mused aloud. Head over heels in love with her husband, she wished for a happy ending for everyone.

The color that filled Annie's cheeks answered the question before she spoke. "I might have asked Serena to take my place because I hoped she and Bailey would hit it off."

"And she was right," Dana pointed out, obviously trying to ease the tensions between her siblings.

Serena could tell that Bailey wasn't in a mood to be appeased. Not that she could blame him for being angry and upset by the machinations of his brother and sister-in-law. She was none too happy herself—and more than a little embarrassed—to have been so completely caught up in the plot.

"Did you have any part in this?" he asked her now.

She immediately shook her head. "Of course not," she denied, shocked that Bailey could believe such a thing.

And maybe he didn't, but he was apparently too mad to think rationally right now.

He turned to his brother again. "You always think

you know what's best for everyone else, don't you? Consequences be damned." Bailey didn't raise his voice, and his words were almost more lethal because of their quiet fury. "I would have thought you'd learned your lesson about sticking your nose into other people's business thirteen years ago."

When Dan's face drained of all color, Serena realized the brothers were arguing about something more than a feigned illness.

"That's enough," Luke said to his brothers.

But Dan refused to heed the warning. "Maybe I was, in a small way, trying to make up for mistakes I made in the past," he acknowledged. "Maybe I was trying to help you find the happiness you don't think you deserve."

"Contrary to what you think, I can manage my own life," Bailey said. "I don't need anyone's interference."

He turned on Eva now, as if having finally let his emotions loose, he couldn't stop. "And I certainly don't need anyone to set me up with a date on Christmas Eve. If I'd wanted a date, I would have got one myself—but I didn't."

The implication of his pointed words was unmistakable, and Serena flinched from the verbal blow. If she'd ever had any illusions that she belonged here, with Bailey, the vehemence of his response ripped that veil away.

Another, even heavier, silence fell around the room.

"Well," Serena said, clearing her throat to speak around the lump that was sitting there. "I think it's time for me to be on my way."

"But…we haven't eaten yet," Dana pointed out.

"And I've got animals at home that need to be fed," Serena said.

No one said anything else then. No one else tried to stop her. Certainly not Bailey.

She didn't look in his direction as she made her way out of the room. And she didn't hurry, keeping her chin up and her gaze focused ahead of her as she made her escape, so that no one would guess her heart was breaking into a million jagged little pieces.

She found her boots easily enough, but there were so many coats piled onto the hooks by the door, it took her a minute to uncover hers. Of course, her efforts were further thwarted by the tears that blurred her vision.

She'd been a fool to think that they were growing closer, maybe even building a relationship. She'd had reservations about accepting Eva's invitation to spend Christmas Eve with the Stocktons at Sunshine Farm, but Bailey's sister-in-law had assured her that he would want her there.

The silence in the living room had been broken. Voices were raised now, talking over one another so that she couldn't make out what anyone was saying—and she was grateful for it. Finally, she found her coat, shoved her arms into the sleeves, stuffed her feet into her boots and yanked open the door.

She blinked in surprise as she got a face full of snow-flakes. An hour earlier, as she'd driven toward Sunshine Farm, she'd been enchanted by the pretty flakes dancing harmlessly in the sky. The wind had obviously picked up since then and the snow was falling heavily now—no longer appearing pretty or harmless.

Swiping at a tear that spilled onto her cheek, she inhaled a slow, deep breath. The icy air sliced like a sharply honed blade through her lungs, but that pain didn't compare to the ache in her heart.

She unlocked her SUV and climbed in. Shoving her key into the ignition, she cranked up the defroster and turned on the wipers. The snow that had accumulated on the windshield was swept away by the blades, and she shifted into Reverse, carefully backing around the other vehicles parked in the long drive. Cars and trucks that belonged to Bailey's brothers and sisters. Proof that he was surrounded by family. Proof that he didn't need her.

He'd referred to his family, with equal parts exasperation and affection, as nosy and interfering. And what Dan and Annie had done proved his description was apt. But Serena had no doubt that his brother and sister-in-law had acted with the best of intentions, wanting him to find the same kind of happiness they'd found together.

Still, Serena could understand why he was angry, if not the intensity of his anger. Or maybe she could. The day he'd told her about his long overdue conversation with his ex-wife, he'd also told her how much he'd hated feeling as if he didn't have any control over his life after his parents were killed. So maybe it was understandable that he'd be furious about the setup, because regardless of Dan and Annie's motivations, they'd taken control of the situation away from Bailey.

She believed the feelings they had for one another were real, but she could see why the manipulation of the situation might lead Bailey to question the legitimacy of his emotions. And that was something he needed to figure out on his own—if he even wanted to. Obviously the Stockton siblings had some other issues to work through, but she had no doubt that they would do so, because no matter their differences, they were a family who cared deeply about one another.

She thought of her own family—of herself, her mother and her grandmother. Three generations of women who had been through so much—and nearly let their trials tear them apart. But even the deepest wounds eventually healed, and for the first time in a lot of years, Serena felt optimistic about her mother's recovery and the relationship they were gradually beginning to rebuild.

Amanda was with Mark today. He understood that Christmas was a particularly difficult time for her and was happy to give her whatever support she needed to make it through the holidays without falling apart—or falling back into old habits.

Serena would celebrate this year the same way she'd done last year and the one before that—with Marvin, Molly and Max. She didn't need anyone else. Certainly not some stupid man who didn't know how lucky he was to have her.

And yeah, maybe she didn't need Bailey, but she couldn't deny that she loved him.

And it hurt to know that he didn't love her back.

Fresh tears filled her eyes, spilled onto her cheeks.

She didn't lift her hands from the wheel to wipe them away, because the snow was coming really fast and heavy now, and she felt her tires slip on patches of ice beneath the fresh snow. Her mechanic had warned her that she needed new snow tires, but she'd been certain that she could get one more winter out of them. She silently pleaded not to be proved wrong now.

"The Christmas Song" was playing on the local radio station she always listened to, and when Nat King Cole finished singing, the deejay's voice came through the speaker.

"I hope everyone's enjoying their Christmas Eve—and staying off the roads. Our local law enforcement has issued the following weather warning and travel advisory—heavy snow with significant blowing and drifting is imminent or occurring. Snowfall amounts up to eighteen inches with blizzard to near-blizzard conditions likely in many areas, making travel difficult or dangerous with road closures possible.

"So if you don't have to be out and about, pour yourself a glass of eggnog and sit back with your feet up by the fire and listen to the sounds of the season. I'm here to keep you company all night long."

It was good advice, and Serena vowed to do exactly as he suggested as soon as she got home.

But first she had to get home.

A flash of something caught the corner of her eye. She eased up on the gas and turned her head just in time to see a white-tailed deer leap up out of the ditch and onto the road ahead.

She instinctively hit the brakes to avoid hitting the majestic creature, but she braked a little too hard for the conditions. Her tires slid on the slick road, and the back end of her SUV fishtailed.

She immediately tried to steer into the skid, but her efforts had little effect. The vehicle continued to spin, as if in slow motion, then slid into the ditch. Because the point of impact was at the rear, the airbag didn't deploy, but she was thrown against her seat belt and then, when the SUV abruptly listed, she smacked her head against the driver's side window.

She winced at the explosion of pain and felt a trickle

of something wet sliding down the side of her face. Had the window cracked? Was it snow?

She wiped it away, then saw the back of her hand was smeared with red.

Not snow.

Blood.

Merry frickin' Christmas to me.

Chapter Fourteen

She didn't get out of the vehicle. There was no point. She could tell by the angle of the hood sticking in the air that she wasn't going to get out of the ditch without a tow cable. So she unclipped her seat belt to retrieve her purse, which had slid off the passenger seat to the floor. She winced a little, realizing that her shoulder was tender from the restraint. Thankfully, she hadn't been driving too fast, but she had no doubt she'd have plenty of bumps and bruises the next day.

She found her phone and swiped to unlock the screen. It remained blank.

Fresh tears burned her eyes. She was heartbroken, frustrated and angry. It was Christmas Eve and she just wanted to be home with Molly and Marvin and Max. Instead, she was stranded in a snowbank on the side of the road with a dead cell phone.

She never should have accepted Eva's invitation to spend Christmas Eve with the Stocktons at Sunshine Farm. She should have known that Bailey not asking her wasn't an oversight but an indication that he didn't want her there. She should have been satisfied with their friendship-with-benefits and not allowed herself to hope and believe the relationship could turn into anything more.

She dropped her forehead against the steering wheel as hot tears spilled onto her cheeks. She wasn't really hurt—not physically. But her heart was battered, her spirit beaten down. And because it was Christmas Eve and the whole town was experiencing blizzard conditions, she estimated the chances of another motorist passing by were slim to none.

Thankfully, she kept a spare charger in her center console. She also found a travel pack of tissues there. After plugging the charger into her phone, she pulled out a couple of tissues and pressed them to her temple to stanch the flow of blood.

Squinting through the window, she saw lights in the distance. Could it be...? Was that another vehicle coming her way?

Her bruised heart gave a joyful little jump.

Maybe her luck was turning around. Maybe something was finally going to go her way today.

She used the sleeve of her coat to wipe condensation off the side window—not that it helped much. She could barely see anything through the blowing snow, but she was almost certain now that there were headlights drawing nearer.

Apparently she wasn't the only resident of Rust Creek Falls who had disregarded the travel warning.

Although, in her defense, she'd been unaware of the warning until she'd left Sunshine Farm and was already on her way toward home. Not that she would have stayed, even if she'd known about the road conditions. Not after Bailey had made it clear to everyone that she wasn't wanted.

She rubbed a hand over the ache in the center of her chest. Yeah, the truth hurt, but she would get over it— and him. It might take some time, she knew, but her heart had already proven its resilience, time and again.

As the vehicle drew closer, she saw that it was a blue pickup. Like Bailey's truck.

And her bruised heart gave another little jump.

She immediately chided herself for the reaction and dismissed the possibility. It couldn't be Bailey's truck. He'd made it clear that he didn't want her at Sunshine Farm, so there was no reason to suspect that he might have followed her when she'd gone.

Of course, it was possible that he'd left the ranch for another reason, although she couldn't imagine one that would compel him to venture out in such nasty weather.

But as the truck drew nearer, she realized that it *was* Bailey's truck.

So much for thinking this was a lucky break. She already felt like a fool. The absolute last thing she needed was for the man who'd callously broken her heart to ride to her rescue. Because of course he would stop, and then he would insist on driving her home. And every mile of the journey would be excruciating painful.

If I'd wanted a date, I would have got one myself.

She winced at the echo of his words in her head.

His vehicle slowed and carefully eased over to the side of the road behind her incapacitated SUV.

Serena swiped at the tears on her cheeks, not wanting him to know that she'd been crying. Not wanting him to think that she was crying over him.

Before she could catch her breath, her door was wrenched open from the outside and a blast of cold swept through the interior of the cab and stole her breath.

"Oh my God, Serena—what happened? Are you hurt?" He sounded genuinely concerned, maybe even a little panicked. "You're bleeding," he said, then lifted a hand to her chin and gently turned her face so that he could inspect the gash above her eye.

"I braked to avoid hitting a deer," she confided.

"Of course, you did," he said, shaking his head. "Without thinking about the potential danger to yourself."

"It was an instinct," she said, a little defensively.

"Do you need a doctor? An ambulance?"

This time she shook her head, wincing as the movement escalated the throbbing inside her skull. "I'm okay. Just…stuck. I was going to call for a tow when I saw your headlights."

"It might take a tow truck driver a while to get out here, if you can find one willing to venture out in this storm. Everyone's being advised to avoid nonessential travel."

"I heard that on the radio…while I was driving," she admitted. "But why are *you* out on the roads?"

"Because I'm an idiot," he said. "And I'm sorry."

He reached into the cab to pull her into his arms and hold her close.

Serena remained perfectly still, not sure how she was supposed to respond to this unexpected show of concern. Not willing to let herself believe that anything had changed in the short time that had passed since she left Sunshine Farm.

"I'm so sorry, Serena." He whispered the words close to her ear, his tone thick with emotion.

"Why are you sorry?" she asked cautiously.

"Because I'm an idiot," he said again, his arms still wrapped tight around her, as if he couldn't bear to let her go. "I got mad at Danny for butting in, because I'd finally started to believe that I was back in control of my life, and finding out that he'd manipulated the situation... Well, it set me off," he admitted. "But obviously I do need someone to tell me what to do, because I just seem to screw everything up otherwise."

"You don't need to apologize for your feelings," she responded stiffly.

He loosened his hold enough to draw back to look at her—or maybe so that she could see the sincerity in his eyes. "I'm not apologizing for my feelings. I'm apologizing for *denying* my feelings—and for letting you get caught in the middle of an old dispute."

She shrugged, still reluctant to let herself hope. "I shouldn't have been where I obviously wasn't wanted."

"But I *did* want you there," he insisted. "And I was afraid to admit that I wanted you there. I was afraid to admit how much I want our relationship to work, so I sabotaged it instead. Because letting you go seemed easier than letting you into my heart."

"Then...why did you follow me?"

"Because the door had barely closed behind you when I realized that you're already in my heart, and I don't ever want to let you go." He lifted his hands to frame her face. "Maybe Dan and Annie manipulated the situation, but my feelings are real. I love you, Serena, and I want to spend not just this Christmas but all Christmases for the rest of my life with you."

His declaration—so unexpected and unexpectedly perfect—brought fresh tears to her eyes.

"Don't cry, Serena. I know I hurt you, but it can't be too late. Please tell me it's not too late."

"It's not too late," she assured him. "These are happy tears."

"Do they mean that you forgive me?" he asked hopefully.

"I forgive you. And I love you, too."

His lips curved. "Yeah?"

"Yeah," she confirmed. "For now and forever."

"Will you come back to celebrate Christmas with me and my noisy, nosy family?" he asked.

"Will you do me a favor?"

"Anything," he promised.

"Give me a ride," she said. "Because my vehicle isn't going anywhere anytime soon."

So they returned to Sunshine Farm, where the rest of the Stockton family was relieved to see her—although distressed by the sight of her injury. But after Annie and Eva had finished fussing and cleaning and bandaging her wound, they all *finally* sat down to dinner.

"I've already apologized to Serena," Bailey told his siblings, after the food had been passed around and everyone had loaded up their plates. "But I want to apologize to all of you, too, for my ill-mannered outburst."

"Since you apparently came to your senses and got back your girl, I guess we can forgive you," Jamie said.

Bailey smiled as he slid an arm around Serena's shoulders. "Did you hear that? You're my girl."

"I heard," she confirmed. "And I think that's a title I can live with."

"Good. Because I don't want to live without you." Then he glanced across the table at Dan and Annie. "And I guess I should thank both of you for introducing me to Mrs. Claus…" He paused then and turned back to Serena. "Or maybe…the future Mrs. Stockton?"

Serena stared at him, stunned. "Are you…" She let the words trail off, unwilling to complete the thought, in case she was wrong.

"I'm asking if you'll marry me, Serena."

She wasn't wrong. And with those words, her heart filled with so much happiness and love, she could barely breathe never mind respond to his question.

"Yay!" Janie immediately cheered. "There's going to be another wedding."

Henry, Jared and Katie—likely picking up on the excitement of their cousin's tone more than understanding her words—responded by clapping their hands.

"While I appreciate your enthusiastic support," Bailey said to his nieces and nephews, "Serena hasn't yet answered my question." Then he turned his gaze back to her. "What do you say?"

"I say yes," she told him. "Definitely yes."

A quick—and decidedly relieved—grin creased his face for an instant before he kissed her.

And then everyone was cheering and applauding.

"I know it's impolite to eat and run," Jamie noted, peering out the window as the table was being cleared a long while later. "But it's really snowing out there."

"It really is," Fallon agreed. "We should get the kids bundled up and make our escape while we still can."

"*If* you still can," Eva said, looking worried.

"Why don't you spend the night here?" Luke suggested as an alternative. "After all, we have plenty of cabins."

"Because Santa Claus is coming tonight," Fallon reminded them all.

"And we're not going far," Jamie pointed out. "Not to mention that Andy and Molly would be very unhappy to be left alone overnight," he said, referring to the puppies he'd adopted out of the litter of seven that he'd rescued two years earlier.

"What about Marvin?" Bailey suddenly asked Serena. "What if his doggy door gets blocked by the snow?"

"I already called Dee," she said, referring to the neighbor who occasionally checked in on her animals when Serena had to be away for any length of time. "She'll make sure the animals have everything they need."

"Does she know to give Max his apple wedge treat? And to fluff Molly's pillow?"

"She knows," Serena assured him.

But in that moment, she knew that if she hadn't already been head over heels in love with him, Bailey's concern for the welfare of her furry companions would have made her tumble.

"So they'll be okay if you stay here with me tonight?" he prompted.

"They might miss me, but they'll be okay" she assured him.

"Good," he said. "Because I'd miss you more if I had to spend the night without the woman I love."

"I've decided that Christmas is my favorite time of year," Bailey announced to Serena the next morning.

"And when did you arrive at this conclusion?" she asked.

"Just now, when I woke up and you were here, and I had the incomparable pleasure of making love with my beautiful fiancée on December 25."

"I've always loved Christmas," she reminded him. "But you've given me even more reasons to love it— and to look forward to all the Christmases we'll share together."

And as she snuggled in his arms and listened to the strong steady beat of his heart, she couldn't help but think of her sister and hope that wherever Mimi was— because with all of her heart and soul, Serena believed that her little sister was out there somewhere—she was also celebrating the holiday with someone she loved.

"I'm still not sure this is real," she said. "It seems like a dream."

"My dream come true," he told her.

"You really do want to marry me?"

"Why would you doubt it?"

"It just seems like everything happened so fast and—"

"Do *you* have doubts?" he interrupted to ask her.

"No," she immediately replied. "But I also never said that I'd never get married again."

"I did say that," he acknowledged. "Because I was sure it was true…and then I fell in love with you."

"So your proposal wasn't just an impulse?"

"The timing was a little impulsive," he admitted. "I probably should have waited to ask until I had a ring, but I promise as soon as stores open on December 26, I'll fix that oversight."

"I should probably say that I don't need a ring, but I want one. I want a visible symbol to show the world—or at least the rest of Rust Creek Falls—that I'm engaged to marry Bailey Stockton."

He shifted so that he was facing her, then lifted a hand to brush her hair away from her face and gently stroke her cheek. "I love you, Serena."

She smiled. "I love you, too."

They sealed their promises with another kiss, which might have led to more except that Bailey's cell phone buzzed on the bedside table. With obvious reluctance, he eased his lips from hers and picked up the offending instrument to read the text message on the screen.

"We're being summoned to the main house for breakfast and then gifts."

"Maybe I could borrow your truck and head back to my place to check on Marvin, Molly and Max," Serena suggested.

"If you're worried about them, we'll both go," he said.

"I'm not really worried," she admitted. "I just thought I should give you some time with your family."

"You're part of that family now, too," he reminded her.

So they got dressed and headed over to the main house, where everyone else was already gathered around the table overflowing with tasty offerings: platters of scrambled eggs, bacon and sausage, stacks of toast and bowls of fresh fruit.

"You're late," Jamie said when Bailey settled into a vacant chair beside him.

"I'd say I'm right on time," he countered, as Eva added a plate of sticky buns, fresh out of the oven, to the assortment of food already on the table.

"I want to know when it's nap time," Fallon confided. "We've been up for hours already with the triplets, and when we finish up here, we're heading over to my parents' place for Christmas Day—round three."

"I'm glad you were able to squeeze this into your schedule," Bella said sincerely.

"Are you kidding? This is the best part of the day," Fallon said to the woman who had been her friend long before she was her sister-in-law.

"It is special," Dana chimed in. "To be able to celebrate the holidays with all of you."

Of course, everyone was aware that the group was incomplete. Unless and until Liza was found, there would always be something missing. But for now, they focused on the joy of being together. And when everyone had eaten their fill, they retreated to the living room to disperse the presents that were piled under the tree.

"It's amazing, isn't it?" Annie said, nudging Bailey with her shoulder as the triplets attacked an enormous box that had all their names on it.

"What's amazing? The noise? The mess? The chaos?"

His sister-in-law laughed softly. "Well, all of that," she acknowledged. "Because it's all part and parcel of being a member of this family. But I was actually referring to the difference that a year can make."

"This time last year, you and Dan were newlyweds," Bailey noted.

"And you'd just returned to Rust Creek Falls, a bitter and cynical Grooge, certain you weren't going to stay."

He couldn't deny that was true—or that, until only a few weeks ago, he'd remained mostly bitter and cynical and unconvinced that there was a future for him in this town. And then his brother and sister-in-law had conned him into donning Santa's hat and coat.

He'd totally been faking it that first day. He'd had no Christmas spirit of his own to share with the kids. Serena had helped him find not just that Christmas spirit again but closure on his past and hope for his future.

She'd changed everything for him.

"It's true," he agreed. "A lot can change in a year—or when you finally find the one person you're meant to spend the rest of your life with."

"You're welcome," Annie said.

"Yeah, maybe I do owe you for that," he acknowledged.

"And I know just how you can pay me back."

"How?" he asked, a little warily.

She smiled. "Be happy." Then she kissed his cheek and moved away to find her husband.

But Bailey knew that he already was.

As he looked around the room, he was grateful and humbled to be part of this crazy family whose connection and affection had not only endured but grown stronger over distance and time. Of course, their family had grown in size, too, with so many of his siblings pairing up and having babies. Or, in Dan and Annie's case, an almost-teenager.

He found Serena in the crowd, and felt his heart swell to fill his whole chest. She was sitting on the floor by the fire with Jared—or was that Henry?—on her lap. The nephew had a gingerbread cookie in his hand, which he would gnaw on for a while and then offer to Serena, and she would gamely take a nibble of the soggy treat before the little guy shoved it back in his own mouth.

She fit so perfectly here. With his family. With him.

Annie was right—a single year could make a world of difference. And he hoped that by next Christmas, Serena would be his wife rather than his fiancée. And maybe, not too long after that, they'd have a child of their own to contribute to the mayhem.

That thought gave him a moment's pause.

Henry—or was it Jared?—toddled over to his brother with two chunky toy trucks clutched in his fists, obviously hoping to entice him away from his cookie to play. His brother was happy to abandon his snack, but he kissed Serena's cheek before sliding from her lap, and she smiled as she watched the brothers move away.

Bailey found a napkin on a nearby table and offered it to her. She wrapped the remnants of the soggy cookie, then wiped the crumbs from her hand.

"You looked deep in thought over there," she commented, as he sat down beside her.

"I was just wondering how long it takes to plan a wedding," he said, sliding his arm around her shoulders.

"You can't be talking about our wedding."

"Why not?"

"Because we only just got engaged."

"Do you know why I asked you to marry me?"

"Because you love me and want to spend the rest of your life with me?"

"All of that," he agreed. "And because I want to start our life together as soon as possible."

"I want that, too."

"So let's set a date," he urged.

"Okay," she agreed. "June 25."

"That's six months away."

"I figure it will probably take that long to plan a wedding."

"Unless we get someone to do it for us," he noted. "Caroline Ruth did a great job with the Presents for Patriots event."

"She did," Serena agreed. "And now that you mention it, Sawmill Station would be the perfect venue for a wedding."

"Then I suggest we reach out to her as soon as possible to get started with the planning."

"What's your hurry?" she wondered.

"Well, I was thinking—" he tipped his head toward hers, his expression filled with cautious hope "—the sooner we get married, the sooner we can get started making a baby."

Her heart fluttered, yearned. "In that case," she said, her eyes growing misty, "the sooner the better."

It was an almost perfect day.

Of course, spending Christmas morning with his siblings, it was natural that Bailey would think about the parents who were no longer with them. And while their absence tugged at his heart, he felt certain that Rob and Lauren Stockton were looking down on their children, happy to see them celebrating together.

Of course, they weren't all together. Not yet. But some of Serena's eternal optimism must have rubbed off on him, because he was starting to believe that the reunion of his siblings would soon be complete.

That thought had barely formed in his mind when the doorbell rang.

The sound didn't interrupt the festivities. Several of the adults exchanged curious glances, silently wondering who would be visiting on Christmas Day, then Luke went to discover the answer to that unspoken question.

A few minutes later, he returned with an unexpected but very welcome guest.

Bailey's heart hammered against his ribs as he reached for Serena's hand and linked their fingers together.

"Liza."

It was Bella who first ventured to whisper the name, and the younger woman's familiar blue eyes immediately filled with tears.

Then, more loudly for the benefit of those who hadn't realized that someone new had joined the party, Bella announced, "Liza's home."

The rest of her siblings all rushed forward to embrace the long-lost sister who had finally returned.

Serena decided it was an appropriate time to extricate herself from the family gathering. Though she was thrilled for Bailey and all his brothers and sisters, their impromptu family reunion was a painful reminder that her family was still in pieces. Yes, she was starting to rebuild a relationship with her mother, but she still felt the loss of the father who'd walked out of her life fifteen years earlier and, even more deeply, the absence of the sister who had disappeared without a trace a year previous to that.

But Serena's efforts to slip away were thwarted by her fiancé.

"Where are you going?" Bailey asked her.

"Home," she said. "I've already been gone longer than I intended to be."

"Your SUV is in a ditch," he reminded her.

She held up the keys in her hand. "Eva's letting me borrow her vehicle."

"That's not necessary," he said. "I can take you."

"I know you can, but you've been waiting for this reunion a long time."

"And you're still waiting for yours," he realized.

"I am," she admitted. "But seeing you with your siblings, knowing you found your way back to one another after so many years apart, gives me renewed hope that I'll find Mimi again."

"You will," he said confidently.

"But in the meantime, my pets are waiting for me," she told him.

"So we'll go get Marvin, Molly and Max and bring them back here," he decided.

"Don't you think that will be a little...chaotic?"

"No, I think it will be *a lot* chaotic," he acknowledged. "But it's Christmas, and family should be together on Christmas."

"You got more than you bargained for, didn't you?" Serena remarked later, after she and Bailey had returned to the relative quiet of his cabin following dinner with his family—and hers. Because Amanda and Mark had been at her apartment when they went to get her pets, and Bailey had persuaded them to join the festivities at Sunshine Farm.

"It was every bit as chaotic as you promised," he confirmed. "And I wouldn't have changed a minute of it."

Marvin, Molly and Max might have agreed with his

assessment, but they were already snuggled up together and asleep in the dog's bed, exhausted from so much attention and excitement.

"Grams didn't even protest being dragged away from her celebration on the beach to hear the news of our engagement," Serena noted.

"Although she did request that we plan a summer wedding."

"June 25 is summer," she pointed out, referencing the date she'd originally suggested.

"And it's a long time to wait to make you my wife," he grumbled.

"I know you're eager to get started on a family of our own, but a June wedding ensures we'll have lots of time to practice our baby-making technique."

"Are you suggesting that I need practice?" he asked, his tone indignant.

"Of course not," she soothed. "I'm only suggesting that I would very much enjoy practicing with you."

"Okay, then," he relented.

"In fact…I was kind of hoping we might practice tonight."

And that's just what they did—all night long.

Epilogue

"**D**id you hear the news?" glowing newlywed Vivienne Shuster Dalton asked her recently engaged friend and colleague Caroline Ruth.

"If you're referring to the news that Bailey Stockton proposed to Serena Langley on Christmas Eve, then yes, I did," Caroline confirmed.

"That's six engagements in the past six months."

"Love is definitely in the air in Rust Creek Falls," Caroline agreed.

"Fingers crossed—" Vivienne demonstrated with her own "—we're going to be planning a lot of weddings in the upcoming year."

"But there are still a lot of single men and women in town," Caroline noted.

Vivienne clapped her hands together gleefully. "Which promises even more business in years to come."

Although Caroline shared her business partner's optimism, she felt compelled to issue a word of caution. "Some of them might need a little nudge to set them on the right path."

"Oooh, you're right." Vivienne considered, then nodded. "That's a great idea."

Caroline wasn't sure how to respond to her colleague's unbridled enthusiasm. "What did I say? What's a great idea?"

"Adding matchmaking to our list of services."

"That wasn't my idea," she immediately protested.

But now that it was out there, the possibilities were undeniably intriguing...

* * * * *

COMING SOON!

We really hope you enjoyed reading this book. If you're looking for more romance, be sure to head to the shops when new books are available on

Thursday 13th December

To see which titles are coming soon, please visit
millsandboon.co.uk

MILLS & BOON

Coming next month

HER BROODING SCOTTISH HEIR
Ella Hayes

'I'm sorry I didn't introduce myself. I was too busy trying not to step on your evidently capable toes.' He shrugged. 'I'll admit I'm not much good at small talk, but I listen, and I notice things.'

'Such as?'

'The Aurora. You really should look up.'

The lights were in full spate now – glowing curtains of emerald green, pulsing and shimmering. Time stretched and for a moment it felt to Cormac as if they were the only two people on earth. When Milla finally spoke, he heard a catch in her voice.

'It's beautiful, Cor, don't you think?'

She kept calling him 'Cor' and it sounded sweet from her mouth. He looked at her face, the tiny lines wrinkling her forehead as she gazed at the sky, the smile playing on her lips. She was luminous and the urge to touch her was overwhelming. His voice emerged as a whisper. 'Amazing.'

She seemed to sense that he wasn't looking at the sky and turned to meet his gaze. 'You *were* talking about the lights, right...?'

He watched the reflections dancing in her eyes and hesitated. 'I was talking about the view.' He didn't know why he'd laid himself bare like that but saw an answering glimmer in her eyes that felt like an invitation.

Slowly, he lifted a hand to her cheek, traced the line of her jaw with his fingers and then, as another flash lit the sky over their heads, he stepped closer. He couldn't stop himself now. With infinite slowness he tilted her chin and lowered his mouth to hers and as their lips touched, he felt her soften and rise to meet him. She wanted him too and the relief of it filled him with joy. Gently, he pulled her closer, felt her body warm against his, her lips opening as he deepened his kiss.

Continue reading
HER BROODING SCOTTISH HEIR
Ella Hayes

Available next month
www.millsandboon.co.uk

LET'S TALK
Romance

For exclusive extracts, competitions
and special offers, find us online:

- facebook.com/millsandboon
- @millsandboonuk
- @millsandboon

Or get in touch on 0844 844 1351*

For all the latest titles coming soon, visit
millsandboon.co.uk/nextmonth